THE BAY PHANTOM

FEAST OF THE CANNIBAL GUILD

AIRSHIP 27 PRODUCTIONS

The Bay Phantom-Feast of the Cannibal Guild
© 2018 Chuck Miller

Published by Airship 27 Productions
www.airship27.com
www.airship27hangar.com

Interior illustrations ©2018 Kevin Paul Shaw Broden
Cover illustration © 2018 Adam Shaw

Editor: Ron Fortier
Associate Editor: Gordon Dymowski
Marketing and Promotions Manager: Michael Vance
Production and design by Rob Davis.

ISBN-13: 978-1-946183-44-6
ISBN-10: 1-946183-44-X

Printed in the United States of America

10 9 8 7 6 5 4 3 2 1

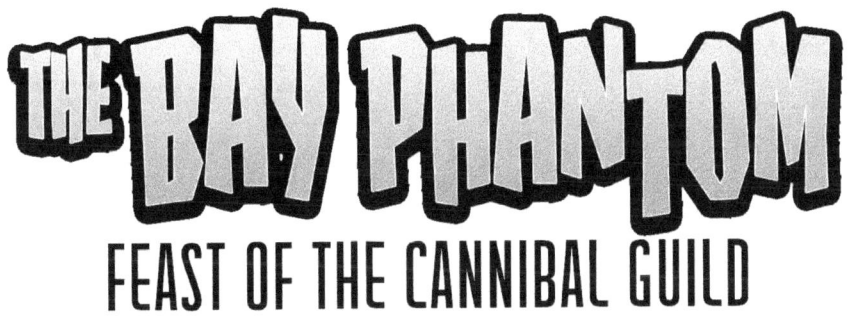

THE BAY PHANTOM
FEAST OF THE CANNIBAL GUILD

by Chuck Miller

PROLOGUE

"What you're doing is against the law, you know," said the Black Embalmer. "Holding me here in this lovely facility, I mean, even though it is more or less consensual. I'm wanted for God alone knows how many crimes, so you're harboring a fugitive. Not that I care, I'm just pointing it out. Doesn't bother me a bit. But you come across as so upright and forthright and—oh, just plain damn *right*—that it seems inconsistent."

The Bay Phantom sighed behind his black mask. "Don't think I haven't struggled with that," he said. "But if I turned you over to the police, you wouldn't stay incarcerated for very long, and you would kill quite a few people while escaping. The system is not capable of dealing with you."

The two men were sitting in a small, clean, well-lighted room. They occupied folding chairs on either side of a card table, upon which sat an untouched chessboard. The Bay Phantom was clad in his "working clothes," complete with mask, cloak, and slouch hat. The Embalmer, on the other hand, was dressed casually in a pair of denim dungarees and a gray flannel shirt. His face, now almost completely healed from the beating given to him a few months before by the hulking Shorty Red, was unmasked. He was a young man, surely no more than twenty-five, and might almost be called handsome. It was his eyes that prevented it. There was something behind them that made one want to either turn away or try to discover their secret. Most people wisely chose the former course.

The two of them had these little meetings on a regular basis, here in a private clinic across the Bay from the city of Mobile, Alabama, in which the Phantom's alter ego, Joseph Perrone, owned a controlling interest. After the events of the previous year, when the Embalmer had been involved in a vicious gang war between the criminal Carter family and a resurgent Ku Klux Klan, the Phantom had decided it would be best to keep the madman under close observation.

He hadn't anticipated the unusual relationship that had developed between them. It wasn't really a friendship...

Or was it?

"You understand me," the Embalmer said, smiling. "To an extent, in a superficial way. Still, I like that. It's a start. Unlike most people, you know

5

you can't force your paradigm on me."

"It would be a waste of time to try. Lord knows you're capable of untold mayhem, but you're not entirely to blame for that. You're not well at all."

"And you *are*? People like you and me, we're not like the rest of them out there." He waved a hand at the barred window. "The rules don't necessarily apply to us."

"I'm just a man in a mask," said the Phantom.

"No, there's a lot more to it than that. You're a man in a mask even when you don't have a mask on, just like me."

"I don't understand that remark."

"Yes, you do. You're just scared of it. I mean, look at what you spend your time doing. Are you crazy?"

"I don't think so. I must confess, I have had my doubts. But after much soul-searching, I have come to the conclusion that I am doing what is right. I may *not* be entirely sane... But I am necessary."

"Maybe. And if you are, then so am I."

The Phantom shook his head. "I believe I understand what you're getting at," he said. "But that's pathological. You are insane. I thought you had come to accept that."

"Well, see, people who are insane never *think* they're insane. That's a bit of a paradox for me. Knowing something and believing it are not the same thing. You say I'm insane, and you certainly have the right to your opinion. I regard myself as *interesting*. Unconventional, yes. Controversial, absolutely. But *insane*? Maybe I'm just evil, did you ever think of that?"

"Of course," said the Phantom. "But there's no reason you can't be both."

"Maybe. But what does that make *you*? You think killing is evil, but you do it anyhow."

"That's right. I do it to save innocent lives. I make a conscious choice. I will commit an evil act to save an innocent life, and I accept whatever consequences result from it."

The Embalmer chuckled. "That's very good," he said, wagging a finger at the Phantom. "That is almost airtight, I'll admit. But tell me this: how do you know the people you save are innocent? Because they happen to be standing in a particular location minding their own business? Evil people have to go to the grocery store too, you know. Perhaps that sweet little old lady whose life you saved by blowing that mugger's brains out is a serial poisoner with a hundred victims to her credit."

"I think you're missing the point."

"Really? I think *you* are."

"Perhaps we *both* are. You imply that I have it in me to understand you. That's what you're getting at, isn't it? And that if I allowed myself to understand you, I would see that you and I are alike. For the sake of argument, then, let's grant that premise. But it should go both ways, shouldn't it? Do *you* have the capacity to understand *me*? On anything but the most superficial level, I mean."

The Embalmer thought about it. He thought about it for a long time, at least ten minutes, before he spoke again:

"Okay, the answer is no, I do not. It's kind of painful to admit it, since I have always considered myself something of a genius, but there it is. "

"You're very intelligent," the Phantom allowed, "but wisdom and understanding do not necessarily come with intelligence."

"They don't necessarily *not*, either. There are different kinds of wisdom. You're only familiar with one or two. I've got lots more."

"You should let me teach you how to play chess," said the Phantom, changing the subject to something a little less fraught.

"No," said the Embalmer, shaking his head. "Too cerebral for me. I'm a creature of instinct and impulse. When I look at chaos, I see order. When I look at order, I see nothing."

"Nonsense. You're a brilliant strategist."

"No, it just comes out that way. I do not think ahead, I do not plan my actions with a definite goal in mind. That is to say, I do have goals that I work toward, but I don't know how I'm going to achieve them until I get there."

"You may think that's true, but I wonder."

Suddenly, apropos of nothing, the Embalmer asked, "Remember when you pretended to be that Roy Markham character?"

"Of course," said the Phantom. He had very briefly adopted the identity of a fictitious criminal, in order to gain access to the Embalmer in the Mobile city jail.

"Do you remember using profanity?"

"Certainly not! I never do that."

"I know. It's a sort of running gag with you. But you did it when you were being Markham. You said 'hell' and 'sonofabitch,' and maybe one or two others."

"Did I really?" the Phantom said, slightly taken aback.

"You absolutely did. And that tells me something."

"What does it tell you?"

"It doesn't really matter. I'm crazy, remember? What matters is... what does it tell *you*? Just think of what Roy Markham could do that *you* cannot."

The Phantom was silent for a long while. Then he said:

"Well, you've given me food for thought. You take care, now, and I'll see you again in a few days."

The Bay Phantom was almost certain that the Embalmer would remain an enigma beyond his understanding. He would continue his efforts, but did not entertain high hopes.

And then there was the other mystery patient there at the clinic. The strange man Perrone had rescued from Hector Sams' clutches a few months earlier.

Perrone believed that the man was actually Paul Darcy.

Mirabelle Darcy's father.

Paul Darcy had come his way during the same case that had brought the Phantom into contact with the Embalmer. Perrone did not know what had happened to the elderly man, or where he had been since his disappearance and presumed death so many years before. Evidently, he had been held captive for many years by Klan leader Sams. Poor Darcy's mind had seemed all but gone.

According to Doctor Ambrose V. Atticus, one of Perrone's confidantes, Darcy was making progress, and had even spoken a few words. But he gave no indication that had any memories of his earlier life. His cognitive functioning seemed to be improving slowly, so there was hope.

Perrone still hadn't decided what he ought to tell Mirabelle...

CHAPTER ONE
MADEMOISELLE DELACROIX TAKES A JOURNEY

"Few men have virtue to withstand the highest bidder."
  —George Washington (1732 - 1789)

JANUARY, 1932

"It's a shame you won't be in town for Mardi Gras," Joe Perrone said.

"Not really," Mirabelle Darcy replied. "I don't like Mardi Gras. I never have."

They were in the front room at Tull House, the strange old place Perrone had purchased the previous year, as both a home and a base of operations for Perrone's activities as the Bay Phantom, Mobile's one and only masked crime fighter. Mirabelle, short and slender, with very dark skin, was dressed a bit more formally than usual, in a long skirt, gray blouse, and a brown jacket, a small hat pinned into her hair.

"Yes," said Perrone, "but have you seen this piece in the paper about the most popular costume this year? It should interest you."

He was almost a foot taller than Mirabelle, with very pale skin. The visual contrast between them mirrored their inner differences. They were two very different people, held together by very powerful bonds.

"Why?" she asked.

"Well, according to the society editor of the *Press*, all the smart young ladies will be dressed as Paper Bag Girl this year."

"Aw *shit*!" Mirabelle exclaimed, horrified. "Tell me you're joking!"

Paper Bag Girl was an impromptu identity Mirabelle had publicly adopted, very briefly, during the Battle of Cathedral Square the previous year. It had been a quick, disposable way to protect her own identity and the Bay Phantom's secrets, but had, for some incomprehensible reason, caught the public's imagination.

This year's Mardi Gras season was in full swing. It had actually started back in November, with the endless balls and get-togethers, but the parades hadn't begun until January. Perrone had no real interest in any of it, but, unlike Mirabelle, he didn't find it distasteful.

Mirabelle was ostensibly Joe Perrone's housekeeper, but in reality, she was both less and much, much more. She might occasionally turn her hand to cleaning or cooking, but such pursuits were on an as-needed basis. Most of her time was spent on arcane scientific research and the crafting of weapons and other devices for the Bay Phantom.

"If it will make you feel better," Perrone said, "*I'm joking.* But I'm not. Here it is, right here. There is a new krewe this year, in fact: The Paper Bag Girls. They'll have their own float."

He waved the newspaper at her.

"I don't wanna see that bullshit," she grumbled. "All I did was pull a damn paper bag over my head. Jesus! Anyway, Mardi Gras isn't Halloween. You're supposed to wear certain kinds of costumes, not just dress up as whatever the hell you want to!"

Perrone sighed. "For heaven's sake, Mirabelle, I thought we agreed you'd watch your language."

"*You* agreed it. I never said a goddamn word. You need to watch those unilateral 'agreements' of yours."

Perrone sighed again.

"I suppose there are worse habits you could have," he said philosophically. "Are you ready? We need to get you to the train station."

"I've been ready all morning, Mister Perrone."

"There's another thing. I thought you were going to start calling me Joe."

"I did, Mister Perrone. I may again one day, if the spirit moves me."

Perrone sighed once more. "All right. I know old habits die hard."

"Yes, well, this goes a little beyond folksy homilies. You know that, I've explained it. Anyhow, if you're all for freedom and equality, why can't I just call you what I want to call you, and leave it at that? And while we're at it, I wish you'd quit sighing at me all the time. It's downright annoying. I certainly won't miss *that* while I'm gone."

It was out of character for Mirabelle to go off on trips, and Joe Perrone took her impending vacation as a good sign. The events of the previous year could have traumatized the young woman, but they seemed instead to have energized her. It would be a bit difficult for him to get along without her, but the potential benefits to Mirabelle outweighed any such concerns.

Though she seemed lighter and more cheerful most of the time, she had taken to spending increasingly long hours by herself, in her private rooms. She said she was working on a number of different experiments, and he had no doubt that she was, but she often emerged from her solitude looking weary and worn. Perrone wondered if she was having trouble assimilating some of the things she had learned and experienced. Perhaps her good cheer was a false front. It would be just like her to conceal any difficulties she might be having.

Even so, *something* had changed, and he was optimistic enough to believe that it was for the better. But there might be... difficulties.

"You're leaving me alone with the ghosts, Mirabelle," he said playfully.

"They won't bother you. Just don't feed them."

"Maybe I'll get an expert to come in and have a look while you're away."

"No! You know how I feel about psychical research. The field attracts more crackpots and charlatans than serious scientists, and that's a damn shame. A dedicated, well-funded group could probably find answers to a lot of troubling questions, given sufficient time, but I don't know of anybody like that. Harry Price is the closest thing, but he's in England. Just leave the ghosts alone. They don't bite."

"Whatever you say, Mirabelle."

"Damn right. And don't you dare sigh again, either."

He drove her to the train station. Her trunk was handed off to a porter, and she kept a large satchel with her.

In the concourse, Perrone bent and kissed her on the cheek, and she returned the gesture, fully aware of the looks of distaste that other travelers were giving them. Perrone didn't care about that. Mirabelle shouldn't have, but it got her goat just the same. What the hell business was it of theirs?

"I'll see you soon," she said. "Take care of yourself... Joe."

He smiled broadly. "Will do, Miss Darcy."

She laughed and waved at him as he walked away. He was awfully sweet, and she knew he meant well. But, like a lot of more liberal white people in the South and elsewhere, he seemed to think he understood more than he possibly could.

Or maybe it was all her. She just didn't know. Whatever genius she supposedly possessed, it could not penetrate the secrets of a human heart, not even her own.

She was dubious about Sigmund Freud's assertion that she was the "ninth smartest person in the world." How could he possibly know that? Most likely, it was an estimate, possibly based on some kind of demographic research. Or else he just made it up. It sounded like something out of a comic strip.

But she was not just smart, not merely a genius. Mirabelle Darcy was a super-genius. There was no getting around that.

In recent months, confronting certain memories that had been retrieved during hypnosis sessions with Doctor Freud, she wondered if she might not have some cause to doubt her sanity. But she decided that wouldn't be practical, so she denied herself the luxury. She remembered things, and the memories had led to new discoveries.

Some of the things she had learned last year—about herself, and about Joe Perrone—demanded action. And that was the real reason for her trip.

She had told Perrone she would be visiting relatives in Zenith. In fact, so far as she knew, none of her extended family lived in that most peculiar of American cities. Once she was certain Perrone was gone, she spoke briefly with the porter, then purchased a ticket to Kansas City. She had no relatives there. But she did have a purpose.

It was an almost-universal truth in this country that a Negro need not seek to be treated with respect even by members of the lowest classes of white society. But it was equally true that a Negro who had enough money could purchase at least the illusion of respect from almost anyone. Only the most die-hard proponents of "racial purity" would willingly forsake financial gain for love of their principles.

As it happened, though Mister Perrone was more than generous with her, Mirabelle Darcy was a wealthy woman in her own right. Just not under her own name. Associates in different parts of the world, with whom she regularly corresponded, had taken out patents on several of her inventions. They split the proceeds with her, fifty-fifty. That was her idea. Most of them wanted to give her full credit and remuneration, but Mirabelle insisted on her arrangement. She wanted no notoriety of any kind. She preferred to be an invisible woman—or maybe more of a human iceberg; only a tiny portion of her was visible to the world at large.

Today, Mirabelle was traveling under an alias, presenting herself as one Monique Delacroix, a resident of Paris, France, and a well-to-do young lady.

Mirabelle had noticed that most white Southerners didn't quite know what to make of the anomalous creatures they referred to as "foreign niggers." In some strange way, they were exotic enough to evoke more puzzlement than scorn. At the very least, they were somebody else's problem. Thus the identity of Monique Delacroix provided her with an extra layer of insulation.

She had once toyed with the idea of moving to France. Things were different there. Josephine Baker said she had finally felt liberated after becoming an expatriate. But Mirabelle had ultimately rejected the notion. She could not accept the kind of liberation that she'd have to travel five thousand miles across the Atlantic for.

Though it was hardly necessary for her current audience, who would surely not know the difference, Mirabelle spoke French better than most natives, with an impeccable Parisian accent. Sadly, her consummate performance would be lost on her unrefined audience.

***

Once she was in her private compartment, she removed her hat and jacket and made herself comfortable. As usual, she felt better when she was by herself, away from other people.

The train moved north, skirting the edge of downtown. To her left, Mirabelle could see the construction equipment on Dauphin Street. Another never-ending public works project. How long had they been at it this time? Wasn't it another "drainage improvement" boondoggle? Something like that. And when they were done, the drainage would still be terrible, as always.

She opened her satchel, and took out a large, folded sheet of blueprint paper.

Smart as I'm reputed to be, why the hell am I doing this?

Well, it isn't stupidity, it's insanity. Gives a defense lawyer something to work with.

Mirabelle unfolded the paper. It had a detailed diagram printed on it. She pored over it for more than two hours, occasionally drawing an arrow here or a dotted line there.

"This shouldn't be too difficult," she muttered at one point. "I may be eaten up with hubris, but I still believe I can do it."

She set the diagram aside, unfolded another similar sheet, and studied it for an hour, again making pencil marks at various points.

Mirabelle smiled. With just a little bit of luck—or, rather, with the absence of any catastrophically *bad* luck—she ought to be able to sneak right into the United States Penitentiary at Leavenworth, Kansas.

CHAPTER TWO
SOME OF THE PHANTOM'S MEN

Louis Rickert did not consider himself a "good person," though he knew for a fact that he was far from the worst that humanity had to offer. He had been a criminal almost since he learned how to walk.

And now, here he was, working for a mysterious crime fighter! Life did indeed throw some curve balls at times.

Well, you don't necessarily have to *be* good to *do* some good. He would never be a genuinely honest man, he knew, but his work for the Bay Phantom seemed to him to mitigate some of his other activities.

Anyway, he wouldn't be much use to the masked man if he didn't occupy a modest position in Mobile's criminal underworld. He couldn't do that and keep his nose totally clean at the same time. That just stood to reason.

Tonight, he was sitting in a speakeasy downtown. It wasn't the sort of place an ordinary fellow would take a date, but it wasn't packed to the rafters with murderous hardcore gangsters either. Had Rickert been a bit more knowledgeable about religious doctrine, he might have thought of the joint as a sort of limbo.

Louis was sitting at a small table, drinking with a man who should have been one of his most feared natural enemies, a shark who could pick off a bottom feeder like Louis Rickert without any effort at all.

Shorty Red, who was closer to seven feet tall than six, and almost as colorless as an albino, sipped at a glass of club soda, while Louis consumed one shot of whiskey after another. Both Shorty and the Bay Phantom had cautioned Louis about his drinking, but he was a grown man and could do whatever he pleased. One of the few things he had never been arrested for was public intoxication, or any other kind of alcohol-related infraction. Anyhow, it had never once interfered with his ability to perform his duties for the Phantom—except for three or four isolated incidents spread out over a period of several weeks.

"Something's going on," Shorty was saying, "and the Phantom wants us to look into it."

"What's the big deal?" asked Louis. "Sounds like an ordinary protection racket to me. What does he care about that?"

Shorty sighed. "He cares about everything, and he's right to do so.

You've got a bad attitude, Louis. We've talked about that before. If you don't like the job, you should stop taking his money."

"I didn't say I wasn't gonna do it," Louis replied indignantly. "I just wonder about it. Is that against the law? What am I, a zombie?"

"No, you aren't a zombie," Shorty said, turning his cold, colorless eyes on Louis. "Are you implying that I am?"

Louis flinched, even though he knew by now that Shorty Red did not and would not ever represent a physical threat to him. The hulking ex-enforcer for the Carter crime family had undergone some kind of transformation over the past few months. Shorty had been one of the most violent and unpredictable criminals on the Gulf Coast—before he met the Bay Phantom. Though he wasn't exactly a pussycat these days, he seemed a lot more thoughtful and sensitive, which was a good thing for Louis, who had quite recently beaten the living hell out of Shorty with a crowbar. The giant didn't seem to carry a grudge over it, and Louis knew full well that the Bay Phantom was the reason for that.

"Hell no, Shorty, I ain't implying nothing," Louis said. "All's I'm doing is... Oh, never mind."

"I won't. Listen, this is serious business, Louis. The Carter family has been in disarray since Caleb disappeared and Penny resurfaced. And it looks now like a small and mysterious group has managed to gain a foothold. The Carter organization has been quiet. This new bunch has been strong-arming restaurants, and nobody wants to talk about it. Could be protection, could be something else. Most of them are completely legit—not speakeasies or gambling fronts. They're frightened, that much is certain. The Phantom wants to know what's going on and what they're so afraid of."

"I got no problem with that," Louis said. "My problem is that I could use some more money. Especially if I'm gonna be doing dangerous duties, you know? Hazard pay, I think they call it."

Here was the crux of Louis' current dilemma. He had quite a knack for keeping his own best interests at the forefront of his mind, no matter what was going on around him. And what was bugging him now was money. It preoccupied his thoughts to the near-exclusion of everything else.

But money was not an end in itself. It was only the means by which he believed he could achieve his true goal.

Gladys Turnbull. He had met her the previous year, during the series of events that had led to his employment with the Bay Phantom.

He had saved her life. Or she had saved his. Honestly, his memories of the whole thing were a little hazy, but somebody saved somebody's life, and then Gladys invited him to have a drink with her. Yes, he had been smitten. Why the hell not? She was a cute kid, blonde and dainty-looking, but tough inside. Maybe too tough.

Gladys' interest in Louis had lasted for all of ten minutes. Her current indifference was not reciprocated. Louis was still interested in her, and it was making him crazy.

He couldn't figure out what had made her turn on him. He wasn't even slightly balding, and he had almost all of his teeth.

It had to be about money, he reasoned. That's what it was always about with women. It was a real shame, but that's how the world worked.

Shorty Red had suggested to him that perhaps a woman like Gladys, who was well-educated and held a responsible, respectable job as a newspaper editor, might not have very much in common with a semi-literate petty crook. That was just plain nuts. The rules of attraction didn't pay attention to stuff like that.

It was money. Had to be.

"Louis, you aren't grateful for anything, that's your problem," Shorty was saying. "You can be so hard-headed. You remind me of my Uncle Reynard."

"What about him?"

"He got hit by a shell fragment in the Great War. They had to put a steel plate in his head."

"Aw, horsefeathers! That ain't even possible!"

"Of course it is. A lot of wounded men had it done."

"I dunno. It sounds like Buck Rogers stuff."

"Think what you like, you're just proving my point. Anyhow, Louis, you won't have to do much of anything, not right now. The Boss wants us to stake out a couple of restaurants. He can't predict where this bunch will strike next, so he wants us to keep an eye on a couple of likely prospects. I'm going to take the Bumblebee Inn, and you will cover Max's Restaurant. You do remember Max's Restaurant, don't you?"

Louis shifted uncomfortably in his seat. Max's Restaurant had been the scene of a certain crowbar beating, back before Shorty started working for the Bay Phantom.

"You're to meet him at Max's tomorrow night," the giant said, looking at his watch. "He'll be here soon with details."

"Ah. Well, that ain't so bad. I could use one of them shrimp dinners Max does."

"You won't be there for a dinner."

"We'll see. And what will *you* be doing?"

"The same thing you'll be doing, only somewhere else and by myself."

"Ha! I guess the Phantom would rather it was me that had his back, huh?"

"More likely he knows better than to trust you on your own, but believe what you want to, Louis."

"I will."

"Louis, you know I appreciate your many...qualities," said the Bay Phantom. Louis jumped at the unexpected voice, the sudden presence. The Phantom seemed to have materialized out of nowhere. One moment he and Shorty were by themselves, the next moment the Phantom was sitting in the third chair.

"Good evening, fellows," the masked man said smoothly. "You're both doing well, I trust?"

"Ah, well, Boss, since you mention it," Louis began, "I could really, uh, use a..."

"We're *just fine*, sir," Shorty forcefully interrupted. "*Both* of us."

"Good to hear," said the Phantom. He handed each of them an envelope. These would contain the standard weekly stipend. It was good money, but... Louis screwed up his courage and prepared to take the plunge. He took a deep breath and turned to the Phantom...

... who simply was not there any more.

Dammit.

"I wish I knew how he does that," Louis said.

"No, you don't," Shorty assured him.

"Yeah, probably not. I need another whiskey."

"You'd have more money if you didn't spend so much on whiskey."

"If I had *more* money to *begin* with, I could spend all I *want* on whiskey and still have plenty. That's a better way to look at it. That's capitalism, Shorty. If people were satisfied with what they have, there never would be any *progress*. You just don't understand how the world works."

"No, Louis, of course I don't. My understanding will never equal yours. Now, open your envelope. There may not be enough money in there to suit you, but your instructions for tomorrow night will be in there too."

"Ah, fooey."

CHAPTER THREE
POOR KATYDID

"It's a hell of a thing, Sarge," said the uniformed cop. "What could have done it to him?"

Detective Sergeant Tom Dart made no reply. He stood and looked down at the body sprawled on the concrete floor of the warehouse. It appeared to be the remains of a white male, clad in a security guard's uniform. The corpse was on its back, limbs drawn up, skin dry and brittle, like an empty katydid shell.

"Wow," the cop went on. "It kinda reminds me of what that Black Embalmer did to people. You reckon he might have done it? He was never caught, you know."

"Oh, I don't need to be reminded of that," Dart said thoughtfully, kneeling beside the body. "But this looks different. Almost like he was *burned*, but there's no evidence of any fire, and his clothes are undamaged." He touched the desiccated neck and wrists lightly with the tips of his fingers. "He's all... dried out."

"Damn, just when it seemed like things might be getting back to normal. What could *do* that?"

"I haven't got a clue, Matranga." Dart stood up and rubbed his hands on his pants. "Never seen the like. Maybe the doctor will know more than I do."

He didn't. When the coroner arrived, he knelt and gave the body a quick examination. Then he gave it a more thorough examination. Finally, he stood up straight, shaking his head.

"This is a new one on me," he said. "You're sure this man was alive earlier today?"

"Yep," said Tom, "no doubt about that." The guy that ran the filling station across the street had confirmed it. This watchman lying here shriveled to a crisp had arrived at his usual time, just a few hours ago.

Doctor Klein shook his head again. "If this body were brought to me without any information, I'd say it had been lying in the desert for a few months."

"Hell!"

"Or there, yes. The corpse is desiccated to an astonishing degree. In fact, extreme dehydration may be the cause of death; I can't be sure just now. I cannot imagine how such a thing could happen here, in this warehouse."

"Lord have mercy," Dart said, shaking his head. "We've got another weirdo."

There was a thin layer of yellowish, greasy residue on the floor, all around the corpse. The doctor didn't know what it was; he scraped some of it up and put it in a test tube. Tom did the same.

"Who called this in?" Dart asked the uniformed cop.

"Search me, Sarge," said Matranga. "Dispatch called us, then they called you. You'll have to ask them."

He picked up a phone and did just that. The dispatch operator was evasive. He hemmed and hawed for a while, then claimed the information had come from an anonymous phone call. He said he got the impression that some derelict had gained entry to the building, seen the body, and decided to call the cops.

Maybe.

Nothing had been taken from the warehouse proper, as far as they could tell, but the office showed unmistakable signs of having been burgled. A small safe had been blown open. There was no way to determine what had been taken. The owner of the building—a corporation called All-South Storage—could not be reached. The manager, according to a small stack of business cards on a desk in the office, was someone called Tim Ridley. Dart sent a couple guys out to try and track him down.

He didn't think they would. Dollars to donuts, this place was among the extensive holdings of the Carter family. If so, there was more to this murder than met the eye. And what *did* meet the eye was more than enough to keep him busy.

A guy had basically been mummified to death, within the space of a few hours, maybe quicker than that.

This whole thing already had a familiar smell to it. Dirty laundry carried an aroma that was unmistakable.

So did dirty money.

CHAPTER FOUR
MEN IN BLACK

L ouis Rickert met up with the Bay Phantom the following night at 8 p.m., at Max's Restaurant in Bayou La Batre. Louis had been there for fifteen minutes when the Phantom appeared.

"Maybe they'll leave Max alone," Louis said hopefully. "He's kind of off the beaten path."

"No, I think they'll strike here, and soon," The Bay Phantom contradicted him. "This place is popular. There isn't much of a pattern to the gang's activities, but they've exhausted most of the potential targets within the city limits. The murder of Charlie Tate, which I believe to have been their work, proves that they are prepared to stop at nothing. And now, they will either be content with what they have, or they will start branching out."

"I've never known a gang of crooks to be content with anything," Louis opined, speaking from long experience as a chronic malcontent. In fact, he was hoping that tonight would provide him with an opportunity to raise once again the subject Shorty Red had prevented him from discussing with the Boss the night before.

He had been trying to work up the nerve to ask the Phantom for a little raise, but it just never seemed like the right time. Oh, the masked man was more than generous, but Louis ran some awful risks at times, and it could be argued that he might possibly deserve a little bit more remuneration. Hell, it was a free country, wasn't it? And didn't employees have the right to bargain with their employers? Louis seemed to dimly recall that someone somewhere had once died for that right. John Henry, or somebody like that, he thought.

Not that Louis was a high roller or anything, but he thought he needed some extra money for clothes and things, if he ever wanted to impress Gladys Turnbull.

"Precisely," the Phantom said. "Also, Max's reluctance to submit to demands is well known. They'll want to bring him in line, if only as an example."

"Oh yeah. I hadn't thought of that."

Max himself, an older man, pear-shaped, with dark hair and a bushy moustache, emerged from the kitchen. The Bay Phantom greeted him in a friendly manner.

"Are we going to have another Wild West act like we did last time?" the restaurateur asked worriedly. "I mean, I appreciate what you've done and what you do, Mister Phantom, but I *am* trying to run a business here."

"Of course you are," the Phantom said, clapping Max lightly on the shoulder. "That is as it should be. You have the right to conduct business, free from the depredations of criminals. And that is why I am here."

"Right, depredations, sure," said Max. "Well, I don't mean to tell you your business. You want something to eat or drink while you're waiting?"

"I wouldn't say no to a grape Nehi, Max."

"What about you, Louis?"

What Louis had in mind was a nice shrimp dinner, with a few bottles of beer. But, with the Phantom standing right there, it seemed prudent to temper his ambition.

"Uh, how about an Orange Crush?"

"Okay, fellas." Max walked over to the cooler and got the drinks. The Phantom handed him two nickels, which he unsuccessfully tried to wave away.

The Phantom pushed his mask up far enough to expose his mouth so he could drink. Louis looked away. For some reason, it made him uncomfortable, like seeing his mother in her underwear.

A car pulled into the lot. Louis and the Phantom went to the front window and peered out from between the blinds. Two men got out. They were well-dressed, in somber black suits and flat-crowned hats.

"They look like preachers," Louis remarked. "Hope we don't have to listen to some spiel."

As far as Louis was concerned, he had had his religious apotheosis a few months earlier in the Cathedral Basilica of the Immaculate Conception. It was a done deal, and he saw no need to belabor the point by going over every word in the Bible time and time again. Best to just get on with life. After all, you could spoil a good thing by overdoing it.

The men walked across the parking area, side by side, toward the front door. The one on the left was about six feet tall; the one on the right, considerably shorter. Their faces were soft, yet mask-like, and they walked slowly and deliberately, looking neither right nor left as they advanced. Louis watched them intently; there was something not quite right about the pair. They were no preachers, he decided, though they seemed to have a vaguely ecclesiastical air of menace about them. Each had a small flower in his lapel, which did nothing to dispel the sinister aura.

Louis noticed a third man, who had remained in the car, behind the wheel. He couldn't tell anything about this one, except for the fact that he must be really tall, the way his head was pressed up against the inside roof of the car.

"I'll just duck down behind the counter," said the Phantom, "and we'll see what happens. They might be ordinary customers. Don't be nervous, Louis."

"Who's nervous?" Louis asked with a bit of unconvincing indignation in his voice. He made a conscious effort to prevent his gun hand from trembling. Something about these guys was making him jittery. He couldn't have said what it was, but it was there. He sat down at a table so his pistol would be out of sight, and waited.

The taller man pushed open the door, and the pair stepped inside.

"Who is in charge here?" the shorter man asked. He had some kind of an accent. Not English or French, Louis thought, but one of those others.

"That would be me," Max said nervously, casting a quick glance at Louis. Dammit, one of those ghouls might have noticed, and they'd be on to him. Louis lifted his pistol from his lap, still keeping it out of sight. But neither of the men looked in his direction.

"Then it is you to whom we must speak. It has come to our attention that you are not part of our new distribution system. We must assume that this is an oversight on your part, and have come to help you set up your account."

"And who are you?" Max asked.

"We represent a distributor. A purveyor of the finest meat available on the Gulf Coast. We will supply you with the best tasting, most flavorful beef you've ever had, truly in a league of its own. We also handle pork products, five star gourmet quality, that belong in a very, *very* select category of restaurant, such as your own fine establishment here."

"I don't think I'm interested, fellas. I get my meat from—"

"Us," the tall man said, forcefully enough to silence Max. He sounded American, but not Southern. "You get your meat from *us*." He punctuated this statement by pulling a pistol from his jacket pocket and pointing it in Max's general direction.

The short one produced a pistol of his own. Louis remained very still, as ready as he could be for whatever was to come.

"We are pleased to sign you up," said the short man. "I have with me a complete price list, and I assure you that you will not find our terms onerous. I daresay you will save a bit of money by switching from your current distributor. And there is an added incentive: your erstwhile supplier will not put a bullet through your head when you cancel your contract with him. But there is every possibility that we *will*, should you unwisely reject our very special offer."

Louis slowly and silently rose from his seat, gradually pushing the chair back with his calves.

And then—

The Bay Phantom rose up from behind the counter, a gun in each hand, covering both of the men. It was an awe-inspiring sight, Louis had to admit, like something out of a movie or a scary Bible story. The Boss looked like he was ten feet tall. He hopped smoothly up onto the counter, then down onto the floor in front of it.

"And who might you be?" said the tall one, unruffled, as though a sudden appearance by a masked, cloaked, armed man was something he saw every day.

"I am called the Bay Phantom. I'm glad you men showed up here tonight, because I'd like to talk to you."

"Then talk."

"I would appreciate it if you two dropped your weapons. I will retain mine. As I am an invited guest and you are not, I think the rules of etiquette are on my side."

Unobserved by the two newcomers, Louis rose from his chair, pistol ready.

The men dropped their guns. The Phantom relaxed his guard for just a fraction of a second, an almost involuntary reaction. But it was enough for the short man. He made a whipping motion with his right arm, and a gun appeared in his hand.

It was a tiny gun, containing no more than two or three shots.

This much the Phantom determined, as the man dashed toward him.

There was no time for the Phantom to dodge the bullet or to fire on the man, but he managed enough of a turn to the right that the slug caught him in the left shoulder, rather than the chest. It was a small-caliber round, but it stung like the devil, and would have been fatal had it found his heart.

The pain from the initial impact was so intense that the masked man was, for three-quarters of a second, virtually blinded and paralyzed. It was all he could do to lift a foot and kick the short man, sending him staggering back almost to the table where Louis was. That gave the taller man his opportunity. He proved himself to be a very poor sport by slithering up close to the Phantom and delivering a savage punch to the new bullet wound. The crime fighter's head spun from the pain, and he almost threw up in his mask.

Oh, that would never do. Need to start carrying an antiemetic with me, just in case.

But he recovered quickly, hopping backward a few steps away from his foe while his senses righted themselves. Then he stepped forward, dodged a hasty jab from the taller man, and whacked him on the side of the face with the butt of one of his pistols. The man staggered back, clutching his bleeding cheek.

Meanwhile, Louis took a shot at the shorter man, who was still disoriented by the Phantom's kick, putting a slug into his right thigh. He didn't really like the idea of shooting a man from behind, but there were other things he liked even less, and this seemed like the best way to avoid them.

The guy twisted around and took a shot of his own, uttering a few words Louis didn't understand. Louis had already ducked, and now he flipped the table up and flung it at the short man.

"Hey now *hey!*" Max shouted.

The table hit its mark, disarming the short man and sending him staggering back in the direction from which he had so recently staggered. His momentum sent him right into the Bay Phantom, who was grappling with his wounded opponent. All three crashed to the floor and began flailing madly at one another.

Louis cursed. He couldn't get a clean shot with all of them thrashing around in a knot like that, and everybody wearing black.

Then the tall man rose above the other two. Louis was about to take his shot, when he was startled into inaction by an angry voice:

"No more shooting in my restaurant!"

The melee was brought to a conclusion by Max Santorelli, who had dashed back into the kitchen to fetch a heavy iron skillet, which he swung like a baseball bat, striking the side of the tall man's head with terrific force.

This sent the man skidding across the room and into the overturned table. Astonishingly, he remained conscious and got to his feet pretty smoothly. Louis drew a bead on the guy, but Max threatened him with the skillet if he dared to fire another shot inside the restaurant. The tall man skedaddled, hitting the front door as though he'd been shot out of a cannon.

The short man also took the opportunity to make tracks, moving very quickly for someone with a slug in his thigh. He was out the door right behind his companion.

Hell, let 'em go, Louis thought. He was worried about the Phantom, fussing over the masked man until he seemed fully alert and was back on his feet.

Unfortunately, he had to report to his chief that the two men had gotten away clean.

"Well, not *clean*," Louis amended. "They were bloodied up some. I put a slug in the little one's thigh, and of course Max done what he done to the big one."

"*Did*, Louis. *Did* what he *did*."

"Right, yeah. Hit him over the head. That's what Max done. I'm the one what shot the other guy."

"Louis..."

Max brought the Phantom a towel soaked in cold water to place over the wound until it could be given proper attention.

"Are you okay, Boss?" Louis asked nervously.

"I'm fine. I just got shot, that's all."

From anybody else, that would have been a wisecrack. But Louis knew the Phantom was completely serious. The Phantom was always serious; Louis doubted the guy had ever cracked a joke in his life. The Phantom genuinely didn't think a bullet in the shoulder was any big deal.

"Well," said the partially-reformed criminal, "maybe you better get someone to look at it."

"Don't worry, I will." He straightened his jacket. "Those men were not familiar to me."

"Me neither. Never seen 'em before. That blonde-headed one musta been a foreigner. He was speaking Spanish or something."

"German. He was speaking German. Spanish is one of the Romance languages, Louis, while German comes from a different—"

"Uh, sure, Boss, but about that shoulder of yours—"

"I believe the bleeding has stopped. I'll have it seen to, Louis. Do you think you'd be able to provide a good description of those men?"

"Yeah, sure."

"Good. You might want to start asking around."

"I will, Boss. They didn't look like hoods, though. Maybe I should check with some of the funeral parlors, huh? They looked like a couple of stiffs."

"Hmmm. Colorful, Louis, but accurate. And there was something else. Did you notice the sound it made when Max hit the tall one? It was like metal on metal. As though the man—"

"Had a metal plate in his skull," Louis finished.

"Precisely. You're becoming quite the detective!"

"Well, it would explain why that whack Max gave him didn't put him under. Hey, you figure he got that in the Great War?"

"Not an unreasonable inference. There are depths to you, it seems."

"That's right, Boss, I ain't as dumb as I look."

"I never thought you were. Well, I'd best be getting along now, I need to have this wound seen to. Take Care, Louis. I'll be in touch."

"Sure, sure. Uh, say, I was just wondering—"

"Yes? Can you make it quick, Louis? This shoulder—"

"Aw, nothing. I'll talk to you about it later. You go get patched up."

The Phantom was a bit concerned about driving, after taking a bullet the way he had, but it wasn't troubling him all that much. He put a compress over it and headed back to Tull House. On the way, the wound actually slipped his mind once or twice. After he got home, he started to the kitchen for a glass of milk before he suddenly remembered he needed medical attention.

The wound wasn't bad at all, nowhere near what he had feared. He could have sworn at the time that the bullet had done more damage. Certainly, an unusual amount of blood had soaked into his suit jacket.

Removing the jacket and his shirt, he discovered something curious. It appeared that the slug had fallen out of the hole it had made in his shoulder. He found it in the folds of the blood-soaked shirt.

"How very queer," he said.

Ah, well. Just accept your good fortune and carry on.

Joe Perrone went into the kitchen and fixed himself a cheese sandwich and another glass of milk. He carried his repast into the front room and sat in his usual chair.

The house seemed cavernous and a little inhospitable without Mirabelle.

After he ate, he picked up the newspaper from the side table and thumbed through it, stopping on the obituaries page when a familiar name caught his eye.

Toby Zinfandel. He was Perrone's age. The cause of death was listed as heart failure.

This was the second such death in as many weeks.

First Norville Perrin, and now Toby Zinfandel.

Both obituaries had been vague as to cause of death. Just how natural could "natural causes" be, in the cases of two active men in their late 20s?

They would likely be members of Perrone's own social set, if Perrone had belonged to one. But he had known both of them when they were all children. He had money in common with them, and a little bit of shared history, which he supposed made them friends.

By the time he was ready for bed, his shoulder wasn't bothering him a bit; in fact, he had all but forgotten about it.

As he climbed the stairs to his bedroom, he heard soft, strange murmuring, accompanied by light tapping, coming from somewhere on the second floor. He had heard it before; so had Mirabelle. They had never been able to pinpoint its source. It would sound as though it were coming from a particular room, but when they went there; it would sound as though it were coming from the hallway or one of the other rooms. The murmuring ghosts seemed to enjoy hide-and-seek.

Mirabelle accepted the reality of the ghosts without adopting a theory as to their true nature. "Not enough data," she had said more than once. She was disinclined to think they were the spirits of dead people, but admitted that she could not advance an alternative hypothesis.

He lay awake for ten minutes, listening to the wordless whispering, until everything faded away.

CHAPTER FIVE
GLADYS PITCHES IN

The following day, Joe Perrone received a visit from Gladys Turnbull, an editor with the *Mobile Press*, and one of a small handful of people who knew that Perrone was the Bay Phantom.

She knocked on the door of Tull House at ten in the morning. Perrone had been awake for about an hour. He had completely forgotten about his recent bullet wound.

"You need someone to look after you a little bit while Mirabelle's gone," said Gladys, after Perrone had ushered her inside. "Someone who knows what you do."

"Gladys, I appreciate the gesture, but..."

"Never mind all that. Look, Joe, I wouldn't be a newspaper editor if not for you. In fact, I'd be a goddamn corpse."

"Gladys..."

"Yeah, I know, *language*. Sorry. I'll try to curb my evil tongue in your presence."

"I appreciate that, but it really isn't necessary for you to look after me while..."

"I know it isn't *necessary*," she interrupted, "but I *want* to do it. I owe you, and I don't take things like that lightly. I still feel bad about what I almost did to you."

"You don't have to."

"I know that, but at the same time, yes I do. We can call it penance, and I need it, for the sake of my soul."

"Well, I wouldn't want to interfere with that."

"Good. It's settled then. I've got a ton of vacation time, and I might as well use it on this."

"Very well. I'm grateful, Gladys."

"I'm not a genius like Mirabelle is," she said. "So don't expect any of *that* out of me. I can't help it if I'm not as smart as she is."

"According to Sigmund Freud," said Joe Perrone, "there are only eight people in the world who are smarter than Mirabelle. I am not one of them. Mirabelle is smarter than I ever had any hope of becoming."

"It's good that you can admit that. A lot of men never would, even under penalty of death. White men, especially."

"Yes, quite. Well, I don't labor under illusions of that kind."

"That sets you *way* apart. So, what's going on? Any interesting Bay Phantom business?"

"Mmm. We seem to have a new gang attempting to move into town. This new outfit, whoever they are, have shown an interest in restaurants. Especially those that do catering, but all other kinds as well."

"Bootleg liquor?"

He shook his head.

"Strangely, no. Not a hint of that. Foodstuffs. Meat."

"Meat?"

"Meat. Pork and beef. No poultry. Several restaurants are now buying these products, and none of them want to talk about it. The police have

"Do they have some kind of farm here in the city?"

done nothing. Oddly, the prices being charged are somewhat below current wholesale rates. Even so, there was resistance, which was met with threats and the fulfillment of threats. The late Charlie Tate, for example. I have attempted to trace the food to its source, with no success. I don't believe it's being brought in from out of town."

"Huh. Do they have some kind of a farm here in the city?"

"Possibly. If so, it is very well-hidden. And their distribution system has so far proved untraceable."

"That's... peculiar."

"Yes, it is," Perrone agreed. "And disturbing in a way I can't quite define. I just have this feeling... There is a deep *unsavoriness* to this thing. I do not know as much as a man who presumes to take the law into his own hands ought to know, and that troubles me."

"Good. That reassures me in a way I can't quite define. Actually, I *can* define it, but I thought that sounded cute."

"Anyhow, they started out small, but expanded their operations very rapidly. Evidently they have a lot of money, and they've been making free with it at City Hall. None of the complaints made by restaurant owners to the police have been properly investigated. And the Carters seem to be staying out of their way. Penny is playing some kind of a game, I'm sure."

"Oh, God help us," Gladys said.

CHAPTER SIX
THE ART COLLECTOR

Rickey Harvard was feeling the full weight of his seventeen years. His life was going nowhere, and there was nothing to indicate that it would ever go anywhere else.

He had a job, sure. That was something. But it wasn't much of a job, and he didn't need to know anything or be good at anything to do it. A monkey could probably discharge his duties just as well as Rickey did.

His youth was working against him. If he were an old man, he wouldn't have much longer to go before he died, and that would be that. But he might live for fifty or sixty more years; that was a long time to do nothing and be nobody.

What did he have to look forward to? Girls weren't interested in him.

That was a huge problem, because Rickey was interested in them. Very interested.

He had thought that drinking liquor would help with that. It certainly made it easier to talk to girls. But it made too many other things not only easy, but inevitable. On every occasion when he had tried, with the help of some bootleg whiskey, to make time with a pretty girl, Rickey had done or said something horribly embarrassing, and ruined whatever chances he might have had.

So it was a good thing he had a job where he wasn't likely to run into anyone he knew. In fact, he had plenty of privacy, which made it possible for him to pursue his new hobby away from prying eyes.

Rickey had become an art collector. Not paintings or statues, but fine photography. Studies of the human form.

Pictures of girls. Girls in bathing costumes, girls in their underclothes, and—best of all—girls *out* of their underclothes. The Great Mystery revealed. Rickey had been taken aback at first; he had envisioned things a bit differently. But it hadn't taken him long to become accustomed to the reality, then to appreciate it, then to crave it.

Today, he was going to make some new acquisitions. The art dealer he patronized worked out of a little stationery store on Saint Emanuel Street. Of course, discerning customers like Rickey didn't just walk in the front door. No, the special customers who came seeking the special items had to make arrangements by telephone, and meet the dealer in the alley behind the store. It might have seemed a little seedy, if a person didn't know better, but the dealer—a little fellow named Antoine—assured Rickey that this was how it was done in the finest galleries and salons.

"The law is unenlightened," he had said, "but true art will win out!"

Antoine, a man about the size of a large raccoon, with slicked back hair and an enormous wart at the side of his nose, met Rickey at the back door, as usual. And, also as usual, Rickey handed over his money. The pictures weren't cheap, but nothing worth having ever was. Antoine counted the bills twice before handing Rickey the now-familiar plain brown envelope.

"Got some real good ones today, Rickey," said the art dealer. "A new girl I have not seen before. She has a fine aesthetic."

"Howdy there, Rickey," someone said.

Rickey turned his head to look. Here came Eddie, ambling up the alley, grinning like the wooden clown at the peanut shop. Like the clown, Eddie had dead eyes, and his smile seemed to be coming from something other than happiness. It was there on his face pretty much all the time, and one side of his mouth went up higher than the other, like he wasn't entirely sure about it.

Eddie was from up North somewhere, and he talked funny, the way people do up there. Rickey thought he had said he was from Wisconsin or some weird foreign state like that. But if it hadn't been for his accent, he could have been any old common Alabama hillbilly, albeit a strange one.

He was twenty-five or thirty years old, probably, and had roomed for a while in Rickey's father's house, before he got a good job and moved into new quarters somewhere else. According to Eddie, he had come down South to see how interesting it was, and maybe to find better work than he was able to get in whatever place he was from.

Rickey and Eddie had formed a friendship, largely based on the fact that nobody else seemed to want much to do with either one of them.

"Oh, hey, Eddie," Rickey said. "They got some good ones today. Brand new girl, Antoine says."

He tore open the envelope and extracted a small stack of cards. He looked them over, and showed one to Eddie.

"Wow, look at that!" Rickey said.

"Hey, that's nice!" Eddie said. "I bet she's a redhead. Can't really tell in black and white, but she looks like a redhead."

"Yeah, she sure does," Rickey agreed. Eddie was right. Redheads had a certain look about them, even when you couldn't see the color of their hair.

Antoine spoke up then:

"Okay, fellas, you know the rules. This is not what we do out of doors, right? Eddie, you make your purchase, then the two of you quickly go elsewhere. If you can't be discreet, I cannot do business with you."

Eddie paid him and received a brown envelope of his own.

They went over the new pictures as they walked up Saint Emanuel Street, and much discussion was devoted to the redhead:

"She looks kind of mean, you know?" Eddie remarked. "Like she don't take no guff off of anybody. My mama's like that, but she wouldn't never pose for pictures like these."

"That's good."

"My mama would kill me if she knew I was looking at this type of pictures," Eddie rambled on. "She's a godly woman, that's for sure, and she knows all about the fallen women in the Bible, and the ones that's still out and about in the world today. I ought to listen to what she has told me, but I'm just too powerfully interested in women. What they look like underneath their clothes and what makes them tick, you know?"

"Mmm-hmm."

"Well," Eddie said in his goofily cheerful way, "back to the old salt mine. That's a joke. I don't really work in a salt mine. There ain't any salt mines around here, I wouldn't think."

"Mmm-hmm," Rickey replied absently. Wow, this redhead was the cat's pajamas! Gosh, look at what she's doing in *this* one!

"They got oil wells in Louisiana," Eddie added. He had a penchant for irrelevant observations, which he scatted randomly throughout his conversations.

"That's good," Rickey muttered, imagining the redhead walking up the street where he lived with his father and knocking on their door.

"I'll see you later, Rickey."

"Sure, Eddie, sure, sure..."

Then Eddie was gone, and Ricky didn't notice his absence any more than he had noticed his presence.

Coming around the corner onto Conti Street, Rickey ran right smack into a guy. He dropped his postcards, and quickly stooped to pick them up.

"Sorry, Mister, sorry," he muttered.

The guy he'd run into said, "Why can't you watch where you're going, you little mutt?" He squatted down to help gather up the cards.

"Hey, leave 'em alone, I'll get 'em!" Rickey yelled, grabbing for the cards.

The man stood up and stepped back, outside Rickey's reach, and examined the cards.

"Well, well, look at this! Hey, she's something. I'll bet she's a redhead."

"Give 'em here!" Rickey wailed, his voice almost breaking.

"Where did you get these?" Louis Rickert asked.

"I ain't telling you!"

"Well," Rickert said, adopting the manner of a police officer, "I might have to confiscate them. This is harmful material in possession of a minor. You could go blind. How old are you, anyhow?"

"None of your beeswax, that's how old I am. How old are *you*?"

"Look, kid. If you tell me where you got these, I might let it slide."

"No, I'm not telling. They'll quit selling to me if I do. Anyhow, you ain't a cop, I know you, you're just a cheap hood. So you can't consecrate nothing. Gimme back my stuff."

"Well... How much did you pay for 'em?"

Rickey told him the truth. Rickert let out a low whistle.

"Are you serious? Where do you get that kind of money?"

"I pull it out of my ass," Rickey snarled defiantly.

"Watch your mouth, kid. Here's your dirty pictures back. Get lost."

Rickey snatched the cards out of Rickert's hand, stuck them into his pocket, and ran off down the street, shooting poisonous looks and muttered curses back over his shoulder. It would have been worse had he been aware that Rickert had slipped one of the pictures of the redhead up his sleeve.

Wheels were turning in Rickert's head.

There was money to be made from pictures like these.

It was something to think about...

Gladys went out and collected the day's post from the box. There were three or four circulars addressed to Joseph Perrone, and sixteen pieces of mail for Mirabelle Darcy. Mirabelle received all manner of mail from all over the world.

Joe Perrone received virtually nothing.

Gladys placed Perrone's meager correspondence on a little table by the front door; Mirabelle's went into a safe in the pantry.

When Perrone came back home from whatever he had been doing to occupy himself, he paused at the little table, and went through his mail, such as it was.

"I've been invited to a get-together," he said, holding up a card. "The German-American Friendship League, or whatever it's called."

"Oh, you mean the Patriots Guild," Gladys corrected him. "I've heard a bit about them. They've set up shop here in Mobile. *Transatlantic* Patriots Guild, to be exact."

"Yes, that's what it says. Seems like a bit of a contradiction, doesn't it?"

"Well, they're pushing the idea of greater friendship and cooperation between the United States and Germany. Based on *something*, I'm not sure what. Nationalism, and probably racial 'purity,' given the current political climate in Germany."

"Perhaps they wish to forestall any further conflicts. If Germany re-arms itself, which I understand it is doing, then war with our allies in Europe becomes likely."

"Yes, and I think it would be to Germany's advantage to keep America out of any wars over there."

Perrone nodded. "And who is behind this ambitious project?"

"One of them is Johnny Till," Gladys said. "The big hero from the Great War. You remember him."

"Yes, I believe so."

"He was lost in No-Man's-Land, presumed dead until he turned up in... Where was it? What was it that he did? I can't remember, but it was a huge deal at the time. Oh, I wish I knew more about it. Mirabelle would."

"Gladys, I do not expect you to be Mirabelle. What we have here is *not* Gladys Turnbull trying to fill Mirabelle Darcy's shoes. We have Joseph Perrone, who happens also to be the Bay Phantom, working with Gladys Turnbull, who is a good friend and a capable ally. Miss Turnbull enjoys Perrone's full faith and confidence. Let us be clear on that."

She almost blushed.

"The fact is, Gladys, that neither of us comes off particularly well in comparison to Mirabelle. Therefore, I suggest that we avoid such comparisons."

"You're right. And I forgot for a moment that I have my own resources. All I have to do is call the city room. I can talk to Myrtle Cobb and she'll tell me whatever I want to know. She's been working on a feature about these guys."

She went to the phone alcove in the hall and placed a call. She stayed on the phone for twenty minutes, jotting notes on a pad of paper.

"Funny, Myrtle wasn't there. Hasn't been in since yesterday. Didn't call in either. That's not like her. One of the copy editors gave me some info that was in the file, though.

"Like I said, one of the head guys is Johnny Till. The other is Hans Kebler."

"That sounds German."

"Uh-huh. That was the big story I couldn't think of before. He and Till were both stranded in No Man's Land. They both somehow got separated from their units. Each of them lost a leg: Kebler his left, Till his right. But, working together, they managed to survive. It was really played up in the press in America and Germany, after the war was over."

"Yes, I recall hearing about it in 1919 or 1920."

"Right. Well, they stayed together after the war, and founded this Guild. They raise money for their 'cause,' but nobody seems to know what the cause is, or where the money goes.

"And then there is Madame Irene Maude. She is a sort of hanger-on. It doesn't look like she's an official member of this Guild, but she follows them around and helps them in various ways. She's a self-styled psychic. You know, Spiritualism. Table-tapping and ectoplasm and so forth. I thought that stuff went out with hoop skirts."

"There was a surge in popularity during the Great War," Perrone said. "Understandable, really, with so many young men going off and dying."

"A lot of young *women* died too."

"You're right. I apologize for the omission. As for this invitation... I think I'll accept."

He found himself strangely intrigued by this organization. Something was gnawing at his mind. The two men at Max's—an American and a German, one of whom may have been seriously wounded in the Great War. It wasn't much of a connection. He shouldn't have found it as compelling as he did. Perhaps it just looked like a possible port in a mysterious storm. Well, a brief jaunt ashore wouldn't hurt anything.

CHAPTER SEVEN
DINNER PARTY

The Transatlantic Patriots Guild soiree was being held at the home of Madame Irene Maude, the self-proclaimed psychic.

She was renting a place on North Conception Street. Mauvais Rêve, as it was called, was a square, antebellum brick townhouse, constructed in 1844, in the Late Federal style with Greek Revival influences. The fellow who had built it for himself and his young bride was a Frenchman whose character was reputed to be much lower than his bank balance. This was proven in 1855 when he murdered both his wife and his mistress, then hanged himself in the main dining room. The following year, the place had been purchased on the cheap by Abner Grandine, a Kansan who had been associated in some way with the infamous John Brown. Grandine had wisely chosen to leave Kansas after the Pottawatomie Massacre in May of 1856.

Perrone parked his car at the curb half a block away and walked up the sidewalk, under the boughs of the great live oak trees that lined the street. He mounted the steps to the front porch and knocked at the door.

He was admitted by a Negro in old-fashioned livery, who spoke with a marked British accent.

Perrone was ushered into a large parlor, where people stood and sat around, sipping drinks and chatting.

He recognized Roger Addison, with whom he had attended grade school, and a few others.

And, oh, dear—There was Penny Carter.

Tall, angular, redheaded, with a smooth, lovely face, and fierce green eyes that dominated everything her gaze touched, promising cold destruction and terrifying affection. She was wearing a clingy dress of some shimmery, dark green fabric. Perrone swallowed hard. Penny had a certain effect on him, and he was feeling it now. It rose in him from down deep, blooming up into his chest, and, for a few seconds, seemed like it was going to get into his throat and strangle him. He swallowed again and took a deep breath, forcing the thing back down.

She had seen him, and was heading his way. Joe had successfully avoided her for several weeks, but now he was most definitely cornered.

Ah, well. Once more unto the breach, then.

"Penny! How are you?"

He saw now that she was wearing dark green lipstick.

How strange. Strange, and... stirring.

"Well, well!" she said brightly. "If it isn't the Hermit of Tull House! You've been avoiding me, don't deny it."

She touched his arm and his left eyelid twitched involuntarily.

"Oh, no, Penny, it's just that I..."

"Never mind, I understand perfectly. I sympathize with you. But here we are, and you can't get away smoothly." She raised her right hand with three fingers extended, like a Boy Scout. "On my honor, I won't flay you alive and drink your blood."

Perrone, eager, not to say desperate, to change the subject, said. "And this Madame Maude is a spirit medium or some such thing?"

"Yes, some such. I spoke with her earlier. She seems quite interesting. Maybe I can get her to explain to me how I came back from the dead."

"Penny, you didn't come back from the dead. You never *were* dead, you said so yourself. I wish you'd tell me the truth about that whole thing."

"No matter what I said, you wouldn't believe it. You know who I blamed it on, Joe. You know I was kidnapped. You were right there when they nabbed me. Anyhow, if *you're* not going to tell the truth about what *you* did that night, then why do you think I ought to?"

Penny had been present at the Klan rally last year when Perrone had rescued Paul Darcy. She had been taken by the villains, and presumed dead for a short time.

"As usual," Perrone said, "I don't know what you're talking about."

Penny knew or suspected that Joe was the Bay Phantom. Joe was certain that Penny was the head of a powerful criminal organization, having taken over from her brother at the time of her "resurrection."

Why would he go through this kind of charade with her? Why did he play her game?

And, perhaps most importantly... why did he *enjoy* it? That was where the danger lay. He was undoubtedly attracted to her, in spite of everything he knew. He should have found her absolutely repugnant. He had managed to avoid her for a while, but now that he was in her presence once again... Oh, it was terrible. She could fool him, manipulate him. She couldn't *change* him—but she didn't have to, because his fascination with her was a part of who and what he was.

"You're glad I'm not dead, aren't you, Joe?" she asked, sounding like a little girl seeking confirmation of an adult's esteem.

"Well, of course I am, Penny."

"Hm. I wish I could be sure, Joe. But do tell me what it was about this little get-together that persuaded you to come down from on high."

"Oh, well, I'm interested in this Transatlantic Patriot's Guild, you see, and..."

"Wait. Are you just *interested* interested, or are you *Bay Phantom* interested?"

"Penny, I have no idea what you're talking about. I'm afraid you've lost me once again."

"No, I've *found* you once again. I know you're not going to admit anything to me, but you need to be aware that I'm smarter than I look."

"You don't look unintelligent at all."

"Exactly."

Perrone said nothing. He was too busy appreciating the awful truth in what Penny had just said.

"This house has quite a history, you know," she remarked.

"I imagine it does. It has lived through eventful times."

Perrone studied the other guests in the room, one by one. Some of them he knew, some he didn't. There was only one who stood out as suspicious.

The man, of average height and probably middle age, wore an enormous ginger moustache and a pair of very thick spectacles.

The disguise was just a hair this side of absurd.

The others were people who might be considered Joe Perrone's peers. People his own age, some of whom he had attended school with, none of whom he ever saw socially. He nodded politely at Roger Addison, who sat in a chair in the middle of the room. Addison was sipping a highball. Three empty glasses stood in a row on the table at his elbow.

All heads turned as a woman entered the room through one of the side doors.

She was tall and heavy-set, with shrewd, opaque eyes, a prominent nose, and a thin-lipped, determined mouth. She held her chin up, and managed to look regal without straying into haughty. She moved smoothly across the room, like a clipper ship with just the right amount of wind behind it, looking from side to side and nodding at her guests.

In her wake came a man. Tall and dark-skinned, his massive frame was draped in a purple robe, and he wore a turban of the same color on his head. With his hooded, deep-set eyes, broad nose, and wide slash of a mouth, he bore a distinct facial resemblance to Boris Karloff.

"Hello, everyone," the woman said. Her voice was deep for a woman, and her accent was French—probably Parisian, Joe Perrone thought.

"That's Madame Irene Maude," Penny whispered, pronouncing it *ee-rayna maw-day*. "The iceberg she's towing is her stereotype. I believe his name is Mohammed, and he is the obligatory inscrutable servitor from the Far East. A eunuch, if he knows what's good for him."

"Ahem. Well, he does look the part. Of inscrutable servitor, I mean."

Mohammed, if that was in fact his name, could easily have stepped directly off the set of some exotic Hollywood thriller.

Everyone was herded into the large dining room, where they found seats around the massive table. Seating had not been assigned. Perrone picked a chair at random, and Penny picked the one next to him.

He realized that he could have made an effort to avoid her, but he hadn't.

Expensive-looking place settings were there to greet the guests, and as soon as everyone was settled in, more Negroes in livery appeared, bearing platters of food.

Perrone, who was unaccustomed to being served by anyone, was considerably more solicitous toward the "help" than Southern social etiquette called for (or tolerated). This earned him a number of eye-rolls, head-shakes, and suppressed giggles from the other guests.

He accepted boiled potatoes, green beans, bread, and salad.

"Don't you want any of that roast?" Penny said. "It looks awfully good."

"I'm a vegetarian," Perrone informed her.

"Since when?"

"Oh, a few years now. Ever since I spent time with Gandhi."

"My goodness. I never knew you spent time with Gandhi. You are full of surprises. Well, if you're not going to eat meat, then neither will I."

"That's hardly necessary, Penny. I'm not evangelizing, I just have my own reasons, both ethical and medical."

"Me too."

Perrone sighed, which made him think of Mirabelle. He hoped she was having a better time than he was right now.

"Suppose vegetables were to suddenly become sentient," Penny said. "What would you do then?"

"I do not anticipate that happening, Penny."

"And how often does what you do not anticipate go ahead and happen anyhow?" she asked.

She did not receive an answer.

After dinner was concluded, a butler appeared and led the guests upstairs, to a large, open room that had been fitted out as a Spiritualist's den. Embroidered draperies covered all the walls, bearing strange devices and sigils, representations of fantastic creatures, astrological symbols, and so forth.

A dais stood at one end of the room, with straight-backed wooden chairs arrayed in rows facing it, as in a theater.

As the guests began taking their seats, Perrone wandered over and spoke with Roger Addison.

"Well, old man, how's life treating you?"

"Oh, you know how it is, Joe," Addison said. He was draped casually over his chair, running his finger around the rim of a champagne glass on a small table at his side. "Busy, busy."

Perrone doubted that. Addison had never done an honest day's work in his life. In fact, all the work he had *ever* done in his life, laid end-to-end, wouldn't stretch all the way across an eight-hour span. But Perrone also knew that Addison believed what he said; that he was, in fact, a busy, important man. But the keen foresight he had shown by being born into a wealthy family was the full extent of his business acumen. Most of his hardly-earned money went to expensive food and liquor, expensive girls, and the odd expensive boy, if certain tales were to be believed.

"Yes," Perrone said dryly, "you're looking dreadfully overworked. Too many Mardi Gras balls this year?"

"Absolutely. The season can be utterly grueling, but one does what one must, eh? Still, it's nice to have a night off, as it were, to come to a soiree like this. And, since it's for a good cause and all—"

"What cause is that, Roger?"

"Well, I think members of the white race ought to stick together, Joe, don't you? I mean, do we really want a world run by darkies and chinks?"

Perrone did Addison a favor by not replying as he wished to.

"Is that what this Patriot Guild is about?" he asked instead.

"Something along those lines, if I'm not mistaken. And I know they're staunchly anti-Bolshevik. Can't stand those socialists, Joe, or communists, or whatever they call themselves. Imagine us being made to give our money to those who haven't earned it."

"Indeed. There is nothing more despicable than worthless idlers who live on the fruits of other people's labors."

"Well, we agree on that, old boy. My father often says the same thing."

✳✳✳

Perrone and Penny took seats on the back row. Madame Maude stood behind the dais.

"And now, folks," she said, "please welcome our guests of honor, a couple of real heroes: Mister Johnny Till, and Herr Hans Kebler."

Two men entered the room from behind a curtain, to restrained applause. Both men walked with slight but noticeable limps. Madame Maude told the guests which one was which, pointing to each in turn, then went to a chair on the front row and sat.

Johnny Till was tall, slim, dark, and clean-shaven, with a thin, sharp-featured face. There was something quintessentially American about him, something earthy and jovial, hale and enthusiastic, the sort of man Sinclair Lewis wrote about. Hans Kebler was shorter and a bit stocky, with blonde hair cut very short, and a small toothbrush moustache. His posture was rigid, his rather doughy-looking face carefully composed into a bland yet forbidding mask, suggesting a lifetime of Prussian self-discipline.

Till took Madame Maude's spot behind the dais. Kebler stood off to one side.

"We are fortunate," said Till, "to have made the acquaintance of Madame Maude. I have no doubt that she has access to the world beyond this one, and can communicate with its denizens when conditions permit. And all of our brothers—and sisters—lost during the Great War, those on both sides, bring us one message: NEVER AGAIN!

"It makes no sense for Americans and Germans to fight one another. Rather, we must *nourish* one another, *sustain* one another. My friends, it is the only way that our Western ideal of civilization can survive.

"And, make no mistake, the Western ideal is in grave danger. Degenerate elements seek to promote their own ideas about equality and brotherhood. So-called intellectuals seek to undermine the principles of hard work and self-help. The state, they say, must bow down before the weak and the unproductive, and take from the strong, and squander the treasure we have earned with our muscles and our blood. The fruits of our labors should be given freely to all, they say—given to those who have not earned them, who are unfit to govern themselves. To this we say: *Never!*"

Here he bowed slightly, which seemed to be a cue for the audience to applaud, which they did, with varying degrees of enthusiasm. Roger Addison, who had finished off three glasses of champagne during Till's address, clapped the loudest.

"Till speaks as though he were negotiating a minefield," Perrone whispered to Penny. "But this sounds an awful lot like that Klan claptrap."

"Oh, it's Nazi claptrap now, Joe," she whispered back. "You know, Hitler and that bunch. They've got Jews instead of Negroes to blame everything on, but it's the same thing."

Kebler then took Till's place at the dais, delivering much the same speech as Till, adding a few things, rearranging some components, and making liberal use of synonyms and Teutonic metaphors. He was just a tad more specific, touching on anti-Semitic themes, and general disdain for the "darker" races. Jews were blamed for a substantial number of the world's ills, while Negroes were dismissed as being of little importance.

Sales pitch concluded, the two hucksters—for that was how Perrone had decided to characterize them—circulated among the guests. Perrone and Penny got up from their chairs and moved to stand near the curtained front window.

Eventually, Kebler and Till approached them. Introductions were made, then:

"Do you wish to contribute anything to our cause, Mister Perrone?"

"I don't believe so, Herr Kebler. I found the presentation a bit distasteful, I'm afraid. At any rate, I prefer to make my charitable contributions closer to home."

"I see. What about you, Miss Carter? Can we count on some support from you?"

"Oh, I'd be delighted. I'll put you down on my list of charitable endeavors, right after my project to send a shipment of snow shovels to Hell."

Kebler's cold eyes got even colder. "I fear I do not understand what you are suggesting."

"I'm suggesting you take your International Friendship Club and use it as a suppository."

"Oh, Penny!" Perrone exclaimed.

Kebler gave her an icy smile. Till couldn't even manage that much.

"That is extremely amusing, Miss Carter," Kebler said in a brittle voice. He gave her a small bow and both men walked away.

"You make friends wherever you go," Perrone said.

"I thought you were interested," Penny said. "*You* sure gave them the brush-off too—just more politely than I did."

"I should have said *curious*, rather then *interested*."

Kebler and Till gravitated toward Roger Addison. Well, if they could persuade him to donate to their cause, it would be worth the effort. Perrone didn't think it likely, though, unless some very unlikely perks were offered. Yes, Addison seemed enthusiastic now, but whether or not he would even remember it when he sobered up was another matter.

✳✳✳

"And now," said Madame Maude, "we will have a small demonstration of my own modest powers as a spirit medium."

The dais was taken away and replaced with a straight-backed chair. Madame Maude sat down on it and placed her hands in her lap. The lights in the room were extinguished.

"Do you think she'll puke ectoplasm?" Penny whispered to Perrone, as they resumed their seats.

"One can but hope."

"Oh, I hope she does a floating trumpet. I've always wanted to see one."

The room got quiet. Madame Maude, who had bowed her head as though in prayer, looked up at her audience.

"Does anybody have a question?" she said. "The spirits are ready to provide answers."

A woman near the front spoke up:

"My—My son died two weeks ago. His name was Norville. He was interested in the Guild. He was—He was a good boy."

That would be Norville Perrin's mother. She was right about her son; he *had* been a good person, so far as Perrone knew. He and young Norville had been thrown together often when they attended grade school, thanks to the similarity of their surnames. They hadn't maintained contact in later life, though.

"I hate to bring up a matter like this," Mrs. Perrin said, "but we've been a bit frantic. Norville had a—he had a rather large sum of money that has gone missing, and we—I know we can't get our boy back, but we'd like to know where—"

"I understand," said Madame Maude. "I cannot guarantee a response, of course, but we shall see."

She got quiet and let her head loll backward. Her lips began to work, but no sound came out. Not at first. This went on for almost a minute.

"Joe," Penny whispered, leaning close to him, "it is me, or did the temperature in this room just drop about ten degrees?"

"More like fifteen, I should say," Perrone whispered back.

"Well, this dame goes all out."

Madame Maude raised her head. Her eyes rolled back until the irises were barely visible. "There is a man here who is not what he seems," she said, in a voice that seemed not to belong to her. It was very deep, though not entirely masculine; its timbre quite unlike Madame Maude's ordinary speaking voice.

"He is not one man, but two. And yet, he is less than a whole man. He is compromised. What he is doing serves no good purpose. I have a plea for this man, a plea from beyond. The spirits say—They say—Please stop all inquiries here. For the good of your soul—Please stop all inquiries here."

Interesting, Perrone thought, though not very helpful to poor Mrs. Perrin.

A slight noise, the scraping of a chair leg on the floor, caught his attention. Turning his head, he saw the poorly-disguised man stand up slowly, and surreptitiously leave the room. Something about this called to him. Perrone waited a few moments, then rose, touching Penny on the arm and putting a finger to his lips, and quietly made his own exit.

That was one good thing about Penny: He didn't have to worry about her asking awkward questions at the wrong moment. Her own deviousness was an occasional blessing.

There was nothing to see in the upper hall. Everything was dark. A bit of light shone from downstairs, faintly illuminating the staircase, but the house was quiet. He wondered if the servants had left.

Where had the fellow gone? A slight noise ahead alerted him. He moved toward the rear of the second floor, where he found a second, much narrower staircase. Listening intently, he heard the soft padding of feet, going down.

Perrone waited until the footsteps faded away, the waited five minutes more, before making his own way down the stairs, where he found himself in an old-fashioned kitchen. It didn't look as though any meals had been prepared there in recent memory. The food they had eaten earlier must have been provided by a caterer.

At the back of the kitchen he found a door standing slightly ajar. He stopped and held his breath, waiting. Presently, he heard the sound of footsteps coming up a flight of stairs.

The odd man stepped out into the kitchen, pushed the door shut, and applied what appeared to be a skeleton key to the lock. Then he tried the knob. Satisfied that the door was secure, he started back for the front of the house, passing within two feet of Perrone, who had pressed himself back against the wall next to icebox.

When the man's footsteps had faded away again, Perrone went to the door he had used. Perrone quickly picked the lock and descended the stairs he found on the other side of the door.

This was strange. Houses in this part of town had never been built with cellars. But the stairs did not appear to have been of recent construction; they were of a piece with everything else he had observed in the house. Had the original builders undertaken such a complicated and expensive extension? It would have to be very well-fortified, this close to sea level. Well, someone had done the same thing at Tull House, after all, and Perrone's home had been built much earlier than Mauvais Rêve, and much closer to the water.

At the bottom of the stairs was a large, open space. The floor was dirt, but walls were of stone, and had obviously been in place for decades. Three of them were blank; the one at the far end was equipped with a crude opening, just about the same height, and twice as wide, as a standard doorway.

Mounds of dirt were piled up next to it, along the wall.

Going to the doorway, Perrone saw evidence that the piled dirt had been dug out of a short tunnel that lay beyond. Floor and walls of the tunnel were dirt, while the ceiling, such as it was, consisted of rough timbers, held in place by heavy beams braced against the bottom and sides of the passage. Someone had been digging in here, and then shoring it up with the wood.

The crude tunnel was some ten feet in length. Perrone walked to the end and placed his hand against the dirt wall.

He heard faint sounds that seemed to come from the other side of this excavation. He leaned forward and pressed his ear to the earthen barrier. It was music. It sounded like an old pipe organ. Yes, that's what it was. He held his breath and concentrated on the music.

It took him a moment to identify the piece, because he was accustomed to hearing it performed on a piano, not an organ. It was Beethoven's *Moonlight Sonata*. A beautiful, if mournful, piece of music, it now took on a sinister cast. It seemed to Perrone that some of the notes were wrong, and the cadence was slow and heavy, like a dirge. The sweet sadness was twisted and abrasive. At the point where light and hope are supposed to rise up out of the melancholy, things just got worse. It brought up gooseflesh on his arms. Someone had transformed the piece into a thing of lumbering horror.

Where was it coming from?

He stepped back out of the tunnel. Digging equipment was ranged against the wall, close to the opening. Two pickaxes and three large shovels. He squatted to examine them. One of the shovels was shiny and new, reflecting the room behind him in the dim light. He could see his own figure, tiny and indistinct. Then, suddenly, he saw a large figure loom up behind his reflection.

He did not have time to turn. That split-second glimpse was all he got before his world went black.

Awareness gradually returned, pulling him out of the blackness, though a region of vague and disjointed dreams, back into the waking world. He opened his eyes. His surroundings were familiar, yet jarring. He had been here before. That dresser, that lamp, this pillowcase under his cheek...

Penny Carter's bedroom.

He sat up. Someone had undressed him.

He looked around. There was no one else in the room, and he saw his clothes, neatly folded on top of a chair. Maybe he could...

"Well, hello."

Penny stepped into the bedchamber from the adjoining lavatory. She was clad in some sort of filmy negligee—which, in this situation, was better than nothing.

"You had a little spell," she said.

"Uh, hello, Penny. My, this is a bit, ah, awkward, wouldn't you say? I confess, I'm not entirely certain how I've come to be here."

"I brought you here. And put you to bed."

"Ah, I see, but how did—"

"Like I said, you had a little spell." She moved closer. "That big goop Mohammed said he found you outside one of the bathrooms on the first floor."

"No, no. In fact, I believe this Mohammed hit me over the head. That's why I lost consciousness. He snuck up on me, and—"

"How could that character sneak up on anyone? He's forty feet tall!"

"Nevertheless, Penny—"

She came and sat on the bed, next to him. He lowered his head back onto the pillow and pulled the covers up to his chin.

"What happened?" Penny asked him. "What do you remember?"

"I was down in the cellar of the house—"

"Joe, you know they didn't build houses with cellars in that part of town. It's practically sea level."

She lifted the bedcovers and slipped herself underneath them, stretching out beside Perrone.

"Nevertheless," he said, "I was in one. It was toward the rear of the place, and there was what looked like a tunnel, or part of one. It was under construction, perhaps, because I saw shovels and piles of dirt."

"And Mohammed—or somebody—struck you over the head."

"Yes, precisely."

"You don't have a knot on your head."

"Really? That's odd." He probed his scalp with his fingers. Nothing unusual. No sore spot, no lump.

"No swelling at all," he said with astonishment.

How could that be?

"Oh I wouldn't say *that*," Penny purred.

"Penny, what are you... Oh."

"Uh-huh. I *knew* you were happy to see me again. And now I've got the proof right here in my hand."

Oh my goodness...

CHAPTER EIGHT
FORT

Penny had made certain demands, and Joe had been unable or unwilling to resist them. Four times last night his resolve had failed him utterly. It had required a Herculean exercise of willpower for him to extract himself from her bed and her apartment several hours after sunrise.

Penny was simply too dangerous. He would have to avoid her.

Back home, he instructed Gladys to tell Penny, should she call, that he was out and wasn't expected back any time soon. Then he went to his room for some needed sleep.

Late that afternoon, Perrone placed a long-distance call to a friend of his in New York, a man named Charles Fort.

"Hello, Joseph," Fort said, when they had been connected and Perrone had identified himself. "How are you?"

"Quite well, Charles. I trust you are the same?"

"Your trust is misplaced. I fear that my health is failing. Evidently, clean living is no guarantee of anything in this life. Perhaps I should have enjoyed myself a bit more."

"Is there nothing that can be done for you?"

"I don't think there is. Why should I pay a doctor—a member of a profession for which I have only profound distrust—good money to simply prolong the inevitable? It's more important that I finish what will be my last book. *Wild Talents* is the name I've decided on. However it turns out, it will be my *magnum opus*, or at least my *finalis opus*—destined to be utterly forgotten by countless future generations of readers."

Charles Fort was a collector of data, the kind of data most people—especially scientists—preferred to ignore. He collected accounts of strange phenomena, inexplicable occurrences, things that could not have happened, but did. Strange objects seen in the skies; rains of frogs, fish, and stones; artifacts found in places where they have no business being.

He assembled material that had been resented, insulted, and rejected by scientists and logicians into thick books, three of them so far: *The Book of the Damned*, *New Lands*, and *Lo!* These were Fort's way of giving a home to the bothersome, unloved facts that continued to manifest themselves year after year, in spite of their impossibility. Fort believed that someday someone would crack the riddle posed by his compilation of anomalous data. He knew it wouldn't be him—his time was too short. Of course, three lifetimes would probably be too short. But if future generations could build on the foundation he had constructed...

Perrone chatted with him for a while, avoiding any discussion of Fort's health. Perrone was deeply concerned, but he knew remonstrating with his friend would do no good. It was what it was. Why waste the time that grew more precious with the passing of each second?

"Do you know anything of a woman called Irene Maude?" Perrone asked him.

"I've heard of her, yes. You know, ghosts and Spiritualism aren't really a part of my self-imposed mandate, but there is enough dove-tailing that I encounter such things without even trying. Madame Maude has been in the game for a while. She and her parents did some sort of Spiritualist act, or 'demonstrations,' as devotees call them, when she was a child, before the turn of the century. She dropped out for quite a while, then resurfaced as a solo act a few years ago in Europe, and made a name for herself again— first in Berlin, then London, I think, and Paris at some point. That's about all I know, I'm afraid."

"That's helpful, Charles, thank you."

"I'm still looking for material about your house," Fort said. "I'm hopeful that I'll be able to locate some documents here that aren't available to you in Mobile. If your phenomenon has been going on for a while, perhaps it was investigated by one of the psychic research societies that flourished in the second half of the last century."

"I appreciate it, Charles, but if you're not feeling well..."

"There's nothing for it, Joseph. Whatever time I have left will be spent working. On my own book, and whatever I can find for you. The two are not incompatible, you know."

"I can't talk you into taking it easy," said Perrone. It wasn't a question.

"No, I cannot be swayed, I fear. If you need something to make you feel better about it, you can give me your assurance that you will help keep the work going after I'm gone."

"I will, Charles, you have my word. I will allocate resources to the continuation of Fortean scholarship."

"*Fortean.* Ha! That's an incredibly silly word. I like it, I think. I doubt it will ever catch on, though part of me hopes that it will. Not many men get to come back as adjectives after they die."

CHAPTER NINE
A POLICE REPORT

S omething bad was going on—again. Detective Sergeant Tom Dart was sure of it. Another mysterious gang was making moves in Mobile, snatching power away from the Carter family, and meeting very little resistance. That part puzzled him a little, but he supposed that it might represent some devious strategy on the part of Penny Carter.

Whoever the new players were, they had a fix in at City Hall. They must have, he reasoned. Any investigations that might lead to this new outfit's exposure were being derailed, while top priority was given to cases that were dodgy at best.

Mysterious "informants" had pointed police in the direction of a group of minor, independent bootleggers, whose output wouldn't amount to one-tenth of one percent of the illegal booze in the county. Top priority had been given to these investigations.

Tonight, he sat alone in his office at police headquarters, assembling facts and suppositions.

Dart was looking for patterns. He didn't like the fact that his police department was being manipulated again, used as tools and patsies by some unknown cabal of criminals. Of course, there were plenty of guys on the force who didn't need to be manipulated, who were more than willing to be tools and patsies, if the payoff was sweet enough.

He was accustomed to the home-grown corruption represented by the Carter organization, and it made him nervous when outside entities began moving in.

Whoever this new bunch was, they were ruthless and well-financed. This wasn't a bunch of upstarts coming in at the bottom and working their way up; this was a well-oiled machine bludgeoning its way into the penthouse.

And meeting with virtually no resistance.

The outwardly respectable members of the Carter family seemed to have vanished. Penny was the only one visible these days. Caleb had gone missing months before, and Tom Dart did not believe that he would ever resurface. Penny had either had him killed, or had done it herself, the detective was sure. And he was equally sure that nobody would ever be able to prove it.

Word on the street was that she shutting down all her family's illegal activities. Why was that? Because Penny was crazy and couldn't hold things together? Not likely. Penny was crazy, sure, but not the kind of crazy that prevents you from running a criminal organization. And she wasn't one to cave in under pressure of *any* kind. City Hall seemed to have turned its back on her. That was foolish of City Hall. If she was being squeezed out by somebody, and she appeared to be sitting still for it, something terrible was going on inside her head. She was playing a game, minding her manners, and no doubt plotting bloody retribution, waiting until the time was right. And when that time came, *everybody* would pay.

And there were other things. Strange shakeups in city government. Five members of the Public Works Commission had suddenly resigned, citing "personal difficulties," whatever the hell that meant.

They had been quickly replaced with men nobody had ever heard of. Was it just the usual graft—somebody's worthless brother-in-law installed in a high-paying, work-free sinecure—or was it something else?

The mayor, old what's-his-name, had recently purchased a fine new home out in Spring Hill. That spoke volumes to Tom Dart.

There had been a sharp uptick in missing persons reports. These were not being taken seriously because of the nature of the persons who were missing: Prostitutes, tramps, and petty criminals. Reports filed by concerned mothers, parole officers, and pimps were left to gather dust.

Something was going on, and it needed to be stopped.

The Mobile police *wouldn't* do it, and Tom Dart *couldn't* do it.

Maybe the Bay Phantom could. Tom had become involved with the masked man during the previous year's gang war, and knew him to be on the up-and-up.

So Dart was assembling a dossier. All the suspicious, inexplicable things, the things that didn't quite make conventional sense.

He wasn't aware, of course, of the close resemblance between his own activities and those of Charles Fort.

Just as Fort believed that someday someone would crack the riddle posed by his compilation of anomalous data, Dart was confident that the Bay Phantom would discern a pattern.

Or *hopeful*, anyhow.

These days, Senior Detective Alvin Branch was giving Dart his assignments. Branch had been a sort of mentor to Tom during his early days on the force, and had taken a paternal interest in him ever since.

Dart had been given a free hand in his investigation of the warehouse burglary and the inexplicable murder of the watchman. That probably meant he could never possibly solve it, for whatever reason. He had no doubts about Branch, his immediate superior, but Branch took his own orders from higher up. The case would keep Dart busy; prevent him from paying much attention to anything else. And, as far as anyone knew, he was putting everything he had into the investigation. He would not be seen as a danger to whoever was feeding money into the slot this time around.

Of course, he had made no progress at all. The crime scene itself had yielded nothing in the way of clues. The putative owner had finally been traced; he was currently in Brazil. The web of corporations and contracts that Dart was sure would lead back to the Carter organization could not be navigated.

The cause of the watchman's death was still a mystery. The autopsy had yielded the fact that the whole body had been dried out—every muscle, every organ, every bit of tissue. The process had killed the guy, of course, but the exact mechanism of death could not be determined. The skin had been so brittle that it broke apart into confetti when it was removed. The bones were darkened, as if by exposure to intense heat, and all the marrow had shriveled and become as hard as granite.

The source of the heat was a puzzle. As far as could be determined, there was no scorching or burning on the surface skin, or anywhere else. Something had boiled away the bodily fluids and petrified the soft tissue, but what was it and how had it worked?

A case that *wasn't* on his plate was the decapitation murder of Charlie Tate. That one had been given to Dave Poitier, a detective who could be counted on to make absolutely no progress on such a puzzling killing. Whether this was by design, or just luck of the draw, Dart couldn't say.

Tate's murder might have been connected to the strongarm stuff going on with the local restaurants, but it was pretty extreme. Decapitation murders were rare, but not unheard-of in the Port City. However, you usually found both pieces in the same place. Once in a while the head would be missing, and it might or might not ever turn up.

But this time, it was the body that had been taken away. That had never happened before. Tate's head had been found sitting on a table in the front of his restaurant. There were no suspects, no leads. There were only murmurs of gossip. *Charlie was killed because he tried to buck some dangerous men.*

Well, that was a pretty common thing, wherever one might go or whoever one might be. Dart himself had felt that hot breath down his neck more than once, and probably would again. The deck was almost always stacked against relatively honest and reasonably decent men, especially those who were prone to defiance.

But the Bay Phantom was back, and the odds were starting to swing around. Dart would do what he could to help the masked man remove some of the lethal booby traps from the playing field.

He had gone over all his material, and was now writing his report, longhand, on sheets of yellow legal paper.

Tom had almost finished his labors when Alvin Branch poked his head through the office door.

"I thought I heard you in here," he said. "Burning some midnight oil, eh, son?"

Branch was sixty years old, rather short for a man, built like a barrel. He had what Tom Dart thought of as a "good face," lined and careworn, but still retaining a stubborn, indestructible youthfulness and good humor. His close-cropped black hair contained not a speck of gray.

"Paperwork," Dart said with a rueful smile. "Seems like detective sergeants have a lot more of it than plain old detectives."

"Hey, you earned that promotion, so you've only got yourself to blame," Branch said. "Wait'll you end up in *my* chair."

"Paperwork," Dart said with a rueful smile.

"Give me another thirty years. It'll take me that long to make any sense out of this warehouse murder."

"Well, keep at it, Tom. I've got faith in you."

"That makes one of us. What are *you* working on these days, Alvin?"

Branch frowned. "Hm. I really can't say, Tom. We may be about to break something big. If that happens, you'll know all about it, but right now... Well, you know how it is."

"Sure."

"You're here kinda late, aren't you, Tom?"

"So much paperwork, Alvin. You know how it is."

"The curse of the detective class. Sometimes I envy that Bay Phantom. He does as he pleases, answers to no one, and never has to look at a police report."

"If there even *is* such a person," Dart said. "I'm not convinced."

"You think it's a gag? Well, if that's the case, I *still* envy him. Good night, Tom."

Dart finished his report, put it into a large manila envelope. In the morning, he would follow the instructions the Bay Phantom had given him for passing along interesting packages.

CHAPTER TEN
HAUNTED

Joe Perrone had told Gladys that Tull House was haunted. That, she might have taken with a grain of salt. After all, Perrone seemed to have a very strange sense of humor, and he believed a lot of peculiar things. He also lapsed into weird metaphors from time to time. But Mirabelle Darcy had told her the same thing, and Mirabelle was a different story altogether. She meant exactly what she said and vice versa. And Gladys had heard the noises in the house, the tapping and whispering, at all hours, but usually late at night.

Well, Gladys didn't know about ghosts, but Penny Carter's constant attempts to storm the gates certainly qualified as a haunting.

The phone rang non-stop during certain hours. Gladys had answered it three times. Three times, she had told Penny that Perrone was not available. After that, she had just let it ring. Nobody else ever called Tull House, anyhow.

Penny had shown up in person on two occasions. Gladys had not answered the door.

Maybe there *were* ghosts—but maybe something *else* was causing the strange noises and murmuring voices Gladys heard. Maybe it was some kind of radio. Maybe Penny Carter had planted something in the house, maybe more than one thing, to listen in on Mister Perrone's business. She was sure the technology existed.

"I want to talk to you about something," she said to Perrone one evening, as he returned from a mysterious, probably Bay Phantom-related, errand.

"What is it, Gladys?"

"Well, I think maybe—"

She stopped short, then put her finger to her lips.

Perrone gave her a quizzical look. Gladys moved closer and whispered into his ear:

"I'm not sure, but I suspect that our conversations here might not be private."

Mildly surprised, Perrone nodded and motioned toward the front door. When they were out on the lawn, looking over Mobile Bay, Gladys continued:

"I don't have anything concrete. I've looked around and haven't found anything, that's true, but I'm not clever that way. And I just have a feeling that we're being *observed* somehow."

"I often experience such a sensation. It could be the ghosts."

"Yes, but it could also be something else. Like microphones and radios and who knows what. And if that's the case, I'm betting your little admirer, Miss Carter, is behind it."

"Perhaps. I'm skeptical, but I suppose it could be."

Gladys had to smile. Perrone accepted the idea of ghosts without question, but when it came to the perfectly logical prospect of electronic eavesdropping, he was "skeptical."

"All right," Gladys said, "but will you please just *indulge* me? It'll make me feel better."

"Of course. And I'm not dismissing your concerns. I'm aware that Penny can be a little bit... devious."

"That's like calling Napoleon a little bit ambitious."

To stem his growing discomfort, Perrone changed the subject:

"Gladys, have you heard anything from your friend, Miss Cobb?"

"No, and I'm worried. Nobody has heard anything. Her mother filed a missing person report."

"Do you know where Miss Cobb lives?"

"Of course. But she's not there. The cops have been by there, and so has her mother."

"Yes, but there may be something there, something to indicate what she was working on. Something that nobody would be likely to recognize. But you work with her—you might."

"What are you—Do you suspect something, Joe?"

"Not necessarily, but one never knows."

They planned an excursion to Myrtle Cobb's apartment. They had no idea whether the place was under surveillance, by the police or anyone else. It was unlikely, but it would be foolish not to employ stealth. Perrone would be "in uniform," of course, as the Bay Phantom.

"You should probably wear a mask," he told Gladys, "in case we're seen."

"Oh boy!" she exclaimed, patting her hands together. "Hey, can I have a crime fighter name too? Something like... Oh, how about the Phantom Lady? No, I know!" She plucked at her hair. "The Blonde Phantom!"

"I wouldn't recommend using either of those," Perrone said. "This will be a one-time-only arrangement, Gladys."

"The Phantom Reporter?"

"No!"

They waited until one in the morning to pay their visit. The Bay Phantom was decked out as usual, and Gladys had put together a rather striking ensemble, consisting of a black, belted overcoat, a wide-brimmed black hat, and a dark-colored, mannish suit. She topped it off with a black domino mask, decorated around the edges with green and purple frills—a typical Mardi Gras adornment, purchased at a shop on Royal Street.

"I am Phantomah!" she had announced.

"No, you are not."

The Phantom parked his sedan on the street, one block over from the house where Myrtle Cobb rented a small apartment.

The interior of the house was quiet, all the other tenants asleep. They crept up the stairs to the second floor and found Myrtle's door.

The lock was almost laughable to someone as skilled as the Bay Phantom. With his lockpick, he got the door open faster than a legitimate tenant would have been able to with the proper key.

Stepping inside, Gladys right behind him, he closed the door and flipped the light switch.

Myrtle occupied a single large room with a kitchenette in one corner and a twin bed in another. She would no doubt use a communal bathroom somewhere down the hall.

There were pin-up pictures on the walls, clipped from movie fan magazines. Robert Montgomery and Lynne Fontaine gazed dreamily across the small, cluttered living space at Joan Crawford and Ramon Novarro. The inexpensive furnishings, probably the property of the landlord, were piled with newspapers and neatly-folded clothing. A small radio sat atop a bookshelf full of dictionaries and paperback novels. A Mardi Gras banner was tacked up over the single window.

It was, he supposed, a typical example of the dwelling of a young, unmarried woman. Not that he had much experience with such, apart from Penny Carter, who was anything but typical.

"I think this place has been searched," the Phantom announced, after he had made a quick tour of the premises, "by someone who knew what they were doing."

"I can't tell that anything's been searched."

"My point exactly."

The Phantom took an interest in a small tin wastebasket over near the room's single window. He peered down into it, probing the contents first with a small flashlight, then with a gloved hand.

"It looks like someone made a small fire. Hmm, whatever was in here was burned pretty thoroughly, then water was poured over it. It's just mush. No, wait a moment—Here's a little scrap, and there seems to be writing on it."

The bit of paper was no more than two inches square, badly scorched and water-damaged, but a few words could be made out.

Perrone held it up so that he and Gladys could look at it together.

"*Donner-Purdy,*" Gladys read. "And what's this down here? it says... What's that word? I can't make it out."

"I believe it says... *Typee.*"

"What does *that* mean? Someone to whom something is typed?"

"Ah... It probably says something else. It's so smudged, you see. I don't think this can tell us much."

Nevertheless, the Phantom slid the scrap carefully into a glassine envelope and tucked it into his breast pocket.

He was being evasive, and hoped it wasn't too obvious. He had an idea, but it was much too shocking to share with Gladys. And he may have been on the wrong track entirely. He hoped that was the case. He would have to learn a lot more before he could begin theorizing in earnest.

They looked around a little longer, but there was nothing else to be found.

"Do you think she's okay?" Gladys asked.

The Phantom did not answer.

CHAPTER ELEVEN
THE GRIM REAPER

"Roger Addison is dead," Perrone announced the next morning. He waved a copy of that day's *Mobile Press* in Gladys' direction.

She turned from the kitchen sink, where she had been dealing with a stack of dishes that had been there for God alone knew how long. Mirabelle Darcy was a housekeeper in name only, and Joe Perrone didn't even make that much of a pretense. The state of the kitchen was not far short of what most people would call outright squalor. Well, Gladys supposed that when you had a super-genius and a—whatever Joe Perrone was—living together in a house, you couldn't expect much attention to be paid to the mundane.

They evidently had not tried to hire another girl to help out, after what had happened last year. The maid they hired had actually been Gladys Turnbull, undercover, looking for a story. This was after Gladys had accidentally discovered the Phantom's secret, and before she had formed her alliance with him.

She still felt guilty about that too. She was grateful for the chance to help put the place in order.

"You mean Charles Addison's son?" Gladys asked.

Perrone nodded, put the paper on the little dining table, and looked down at the scrambled eggs on his plate. "Quite sudden it was, according to the paper. Funny, I just saw him at that Guild meeting."

Gladys switched on the radio, moved close to Perrone, and spoke in a low voice:

"You think there's a connection?"

"I'll need more data before I can make such an assertion," he replied softly. "But here's something interesting: Roger's arrangements are being handled by an outfit called the Donner-Purdy Funeral Home."

"Donner-Purdy? Like in Myrtle's notes?"

"It must be. I can't imagine there are very many of *those* lying about. Gladys, if you would, please bring me the last few weeks' worth of the *Mobile Press*. They're stacked up in the back of the pantry. A month should do it."

"There have been several surprising deaths among Mobile's more affluent citizens over the past few weeks," Perrone said half an hour later. "And I've noticed that they all have one thing in common, apart from money. All of the bodies went through the Donner-Purdy Funeral Home."

"Yes," Gladys said. "And while you were going through the papers, I checked the phone directory and the city directory. 'Donner-Purdy' could not possibly refer to anything other than that funeral home. So Myrtle was interested in them for *some* reason."

"Yes. And if it had anything to do with her investigation of the Patriot Guild, then there's our possible connection."

The Donner-Purdy Funeral Home had been in business for six months. It occupied a large, pre-Civil War era house on Joachim Street, just north of downtown.

The house had been built in 1856 or 1857, and was much larger now than it had been originally. Subsequent owners had added room after room, building backward from the street. The place was fairly narrow, but it ran deep.

Perrone learned that the property had been leased by one "John Smith," presumably the same John Smith whose name appeared on the funeral home's incorporation papers. Of course, it could be legitimate; there *were* people named John Smith, after all. But, if so, who were Donner and Purdy?

The whole situation was peculiar, to say the least.

Perrone went to the Donner-Purdy Funeral Home at six o'clock that evening for Roger Addison's viewing.

He stepped through the front door into a wide foyer, with an office to one side.

It was chilly in here. The air smelled of cleaning products, flowers, and something else—something incongruous.

A man named Carlos Momia emerged from the office, introduced himself, and informed Perrone that he was the funeral director here. He led Perrone across the foyer and through a curtained archway into what he called the Viewing Room. This was a sort of parlor, at the rear of which was a cloth-draped bier. Resting on top of this was a bronze casket with the upper part of the lid open. Several living people also occupied the room, standing around or sitting in chairs, chattering to one another.

Perrone approached the casket for a look.

Addison looked no better and no worse in death than he had in life. He simply looked a bit different. Someone had applied powder and rouge to his face. The effect was a bit grotesque, but Addison had always been a little fey, not to say effeminate.

Perrone circulated, nodding and speaking to the other mourners, Addison's cronies, most of whom he recognized, none of whom he knew at all.

The "Gang," as they called themselves, a sloppy confederation of wastrels, ne'er-do-wells, and young ladies whose lack of virtue was flaunted like a civic or military award, seemed to regard this viewing as a sort of gay party. They maintained a bare minimum of decorum, but there was plenty of giggling and a few off-color remarks. The dead man inspired no reverence among the survivors.

Perrone sat down and looked around the room. There was a red door in the wall, behind and to the right of the bier. There was a man standing next to this door, and he looked awfully familiar. He stood there in front of the drapes, hands behind his back, like a soldier at parade rest. He didn't look like the sort who had ever submitted to military discipline, though. He was both hard and soft-looking at the same time, the hallmark of the career criminal.

Molloy, that was his name. He had a rather sanguinary reputation, as Perrone recalled.

Perrone knew that he was more formidable than he looked. He was tall and very thin, with a bland, unexpressive face. His height was not particularly impressive in the overall scheme of things. He looked as though a stiff wind might give him problems.

But, in fact, Molloy was in excellent physical shape, though one couldn't tell that just by looking at him. Underneath the somber black suit he wore, Molloy had a lean but well-muscled physique. He was not a bludgeon. His fearsome reputation came not from raw strength, but from his uncanny physical prowess. He had, over the years, mastered a handful of exotic martial arts disciplines, most of which were largely unknown in the United States.

Perrone took a handkerchief from his breast pocket and mopped nonexistent moisture from the corners of his eyes.

Carlos Momia bustled in from the foyer, approached Molloy, and said something to him. The gangster scowled and shook his head. Momia drew himself up and said something else. Molloy laughed, loud enough to attract the attention of some of the "mourners." Momia held a finger to his lips.

Perrone could not see Momia's face, so his lip-reading skills could provide no enlightenment as to the nature of the argument. Thus far, Molloy, whose face was plainly visible, had not spoken.

The funeral director raised a fist and said something else to Molloy, and the gangster responded. Perrone had no trouble deciphering this utterance. Molloy had called Momia a name that Perrone would never dream of saying out loud.

Momia moved back, shocked. Molloy walked away, across the Viewing Room and into the foyer. Momia followed. Soon, Molloy's place by the red door was taken by a little fellow clad in an ill-fitting tuxedo suit.

Perrone supposed that the fellow was young, probably in his twenties, but he had the ageless air of the congenital idiot. No matter how old he got, he would remain a child. The expression on his face was almost completely vacant, but for a trace of mild amusement that probably had no objective cause.

Momia appeared again, and he could not be still. He scurried back and forth, from the little office in the front to whatever was behind the door. Every time he passed through, he had to unlock it; he opened and shut it quickly, and when he was through, he locked it again. Every single time.

Perrone would love to have a look behind that door, but it was impossible.

He sat. Molloy did not reappear.

Presently, the Gang decided to repair to the veranda for "a few snorts." They extended Perrone a halfhearted invitation, which, to everyone's relief, he declined.

Now.

He was unobserved at the moment, but would not remain so for long. He acted quickly. There was one thing he *could* do, and this was his chance. He stood up and went to the bier.

Leaning over, as if to get a better look at his departed friend, he reached into the coffin with his left hand, to brush an imaginary bit of fluff off of Addison's lapel. Simultaneously, with his right, he reached into his jacket pocket and produced a hypodermic syringe with a needle attached. This he slid into Addison's carotid artery and pulled back the plunger, filling the reservoir. It took him less than five seconds, with another three-quarters of a second to stow the hypo away in his pocket again.

Shaking his head sadly, as though in disbelief over young Roger's untimely demise, he stood up straight again and studied a beautiful display of purple flowers.

The other giggling mourners soon filed back into the room, a couple of them walking unsteadily.

Perrone announced that he had to be going, to the complete indifference of the others. His good-bye wave was ignored.

"Thank you sir," said Carlos Momia, emerging from a little office next to the foyer as Perrone reached the front door. "Please come again, and tell your friends about us."

Perrone's eyebrows went up. What a peculiar thing to say. Was it some kind of bizarre joke? The little fellow seemed absolutely serious.

"Uh, yes, certainly. Good night."

Momia bowed him out the door.

Perrone had almost reached his car when something occurred to him. He looked back at the funeral home, then up and down the street.

"By gosh, I think so," he said out loud.

He had to walk around the block twice, to make absolutely sure.

The Donner-Purdy Funeral Home was directly behind Mauvais Rêve.

He took the fluid he had extracted from the corpse directly to Doctor Ambrose V. Atticus, at his home/office in Prichard.

Doctor Atticus was fifty-five years of age, a dark-skinned man, with graying hair and a pair of wire-rimmed spectacles perpetually perched on his nose. He was a brilliant man with lots of unusual knowledge, and Perrone often wondered about his past. Where had he studied? What had he studied? Though he was a practicing physician, a general practitioner, he had the makings of a fine research scientist, and his knowledge and enthusiasm encompassed a wide range of subjects and scientific disciplines.

He had been a friend of Mirabelle Darcy and her family for many years, and Perrone suspected that the older man might have, at some point, acted as a mentor to the brilliant young lady. And it had probably ended rather quickly, with the pupil leaving the teacher hopelessly behind.

Which did not mean that Atticus wasn't brilliant himself. He was. It was rumored that he had been offered a scholarship to a medical school in Europe, a place where his pigmentation wouldn't have made any difference to anyone, but he had turned it down. He needed to stay where he was, he had said, with his family and his community.

Perrone had confided in Atticus, to a degree. Though he had never explicitly stated to the doctor that he, Perrone, was the Bay Phantom, he had to assume that Atticus had to assume it.

He waited for an hour while Atticus tested the sample in his small laboratory.

When Atticus emerged at last, he brought information with him.

"It was blood, not embalming fluid," the doctor said. "And it was still liquid. The body you took that sample from had never been embalmed. And the blood was indeed adulterated."

"With what?"

"It appears to be a poison, but there is an odd biological component. Something similar to a virus, I think. But it doesn't conform to any disease I know about, and I'm not sure what it does."

"Well, then..."

"Wait. I said I'm not sure, but I have a theory. This is based on inference, since I didn't have time for a thorough testing. It seems to me that this organism, whatever it is, exists to destroy the poison—to break it down and render it inert. Once that is done, the organism itself dies. It is separate from the poison, but acts in conjunction with it. I would theorize that they are introduced into the body at the same time. The organism starts breaking down the poison, but not before it does its job, by killing the person. Then the organism..."

"Covers the tracks of whoever administered it," Perrone interjected. "Eliminates all the evidence."

Atticus nodded. "From what I've learned, it seems that the whole process should take approximately three days. By this time tomorrow, that sample will look just like ordinary, unadulterated blood."

"Well, I'll be. That's something new."

"Another thing... You say you got this sample from a dead body that had already been prepared for burial, right? Well, the sample contained the things I have just described, along with liquid blood."

"Yes, as you said earlier."

"It bears repeating. You see, that's the thing: There shouldn't have *been* any blood in that body—just embalming fluid."

"By golly, you're right! I ought to have thought of that."

"It's fortunate that you didn't, or you wouldn't have secured the sample."

"There can be a certain strength in ignorance, I suppose. Or absent-mindedness. One would think I'd have embalming procedures firmly in mind, after the events of last year. I suppose I've been a bit distracted."

"Hm. Also, the blood should have been coagulated if it had been more than a day after death. Something about that compound must have kept it in a liquid state. I have to assume that, but I can't explain how. It may go ahead and coagulate when the chemical reaction has run its course—we'll have to wait and see."

CHAPTER TWELVE
MEAT GRINDER

"So now we have to watch a funeral home," Louis Rickert grumbled.

"That's right," Shorty Red replied.

They were in Shorty's dark sedan, parked at the corner of Congress and Joachim Streets, with a good view of the front of the Donner-Purdy Funeral Home.

"I don't like funeral homes," Louis said.

"Nobody does, except the people who own them."

They watched and waited. Hours passed. Louis fidgeted and made a wide variety of complaints. Shorty ignored him, keeping his attention riveted to the front of the funeral home.

His patience was rewarded at 8:24 p.m. The front door opened and a man stepped out.

"Holy Christ," Louis breathed. "Meat Grinder Molloy!"

"Mmm-hmm. The Boss said to keep an eye out for him. And if he goes anywhere, we are to follow him."

Molloy trotted down the walk to the street and got into a dark green touring car that was parked at the curb.

"It looks like he's going somewhere," Louis observed.

"Then so are we," Shorty said, starting the car.

"Maybe the boss'll wanna try to reform him," Louis speculated.

Shorty shook his head. "Meat Grinder Molloy can't be reformed. He's not a human being."

The touring car pulled away from the curb. Louis and Shorty followed it south down Joachim Street, working their way around the construction on Dauphin, and on to Government. There, Molloy headed west. A few minutes later, he pulled to a stop at the curb in front of a modest clapboard house. Shorty pulled to the curb a block behind.

"I know about that place," Louis said. "That's a cathouse."

"What a disgusting euphemism," Shorty said, making a face. "It's a house of prostitution."

"That takes longer to say. About three times longer."

Molloy shut off his headlights and got out of the car.

At that moment, another large touring car pulled to the curb behind him. Three men approached him. Two were tall and lean, the third short and plump.

The short, plump one had a gun. He was pointing it at Molloy.

"Well, look at that," Louis said.

The three men had a few words with Molloy, then led him back to their touring car. Everyone got in, and the car pulled out.

"Here we go again," Louis said.

The Phantom's agents followed the touring car to a neighborhood in the Crichton area. There, they turned onto a short, dead-end street.

Shorty continued for another block, then parked. He and Louis walked back to the dead-end street. There were no houses, just empty, overgrown lots on both sides. About fifty yards from the corner, almost at the end of the short street, the touring car was parked next to a little shack of some sort. An old garage, maybe. It was small and cheap, weather-beaten from years of wind and rain endured without a drop of new paint. The boards were warped, and there were small chinks of light showing here and there.

"This doesn't look right," Shorty said.

"How the hell is it *supposed* to look?" Louis asked.

"Come on," Shorty said, "let's try to see inside. First, though, I need to get a message to the Phantom. You go on ahead. Be careful and be quiet"

Shorty's car was equipped with a small, powerful radio transmitter. The signal would be received in two places: Tull House and the Phantom's automobile. The message would be heard or recorded, and relayed to its intended recipient as quickly as possible.

Shorty gave his location and used the phrase "code two." That meant that the Phantom was to get to where Shorty was as quickly as possible. Shorty didn't wait for any acknowledgement. The Phantom would either get the message or he wouldn't. If the latter, Shorty would have to improvise.

He joined Louis behind the shack.

"What's happening?" he whispered.

"Those guys have been beating hell out of Molloy. And he ain't fighting back."

"That's curious. No will to resist? What on earth is he involved in?"

Shorty put an eye to one of the cracks. He saw Molloy, sitting on a metal drum, his face bloodied. The three men stood around him.

A door at the rear of the shack opened and another man stepped in. He was wearing a tan boiler suit, with a thick leather apron, and what looked like a welder's mask covering his face.

"Who the hell's that?" Louis breathed. "Why's he dressed like a welder?"

"I wouldn't know," Shorty softly replied.

"He's not very big," Louis observed.

"Be quiet," Shorty whispered.

✳✳✳

"So," said the strangely-garbed man, "you don't want to play ball, eh? I'm surprised, I really am, given your... proclivities. I thought you'd take to all this with more enthusiasm than anyone else."

"Look," Molloy said, "what I do is one thing. It's rough, but it's business. That's all it ever was."

"So is this."

Molloy vigorously shook his head. Blood came from his nose, whipping back and forth over his trousers. "No. It goes—I mean, it's too—What's the word I want? *Indiscriminate*, that's it. You see what I mean, don't you? Keeping it among the guys in our business, you know, that just makes sense. Yeah? Right? But you can't—We can't just go out there and—"

"You're not going to convince anybody of anything here, Molloy. You've already threatened to go to the authorities. That was your death sentence. There's a new world coming, and it's going to have new rules. If you're not willing to adopt them, well—"

"And the thing with the tunnel! That's just crazy!"

"It was a mistake letting you know about that. Anyhow, that's only a contingency, in case everything goes sour. Which it won't. They know what they're doing, but they believe in being careful. *Very* careful. That's why you have to go."

The other men got Molloy onto his feet and pushed him into the center of the room, then stepped back. Molloy stood there, very straight, like a hanged man at the end of an invisible rope, his feet just touching the floor.

The masked man unhitched something from his belt. It was a black box, about the size and shape of a small shoebox, with a pistol grip and a trigger at one end. A thick black cable connected it to a bulky backpack the man wore.

"Aw, no, come on now," Molloy pleaded. "This ain't necessary."

"Of course it is."

"Listen, I was maybe a little hasty. We can just forget the whole thing and go back to how we was before. I'll toe the mark, and I'll..."

No one would ever know what further concessions Meat Grinder Molloy was willing to make. The man in the welding mask pointed his device at Molloy and squeezed the trigger. There was a loud popping sound, and a pair of tiny projectiles shot from the front of the weapon, trailing thin wires behind them. The small, barbed missiles embedded themselves in Molloy's chest. A loud electrical hum issued from the backpack the masked man was wearing.

Molloy started to jerk and twitch. His mouth opened wider than it should have been able to, and the whites of his bulging eyes instantly turned bright red. Then he dropped to the floor and curled up like a pill-bug. A great quantity of heavy yellowish steam oozed from his body.

The smell, which easily reached Louis and Shorty through the crack, was indescribable. It incorporated five or six kinds of vileness that one did not typically encounter all at the same time.

"Well," Louis whispered, "I reckon that's one way to reform him."

"What's the story, men?"

Louis jumped, startled by the whispered query. The Bay Phantom had appeared, in that unnerving way of his.

"There's a guy in there with some kind of strange weapon," Shorty whispered. "Be careful of him. You'll know which one. I think he just killed Molloy."

The Phantom nodded, found the front door, and kicked it open. He entered the shack, Louis and Shorty right behind him.

The man in the welder's outfit whirled around.

"And who are you?" the Phantom asked. "Do you have a colorful name? Is that meant to be a costume, or is it utilitarian?"

The other thugs were startled by this sudden apparition. The Bay Phantom, a giant, and an ordinary-looking schlub, all of them armed and obviously hostile. The crooks briefly weighed their options. The Phantom was known to be deadly. The big guy looked like he could pick up a stack of four or five men in his bare hands and tear them in half. What the little schlub might or might not be capable of was academic.

They ran for the rear door.

The weirdly-garbed man seemed not to notice his comrades' inglorious retreat.

"The Bay Phantom, plus two," he said, raising his weapon. The little projectiles had been retracted into position.

"Hold on a moment," the Phantom said calmly. "I would rather not hurt you. In case you didn't notice, your friends have fled, so it is now three against one. You face three men with four guns aimed at you. I don't know what that thing is that you're threatening us with. Would you care to explain?"

"I'm the Mummifier. I'm called that because of this weapon I invented. It mummifies people. Alive. Well, they're alive when it commences. Obviously, the process is not survivable."

"Like that man on the floor there? You did that?"

Molloy lay in the center of the shack, seemingly fried to a crisp.

The welder's mask bobbed up and down as the man nodded.

"Yes," he said, "with this. That's what it does."

"Well," said the Phantom, "we've already had a criminal in this town with a similar, ah, *theme*, so—"

"No, that was *totally different*," the Embalmer said hotly. "This thing here is state of the art."

"Well, perhaps you're right. How does it work?"

"It's too complicated to explain. Some of it is science most people don't know about yet. Are you going to shoot me down right here?"

"Maybe we should, Boss," Louis suggested.

"I could pull *my* trigger," said the Mummifier, "and get *one* of you, anyhow."

"Yes," the Phantom agreed. "And that would leave two of us alive—and none of you."

At that moment, they heard the roar of a car engine, followed by a terrific crash. One wall of the shed shattered and the touring car poked its nose in through the breach. The "deserters" had merely made a temporary retreat to fortify their position.

The whole shack rocked. It was clear that the ceiling would collapse entirely within the next few seconds.

The Mummifier made a dive for the automobile, sliding in through one of the rear doors, avoiding shots fired by Louis and Shorty, more by luck than design. The Phantom got off two shots that would have killed the driver, had the windows not been bulletproof.

When the door slammed shut behind the Mummifier, the automobile backed out, ripping more timbers loose. The ceiling gave way. The Phantom and his men barely made it out through the front door before the whole building collapsed in on itself. The car roared away down the short street, and skidded out into the avenue beyond.

"Well, shit," Louis said bitterly.

"Now, Louis," said the Phantom. "That really isn't necessary. Come on, we've work to do."

They pulled rubble aside until they reached the desiccated body. Shorty and the Phantom lifted it gingerly and carried it out to a strip of grass next to the ruins.

"I guess we better call the cops," Louis said, still a little astonished to find himself saying such a thing.

"Not the Homicide Squad" said the Phantom. "They may be compromised. I'm going to call Tom Dart. I believe he has had some recent experience with this method of murder."

Returning to his own automobile, the Phantom used his car radio to patch into the city phone system. When he connected with an operator, he gave her Tom Dart's home number.

"Yep," the detective said thirty minutes later, "this is just like the one in the warehouse." He looked at Shorty and Louis. "And you two mugs saw how it was done?"

Shorty nodded. "Yes, but seeing and understanding are two different things." He described for Dart the scene that had led to Molloy's bizarre demise.

"Okay. One of you guys make an anonymous call to headquarters.

Tell them there's a body out here, and *nothing else*. After it's taken to the morgue, maybe I can learn more."

"That sounds good, Tom," said the Phantom. "And if I learn anything more, I'll share it with you, of course. And *only* you."

Dart nodded. "Somebody's got the fix in on something. I don't know who it is or what they're doing, but people in the department are complicit in whatever's happening. In short, business as usual—but the shadow players are new. A lot like last year, but there's something darker about this. I can't say what or why, but I have a strong feeling."

"Yes," said the Phantom, "I've looked over all the material you sent me the other day. Nothing quite makes sense yet, but the threads are coming closer together. And I fear that we are, as you say, moving toward something very, very dark."

"Not too dark for *you*, though, huh Boss?" Louis said cheerfully.

The Bay Phantom made no reply.

To Dart, he said: "You might want to have a discreet look at the Donner-Purdy Funeral Home."

"How discreet?" the detective asked.

"Use your own discretion. I suspect that they are involved in something quite sinister. I believe them to be connected to the Transatlantic Patriots Guild."

"All right."

"It may have some bearing on this gang that's been pressuring restaurants. And there's a woman called Irene Maude. She is involved in some way, but I haven't been able to determine the nature of her involvement."

"I'll keep an eye open and I'll see what I can do."

"Thank you, Tom. I'll be in touch."

CHAPTER THIRTEEN
THE MODEL

It was against the law. Of course it was. So what? Louis was a criminal, right? That's why the Bay Phantom wanted to hire him in the first place, right?

Well, then.

Anyhow, it was a victimless crime. The Phantom couldn't possibly object to it, even if he found out, which Louis would make sure he didn't. It was a sure thing.

All he needed was a few willing girls. But it seemed that he didn't know any women as well as he thought he did. He had tried a couple of girls he knew, and they laughed in his face. A couple of others did worse than that.

Today, the day after the strange death of Meat Grinder Molloy, Louis was on his way to meet Alice Tague, a "working girl" he had known for a year or two. He had never purchased any of her services, but the two often found themselves in the same place at the same time, for a variety of reasons, and they had struck up what one might call a very casual friendship.

She was not, perhaps, the cream of the crop. But you have to start somewhere.

She was to meet him at noon, at the lunch counter at Woolworth's, on Dauphin Street.

Louis arrived a couple minutes early, cursing over the mud he'd gotten on his shoes when he walked past the construction on the next block, and took a stool at one end of the lunch counter. The counter man asked him what he wanted, and he said he was waiting for someone and would order later.

Alice showed up shortly after that, taking a seat next to Louis. The counter man came back. Alice said she didn't want anything. Louis asked her if she was sure, and she insisted she was. Louis said he didn't want anything either. The counter man scowled and went back to his station.

"What do you think about it, Alice?" Louis asked, once he had explained his plan.

"It might fly," she said. "A lot of the girls are scared about going out to work. So many have disappeared lately. Mardi Gras is usually a good time to pick up trade. Lotsa girls come in from Biloxi and Panama City for the season, but this year... New girls show up, then all of a sudden, they're gone. And a lot of girls that live *here* are coming up missing as well."

"No kidding."

"Somebody was saying something about white slavers, but they usually go for the real young and pretty ones. The girls that have been vanishing are like me: old and used-up."

"Aw, you ain't old and used-up. Why, you don't look a day over forty."

"I'm twenty-seven."

"Oh. Well, listen, I can't pay much up front, but once the ball gets rolling..."

"It's okay, Louis. Whatever you can manage, I appreciate it."

"Well.. Okay. I'll get in touch with you later, then. You take care of yourself, Alice."

She laughed, as though the idea were self-evidently absurd. She got up from her stool.

"Sure, Louis. You too." She smiled at him, and for some reason, the gap where her right front incisor had once been made him almost want to cry. "I'll talk to some of my friends and try to get them in on it too."

Louis watched her walk through the store and pass through the glass doors, out into the street, then turned to the counter man. Might as well hit a little lick at earning the peanuts the Bay Phantom tossed to him.

"Say, Luther," he said to the counter man, "you don't know anything about this new gang, do you?"

Luther Stick was thin and tall, with a long face and large hands. He had worked on a farm most of his life, dreaming about a move to the big city. This he had accomplished in 1925. When he had been in Mobile for three days, he had been hired by Woolworth's as a grill man. Seven years later, he was starting to miss the farm.

"I can't say nothing about 'em, Louis," he said. "I never met any of 'em, but they've been here. Forced us to buy meat from 'em, is how I understand it. I don't wanna know nothing about them. These guys play rough. They're okay so long as you go along, but... Well, you know what happened to Charlie Tate. After that, everybody else sure fell in line. Amazing how one beheading can change a whole economy practically overnight."

"Right. They never did find the rest of his body. It ain't every day you just find someone's head somewhere."

"That's how crazy these boys are. Poor Charlie, he hadn't been married but six weeks. He was so proud!"

"Yeah, poor guy. Makes me kinda depressed to think about it. I guess I better have a shot of whiskey and a beer."

"Louis, we don't serve stuff like that at Woolworth's."

"Oh. Well, let me get a hamburger then."

"That, I can do."

Luther went to his cook station and tossed a patty onto the grill.

"Hey, I'll have one too," came an unfamiliar voice.

Louis looked around. There was one other guy at the lunch counter, a really silly-looking rube wearing dungarees, a plaid flannel shirt, and a red plaid cap. Good grief! The guy looked over at Louis and gave him a friendly nod. Louis sneered and blinked his eyes. It didn't seem to bother the hayseed, though; the guy just sat there with a goofy half-smile on his face and a vacant look in his round, colorless eyes. Something about that look gave Louis the creeps, and he turned away.

Luther put another patty on the grill. A few minutes later, he brought Louis his hamburger, on a plate with a handful of potato chips, and put the second one in front of the other guy.

"Oh boy," said the queer little fellow, after he took a bite. "This is one fine hamburger. Best I ever ate, no kidding. Something real special about this here meat."

He had a weird accent, like he was from way up North or someplace. Louis shook his head. Wherever this guy was from, he was one big hick. Probably never had actual cooked food before.

Louis tucked into his burger. Straight away, he bit down on something hard. *What the hell?* He reached into his mouth and gingerly extracted the foreign object. Fortunately, he hadn't broken any teeth on the damn thing. He held it up and was about to yell at the counterman, when he realized what he was holding.

A ring.

A plain, gold ring. It sure *looked* like real gold, anyhow. He quickly slipped it into his pocket and looked around to make sure no one had seen.

Louis finished his hamburger, chewing each bite very slowly and gingerly. He was hoping for a pair of cufflinks or something, but the ring was the only baby in this particular king cake.

CHAPTER FOURTEEN
WHERE IS THY STING?

"One of those guys from the Patriot's Guild wants to come see you," Gladys said, holding her hand over the telephone mouthpiece. "Shall I tell him to get bent?"

Perrone, sitting in his chair in the front room at Tull House, reading the newspaper, looked up.

"Oh, I think not," he said. "Tell him I'll be available this evening."

This was, perhaps, a stroke of good fortune. He had an idea. If he could pull it off, it would kill at least two birds with the same stone.

✴✴✴

At precisely 7 p.m., there was a knock on the front door.

Gladys answered it, and led the visitor into the front room, where Perrone rose to greet him.

Perrone concealed his surprise and gave no sign that he recognized this representative of the Guild.

Here was the tall man who had received the blow from Max Santorelli's skillet! There was still a bit of discoloration around his right temple where the blow had fallen.

He introduced himself as Dale Finster.

"I just wanted to see you in person, sir," he said politely, "and ask you if you had perhaps changed your mind about offering the Guild some support."

"Why would you wonder about that? I think I made myself quite clear the other night."

"Yes, but, if you'll forgive my saying so, I thought you might have been a bit, ah... indisposed. Not quite yourself, as they say. The, ah, *incident*, you know. "

"I don't recall seeing you there."

"Nevertheless, I was. I do hope you're quite all right now."

"Nothing for you to worry about, old boy. Sometimes I don't realize when I've had a little too much, don't you know?"

"I am afraid I don't. Well, if that is your final word, then, I will bid you good day."

They shook hands.

"What a stiff," Gladys said, after she had ushered Finster out the door. "Can I ask you just what that accomplished?"

"I believe I have what I need."

"Which is what?"

"Just this," he said, and proceeded to peel the skin off of his right hand. It came away in one piece, like a glove.

Gladys gasped. Then she noticed, with palpable relief, that it *was* a glove.

"Looks just like real skin, doesn't it?" Perrone said. "It's actually a glove, and it has been equipped with an absorbent pad fixed into the palm. The pad is backed with a thin sheet of metal, so nothing can penetrate to the skin beneath."

"Okay."

"There is a pinprick in the glove, and it looks as though the pad absorbed a little bit of liquid."

"I don't get it."

"I was sure the Guild's emissary would want to poison me, and I knew he couldn't count on my accepting any proffered food or drink. He would have to give me the poison in some other way. It would require physical contact. The only thing that can be counted on in any social situation is a handshake. How could I refuse that? He was wearing a ring with a small barb on the palm side. I believe it was treated with poison."

"Well, that's clever of you," Gladys said with admiration. "I wouldn't have thought of that. And, see, you didn't need Mirabelle to tell you. You're pretty smart all on your own."

"I just modified the glove. Mirabelle made it, in case I ever needed to avoid leaving fingerprints without it being obvious that I was doing so."

"When would a thing like *that* ever come up?"

"You'd be surprised. Now this goes to Doctor Atticus, and we'll see if it contains the same substances he found in poor Roger's blood."

It did. Atticus confirmed it two hours later.

"Extraordinary problems require extraordinary solutions," said Perrone, after he had received Atticus' report. "I believe, Gladys, that I need to die."

Gladys jerked backward as though she had been slapped. "Mister Perrone," she said, "I know Penny Carter is a harpy, but suicide is not the answer."

Perrone laughed. "Oh, it won't be permanent. I'll remain in the grave only long enough to keep Penny out of my hair until I can clear up this current business."

"You can't... Oh, I get it. Well, what do you have in mind?"

"Just this: Our friend from the TPG believes that he poisoned me. Therefore, he will believe it when the story is put out that I fell ill and passed away. I can get Doctor Atticus to help me with the, ah, paperwork. A trifle unethical, perhaps, but no more so than some of the other things

I've called on him to do. I have a plan that may give me an opening into the workings of the Guild, and it will also solve the Penny problem—at least for a while."

"She might just leave you alone if she thinks you've kicked the bucket."

He nodded. "But this charade is not just for Miss Carter's benefit; it will serve other purposes as well. I'm not that concerned about anyone else. I don't imagine many other people will even care. I have no close friends or associates."

Gladys thought that was a little sad. She was his friend, of course, and he was very close to Mirabelle, but what did he have beyond that? There was Louis Rickert, yes, and Tom Dart, and Shorty Red. But they were more like employees, and he only associated with them when he had the mask on. Not for the first time, she wondered which one was the real man.

Maybe both.

Maybe neither.

"Okay," she said. "So, how do we pull it off?"

An obituary appeared the following morning in the *Mobile Press*. Gladys had seen to it that the brief story quickly made it through the hoops necessary for publication.

> *Joseph Alexander Perrone of Mobile died on Thursday at his home, possibly due to complications from Meiringen's Syndrome.*
>
> *He is preceded in death by his parents, Frank and Margaret Perrone, and a brother, Anthony Perrone.*
>
> *Funeral services have not been made as of this publication, and will be announced at a later date.*

The circumstances of his death, as reported in the paper, would inform Mirabelle Darcy that her employer and friend was actually alive and well, should she see the obituary.

On the evening of the day the death notice was published, the telephone rang at Tull House and Gladys answered it.

"Hello, Perrone residence, Grace Munro speaking... Yes, that's right. He passed away last night... You're with who? No, he never said anything about that... Oh, he did? No, I don't believe you're correct there... Well, I was Mister Perrone's attorney, and I would have known if he had... No, there's no point in that, the arrangements have already been made... I'm sorry, I can't divulge that... No, the body will not be embalmed. Mister Perrone had religious objections to that practice, and... I'm not calling you a liar, but if you persist in this, I may change my mind. You had best check your paperwork again, because I'm quite sure no such agreement was ever made... No, that's just absurd. I'm sorry about the mixup, but everything is settled here and... No, sir, I think our conversation is over now. Please do not call back."

She hung up, then switched on the radio.

"Well," she said to Perrone, "he was a persistent little bast—That is, little *so-and-so.*"

"Thank you. What was absurd?"

"Oh, he asked if they could have a look at your body to assess the quality of our mortician's work."

"Ah-ha! Desperation! That's good. We know we're on the right track."

Late that night, in a soundproofed room at the rear of Tull House, with the radio playing loudly, Perrone and Gladys sat with their heads together, conversing in near-whispers.

"And now," Perrone said, "both Penny and the Guild will think I'm dead. We will turn away any representatives of the Donner-Purdy Funeral Home. Thus thwarted, the miscreants will resort to other means to obtain what they want."

"You just used the word 'miscreants' with a totally straight face," said Gladys, her face not totally straight.

"Yes. Is that unusual?"

"Very. But don't worry about it. It's kind of charming."

"Ah. Well, at any rate, this ruse ought to work. If I am correct, members of the Patriots Guild are poisoning certain people, then the Donner-Purdy Funeral Home obtains the bodies.

"Earlier today, I turned up some interesting information. From an

"Well, he was a persistent little bast—"

acquaintance of mine at the Schuyler Funeral Home, I learned the name of the firm that supplies Donner-Purdy with caskets. I employed a bit of subterfuge over the phone, and found out that Donner-Purdy has made several orders for duplicate caskets! I can only assume that, at some point, the caskets containing bodies are substituted for empty ones, which are then interred. Obviously, they use one for the viewing, then quickly switch them before the trip to the cemetery. I feel certain the coffin in poor Toby Zinfandel's grave had never been occupied, not even briefly. I examined it very thoroughly."

"You... dug up his grave?"

"Well, I had to. I don't believe in disturbing the dead, but I needed to make certain. And, of course, my actions didn't cause a disturbance, since there was no body there."

"Someone stole it?"

"No. Remember, I said the coffin appeared to be completely unused. No corpse had *ever* occupied it. And that must have been the condition in which it was buried."

"That is disturbing."

Perrone nodded. "They aren't doing this for monetary gain. They are interested in the corpses themselves."

"Why?"

Perrone hesitated for a moment before speaking.

"I can't be sure about that. There are certain disturbing possibilities, and I would rather keep them to myself until I know more. I would hate to say such things out loud unless I was absolutely certain."

A rather expensive-looking casket sat in the front room of Tull House, on top of a wheeled metal bier covered with a dark blue drape. The lid stood open, and it was evident that someone had been making modifications. Chief among these were two large, metal locks, affixed beneath the interior rim. They had deadbolt-style latches rather than keyholes, the curved bolts corresponding to slots in the lid. They could only be operated from inside the casket.

Perrone and Gladys walked around the thing, examining it, like a car salesman and a prospective buyer.

"Obviously, I will not be taken to the Donner-Purdy Funeral Home," he was saying. "They won't like that. I think they'll still want my body, though. That's why I had it announced that I wouldn't be embalmed. And I will be there when they come for it—just not in the way they'll be expecting. I purchased this from the friend I mentioned earlier, and made some modifications. When they cannot get the casket open, they will take it directly to their lair, and I'll be inside."

"You hope."

"It's more than a hope; it's a calculation. It may be an error, but I don't think so. We had best keep a vigil over the 'body' tonight, in case they attempt something, though I doubt they will. The interment will be early tomorrow, no service, graveside or otherwise. Poor Joe Perrone didn't have many friends."

Gladys bit her lip.

CHAPTER FIFTEEN
GHOULS IN THE MAGNOLIA

Rickey Harvard had a job doing maintenance work at Magnolia Cemetery. His father had made it clear to him that if he was going to keep on living at home, he'd have to start bringing in some money. There hadn't been too many jobs to choose from. It had come down to the cemetery and a meat packing plant. Both positions were low-paying and menial, but at least Rickey had been able to pick.

The cemetery had been more attractive than the meat packing plant, for a couple of reasons.

The plant was dirty and hot and smelled of blood. About a hundred other guys worked there, and half of them were Negroes. The other half were derelicts and bums. Rickey didn't have too much pride, but he had enough not to want to work with people like that.

So the plant was out. Now, the cemetery had its own set of problems, but Rickey had figured out that the problems could actually be made to work to his advantage.

The only thing Rickey Harvard was afraid of was ghosts. Well, the *main* thing. Just a few months before, he had seen an awful black ghost rise up out of a grave in the Church Street Graveyard. That had been bad enough, but a while after that, on the very day of the big riot in Cathedral Square, Rickey had spotted a whole gang of white-sheeted ghosts parading down the street right in front of his father's house! That time, instead of running away, Rickey had picked up a gun and gone after the spooks. Shot one of them too, and knocked it to the ground!

Rickey wasn't too clear in his mind on what had happened from there. He had been a little drunk, after all. The next thing he remembered, he was back home in the little bedroom he slept in on the top floor of his dad's three-story house. The top floor was really more of an attic, with a very low ceiling and just three small windows.

And that miserable little garret was what he was now working to keep from getting thrown out of. And to finance his new hobby, of course. One good thing about it was that his boss, a dried-out little shrimp called Nelson Carr, couldn't have cared less what Rickey did, or when or if he did it. Rickey could hang around in the Magnolia at any time of the day or night, doing a lick of work here and there, just as he pleased. If there was a little house with a cot in it, he could just live there and let his father go whistle for the rent, but there wasn't any such thing.

The reason he liked the idea of working in a cemetery was because of ghosts. Most people would totally avoid places that were filled with dead people, but not Rickey. He knew ghosts were real and he knew they sometimes walked the earth. Graveyards were a good place to see them. And that's what Rickey was hoping for. He wanted to see a ghost so he could walk up to it and look it in the face and have it out once and for all.

He was afraid of ghosts, without knowing why, and he didn't like it at all. It made no sense. Could ghosts actually hurt people? He had never heard of it happening, except in the movies. And, on top of that, hadn't he shot one down just a few months ago? So, the way he saw it, *they* ought to be afraid of *him*.

But he hadn't seen any at all in the time he'd been here. There had just been an interment today, some character named Joseph Perrone had been shoved into a slot in one of the big crypts. Rickey figured he might wander over that way and see if anything was going on. It was almost midnight now, which some people called "the witching hour," and that might apply to ghosts as well.

On the other side of the cemetery, toward which Ricky slowly meandered, strange things were afoot.

A queer-looking figure prowled an irregular course between the silent tombstones, on its way to the Perrone family crypt. The prowler wore a stained white smock, the head and face covered by a dark hood with a plaster false face affixed to the front.

In the left hand was a crowbar; in the right, a .22 pistol.

A group of men, four of them, were clustered in front of the door to the crypt. They were dressed in work clothes and slouch hats, with dark handkerchiefs tied around their faces. The weird figure stopped in mid-stride and stood watching them.

One of the men, the tallest of the quartet, used a large pry bar on the crypt entrance, breaking the lock, and pulling back the wrought-iron door.

"Here we go," said one of the others. "Let's get in there, get what we're after, and get the hell out of here."

The masked figure crept closer, pistol at the ready, crowbar held up like a club.

The men entered the crypt and found the niche in which a new casket had been placed very recently. Each man produced a screwdriver and removed one of the screws that held the four corners of the marble facing to the wall. They lifted it down and set it aside. Inside the space thus revealed was a bronze-colored casket.

"This ain't so bad," said the man who had spoken before. He and his comrades slid the coffin out of the niche and put it down on the floor.

"Just get this open and get the stiff out. Be careful, don't damage anything. We have to leave the coffin and put everything else back like it was."

"I can't open it," said the tall man. He had an Eastern European accent. "Damn thing must be welded shut."

"Well, shit. We can't go back empty-handed. I guess we'll just have to take the whole damn thing."

There was a brief chorus of groans. Crime loses some of its appeal when heavy lifting is involved.

"Nobody will know," said the tall man. "We can put the wall back together and close the door before we go."

"I don't think that belongs to you," came a strange, muffled voice. "You better put it back where you got it."

Inside the coffin, the Bay Phantom made a noise of exasperation.

What now? Something was going on out there, upsetting his careful plans. *Whatever this is, it can't be good.*

Well, there was nothing for it but to crack open the casket and see what was what. Fortunately, he was well-armed and prepared for any eventuality.

Or so he thought, anyhow. One day, perhaps, he might scrub away the last of his hubris and learn to always expect the unexpected. When he undid the interior latches, pushed the casket lid open, and bounded out across the floor of the little crypt, he was greeted with a sight he never could have anticipated.

Just outside the doorway, four men, masked and unmistakably thuggish, stood facing off against a crowbar-and-pistol-wielding Black Embalmer!

"What on earth are *you* doing here?" the Phantom demanded.

The four men's heads swiveled automatically toward the source of the new voice.

"Oh, *now* it's a party!" the Embalmer exclaimed.

"Aw, holy *shit*!" said one of the men. The four drew guns from their belts.

"That's not the sort of language you ought to be using in a place like this," the Phantom scolded.

The Embalmer laughed. After that, for a little while, nobody moved or said anything. The four men gripped their weapons, white-knuckled, afraid to move. The Phantom had them covered from his side, an automatic in each hand, each one aimed at the head of a thug. The Embalmer had drawn a bead on one of them with his slim little pistol, and hefted the crowbar menacingly in his other hand.

Thirty yards away, Rickey Harvard stood gaping and trembling. *Sweet Jesus, it's the black ghost from the Church Street Graveyard!* What was he doing *here*? How many graves could one ghost rise up out of, anyhow?

All of a sudden, the idea of confronting a specter didn't appeal to Rickey one little bit. It was a lot easier to be brave about ghosts when there wasn't one standing right in front of you.

Especially one that was packing two pistols. Good Lord, they were *arming* themselves now! Rickey ought to have known they might, after what had happened with him last year.

Fortunately, the ghost was paying all his attention to the four gangster types, and the guy in the smock and the mask. Hell, maybe that guy was a spook too! He sure looked weird enough.

The best thing would be to get the hell out of here...

The standoff might have continued indefinitely, if not for a bit of slapstick.

Rickey, backing away from the tableau as quietly as he could, stepped on a rake he had left lying in the grass. The handle popped up and smacked him in the back of the head. This made a loud thunk, which was quickly followed by Rickey's wail of pain and terror.

All six of the potential combatants turned their heads in that direction.

One of them recovered more quickly than the other five. The very tall man, having recognized the Phantom as the greatest of the three potential threats, sprang forward to deal with it. The Phantom, turning his head just a split second too late, took a punch to the face, forceful enough to crack one of his blue goggle lenses and knock him backward.

He turned the stumble into a crouch, braced himself with his hands on the ground, and launched himself at his assailant. He kicked the man in the knee, hard enough to dislocate the kneecap. This brought out a howl of pain, and sent the man staggering in the direction of the cemetery gate.

Meanwhile, the Embalmer had whacked one of the other men in the back with his crowbar, knocking him to the ground, and was attempting to crack another one over the head, but the man was dodging like a rodent.

The marauders, though armed, seemed disinclined to fire their guns, and appeared to be more interested in exercising the better part of valor.

"Let's get out of here!" one of them shouted. "The Bosses won't like it, but I ain't tangling with these two lunatics! I heard they can't be killed!"

They all ran for the gate, the tall one dragging his injured leg painfully behind him. The Phantom, still a bit disoriented, his right eye swollen shut, attempted to give chase. All he accomplished, however, was to slam right into the Embalmer, sending both of them sprawling on the grass.

By the time they got to their feet, the men were long gone.

The Bay Phantom grabbed the Embalmer and turned him around, holding the madman by the wrists.

"Well, that was the very definition of a debacle," the Phantom said in a scolding tone.

"Yes, or a fiasco," replied the captive.

"How on earth did you get here, and what were you trying to do?"

"I can't talk to you with this goddamn mask on. Take it off me."

The Phantom obliged. And got a surprise. The face he saw was not the one he had looked at so many times across the idle chessboard.

It was Penny Carter.

"Ha!" she said delightedly. "You've got a look on your face like you just found a kangaroo in your Cream of Wheat. Anyhow, I have to *assume* that you do, since I can't *see* your face. I probably would."

"Well, Miss Carter, you've made quite a mess."

"You know who I am."

"Certainly."

"I know who you are too."

"Well, yes, of course you do. The Bay Phantom is hardly unknown."

"Right, the *Bay Phantom*. How come the *Bay Phantom* just happens to show up here while a gang of goons are breaking into Joe Perrone's crypt?"

"I could ask the same thing about Penny Carter."

"You have me there."

"And this is the Perrone *family* crypt, not just *Joseph* Perrone's."

"Of course. But Joe is the only one who is supposed to have died recently. He was interred today. I didn't get invited. As for why I'm here... I just wanted to pay my respects in private. Joe and I are very close. Notice my verb there."

"I've no idea what you're driving at. Mister Perrone's passing was a shock and a tragedy. I never met him, but I knew him by reputation, you see. I too am here to pay my respects in private."

"You're a terrible liar. It's bad form to repeat a lie someone else has just told you. Should we go in there and check on the new arrival? Make sure he's all comfy and everything?"

"I don't think that will be necessary."

"Oh, I'm not sure I agree. I think we should..."

"Miss Carter," the Phantom interrupted, "this is hardly a fit place for a respectable young lady, especially at this hour."

"I couldn't agree more. Fortunately, I'm something of a hussy."

"Why are you dressed like this?" the Phantom asked.

"It's a costume. Mardi Gras, you know."

"Mardi Gras is not Halloween," he said, echoing Mirabelle. "Were you under the impression that there was to be a parade here tonight?"

She laughed, absolutely unperturbed.

The Phantom closed his eyes and pursed his lips. It was a fact that Joe

Perrone simply could not cope with Penny Carter. And the Bay Phantom was Joe Perrone. Joe Perrone was the Bay Phantom. The only difference was the mask. Though Doctor Freud had had a slightly different take on it, as far as Perrone was concerned, the Bay Phantom was just camouflage, not an identity.

Or so it had always seemed, at least.

Maybe that needed to change. Maybe the Phantom needed to be his own man—the way Roy Markham was. That wouldn't be easy, but it could surely be done, Perrone figured. The Phantom would need a bit of an edge. He could borrow that from Markham. The appearance of it, anyhow. He couldn't let the Phantom actually slip over that line.

A velvet fist in an iron glove, that's what was called for.

He opened the mental box in which he kept Roy Markham, just a crack, and drew a little material from it.

He gripped Penny by the upper arm and snarled, "Listen, sister, I don't know what you think you're doing, but I'll tell you one thing: If you don't lay off, you're going to regret it."

"Now, wait a minute. I just..."

"Shut up! I've had enough lip from you for one night. You need to go home and behave yourself. You need to stay out of graveyards in the middle of the night, and you *especially* need to stay the hell out of my business. Do I make myself clear?"

He shoved the mask at her, and she took it, holding it as though it were a spiny lizard.

"Do I make myself *clear*?" he repeated.

He let go of her arm and she stepped back, shocked. The expression on her face was difficult to read. She seemed amused and frightened in equal measure.

"Wow! Really?"

The Phantom gave her a sharp, dismissive wave of his hand. "You heard what I said, didn't you? Beat it, you screwy dame, before I smack you one!"

Her mouth hung open for a few seconds before she spoke again:

"I... okay, okay... I'm... sorry." She moved toward the gate, gazing back over her shoulder at the dark, menacing figure of the Bay Phantom.

"Move it!" the masked man shouted.

Penny turned her face away from him and broke into a brisk trot.

The Phantom felt weak in the knees, but there was a lightness in his chest that seemed to buoy him up. A sense of great freedom and power moved through him like an electrical current. Behind his mask, his lips pulled back involuntarily into a wolfish grin.

"Well, well," he said softly, with a great sense of wonder, as he watched Penny disappear into the shadows around the front gate.

Once she was gone, he went back into the crypt and secured the coffin, shutting the lid and sealing it, then returning it to its niche, whistling cheerfully as he worked.

He was aware of the other niches, the ones that weren't empty. He knew the remains of his father and mother and brother were there with him, just a few feet away. But he found it comforting rather than upsetting. He felt a sense of kinship, and a part of him even envied them their oblivion. There was a wall between him and them, and he was alone on this side of it.

❊❊❊

But he wasn't quite alone, there in the cemetery. Standing behind a tree two dozen yards from where he performed his labors was a woman. On her face was an expression of deep concentration and concern. She kept her eyes on the door of the crypt, watching the shadows playing on the wall inside. She moved backward when the specter in the black cloak and hat stepped out.

The Bay Phantom shut the crypt door and affixed a large new padlock to it.

Then he paused and cocked his head.

Behind the tree, the watcher had stepped on a twig, snapping it in two.

The Phantom closed the distance with incredible swiftness, the only sound being the whisper of his cloak through the chill air.

The watcher, suddenly confronted, stepped backward and nearly stumbled.

Irene Maude reached into her jacket and produced a large crucifix, which she brandished at the Phantom.

"Whatever you are," she said, "leave me alone."

"I don't mean you any harm," came a muffled voice. "I'd just like to know what you're doing in this place at this time of night."

"You are not a spirit? A devil?"

He leaned forward slightly and touched the tip of an index finger to the crucifix.

"It isn't burning me, you see. I'm just a man."

She shook her head. "You are not just a man. You are not alone. I sense two faces, two identities. Two distinct spirits, perhaps?"

"I don't think so. Again, ma'am, why are you here?"

"I was walking. I could not sleep. Is it against the law to be here?"

"Technically, yes it is, from sundown until 6 a.m. That's a city ordinance, though I doubt it has ever been enforced."

"Well, then. We are both criminals. I don't ask you why you're here, as it is none of my business."

"Ah. Perhaps, then, both of us should go home." The Phantom pointed toward the main gate. The women reflexively looked in that direction. Seeing nothing of interest, she returned her attention to...

... nothing. The cloaked figure was gone.

Shivering a little, Madame Maude put her crucifix away, buttoned her jacket all the way to the top, and headed for the gate.

CHAPTER SIXTEEN
SOMETHING WITH PENNY

The following afternoon, in an office in a building downtown, Penny Carter sat behind her desk, the desk that had once been the property of her late brother, Caleb. The brother who had been making plans to kill her before she turned the tables.

Now the desk was hers, and so was the organization Caleb and the other men in her family had built. Caleb was gone, and the others had slunk away to Europe, broken and demoralized by Penny's assumption of power the previous year. She was talking with her right-hand man, Gus Twombly, a battle-scarred hooligan who had been on the Carter family payroll for many years. He was one of the few old-timers to survive Penny's purge. He appreciated her, and she him.

"When are we gonna do something, Boss?" he was saying.

"When the time is right," Penny replied. "I don't know when that will be, not exactly."

"Some of the guys are getting nervous. This new bunch is gobbling up territory. They're got their grip on all the restaurants, and they may start expanding into other areas. We think they've been distributing dirty pictures. It's just a matter of time before they get into booze and dope."

"That's understandable. But remember, Gus, I always know more than anyone thinks I know."

"Personally, I got no complaints, Boss. You're a lot better at this than your brothers. And you're smart not to run your mouth to the hired hands, myself included. But a lot of the other guys don't understand you the way I do. Not that I *understand* you, mind—but I understand that I *don't* understand, and that you know exactly what you're doing. I figured that out a while back."

"You are a very wise man, Gus. Your faith in me is second only to my own."

She poured whiskey from a crystal decanter into a tumbler and sipped at it.

"But it isn't too early to start making preparations," she said presently. "This business might come to a head soon, Gus. There is a thing going on in a place that could have some bearing on it. Might give us a couple more warm bodies that know their way around. I'll make some calls, see where we are with that.

"Meanwhile, there is *one* thing that we can go ahead and take care of..."

CHAPTER SEVENTEEN
MYSTERY MAN

That night, the Bay Phantom found a reasonably comfortable spot in a large oak tree across the street from Mauvais Rêve, and settled in for his vigil.

The night was cold and quiet. Nothing happened until 11:30. An automobile pulled to the curb in front of the house and a man got out.

It was Mohammed, Irene Maude's mysterious retainer. He walked around to the side of the house and looked up at the second-story windows.

The Phantom was reasonably sure that Mohammed had walloped Joe Perrone over the head the other night, down in the cellar of the house. And he noted with some satisfaction that the man was limping, favoring his right leg.

He had kicked one of the cemetery marauders in the right knee last night, hard enough to cause problems for at least a week. And Mohammed was unusually tall, as was the man the Phantom had kicked. They could very easily be one and the same.

The man, either satisfied or frustrated by his brief examination, giving no indication either way, came back around to the front of the house and went inside.

Another uneventful hour passed. Then another character took the stage.

A man in an overcoat and wide-brimmed hat appeared from the shadows behind Mauvais Rêve. Where had he come from? No one had passed on the street.

The man walked up and down along the south side of the house. At one point, he took off his hat, got down on his hands and knees, close to the wall, and poked at something with a stick.

The Phantom studied the man. He was sure it was the same man he had followed down to the basement of the house the night of the dinner party. Here he was, poking around Mauvais Rêve again, this time on the outside. He stood up and discarded the stick, moving back toward the rear of the house, where he disappeared into the shadows.

The Bay Phantom dropped from the tree, landing lightly on the sidewalk without a sound. He seemed to glide, cape billowing behind him, across the street and around the side of the house. He slowed down and listened closely. A few faint noises told him a little story.

At the back of the property he encountered a short, wooden fence. He had heard the man climbing over it, and he did the same, making no sound at all.

Now he stood in the rear lot of the Donner-Purdy Funeral Home. He kept to the shadows to avoid being noticed by the guard at the back door.

He moved around the building, out onto Joachim Street. Where had the fellow gone? Ah, there he was, just going around the corner to the north, onto Constitution Street.

The Phantom followed him over to North Jackson Street, where the man got into a car—a brand-new 1932 Plymouth coupe, still flaunting its original shine. The Phantom surged forward like a rapidly-lengthening shadow, and climbed onto the back bumper of the machine. He held tight to the spare tire. The engine came to life, and the car pulled away from the curb.

A little yellow dog chased after the vehicle, yipping at the strange passenger on the back, for two blocks before its interest waned and it gave up.

After a drive of some fifteen minutes, the car came to a stop in the driveway of a small house on Old Shell Road, and the driver got out and went inside. The Phantom noted the address, then walked thirteen blocks, to one of the ingress points to his network of tunnels, eventually making his way back to Tull House.

He checked the address in the city directory, and learned that it was the home of Senior Detective Alvin Branch.

Well, this could be a good sign. If the police were working from that end, the Phantom would be free to seek out the other end and try to work his way in from there.

CHAPTER EIGHTEEN
THE PATIENT

The patient's name was Gerald Sams. He was the younger brother of the late Hector Sams. For a brief and terrifying period in 1931, he had been the Werewolf. Something had been done to his mind, and someone had provided him with a bizarre and lethal costume. The list of murders attributed to him was staggering.

The doctor's name was Terry Griggs. He had been working with Gerald Sams for a few months. The patient had not regained consciousness during that time, but his vital signs were good, and he seemed to be in no danger from infections or any kind of organic disease. Toxicology screens were inconclusive, intriguing, and impossible to interpret.

The hospital didn't have a name. It was used by certain government and law-enforcement agencies to treat patients/prisoners who needed to be kept as far from the public eye as possible.

"This is incredibly irregular, Miss Carter," said Doctor Griggs. "I'm not going to try to stop you, because I'm not stupid. But I object to your actions on moral and legal grounds. This man has been injured, his condition is still precarious, and he needs constant medical supervision."

"He'll have it," said Penny Carter.

Penny and four of her employees had arrived at the hospital a few minutes before, and expressed their intention to take charge of Gerald Sams. Griggs had objected, of course, but not too strenuously. Penny Carter could destroy him completely within just a few hours, were she of a mind to. So Griggs knew what the outcome of this confrontation would be, but he had to argue—mildly—to give his conscience something to nibble on later.

"He is also under a court order," Griggs continued. "If and when he ever regains consciousness, he is to be taken into custody by the police and charged with several murders."

"Ah, now that one is a little more problematic. I really don't see it happening."

"The federal government is involved, Miss Carter. You could be opening a very large can of worms if you tamper with this patient."

He was trying valiantly, ramping up the possible consequences, even though he knew none of it would affect Penny's decision. It was like trying to break a plate glass window by pelting it with marshmallows. Even if you had one three feet around, it wasn't going to go through.

"Your objections are noted," she said, "by which I mean ignored and almost forgotten already. This creature is coming with us. You have a story to tell the authorities: I was not here. These men were not here. This patient was taken by men unfamiliar to you. You can put masks on them if you like, or dress them as harlequins. In fact, it could be a gang of women, or children, or purple gorillas. But it wasn't us. You understand that, don't you? You won't try to tell anybody anything different, will you?"

"I... N-no, ma'am, I won't."

"That's what I like to hear."

Penny's men lifted the Werewolf from his bed and placed him on a stretcher.

"Where's the costume?" she asked the doctor.

"In the evidence locker at police headquarters, I suppose. It took us a long time to get the whole thing off of him, and we handed it over to the authorities when we finished."

Penny nodded. "That won't be a problem."

"It's more than just a costume; it's a deadly weapon."

Penny smiled.

"Yes," she said. "Yes, it certainly is."

CHAPTER NINETEEN
THE MOUSE

n the warren of rooms and laboratories beneath Tull House, Joe Perrone brooded. In his very private office, sitting behind the huge old oaken desk that had been one of the few pieces of furniture to survive the fire in

Bayou La Batre so many years before, he turned his current circumstances over in his mind.

For the time being, he was dead. There was no Joe Perrone. He was now the Bay Phantom.

But was the Phantom up to the current task?

He was facing something he had never faced before. Whoever was behind the recent disturbing events was worse than anybody he had ever encountered. Worse than the Black Embalmer; worse, even, than Doctor Piranha.

There were monsters at the bottom of this well. Who were they? What motivated them? How was Irene Maude involved? Involved she must be— she hadn't simply been out for a walk. He hadn't bothered to interrogate her further, having sensed that it would have done him no good. Anyway, he knew where she lived. He would have to speak with her in the near future, but on his own terms. There were things he needed to know first.

His plan had been ruined. He'd have to approach from a different angle.

He would have to get closer.

How do I do this?

Joe was still a Catholic, though a badly lapsed one. And, though he did not accept without question all the teachings of the Church, he firmly believed in the reality of right and wrong; of *good* and *evil*. A certain amount of moral relativism was necessary just to survive in this world, but there *were* absolutes.

When Perrone chose to do what he knew was evil, though he did so to promote a greater good, he could not permit himself to justify it. He could never call his evil by any other name, or he would truly be lost.

In order to penetrate this darkness, he might have to do horrible things. Whoever was behind all this was absolutely vicious and ruthless. There was no doubt about that.

Perrone couldn't do it. It was possible that the Bay Phantom couldn't do it.

But maybe Roy Markham could.

Perrone had used the Markham persona months ago, when he was hunting the Black Embalmer. As Doctor Freud had postulated, neither Markham nor the Phantom were Joseph Perrone, strictly speaking. Perrone had constructed both of them by rearranging components of his own personality into strange configurations, thus creating versions of himself that would be better equipped to face certain challenges.

Maybe the Embalmer had a point. But—did Freud?

Where did Markham come from, really? What was his true lineage? There were things in him that Perrone could not reconcile with anything he knew to be part of his makeup.

What is Markham made of?

How does Markham work?

Does it matter? Or is it enough that he does?

What had worked with Penny might work with these people.

Markham had not been permitted to reach his full potential last year; the operation had been concluded quickly, and it hadn't been necessary. This would likely be a very different thing.

He sighed and leaned back in his chair. It wouldn't do to overthink this, he decided. It had to be done. So he would just do it, and worry about the possible consequences later or not at all, depending on how it turned out.

He caught some motion in his peripheral vision and turned his head for a better look.

On the floor near his desk, squatting on its haunches was a small, dark gray mouse.

"Well," Perrone said, "hello there, little fellow. Or little miss."

The creature looked up at him, whiskers twitching, wringing its little forepaws.

"Are you hungry?" Perrone asked. "I don't have any cheese down here— but Mirabelle once told me your kind don't like it as much as you're reputed to. You prefer fruit and grains, isn't that correct?"

The creature cocked its head and continued rubbing its paws together furiously, a tiny Lady MacBeth. Perrone smiled at the incongruity of this anthropomorphic impression. Surely a mouse had nothing to feel guilt about, no damned spots on its paws that needed washing away. He envied the little beast.

"I'll go up and get you some oatmeal," Perrone said. "That ought to suffice. Just stay put, I'll be right back."

When he returned, the mouse was gone. He dropped the oats onto the floor where the creature had been. He hoped it would come back for the food. The thought of the little rodent starving seemed unbearable to him.

It was time now for the physical transformation. He went into the Changeling Room, as Mirabelle called it, where he stored all his disguise materials.

He injected a certain chemical, developed by Mirabelle, into parts of his face. It would temporarily alter the shape of his cheeks and chin. Very subtle, but all the more effective for it.

A false moustache was the very simple final touch.

Perrone could not be called burly, but by moving in a certain way, he could make it appear that he was. It was really remarkable, the false impressions one could give without the aid of makeup or prosthetics.

When he returned to his office, he saw that the oatmeal was gone. He smiled, went upstairs, and got some more, which he left in the same spot.

Then, he opened the box that contained Roy Markham, removing the lid and setting it aside...

CHAPTER TWENTY
THE WALL

Making inquiries about a fortune teller, or whatever this "Madame" Maude was supposed to be, should have been a very simple matter.

The vice squad generally kept up with palm readers and that kind of thing, as they were often fronts for prostitution. The "squad," a couple of sad sacks named Durrel and Kirk—guys for whom the retirement age ought to be lowered to 35—had been busy for weeks pretending to be doing their utmost to trace the source of the French postcards that had begun appearing all over town a couple months before. So far, they had come nowhere near the source, unless it was to collect bribes. Dart decided to talk to them. They might accidentally know something about Maude.

If they did, they weren't letting go of it.

Nor had he been able to learn anything about the corpse of Meat Grinder Molloy. He was the only one on the force who knew the identity of the decedent—or so it should have been. But the body had disappeared from the morgue, with no report ever filed on it in the first place. Officially, the body had never been found.

He also sought information on the Donner-Purdy Funeral Home. He learned that nobody had anything to say on that subject, either, though a clerk in the records department told him that a couple of criminal complaints had been filed against the establishment by dissatisfied customers. The clerk did not know the nature of these complaints, or why they were criminal complaints, rather than civil. The reports themselves could no longer be located.

***

At the end of his shift, he received word that Branch wanted to speak with him. He dropped by Branch's office.

"You've been asking about a certain Madame Maude, I hear," Branch said. There was something behind those words—something dark.

"Yeah," Dart said very casually, "I got a tip from an informant that she might be involved in something shady. I don't know what, though. But it may have something to do with that Donner-Purdy Funeral Home."

Branch gave him a hard look. He seemed angry for just a moment.

"I can't say anything about this Madame Maude, Tom. I just can't. If I could tell you anything, I would. Strange things are going on. I'm walking a knife's edge right now, and I don't need to be worrying about you as well."

"But, Alvin. I can—"

"For your own good, Tom, don't mix into this. You don't want to get in over your head, son. What do you know about it, anyhow? Where did you get this information?"

"I wouldn't call it information," Tom said. "Nothing actionable, anyhow. I have a few informants around town, they tell me things, but they don't always know whether what they see or hear is important or not."

"Well—Just let it lie, Tom. You've got plenty to keep you busy."

Tom accepted this because he had to. There was no way he was going to try and go over Branch's head. Anybody on that level could be dirty. Hell, *all* of them could. It was pretty obvious that *somebody* was putting pressure on Branch.

Speaking of Branch's head—maybe Branch was in over it himself.

CHAPTER TWENTY-ONE
THE RING

"Aw, Alice, you don't sound so good."

"I just got this cough. I'm okay."

Louis studied her face. There was something wrong with her.

They were in a "loft" at the top of a house on State Street, an unheated dump that wasn't wired for electricity. But there were a couple of high, wide windows that let in plenty of sunlight for taking pictures. None of the girls Alice had spoken to had shown any interest in the venture, but she was on board; the only thing of value that she had right now was the hope Louis had held out.

Now she stood before Louis in a belted overcoat, which she was ready to shed. But she had been coughing all the way up the stairs, and she was very pale, with dark smudges under her eyes. Her cough had been harsh and raw, and it hurt Louis' throat to hear it.

"I don't know," he said. "You better not take your, ah, things off. I don't want you getting pneumonia."

"I need the money, Louis."

"I know, but—Aw, it's too cold in here, Alice. No, we can't do this today." He shook his head, resolute. "Maybe later."

"But, Louis, I was kinda counting on making some money this way. I haven't been feeling too good, and I haven't been able to work very much."

"If you're already not feeling good," he said, "there's no sense in you making yourself sicker."

"Look, Louis, I'll level with you. I'm *really* sick, okay? I need money. The treatment I need is gonna cost plenty, and I want to go back home to my folks in Huntsville. But I can't do anything *broke*. Mom and Pop can't help me; they're practically in the poorhouse themselves."

"Aw, jeez, Alice. I didn't know all that."

She pursed her thin lips. "Don't start feeling sorry for me. I brought it all on myself. I wish I'd never come down here and started... you know. I just want to go home and maybe get better. I can't get much sicker than I already am—not just from being cold for a while."

Louis scowled. What was he supposed to do? He thought for a while, and saw only one way to proceed.

"Look, Alice, here's a few bucks, okay?" He dug into his wallet and handed her most of what remained of his last stipend from the Phantom.

"Louis, I couldn't just—"

"Yes, you could. I'm not running a charity, Alice, I'm just protecting my investment. That is a principle of capitalism. You're my top model, see? If you was to get sick and die, I'd take a terrible loss. So you take that money. It ain't much, but I'll get you some more."

"How?"

That was the question. He had already spent most of his money on film and stuff.

But...

There was the ring. The ring he had found in the hamburger. If it was real gold...

"Alice, I'm a businessman. I got capital. You just go home and stay inside where it's warm, huh?"

"Well... If you say so, I guess."

"I say so, Alice. Go on home, yeah? Get some soup or something, then lie down a while. I'll see you later."

Louis walked around for a couple of hours, struggling against the demands of his conscience, trying to find some kind of loophole. But there was no way out.

He went to Nathan's Pawn Shop on Royal Street. There was no Nathan, and possibly never had been. The place had been run by a twerp named Malcolm for at least the past fifteen years.

"Yeah, this looks pretty good, Louis," said Malcolm, after a quick examination of the ring. "I can probably give you a good price. Just let me take it in the back for a few minutes and run a test."

"Sure, yeah, hurry it up, wouldya?"

He watched Malcolm carry the ring back behind the curtain. Damn, he hated to lose a windfall like that. How many more gold rings could he expect to find in hamburgers? But—poor ol' Alice. She was a good kid. She wasn't like some of the other girls out there on the streets. She wasn't hard and nasty, and she never talked bad about anybody. She didn't deserve the pressure she was under, and to be sick on top of that... Well, it wasn't fair. The ring would surely bring enough money to get her some food and clothes and maybe some medicine, and possibly even a bus ticket back to Huntsville. Yes, it was the right thing to do. He was willing to bet the Phantom would approve.

And maybe Louis could go back to church one day and tell the Lord what he had done for Alice. God might cut him a break and send him another ring. Pretty much the first prayer he'd ever said, last year in the Cathedral of the Immaculate Conception, had been answered almost immediately. He hadn't said any more of them since then, so maybe he had some credit built up. He ought to be good for a *silver* ring, at least.

The bell above the door jangled, startling Louis out of his religious reverie. Into the shop strode a man he knew by sight.

Louis moved over to one wall and feigned intense interest in a dented old trumpet that hung there on a peg.

He could see the man's reflection in the surface of a large silver teapot on a shelf near the trumpet. The guy was *leering* at him; that was the only word for it. The look was both appraising and supercilious, and it made Louis nervous.

Detective Dave Poitier had a bird-like nub of a head, complete with a sharp little beak for a nose, and small, wide-set eyes. He habitually wore cheap, poorly-cut suits. The one he had on today looked like it was made out of tan butcher paper.

Louis' uneasiness increased when Malcolm reappeared through the curtain and exchanged a nod with the detective.

Malcolm handed the ring to Poitier.

"That's it all right," said the pawnbroker. "Tate's name is engraved on the inside."

Louis turned around slowly, keeping his hands in full view. Poitier walked over and put a hand on his shoulder.

"Louis Rickert," the detective said with mean-spirited relish, "you are under arrest on suspicion of the murder of one Charles Tate. You have some Constitutional rights, but they won't be doing you much good."

At that moment, as though responding to some silent signal, two uniformed cops came into the shop.

Louis sighed and held out his wrists for the cuffs. Fighting or protesting his innocence would only make his situation worse.

He had once heard Shorty say that no good deed goes unpunished. But this was just taking it *way* too far.

✳✳✳

CHAPTER TWENTY-TWO
LEAVENWORTH

"It is not possible either to trick or escape the mind of Zeus."
—Hesiod (800 BC - 720 BC)

Mirabelle got off the train in Kansas City, and was met at the station by Lee Rosenberg, a New Orleans-based private detective who had once done some Phantom-related work for Mister Perrone.

Lee had reserved a small suite of rooms for her at a hotel in downtown Leavenworth, Kansas, and another room for himself. Once she had collected her luggage, they made the short trip there in Lee's car.

Months ago, Mirabelle had passed the word quietly among her many contacts across the nation. She wanted to be informed if anybody heard anything that involved Leavenworth.

Good fortune had come her way via Lee. He had gotten wind of plan to break a certain crime boss out of Leavenworth. A ragtag gang of low-level crooks were concocting a grandiose scheme to spring one of their more highly-regarded associates. As soon as she had received this information, Mirabelle had begun her operation.

She had provided a great deal of her own money. Lee had managed to get a man he could trust inside the gang. The mole hadn't come cheap, but if this worked out, it would be well worth it.

The gang had almost given up the plan after the escape plot that had begun to unfold in December of the previous year.

A Chicago-based crook named Harold Fontaine had smuggled guns, dynamite, and nitroglycerine into Leavenworth, hidden in a barrel of shoe dressing. The contraband had entered the prison on December 11, 1931. Shortly thereafter, seven convicts on the inside had used the arsenal to escape. Three had been killed, and the survivors—Stanley Brown, Charles Berta, Thomas Underwood, and Earl Thayer—had been speedily recaptured.

Mirabelle had experienced some anxiety over that. Here was a plan they had been unaware of. It might put the skids to their own plot.

But Lee's inside man had convinced the criminals that it would only aid their own raid. Who would expect another attempt so soon? And this one wouldn't be sneaky; there wouldn't be any infiltrations or preparations for the authorities to get wind of. The gang would remain quiet and isolated until the day they were to strike.

"That's the kind of pretzel logic these desperadoes love," Lee remarked. "The less sense a thing makes, the better they like it."

They spent the better part of a week finalizing and triple-checking on their preparations. The gang's plan, largely crafted by Mirabelle herself and fed to the conspirators by Lee's inside man, stood an excellent chance of succeeding—up to just the right point. There are, of course, no sure things in life, and even fewer when it comes to breaking into maximum-security federal penitentiaries—but the carefully-calculated odds were in Mirabelle's favor.

The convict the gang was supposed to be springing knew nothing of this plot. But the gang would be expecting him and some confederates to have weapons of their own, stolen from the guards, and to be ready.

The leader of the gang believed he had been corresponding with the crime boss they were planning to spring. In reality, his letters had been intercepted by Lee, who had drafted all the responses.

The day arrived. They spent the afternoon in Mirabelle's suite, making their final preparations.

"I have to admit, Mirabelle, that I still have misgivings," Lee said. "I'd hate for someone to get killed."

"We're making sure they can't hurt anybody," Mirabelle reminded him.

"The guards are liable to hurt *them*, though."

"*Af a shlang tor men keyn rakhmones nit hobn*," Mirabelle said.

"I didn't know you spoke Yiddish! 'For a snake you should have no pity.' I suppose you're right."

"Look, Lee, I understand your feelings, but we're doing them a favor. Guys like that don't live very long in the wild, and they kill lots of innocent people while seeking their own deaths. At least we're giving them a chance to live out their spans in relatively humane captivity, without killing anyone else."

They went over the next few steps point by point. Mirabelle repeated details like a catechism. She knew it all by heart, but she had to go over it one more time, because that's what people do. It was better than sitting around watching the clock.

"There will be anonymous calls to several different law-enforcement agencies," she said, "just minutes before the gang is to show up at the prison. We don't want them getting stopped until they're through the gate. After which we want as many cops on the scene as possible."

"It'll be chaos!"

"That's what I'm counting on."

"Of course. Connie and her friends will handle the calls."

Connie was Lee's secretary. She had arrived in Leavenworth the previous evening, with a few friends in tow—a little working vacation.

"Afterward," said Mirabelle, "the prisoners will be locked down. The last thing anyone'll be worried about is the cops at the front gate. The only way I'll get in is if I look like I belong there. That's how come I have the Missouri State Police uniform. That's one agency that *won't* get a call. Even if the uniform gets noticed, nobody will think it's strange. They'll have more pressing matters on their minds."

"Yeah, I get the reasoning there, but even *with* the uniform... I mean, you don't exactly..."

Mirabelle laughed. "That's why I'm gonna have to go in whiteface. It won't be absolutely convincing, but if there are a couple dozen cops hanging around, I won't attract much attention. You stay right here—I'll be back in about an hour."

She disappeared into the bedroom.

"I don't know, Mirabelle, that's pretty damn convincing," Rosenberg said. "If I were standing five feet from you, I wouldn't think a thing about it. Maybe even closer, assuming I didn't know there was anything to notice. Lon Chaney could have taken some tips from you."

Mirabelle stood before him, in her uniform, arms extended like a fashion model. She looked for all the world like an older white man, maybe fifty-five or sixty years of age.

"A lot of it is just how you carry yourself," she said. "My voice probably wouldn't pass muster, but I don't plan on doing any orating."

"Well then—I guess we're ready. Let me just say, I don't know why you're doing this, but I trust you. I know you've got good reasons. Any last-minute qualms?"

She shook her head and reached into the pocket of her police jacket, taking out a small medallion her father had given her a lifetime ago

"I've got my lucky charm," she said.

"Lucky charm? *You*?"

"Don't be so quick to dismiss things that most people call superstition. Those people aren't as enlightened as they may think they are."

CHAPTER TWENTY-THREE
BREAK-IN

The United States Penitentiary at Leavenworth was located 25 miles northwest of Kansas City, Kansas. It was the largest maximum-security federal prison in the United States, and had been since its construction in 1903. People often confused it with the United States Disciplinary Barracks at nearby Fort Leavenworth, a couple miles to the north.

Mirabelle and Lee were parked in the shadows next to a large wooden fence on Metropolitan Avenue in Leavenworth. From there, they had a good view of the long double driveway that led off the street and into the prison compound.

Their car had been painted to look like a Missouri State Police vehicle. Lee also wore an MSP uniform.

"Our man in the gang is going to be dropped off at a filling station," Lee said. "He's supposed to be meeting with some non-existent reinforcements who will ostensibly remain just outside the immediate perimeter, to help the rest of the gang get away when they liberate their men."

Mirabelle shook her head. "And they believed all that?"

"Oh, yes. Stanley's a great liar. Not that he really had to be. As I said before, this gang is not what you'd call a convocation of masterminds."

They didn't have long to wait. They had only been there for a few minutes when the car carrying the gang passed them, and turned right onto the drive.

"There they go." Lee looked at his watch. "The police have already been notified. They'll get in touch with prison officials, of course. If I figured it

"That's how come I have the Missouri State Police uniform."

correctly, the first unit will arrive not long after the gang's car reaches the gate. As soon as we see it, we can fall right in."

The marauders rolled up to the front gate and jumped out of the car, guns at the ready. There were two guards up on the wall. They displayed rifles, aimed them at the armed gangsters, and waited.

It was something of a standoff. The gang seemed to think they had the upper hand.

"Okay, you mugs," shouted one of the gang members. "There's more of us than of you. Just don't get funny, and this'll be over before you know it. Open the gate."

"Kiss my ass!" the guard yelled back.

"Okay, then!" the gangster shouted. "Bosco, you know what to do!"

While the others covered the guards on the wall, the driver got back into the automobile, backed up, then shot forward and rammed the gate, knocking it open and rolling on through, heading straight for the main prison building.

A criminal named Frank Grigware had done something similar in 1910, except he and his cronies had hijacked a locomotive that brought supplies into the prison, rather than a car. Of course, Grigware had been going out, not coming in.

The guards on the wall opened fire on the automobile. Slugs slammed into the roof and the trunk, but the old Ford kept on rolling.

The men on the ground tried to fire on the guards. Fingers tightened on triggers and squeezed.

Nothing happened.

The gang, of course, had no idea that Lee's inside man had switched out all their ammunition. All they had in their guns was dummy ammo, with no powder in the cases. The prison guards had evidently already been informed of this, as it had been part of the information relayed to law enforcement by Lee's secretary, Connie, and her friends, from pay telephones across the county.

One of the guards fired back at the gang on the ground, aiming to scare rather than kill. It worked.

Two cars from the local police department roared up Metropolitan, toward the prison. As they passed the concealing fence, Lee and Mirabelle pulled out and fell in behind them.

They went up the long drive to the gate.

Lee stopped the car right behind a Kansas State Police vehicle. A few cops were milling around, and one of them gave him a quizzical look. Lee rolled down the window and said, "Headquarters got one of them anonymous tips too. They radioed us 'cause we were in this area. Someone sure ratted these bastards out, huh?"

The cop nodded and moved on.

Mirabelle hopped out of the car.

"Okay, Lee," she said. "Great job. Now, ditch this car and get to the rendezvous point. I'll see you when I see you."

"I can't get over your voice coming out of an old white man."

She chuckled, waved, and headed for the gate.

She had a large camera bag slung over her shoulder, and what appeared to be a Speed Graphic in her hands. Just a simple police photographer, nobody important. She stood in front of the ruined gate, raised the camera to her eye, and the flashbulb went off. Then she stepped through.

She trotted up the drive to the front of the complex, and walked around the bullet-riddled car, pointing the camera at it and depressing the shutter button three times, from different angles, changing out the flashbulb each time. More squad cars had arrived, and the area was quickly filling up with uniforms.

The would-be liberators had been taken into custody, and were being led to the police vehicles that would transport them to jail. Months later, they would go to trial, where it would become painfully obvious to them that they had been suckered. By whom, and for what purpose, they would never learn.

Mirabelle nodded to a few of the other officers there, but did not speak. Nobody challenged her as she approached the main building, an imposing four-or-five-story—she wasn't quite sure—edifice in neoclassical architectural style popular in Washington D.C. Atop the blocky central structure sat a squat, featureless, silver dome, which somehow seemed smaller than it ought to be, giving the building an unfinished look.

The wings housing the prisoners radiated outward from this central administration area, one on each side, the others off to the rear.

There was plenty of confusion, and Mirabelle just walked right through one of the front doors. She was a bit surprised herself at how easy it was.

The guards would soon be changing shifts, though the schedule might have been upset by all the action. So much the better.

She squatted in a corner and began jotting things down in a small notebook, appearing to be intently focused on what she was writing, surreptitiously keeping an eye on the activity around her. Nobody approached her.

When she was sure she was unobserved, Mirabelle headed for one of the hallways that led back from the reception area to the administrative offices. Now it might get tricky. None of the locks in this place would give her any problems, but she had to remain either unobserved or unremarked-upon from this point forward.

"Hey, 'scuse me, fellah. You lookin' for something?"

It was a prison guard, coming up behind her—not unfriendly, but mildly suspicious.

"Sure am, son," she said in a gruff voice. "Where's the damn head? I gotta piss like a Russian racehorse."

"Ha! Well, don't bust a kidney, old-timer. It's right over there."

In the restroom, behind the door of a stall, she removed her police uniform. From her camera bag, which was really a small backpack, she removed a guard's outfit, and put it on. She put the white wig into the backpack and took out a brown one. She added a further layer of camouflage to her face, in the form of a false moustache.

Then she disassembled the camera, which was only a painted cardboard shell—the only part of it that worked was the flash bulb. She tucked that into her bag, flattened out the rest of the "camera," and wrapped it in the uniform she had removed. This went into a brown paper bag, which, in turn, went into a trash can.

Then she waited in the stall for half an hour before venturing back out of the restroom.

There was still plenty of activity, of course. She walked around the perimeter of the lobby, nodding politely to cops, avoiding eye contact with prison guards, until she located the corridor she needed next. It was empty, and she started down it. If anyone saw her, no one challenged her.

Once she rounded a corner at the end, she relaxed just a tiny bit.

Mirabelle foresaw a time when every inch of a facility like this would be covered by small, inexpensive television cameras. But that was still fifty or sixty years in the future, by her reckoning. For once, she was grateful to be living in a relatively primitive era.

The guards were sparse in this part of the complex, their movements predictable. Mirabelle flitted from one patch of shadows to the next, working her way closer to her goal.

She was calm, her mind uncluttered and detached. The more self-conscious one is, the greater the probability that one will be noticed by someone else. It was a lesson she had learned long ago, from her father, and it had been buried for years, along with all her other memories of him. But those memories had recently been freed during a hypnotic session with Doctor Freud—those and many others.

And there were other techniques that had been passed along to her by Mister Perrone, who had picked them up during his travels. She had never been able to master them before, but by combining them with her newly-recovered memories, she could make a phantom of herself.

Mirabelle was only partially present in her body right now, and she moved like a ghost, through corridors and up stairwells. She encountered locks, and she was prepared for them. Without stopping to think about it, she applied her lockpicks and skeleton keys smoothly and silently, with no anxiety, no sense of peril. At the moment, there was no difference between a federal prison and a peaceful forest glade.

Fortunately, the party she had come to see was a special case, and was kept well away from other prisoners.

She was fortunate in that her goal was not in the wings of the prison proper, where the regular cells were. It was in the upper reaches of this administration building. Still, she would have to be very cautious. She ducked into a dark alcove to make her final transformation.

Off came the guard uniform revealing her fundamental garb, the close-fitting black stealth suit she had worn during some of her adventures with the Bay Phantom, along with a loose-fitting black blouse. Finally, she removed the makeup and prosthetics from her face. Her natural coloration would do her more good from here on out.

Then she continued, finding the stairwell she needed and ascending three flights, then slipping out into another featureless corridor. Now she would have to work her way toward the rear of the building.

At one point, she was almost spotted. A guard, coming around a corner, stopped dead and stared at the patch of shadow in which she was concealed. She instantly cleared the surface of her mind, became nobody, nothing but dead air. After a moment, the guard shook his head and moved on.

Soon, Mirabelle found a maintenance closet with a locked door. She got it open, went inside, and made herself as comfortable as possible behind a metal shelf full of cleaning products. Here she would remain, while the excitement below died down. The prison would be locked down for a while, security heightened. She believed she could cope with that, but there was no point in getting cocky. She was close now to her goal. Slow and steady.

She remained there for almost 24 hours. She slept and meditated, preparing herself for what lay ahead. The closet was opened only twice during this time, once to fetch a mop, then to put it back. Mirabelle stayed hunkered down in her dark corner, and was not observed.

✻✻✻

She emerged from the closet when she judged the time to be right.

Now she would use some special information she had obtained, details that were not found on any of her maps or charts or anywhere else. They had come to her from a most extraordinary source.

She negotiated a rather bewildering series of hallways, following the path she had committed to memory.

This was not the maximum security section. This was not officially a section at all. Officially, there were no prisoners up here, and no cells to keep them in if there were. The hallways she now trod had not appeared on any of the blueprints Mirabelle had procured. But she had been informed of their existence. She was relieved to find that her informants had been reliable.

Finally, she reached the short corridor that was her destination. At the far end was a door with no markings, and only a small, barred window at eye level. Behind that steel door was the man she had come to see.

It was the toughest lock she had ever tried to crack. It took her almost thirty seconds. When she had it open, she stepped inside, pulled it shut, and locked it behind her. This was much easier, since she knew the lock now.

A man rose from a bunk attached to one wall.

"Don't worry," said Mirabelle, covering the cell's occupant with a flashlight. The room was more Spartan than she would have expected, given this prisoner's unique status. "I won't try to hurt you. I've come a long way and gone to a great deal of trouble to see you, Doctor Piranha."

CHAPTER TWENTY-FOUR
DOCTOR PIRANHA

Doctor Piranha. The man who had tried to destroy the city of Mobile almost five years ago, with a cache of explosives concealed in a network of underground tunnels.

The man who had been stopped by the Bay Phantom.

The man whose official name was "John Doe."

The man whose real name was Anthony Perrone—Joe Perrone's older brother.

The occupant of the cell touched a switch on the wall and a dim ceiling light came on. Mirabelle doused her flashlight.

"I know you," said Doctor Piranha, cocking his head to one side and studying her. "You used to be Mirabelle Darcy, did you not?"

"What a queer thing to say," she replied. "I still am Mirabelle Darcy, of course."

He nodded. "My apologies. I sometimes forget that other people are real."

He smiled at her then; at least, that's what she assumed he thought he was doing. It was more like the meaningless grimace one might see on the cold face of a dead fish.

"Okay," Mirabelle said, "let's just cut the bullshit, shall we? You know who I am, and I know who you are. And you know that I know. You haven't killed me, and I don't believe you intend to. You must know why I came here, what I want to talk about."

"Joe," he said flatly.

"*Joseph Perrone*," Mirabelle said pointedly. "Your brother. Don't worry, I'm the only one who knows that. I know you are—or were, if you prefer—Anthony Perrone. I know you did something to him. What I *don't* know is what it was that you did.

"I assume that you became Doctor Piranha and tried to destroy Mobile and the Carters because you blamed them for the deaths of your parents. Or because it seemed like an interesting thing to do."

The elder Perrones had died years ago in a fire that had most likely been set by a member of the Carter crime family. Joe believed that his brother Anthony had perished as well. Mirabelle had come to the conclusion that he had not.

"A little of both," Piranha said. "Perhaps more of the latter, if I'm honest."

"Uh-huh. Piranha, Perrone. It's kind of obvious, isn't it?"

"Not to anybody but you, evidently."

More silence. The smile had slipped away. Mirabelle forced herself to keep looking him in the eye. She was damned if she'd be the first one to look away. This went on for quite some time.

"Joe doesn't know?" Piranha finally said.

"He does not. Nor will he ever, if I have anything to say about it. He thinks his brother is dead. He may be right."

"You care about him," Piranha said.

"That's obvious. And I think you do too. Whatever you did to him, you thought it was for his own good. I figured that much out. But how do you *know*? How do you know that whatever you did won't kill him in the long run, or screw him up in some way you can't imagine? I want to know what you did. I'm smart enough to understand it, don't worry about that."

"You really are, aren't you?" he said. He sounded genuinely intrigued. "I barely noticed you at all when we were both younger, and your mother worked for our family. You were barely a shadow of a presence in our house. I rarely ever underestimate anyone, but I certainly did in your case. Seeing you now, like this... I am very good at reading people, Miss Darcy. I believe that you are at least as intelligent as I am. You managed to break into a maximum-security federal lockup undetected and made your way to my cell. You are highly motivated, and willing to assume unlimited risk. Your concern for others could one day be your undoing."

"I can live with that. Or die. Whichever."

"You know how to survive, do you not? If people knew what you really are, there are a lot of them who would kill you for it."

Mirabelle nodded.

"Not just a Negro, but a woman to boot," Piranha went on. "They would not suffer a mind like yours to live in such a body. People are so wretched and small-minded, Miss Darcy. Those of us on a certain plane understand how false and foolish are all the distinctions based on race and sex, but there are damn few of us up here. It is fortunate for you that my brother is such a person. Miss Darcy, I do not dislike you. That is about as sentimental as I get, and it is rather rare. You have come to me with a reasonable request, under the circumstances, and I feel more than inclined to grant it. However, you have arrived here at a rather awkward moment—or perhaps it is opportune. I seem to be in a bit of a situation. It occurs to me that you might be able to render me some assistance. I will not make my cooperation with your request contingent upon yours with mine, *but...*"

"But what?"

As if in response, the lights in the cell and the hallway outside winked out. A siren began to sound, and emergency lighting came up. Then the siren abruptly dropped off to nothing, as though something had snuffed it out.

"But without your help," Piranha calmly continued, "I may well be dead within the hour."

CHAPTER TWENTY-FIVE
FRIGHT

"Two people have come here to kill me," Piranha explained. "They go by the names Milton Cabal and Winona Dirge. The odds against me were beginning to seem rather dire. But between the two of us, Miss Darcy, we might be smart enough to destroy them before they destroy me. What do you say?"

"How do you know this?" Mirabelle asked. "That these people are after you?"

"The same way I know a lot of other things I've got no business knowing. Contacts. A huge web of them, out there. Prison is not a hardship to me, Miss Darcy; it's the best place for me. I influence the world outside, and am influenced by it. But there aren't supposed to be any incursions."

"And you believe they're here now? Quite a coincidence, isn't it, that they arrive the same evening I do?"

"It would seem so, yes. There *is* such a thing as coincidence, Miss Darcy, or else there wouldn't be a word for it."

"Huh. You oughtta put that in a fortune cookie."

"Is that your answer?"

Mirabelle sighed, reminding herself of Joe Perrone.

"Okay," she said. "I'll help you. I don't suppose I have much choice."

"Are we playing with him, Milt?" asked the woman. "Because I don't think we should be playing with him."

"We're not playing," her companion said tartly. "I don't play with people like him. We're being careful—very, very careful. We don't know what sort of defenses he has. We know the warden is in his pocket, and God only knows what sort of an infrastructure he has in place. This is not some two-bit rum-runner, Winona. This is Doctor Piranha, the most dangerous man on earth."

They were standing on the roof of the administration building, next to the silver dome.

"*You're* the most dangerous man on earth," said Winona Dirge. She was a tall woman—six feet exactly—with a smooth, pale face that was absolutely symmetrical; the two halves were like mirror images of one another.

Milton Cabal shook his head. He was an inch taller than Winona, and his round face could be called cherubic if you ignored the unpleasant thing living behind his watery blue eyes—which was pretty well impossible to do. He was infected with the sort of malevolence that could not help making itself known.

"Not tonight I'm not," he said, "If I believe that right now, then I'm doomed. If I go at him with the attitude that I'm better than he is, he will kill me. Kill *us*. We have to approach him the way we would approach someone who absolutely cannot be defeated. We take nothing for granted. Any hint of cockiness on our part is a self-administered dose of lethal poison. We are not here to commit suicide."

"That makes sense. But he can't possibly know we're here."

"I'm operating under the assumption that he does. You're correct, there's no possible way he could, but I bet he does anyhow. I may be the most dangerous man in the world, but he isn't a man. He's... something else."

"Seriously? You're that afraid of him?"

"I'd call it respect, but you can call it whatever you want to. We're here, aren't we?"

"That we are," Winona said. "And remind me again why we're here doing something roughly analogous to Russian Roulette. With two bullets in the cylinder instead of one. *Three* bullets."

"Four million dollars."

"Yes, that's it. It still sounds worth the risk—but we're not inside yet."

"No," said Cabal. "And don't forget all the money we were advanced to construct the devices we're using to *get* inside. Those were some very advanced designs we were provided with."

"Yes, and I'd say we put them together in record time—if anybody kept records of things like that."

"Oh, we're very smart and capable, but we've never had this level of resources before. That blimp that dropped us onto this roof didn't come cheap. Well, we launched the initial strike, which should be taking effect, and now the power is knocked out. Time for us to get moving. We've got about an hour. We need to do it in half that time, or less. So let's cut a hole in this roof and get to it."

✱✱✱

"So, what's next?" Mirabelle said.

"I don't suppose we'll have to wait long to find out."

A door in the middle of the hall opened, and a guard came through. Mirabelle watched him through the little window in the cell door.

"There's a guard, but I think something's wrong with him. Either he's drunk, or—"

Piranha stepped up behind her, off to the side, so he could see through the window too.

"No, that's Paulson. He doesn't drink. He doesn't do anything interesting, apart from taking bribes. He does look unsteady on his feet, doesn't he?"

The man staggered up to Piranha's cell door.

"Doctor," he said weakly, "You gotta—Somebody's—"

And that was as far as he got before he lost consciousness and fell to the floor.

Piranha tipped his head back and sniffed the air. Then he said one word: "Gas."

CHAPTER TWENTY-SIX
FIGHT

Mirabelle's backpack contained a few potentially useful items. One of them was a small rebreather, a sort of miniature gas mask that could filter harmful toxins out of the air. She took it out and put it in her mouth.

She watched Piranha closely. He showed no signs of discomfort.

"I think the air is clear now," he said presently. "Must be quick-acting and quick-dissipating."

Mirabelle removed the rebreather from her mouth.

"This begs an interesting question," she said.

"Yes, indeed. I have made certain alterations to my body chemistry. I am not susceptible to most poisons or soporifics. No known toxin can penetrate the blood-air barrier in my lungs, you see."

"Huh. You are very, very interesting, you know that?"

"I can see where people might think that."

"Yeah. Well, what do you know about these assassins? Anything that might be helpful?"

"They sometimes use swords," he said.

"What? *Swords?* What kind of modern assassin uses a sword?"

"This kind, obviously. If what I've heard is true."

"Well," Mirabelle said, "I've studied fencing."

"Under whom?" Piranha asked.

"Nobody. I read a book. And watched some movies."

"I see. No practical experience?"

"I practiced with a broom handle. But I have a vivid imagination; very tactile, and especially sensitive to three-dimensional geometry and spatial relationships. Kinetics and so forth."

"I don't doubt that," said Piranha. "I imagine you can construct a sort of... *virtual reality,* I suppose one might call it, inside your head."

"That's actually a pretty good term. I think of it as my training simulator."

"That works too. I do the same thing, by the way."

"I figured."

"Of course," Piranha said, "neither of us happens to have a sword."

"True," said Mirabelle. "But I didn't come empty-handed. And I'd be very surprised if you didn't have something in here you could use as a weapon. We need to work up a quick strategy while we have a little time."

"First," said Piranha, "we should separate them. They work well together; you and I do not, and we don't have time to learn."

"Okay, that seems sound. I'll deal with her, and you see what you can do with Cabal. Can we agree not to kill either one of them?"

"You're free to do as you wish, of course. I make no promises."

Mirabelle let out a sharp sigh. "All right, whatever, we don't have time to argue. But, as a favor to me, you might at least *try*."

He refused to commit himself. Instead, he said:

"They'll think I'm locked in. They could not possibly know about you."

"Oh, sure, of course."

"I detect skepticism in your voice," he said, as he squatted down and reached under his bunk. "Perhaps a bit of sarcasm."

"Who, me? No, no. Nothing like that."

Piranha turned around. He was holding a metal bar, about four feet long, in his right hand.

"This may suffice," he said. "Depending."

Mirabelle opened the door again. She and Piranha moved out into the short hallway, stepping around the unconscious guard. Mirabelle saw that he was still breathing, which was something.

They stepped out into the wider hallway beyond the short one that led to the cell. It was deserted.

"They'll have to come this way, but from which direction?" she said.

"There are only two to choose from."

"Okay, let's go this way, then," Mirabelle said, heading off to the right.

Mirabelle and Piranha walked to the end of the corridor and turned right, into yet another hallway.

And there they were, moving stealthily up the middle of this hall. A man and a woman.

The woman was indeed brandishing a sword. Mirabelle shook her head in wonderment. It was difficult to become jaded and world-weary when people kept coming up with innovative foolishness like this.

"Shit, he's *out*!" the man exclaimed.

"Who's that with him?" the woman asked.

"What's her name again?" Mirabelle whispered to Piranha.

"Winona Dirge."

Mirabelle nodded. "Prepare for separation," she said.

Then she started running, directly toward the assassins.

"Winonaaaa!" she yelled as she approached. "I know your secret!" She veered to the right, giving the nonplussed killers a wide berth.

"When I get to the end of this hallway, you're *finished*, Winona!" she shouted as she careened past them.

Dumbfounded, Winona looked at Milt for guidance.

"Hell," he said, "Go after her! I'll take Piranha."

Winona whirled around and took off. She pursued Mirabelle around two corners, left then right, and found her standing in the middle of the hallway, feet planted, ready for a confrontation.

"What the hell is a *girl* doing in here?" Winona exclaimed, skidding to a stop.

"Look who's talking!" Mirabelle said.

"I broke in! What are you, the cleaning lady or something?"

"I'll show you a goddamn cleaning lady," Mirabelle said, dropping into a crouch. As if by magic, a pair of long, thin daggers appeared in her hands. The blades had been spring-loaded into special sheaths, one in each sleeve of Mirabelle's blouse. She had released them by twisting her wrists in a particular way.

"Damn," Winona said, impressed in spite of herself. "Where did *those* come from?"

"India. Are you gonna fight, or just stand there and talk shit?"

"Now, hang on a minute. We were hired to come in here and kill Doctor Piranha. Nobody said anything about any colored girl."

"Talk shit, then," Mirabelle said, nodding. "Well, *I'm* gonna fight."

"You said you know my secret," Winona pressed.

"Yeah, I figured that'd grab your attention."

"You don't know anything, then?"

"I wouldn't say *that*. Now, are you gonna fight?"

"Oh, all right, dammit."

Winona advanced and began jabbing with her sword. Mirabelle held her own, but she sensed that her opponent's heart just wasn't in this battle. The sword thrusts were menacing enough, but did not seem to have any deadly intent behind them. No real determination. Mirabelle blocked everything easily with her two smaller weapons, which were more durable than they looked, though she had no opportunities to go on the offensive.

Thrust-parry-thrust

"And you weren't going to do anything at the end of the hallway that would finish me?" Winona said at one point.

"No, not really. Just what I'm doing now."

Thrust-parry-thrust

Thrust-thrust-duck-parry-thrust

"I'm getting tired," Winona said presently. "I don't want to kill you. I don't even know why you're here."

Thrust-parry-thrust-kick-dodge

"Well, I do," Mirabelle replied, "and I can't let you interfere with it."

"*You're* the one interfering! I'm a professional, and this is a professional operation. You don't have any business being involved in it."

"You know, now that I think about it, you may have a point."

"Of course I do. We're getting paid for *one* kill. Even just *fighting* you is a waste of time and manpower. I don't believe in killing people for free, if they're not part of the contract."

Thrust-parry-thrust-duck-kick-twirl

"All I need from Doctor Piranha is information," Mirabelle said. "If I can get that, then I don't really care what you do with him. There's no actual need for us to be at cross-purposes. If you're getting paid for this, it would be pretty niggardly of me to ruin it."

"Ah—Was that a joke? Should I laugh?"

"If you have to ask, then don't laugh."

Thrust-parry-thrust

"I *knew* this didn't have to get ugly," said Winona. "So, if I stop swinging this blade at you, do you promise not to pull any stunts?"

"Sure," said Mirabelle, blocking a shallow swing at her left knee, "why not?"

"Word of honor?"

"Are you serious?"

Winona laughed. She danced back a few steps, outside Mirabelle's reach, and lowered her blade. Mirabelle held her blades down at her sides.

"So," said Winona, "now do we just stand here all night, proving we're not going to kill each other? Everybody in here's going to start waking up eventually."

"No. Let's just go find the boys."

"I guarantee you, he's enjoying himself," Winona said, as they started back the way they had come. "He knows how serious this is, we talked about that, but he's still going to make a game out of it. He can't help himself. He's probably not even aware he's doing it."

"He's kind of a big deal, huh?" Mirabelle said. "I don't guess I've ever heard of him."

"Oh, he's okay. He's not really what I'd call one of the top contract killers, though. He thinks he's the most dangerous man in the world, and I humor him. But he's okay, like I say. He was behind the Milaflores Massacre in 1927, and he killed Arnold Rothstein the year after that."

"No kidding? That's kind of impressive."

"I guess so. They were easier jobs than you'd think."

They went back to the hallway where they had first encountered one another. Doctor Piranha and Milt Cabal were nowhere to be seen.

"Now where did they get to?" Winona said. "This place is like a maze. Maybe Milt killed him already."

"He better not have," Mirabelle said darkly. "Then I'll have to—Hey, wait, listen!"

Sounds of a scuffle came to them from around a far corner.

"That must be them," Mirabelle said. "Come on, let's call a timeout so we can get this sorted."

There they were, grappling hand-to-hand in the middle of the corridor. Piranha's metal bar lay on the floor against one wall.

"What did I tell you?" Winona said, shaking her head. "He's got five different weapons he could have used to kill Piranha from twenty feet away, and look what he's doing! And after he lectured me about not getting cocky and taking unnecessary risks."

"Men," Mirabelle said.

"Hey!" Winona shouted, raising her hand and snapping her fingers. "This young lady and I have been negotiating. That's what smart people do."

The combatants ceased their struggles and stood slightly back from one another, looking over at the women. Piranha was impassive, Cabal irritated.

"Winona—" Cabal began.

"Winona, nothing!" she said. "Listen: She's just here to get information out of him." She jabbed a finger toward Piranha. "She doesn't care what *we* do one way or the other."

"Dammit," Cabal spat, "this is exactly what I was afraid of! If you—"

Cabal's attention was momentarily distracted, Piranha dove across the space between him and his metal bar, snatching up the weapon.

"Shit, *now* look!" Cabal said.

"I'm sorry, Winona," Mirabelle said softly. "You know, I actually kind of like you."

"Well, thanks. But what are you sorry for?"

"This."

Mirabelle whirled abruptly and punched Winona in a spot directly between the lobe of her right ear and her spine. The assassin went down, unconscious, without knowing what had happened to her.

"Seriously," Mirabelle said, "I really am sorry."

"Hell," said Cabal.

"You, I don't like at all," she said, pointing at the bridge of his nose.

Cabal reached into a pocket and took out a small, round, metallic object. Mirabelle thought it might be some kind of grenade. Cabal thumbed a little stud on the thing, and...

... the whole corridor was flooded with intense light. Mirabelle expected the sound of a blast, followed by the shredding of her flesh and the shattering of her bones.

Those things did not come.

She blinked her eyes, and saw blackness, shot through with faint glowing ripples. Flash blindness. Nothing to panic over. There was no pain, no burning. Her retinal pigments had been oversaturated by the burst of light, and her pupils had constricted. Her vision should return very soon.

In the three seconds following the flash, when she was at her most disoriented, she had heard sounds that she now interpreted as Cabal scrambling forward and scooping up Winona, then running off down the corridor.

"Doctor," she said, "can you hear me?"

"Of course. I'm blinded, not deafened."

"So your eyes aren't as impregnable as your lungs."

"Sadly, no."

"It feels like I took some kind of an inner ear jolt too," she said. "I'm dizzy, and my sense of direction is totally scrambled."

"Yes."

The dizziness passed pretty quickly, but it was almost ten minutes before they could see again.

CHAPTER TWENTY-SEVEN
FLIGHT

"I suppose we can just walk right out of here now," said Piranha.

"We?" Mirabelle repeated, her eyebrows raised.

"Yes. From what you've said, I fear that the things I did for Joseph when he was a child may be... *going bad*, for want of a better term. I'm afraid of the psychological effects. His personality could start to fragment.

"That being the case, I need to *see* him. I could not possibly give you all the information you might need under the current circumstances. And then, of course, there are those killers out there somewhere. We should at least try to address that as well."

"This was a hell of an operation," Mirabelle said. "Must have been well-financed."

"I imagine so."

"The timing was very interesting."

"Wasn't it, though?"

"They went to a lot of trouble, just to be thwarted so quickly."

"Must have been quite demoralizing. To whomever."

"Well, shit," Mirabelle said, shaking her head. "Let's go, then."

✳✳✳

The power had come back on, though some areas were still blacked out. The assassins had evidently disabled the alarms. And everyone else in the place was, presumably, still unconscious.

It was surreal, moving through the still, silent building. Was this possible? How had those two assassinations managed to do a thing like this? It seemed impossible. There was a distinct chill in the air that had not been there earlier. Making their way toward freedom, looking at unconscious guards sprawled on floors or slumped in chairs, Mirabelle felt like she was plodding through a dream.

This couldn't be what it looked like. But someone sure wanted it to look this way.

Between the two of them, bypassing failsafes and manipulating locks, Mirabelle and Piranha had little trouble. Piranha, Mirabelle noticed, had a great deal more knowledge about various features of the building than any prisoner ought to.

"Do you think they knocked out Fort Leavenworth too?" Mirabelle asked.

"I don't know. If not, someone from over there will surely notice that something's going on here. It doesn't appear that they have thus far, but we'd better be careful."

It was strange. In a way, Mirabelle felt quite comfortable around Doctor Piranha. In another way, she did not. But she wasn't afraid of him at all, didn't feel that she had to watch her back. She didn't believe in intuition; she knew this feeling was based on things she had observed and analyzed on a subconscious level, and she trusted it.

Of course, Piranha knew more about this impossible break-out than he was telling. She couldn't fault him for that. She also knew a great deal more about things than she let on.

They reached the ground floor and left the building via the front door, just like regular folks.

They made their way on foot into downtown Leavenworth itself, quite certain they were not being observed by anyone.

It surely wouldn't be much longer before some kind of alarm was raised at the prison—*if* the ordinary rules were being adhered to. Fortunately, Lee was close by, waiting at the hotel for word from Mirabelle.

It was only a little after midnight when they arrived there.

Not wanting to alarm the private detective, Mirabelle introduced Piranha as a contact of hers that had offered some last-minute help.

"Did you get what you were after?" Lee asked.

"And then some," she said. "I'll explain in detail later. This whole thing has taken on a rather interesting shape."

"I spoke with our contact," Milt Cabal said.

He and Winona were sitting in a 1927 Model A Ford parked outside an all-night sandwich shop. Cabal had just used the payphone in the shop and also bought two turkey sandwiches on rye.

"And..?" Winona prompted, unwrapping her sandwich.

"And we are to head for Mobile, Alabama. That's around 900 miles from here, depending on what roads we use. Three or four days, maybe. We're not supposed to be in a hurry."

"We're not? Did you tell them what happened? Did you tell them about the colored girl?" Winona took a bite of the sandwich.

"Of course I did," he said. "They didn't seem upset. They didn't even seem surprised. And they want us to go to Mobile."

"And not be in any hurry."

"Right... And they want us to leave a trail."

"I see," Winona said around a mouthful of turkey and bread. "Well. So we're bait of some kind."

"I guess so," Cabal said, looking down at the wrapped sandwich on his lap.

"Are we still supposed to kill Piranha?"

"They said to hold off on that until further notice. They must want him in Mobile, for whatever reason."

"This whole thing is starting to smell funny."

"I don't disagree. But we're still alive, and that four million bucks is still an attainable goal."

Winona swallowed the last bite of her sandwich. "So is the summit of Mount Everest, theoretically. So is the moon, while we're at it."

"No one will ever go to the moon—but we *will* get that money."

"Milt, if you're not going to eat your sandwich, can I have it?"

"Tell me what's going on with Joe," Piranha said.

He and Mirabelle were sitting in her suite, eating sandwiches Lee had brought from an all-night diner nearby. Lee himself had gone on to bed in his own room.

"He heals very rapidly," Mirabelle replied. "At an unnatural rate, in fact. I'm not sure how long it's been going on."

"Yes, that's part of it."

"And I'm afraid his ability to reason has become impaired. These almost miraculous things that happen with him—he doesn't pay any attention to them. When I point them out, he just brushes it off. He's always been so logical, but when it comes to this—He gets angry if I press him. He just won't hear it. You used some kind of hypnosis on him too, didn't you?"

"How did you come by so much information?" Piranha asked.

"Part super-genius, part happenstance. Please answer the question."

"Well, yes, I did. I didn't want him to notice, you see. But if someone such as yourself points it out—Does he become hostile?"

"Almost."

"That should not happen. I thought I worked all of that out after my first test subject."

"What? Your first test subject? Who?"

"Gerald Sams."

Mirabelle dropped her sandwich and leaned forward. "The Werewolf! *You* did that to him?"

"It was a scientific necessity."

"You did experiments on an innocent boy!"

"Not so innocent. That whole family was corrupt. He had it in his blood."

"You destroyed his life! You ought to be ashamed of yourself."

"I never was before. Until quite recently, that is."

"How recently?"

"The last fifteen seconds. You have a way of bringing out the worst in me, Miss Darcy. By which I mean conscience, compassion, and other unspeakable vices. If I am ruined, it will be on your head."

Mirabelle wasn't sure how to take that.

"I told you earlier that it was fortunate for you that my brother is who he is," Piranha continued. "And it is fortunate for *him* that you are what you are. He is very lucky."

He smiled again, obviously attempting to make it more human than his previous effort had been. It didn't work, not at all.

"Wait, now," Mirabelle said. "You're not starting to get infatuated with me, are you? Because if you are..."

"No, no," he said quickly. "I don't—I don't do that. Not with anyone. I am merely stating the obvious."

"Well, then."

"And after this is all done, I'll gladly return to prison."

"Yeah. I believe you will. You want to be there, for whatever reason. I don't suppose you ever do anything you don't want to."

"Not very often. It *has* happened, though."

That remark seemed to be laced with meaning, as it was delivered rather pointedly, but Mirabelle didn't pursue it. She had the odd feeling he would have welcomed questions about it, but she wasn't in the mood right now.

Milt Cabal and Winona Dirge were experts at not leaving a trail. Which mean that they also had some excellent insight in how *to* leave one.

First, they had to let their prospective pursuers know that they were there to be pursued. That was not a problem. Piranha needed to know that they were going to Mobile too—that way, he wouldn't waste time trying to locate them before he hit the road.

The two assassins had watched Piranha and his strange ally leave the prison, and had followed them to the hotel. Where were they likely to go from there? The only place Piranha might conceivably have any business was Mobile. That, the killers reasoned, was probably why their employer had ordered them to make their way there. Piranha could be taken out when they all arrived at their common destination—Cabal and Dirge might even get some backup there.

Piranha was smart, and that colored girl, whoever she was, certainly had more on the ball than either of the assassins would have expected.

There was no way they could allow those two to pick up their trail without it being obvious that that was what they were doing. So be it. They wouldn't even attempt any clever deception. What did it matter, so long as they all ended up in the same place? They would make the whole thing obvious as hell. If an opponent is too smart to pull cute tricks on, don't even try.

All they had to do was make sure Piranha and his friend didn't kill them en route.

That was all.

"That's them over there," Mirabelle said, peeking between the blinds. "Watching the hotel."

It was an hour or so before dawn. A pair of figures who were very obviously Milt Cabal and Winona Dirge stood in the doorway of a closed apothecary shop—right under a street lamp, just in case they weren't being obvious enough.

"I thought they were supposed to be clever," Piranha said, stepping up and looking over Mirabelle's shoulder.

"Maybe they are. Maybe we all are. Too clever for our own damn good."

Piranha did not respond. He returned to the settee, while Mirabelle continued to observe.

After twenty or so minutes, the pair walked halfway down the block and got into in a 1927 Model A Ford. The car pulled away from the curb and disappeared around a far corner.

Mirabelle remained where she was. The automobile drove past the hotel three more times in less than an hour.

Okay, then. If this is how this is played, I can deal with it.

Mirabelle and Piranha drove out of Leavenworth shortly after sunup, Mirabelle at the wheel of a car provided by Lee Rosenberg.

If an alarm had been raised at the prison, they never saw any indication of it. There was nothing about it on the radio.

The 1927 Model A passed them on the road out of town.

"There go the happy wanderers," Mirabelle said.

"Are we following them?" Piranha asked. "Or are they following us?"

"I guess we'll see. Maybe it doesn't matter."

They passed through Missouri, and on into Arkansas, stopping briefly in West Memphis, where Mirabelle picked up a recent copy of the *Mobile Press.*

"It says here that Mister Perrone has passed away," she said, pointing to an item in the obituary column.

"That cannot be," Piranha said, his tone that of a person stating an obvious fact, rather than denying an unpalatable truth.

"You're right, it can't. See here, the cause of death is given as Meiringen's Syndrome. Meiringen is the name of a town close to the Reichenbach Falls in Switzerland."

"Ah, the scene of the bogus 'death' of Sherlock Holmes."

"Right. Mentioned in 'The Final Problem' by Arthur Conan Doyle."

"You mean," said Piranha, "Joe anticipated a situation in which he might have to fake his own death while you were out of town and not in direct contact with him?"

"No, of course not. *I* did." She sighed sharply and swatted her thigh with the newspaper. "He's not dead, but he's certainly in some kind of trouble."

Piranha enjoyed watching the countryside roll by, it appeared. Day or night, it made no difference to him. His head moved back and forth constantly, eyes unblinking, as though committing every mile to memory.

Time seemed to distend. It took much longer than sixty minutes to get from the top of one hour to the top of the next. In spite of this, Mirabelle felt no fatigue.

She and Piranha discussed a wide variety of topics, only touching now and then on the reasons behind their journey. Piranha could speak knowledgeably on just about anything, and Mirabelle enjoyed it. Art, music, medicine, science, religion—he was full of facts and interesting opinions, coldly and bloodlessly insightful. He knew the proper way to argue a point, never getting carried away with himself, or lapsing into logical fallacies. Her interaction with him contained none of the elements that made her so uncomfortable when dealing with other people.

Once the novelty wore off, though, it began to seem a little too sterile. Intellectually, they were just about equal, she thought. But Mirabelle was an inherently emotional creature who had learned control. Piranha seemed never to have been burdened in the first place.

There were long silences too, which Piranha would occasionally break with some peculiar remark or question, such as:

"Have you ever fancied you saw a giant crow perched on top of the moon?"

Mirabelle admitted that she never had.

Another time, as they passed a small, rural cemetery, he said:

"You know, the dead outnumber us, Miss Darcy. Do you think we should fear them?"

She told him she had no opinion one way or the other.

And always, always, there was the 1927 Model A. Sometimes ahead of them, sometimes behind. They might go for hours without seeing it, but then it would appear from around a bend or they would see it parked outside a filling station. It began to seem like some kind of phantom, a land-bound Flying Dutchman.

It passed them on a rutted two-lane road in the middle of Mississippi. They were cutting across the state diagonally, from the northwest corner to the southeast.

"They haven't changed cars," Mirabelle said unnecessarily.

"No," said Piranha. "And there's no way they're as stupid as they're acting."

"They want us to follow them."

"Of course."

"Do you know why, Doctor?"

"How could I possibly?"

"That isn't an answer."

But it was all she was going to get.

***

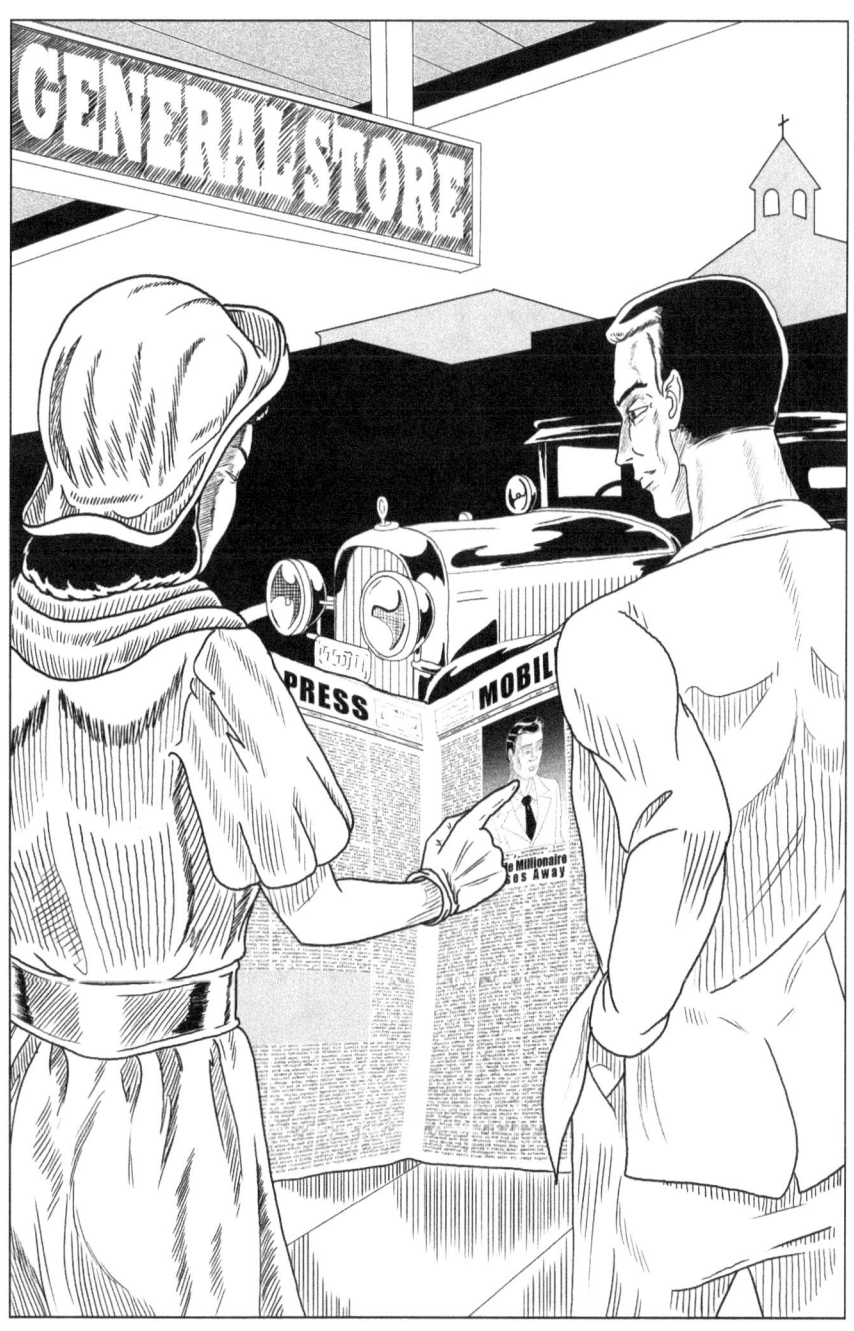

"It says here Mr. Perrone has passed away."

A hundred miles out of Mobile, they were only a few steps behind the assassins, but they made no effort to close the gap. It had obvious for some time that they were being led, or possibly followed, to Mobile.

Neither Mirabelle nor Piranha seemed overly concerned by this. They had both known it, of course, the entire time. Whatever each of them might have been thinking about that, they did not share with one another.

✸✸✸

CHAPTER TWENTY-EIGHT
LOOKING FOR WORK

"The individual does actually carry on a double existence: one designed to serve his own purposes and another as a link in a chain, in which he serves against, or at any rate without, any volition of his own."
—Sigmund Freud (1856 - 1939)

The little speakeasy had no name. It didn't need one, because those who patronized it seldom went anywhere else, and those who didn't patronize it never would.

Except tonight.

Roy Markham pushed open the door, stepped in, and stood looking around the place.

There was very little light. A few bulbs glowed dimly on the wall behind the bar, so the bartender could see what he was doing. A few other bulbs, of lower wattage, were irregularly distributed around the room in fixtures on the walls, providing just enough light for patrons to see what they needed to see, and no more. Mardi Gras did not venture into this place.

Over there, Markham, said a voice in his head. *See that fellow at the table in the far corner? You need to speak with him.*

I know that, Perrone. It was my idea, remember?

Oh, yes, right. I don't know his real name. He calls himself "Solomon."

"Open 24 hours a day," that's his motto. He sells information.

I know all that. Maybe I can get something at a discount.

Don't hurt him.

Well, I might not have to, we'll see. Just pipe down, willya, and let me concentrate on what I'm doing.

Solomon was about seventy years old, and had been for as long as anybody could remember. He had never been known to commit a crime, but he knew everything there was to know about those who did. If you wanted to know who was planning to do what with—or to—whom, or where so-and-so might be found, and if you weren't a cop, and if you had the cash, Solomon was your man.

In spite of his name, he wasn't particularly wise, or even clever. It would never occur to him to suggest cutting a baby in half. He simply had an astonishing native ability for storing, correlating, and trading in information.

Markham approached. Solomon looked up inquisitively. The only people who ever approached him were customers, recurring or potential. He didn't recognize this fellow.

"I'm lookin' for Meat Grinder Molloy," Markham said by way of greeting.

The brutal gangster's demise had not been reported in the press, nor had it spread along any of the established underworld gossip channels.

"So what?" Solomon said.

"So I wanna find him. So you might know where he is."

"I might, but I'm not running a charity. I have to see some benefit for me before I part with anything I know. You get what I mean?"

"Yeah."

"Molloy isn't a guy to be trifled with. I tell somebody something, then something bad happens to Molloy and it doesn't kill him, then he'll wonder who said what to who. I'm not the first guy he'd go to, but he might find his way eventually."

"Right."

"So I'd need to have a lot of incentive."

"Oh, I think I can provide plenty." Markham took his wallet out of his hip pocket and extracted a hundred-dollar bill. "Money is good incentive, right? I can give you some and you can give me information."

That's good, said Perrone. *The carrot is preferable to the stick.*

"Of course, the information may or may not be any good," Markham went on. "And if it turned out not to be, I'd have to come back looking for a refund."

"I stand by what I sell," Solomon said indignantly. "Everybody knows me, I ain't going nowhere. How long you think I'd last around here if I peddled worthless junk?"

Markham handed him the hundred.

"Molloy is with some new outfit these days," Solomon said. "If you want to find him, you'll have to go through them, probably. I suspect that's what you're really interested in, isn't it, my friend? They are reputed to be very generous employers, if one makes the grade. I don't know much, sadly, but I'll share what I've got.

"There's this new company. They say they're looking for day laborers, but they're really looking for muscle. Guys not known to the police. They weed out the ones who aren't... *suitable.* Some of the guys do get actual jobs, to keep the business front going. But if a candidate shows a certain kind of promise, they take him on for the dirty work.

"They want guys with no connections at all. No loyalties to get in the way. You might have to hang around for a couple of days before you get their attention. Just keep at it and don't make a secret of your willingness to get your hands dirty. Not *literally*, mind you."

"I get what you mean."

"All right. I'll give you the address."

Solomon took a little notebook from his jacket pocket and made a notation on one of the blank sheets. He tore the sheet out and handed it to Markham.

"And you're sure this is the bunch that Molloy is involved with?" Markham asked.

"Absolutely certain," Solomon said. "And, ah... I would appreciate it if you wouldn't tell anybody you got the info from me. Those guys play rough."

"So do I, which I think you understand. I know how to keep my trap shut, don't get your knickers in a twist. And—" He leaned forward, stopping when the tip of his nose was less than an inch from Solomon's. "If anybody finds out from *you* that I was *asking*... I will rip your goddamn head clean off. Do you get *that*?"

The information broker nodded dumbly.

Remember the carrot, Perrone scolded. *The carrot.*

"How about you shove your carrot up your goddamn ass!" Markham snapped.

"I beg your pardon?" said Solomon.

Markham, Perrone said, *that is unnecessary and inappropriate. That language...*

"Ah, shut up," Markham snapped.

"What—What did I say?" Solomon whined.

"I wasn't talking to you," Markham snarled. "Mind your own damn business."

Oh, my!

"*Both* of you mind your own damn business."

CHAPTER TWENTY-NINE
JOE BARROW

The next morning, Roy Markham showed up in front of a little brick building on St. Anthony Street. The sidewalk was already crowded with rough-looking men. A sign in one of the large plate glass windows said "GULF COAST DAY LABOR." Underneath that, in smaller type, it added, "Work Today Get Payed Today."

He stood there for a while, getting sidelong looks from some of the other men, not making eye contact or speaking with any of them.

The sun inched slowly higher, and the men waited. Presently, a young Negro, probably in his late teens or early twenties, came up the sidewalk and stopped in front of the little building.

"Is that the end of the line?" he asked the men closest to the door, pointing to where Markham stood.

"Ain't no line," said one of them, an unattractive little weasel of a man, with bad teeth, a shock of red hair, and a stray eye. "You best just keep moving."

"I heard a man could find work around here," said the youth, undeterred.

"May be that a *man* could," said the little weasel. "That don't do you much good, *boy.*"

"Look, mister, I didn't come looking for no trouble, okay? I just need a job real bad."

"Well, you ain't gettin' one here, darkie. But you *are* gonna get something from me to help cure that smart mouth of yours."

Roy Markham stepped forward and said, "Who do you think you're talking to, you dried-out little sonofabitch?"

The dried-out little sonofabitch turned his head to look at Markham.

"I'm talkin' to this little black boy here," he said. "He's fixin' to take a whipping. And if you wanna stick up for him, you can have one too."

"That there young *man* is my partner," Markham said, approaching the group. He didn't like little wise-asses who abused colored folks. "I told him he could meet me here."

"Well, I reckon you done made your choice, then, so you can take your beating right along with him. Come on, boys."

It might be that Markham was jeopardizing his mission, but he had acted on impulse, and now the die was cast. A few of the little weasel's pals stepped forward to confront him.

Three of the hoodlums chose to take on Markham, while the weasel and two others moved to attack the young man.

As it happened, neither Markham nor the young man took anything resembling a beating. But they both dished out plenty to the would-be bullies.

The young man's fighting style was direct and economical. There were no wasted moves, and every punch was deliberate and surgical. This kid must have spent some time in the ring, Markham decided.

Markham did not hold back. These men posed no real threat to him, but he didn't like them, and found it deeply satisfying to give them more pain and damage than was strictly necessary.

Lots more.

One by one, the aggressors dropped out of the fray. Some came to understand what they had gotten themselves into, and took off running; others slunk away, trying to make themselves too small to be noticed. Four had to be carried or otherwise assisted out of harm's way. The dried-out little sonofabitch who had started it was taken home with a broken jaw and half a dozen cracked ribs.

By the time it was over, the crowd on the sidewalk had thinned out considerably. Markham and the young man were at the head of the line, followed by six men who had wisely chosen to stay out of the fight.

"What's your name, kid?" Markham asked.

"Barrow. Joe Barrow."

"I'm Roy Markham. You're mighty good with your fists."

"I reckon. You're no slouch yourself, Mister Markham."

"I'd rather you call me Roy. 'Mister Markham' is what folks used to call my daddy, and I don't like bein' reminded of that worthless sonofabitch."

Joe laughed. "All right, then. My real daddy got put in the nuthouse when I was two years old, then he died a few years after that, so I never really knew him. I don't like being reminded either, even though it wasn't none of his fault."

"Life does that kinda shit to folks sometimes."

"It does, sir, it truly does. I'm originally from Chambers County, Alabama, up around Lafayette. About six years ago, my family and me moved up to Detroit. We figured we weren't safe where we were, because we had got into a ruckus with the guys in white sheets—if you get my meaning."

Joe Barrow was very talkative, it seemed. Markham figured it had been a while since the young man had found anything like a sympathetic ear.

"I do," said Markham. "I don't much care for that bunch."

Joe nodded. "So I was workin' up there, in Detroit, but when the Depression hit, everything dried up—especially if you got a good suntan like I do. I figured I could drift back down here, maybe find something, send some money up to my Ma. I was workin' in a restaurant here for a while. But it... kinda shut down."

"What happened?"

Joe took a deep breath, let it out. "The owner got his head cut off. Or maybe you could say his body got cut off, because the head was all they found. Somebody toted the body off. Who would do a thing like that?"

That was the question, wasn't it?

"How old are you, kid?"

"Me? I'm twenty-five."

Markham shook his head.

Joe gave a sheepish little smile. "Okay, I'm sixteen. But I'm old for my age."

As church bells a few blocks away chimed the hour, the front door of Gulf Coast Day Labor opened, and a man stepped out onto the sidewalk. He was small and wiry, with sharp, dark eyes, and he carried himself with the air of a man who would always be convinced he was better than you were, no matter what. He was dressed in dark blue slacks, a white dress shirt with tiny red pinstripes, cuffs rolled up above his elbows, and a wide maroon necktie.

"I want to see these two pugilists we got out here," he said.

"I reckon that'd be us," Markham said, stepping forward. "Me and my pal, here, Mister Barrow."

"Well, well. And what is *your* name?"

"Roy Markham."

The man's eyebrows went up.

"No kidding? Come inside, you two. The rest of you bums hit the bricks."

Grumbling, the other men wandered off, while Markham and Barrow stepped through the door into a small lobby.

"Markham, I want to speak to you in my office." He turned to Joe Barrow. "You just wait out here on this bench, okay?"

"Yessir."

He ushered Markham into a small office and closed the door, waving Markham to a chair in front of a bulky metal desk. He sat down in a creaky office chair and introduced himself.

The man's name was Feeney. That was all, just Feeney, and it was more than enough for such a little squirt. But he seemed to have a very high opinion of himself, and he spoke in a pompous, condescending manner, wielding an impressive vocabulary that missed its target more often than not.

"I know of you," he said. "Roy Markham. Your reputation exceeds you, and I think you're the right kind of guy, the kind we're looking for. Would I be right in exhuming that you had a similar impression about this place of business?"

When Perrone had created the Markham persona months before, he had let Mirabelle construct a pretty bloody *curriculum vitae* for the career criminal. She had produced phony documentation to back the whole thing up. Louis Rickert had done his part too, spreading tales of the redoubtable Markham through the underworld.

By now, some petty criminals were claiming to have met Markham, to have done time with him, and to have pulled jobs in his company. The legend had grown on its own, and now it was time to reap some of the fruit.

"Yeah," Markham said, "I might have heard something. No details, though, just that a guy like me might be, as you say, the right kind for what you're doing here. I been laying low for a while, but it's got to the point where I need something regular, you know?"

"Yes. Things aren't how they used to be, that's for sure. And what about that colored boy out there, your partner? You can vouch for his bonapartes as well?"

Markham nodded.

"Well, that's fine. I don't believe in being racial. I believe in treating folks equal, and that includes niggers. As long as I don't have to eat or sleep with them, they're just as good as I am. Plus, that kid is one hell of a fighter! Yes, truly exculpatory.

"Now, let me ask you a question. This is strictly a formidable, since you and me already know the answer, but: Do you boys mind doing work that ain't strictly what you would call legal?"

"My friend," said Markham, "I don't give a good goddamn *how* legal it ain't, so long as it pays!"

Feeney smiled.

Markham waited for Joe Perrone to start nagging him again about his language, but there was only silence.

CHAPTER THIRTY
NEW GUYS

Roy Markham was in. So was Joe Barrow. That was good. The kid seemed to be honest, and could be a valuable ally. As Markham made his way to the heart of the gang, he'd need someone on his side, someone good with his fists, like Joe was.

Markham would have to look out for him, make sure he didn't put his foot into anything he couldn't get it out of.

Markham was still on board with Perrone's agenda. He was vaguely aware that he and Perrone were one and the same, but that awareness grew more and more irrelevant as time went by. He would do what Perrone wanted— because he felt an obligation, and because it all needed doing— but he was his own man. Most of the memories and things in his head belonged to Perrone, but Markham saw them differently.

Over the next few days, Markham and his new "partner" were put to work. One the first day, they helped out on what seemed to be a legitimate construction job up in Chickasaw. The day after that, they were transferred to a warehouse, where they loaded and unloaded unmarked crates and canisters onto and off of equally unmarked trucks.

At night, left to their own devices, they took in some Mardi Gras parades downtown. The usual routes down Dauphin Street had been scrapped this year on account of the construction, so most of the activity centered on Royal Street.

Joe Barrow learned all about how Mobile had been celebrating Mardi Gras since before New Orleans started doing it. Locals never seemed to tire of bringing up that fact. People seemed proud of it, like they had somehow been personally responsible.

A couple of times, Markham had gone off by himself for an hour or two on mysterious "errands." Joe Barrow didn't ask him what he was doing, and wasn't particularly concerned about it. There was plenty of fun to be had, and he was in no danger, so long as he stayed out of "whites only" areas. Since the signs identifying them were larger and easier to read than any others, including traffic and street signs, he had no trouble.

"You're going to help guard a certain premises downtown," Feeney informed Markham after a week. "That's all you got to do, keep an eye on the place. You won't be inside, we'll have you in a house up the street. You and your buddy will be sleeping there, to be on hand if you're needed. Extra security, in case it's necessitated by whatever verisimilitudes might arise. This will last for a few days, after which you will be given more extemporaneous duties, provided your performance remains as vociferous as it has proven thus far. Okay?"

"Sure, sure," said Markham. "Thanks."

"There's something about you, Roy," Joe said to Markham one evening. "I don't think you're a bad man, but this bunch we're working for, they ain't no good at all. The more I see, the less I like."

"I know, Joe." he said. "I'll level with you: That's why I'm here. I'm workin' undercover, you might say. These bastards are up to some serious no good. I'm—Well, the truth is, I'm sort of working with the Bay Phantom on this. You know who that is?"

"Wow, I sure do. No kidding, Roy?"

"Cross my heart, kid. The reason I been keeping you close to me is because I think you're a right guy. And you can fight like a sonofabitch. I was gonna tell you sooner or later. So that's what's what. It might be dangerous, Joe. If you want out, go ahead and walk, and I'll make sure you can get away clean."

Joe frowned. "I'll pretend like you didn't say that last part. Sure, I'm in with you, Roy. Yeah, I heard a lot about the Bay Phantom since I been here. They say he treats everybody square, even colored folks. They say he brought down that new Klan leader last year, and you know how I feel about the Klan."

"Right. Okay. I think you're a good man, Joe. I'll look out for you, I promise."

"And I'll look out for *you*. I think the Phantom is a good man too."

"Naw, he ain't, but these guys are worse."

"Well. I also think *you're* a good man, Roy."

"Oh, *hell,* no. Put that out of your head right now, kid."

CHAPTER THIRTY-ONE
LIBERTY

The Black Embalmer was feeling lonely. The Phantom hadn't been to see him for several days. Doctor Atticus was a pleasant enough fellow, but he wasn't really a psychiatrist, and he didn't have any interesting views on life and death and morality to share.

According to the news, the masked vigilante had not been spotted at all during the past week. It was unusual for two or three days to go by without a sighting, never mind *seven* of them.

The Phantom must be working on an important case. That had to be it.

So the madman had filled his time with reading, meditation, and radio. He enjoyed "Little Orphan Annie," and was somewhat addicted to a serial called "Myrt and Marge," about a pair of chorus girls who got themselves into all manner of scrapes. Recently, Myrt had become involved with a man who, unbeknownst to her, was a vicious gangster. The Embalmer was concerned for her safety, and nursed a sickening certainty that the whole thing would end badly for her.

Apart from that, things at the clinic were as they had ever been—always quiet, always peaceful.

Suddenly, one morning, all of that changed.

After finishing his breakfast, the Embalmer became aware of a ruckus of some kind going on at the front of the building. He pressed his face to the little round window in the door of his cell, but he couldn't see anything. He heard yelling, banging, then a woman's scream. Sounded like Nurse Jeffries. He liked her. She was a little bit cross-eyed and wore glasses to correct it.

He had learned all about the lock on his door during his first day there, and he put that knowledge to work now. Extracting a paper clip he'd been keeping in his mouth, tucked between a molar and his cheek, he straightened it out, put a couple of clever little kinks in it, and applied it to the lock.

Five seconds later, he was standing in the hallway.

He tiptoed toward the front lobby, staying close to the wall. At the end of the hallway, he stopped and got a look at the situation.

Four men, dressed in boiler suits, with gas masks over their heads, stood in the center of the lobby. One of them carried a metal cylinder about three feet long and half a foot in diameter.

Gas.

It wouldn't bother the Embalmer. He had immunized himself long ago against any kind of airborne toxins. It had been one of his first great experiments, and a resounding success, though he owed half the credit to that strange, brilliant kid he'd partnered with briefly, more than a decade ago. He breathed in. The gas had a very faint odor that reminded him of lilacs.

It was certainly non-lethal. Otherwise, why would these guys have bothered with gas at all, bullets being so cheap?

Nurse Jeffries was on the floor, and two orderlies were stumbling around, obviously about to join her. As one of them lost his footing and started to fall, one of the gas-masked men caught him and lowered him gently to the tiles.

Interesting. These goons seemed to be going out of their way not to hurt anybody, even slightly.

Some people...

Of course, the Embalmer didn't want to hurt anybody who worked here because he had grown accustomed to them. But strangers? If there were people standing between him and something he wanted, he would not hesitate to dish out at least a *bit* of gratuitous mayhem.

He held back, there in the hallway, and watched the gas-masked figures move to the other side of the lobby, out of his sight. Poking his head around the corner, he watched them go up the other hallway, stopping in front of a particular door.

That room, the Embalmer knew, was occupied by the nearly-catatonic old colored man who had been brought there by the Phantom. He didn't know what the poor elderly revenant's story was, but the Phantom had taken an interest in his welfare.

The men in the gas masks pushed the door open and two of them went inside. A few seconds later, they emerged, propping the old man up on either side, leading him back toward the lobby.

They were trying to make off with the mysterious old man!

No, sir, not on my watch!

The Embalmer looked around, and spotted a fire extinguisher on a peg on the wall behind him. He lifted it off and stepped out into full view, brandishing the device and saying, "Hold! Enough!"

The raiders seemed astonished, both by the Embalmer's sudden appearance, and by his immunity to their gas. This was very much to his advantage, from a psychological standpoint; faced with such a mind-boggling anomaly, most people tended to lose all pretense of control over the situation. It was as though a banshee or a jabberwock had suddenly appeared in their midst, and they had no idea what to do. The two holding the old man let him slip down to the floor and stood there like deer startled into immobility.

Before they could mount an offensive, the Embalmer waded in with his fire extinguisher and laid them out, one after another, in rapid succession. That done, he snatched off all their gas masks, letting their own weapon put them completely under.

"And *that's* how you do *that!*" he exclaimed triumphantly.

He squatted down next to the old man, who lay motionless, his eyes wide open and devoid of intelligence, neither conscious nor unconscious.

"I know the Phantom thinks you're important. He hasn't told me why. I don't suppose it's any business of mine, but I certainly can't let anybody take you God knows where."

Leaving the old man for a moment, the Embalmer located one of the orderlies who lay insensate a bit further down the corridor.

This was good old Larry. That was how all the other employees of the clinic referred to him. "Good old Larry did this, good old Larry did that." The Embalmer couldn't stand good old Larry. Good old Larry was a smart aleck. The Embalmer bent over him and patted his pockets, locating a ring of keys.

Then he picked up the old man, and carried him out the front door, into the parking lot. There was good old Larry's car, a dark maroon two-seater. It was a better car than the irritating orderly deserved. Well, justice would be done this day.

The Embalmer unlocked the automobile, placed the old man in the passenger seat, and got behind the wheel.

"My friend," he said to his inert companion, "you and I are hitting the road! To unpathed waters, undreamed shores!"

He drove himself and his taciturn new companion to one of his old hideaways, a place nobody had discovered during his sabbatical, not even the Bay Phantom. It was quite comfortable, and there was plenty of room for his guest.

Once he had his new charge tucked away on a cot in the back, he sat down in a chair to think about what he ought to do next.

He should find the Phantom, of course, and tell him about everything that had happened on this most fabulous of days.

But, as he learned from a newspaper he had picked up on the way here, the Phantom had not been seen for days.

Where was the Bay Phantom? Nobody knew.

The Embalmer had been to the Phantom's house once, or thought he had, but he couldn't quite recall how he had gotten there. Something about a graveyard and a long underground tunnel. The whole episode had been a bit of an ordeal.

"He might not appreciate me coming back into his house again, anyhow," he said out loud, to an apparently empty room. "Even if I could remember how to get there, it would be better if I didn't. Don't you think so?"

There were people inside his head. He hadn't told the doctor about them, hadn't even mentioned them to the Bay Phantom. He knew how it would sound. And it didn't really matter. He wasn't sure himself that they were objectively "real." That didn't matter either. If he had somehow generated them in his mind, that didn't make them any less real. What was a "person," anyhow? Just a collection of thoughts and impressions.

I think them, therefore they are.

There were a bunch of them, each with a different personality and moral code. Some were even more lax than he was, while others were downright puritanical. He didn't believe they were hidden aspects of his own psyche, and he never let them influence his behavior very much. Mainly, they were just company.

After he inventoried the supplies he had on hand in this bolt hole—food enough to get by for a while, and a well-appointed laboratory, but very little in the way of his *special* equipment—the Embalmer turned his attention to the old man.

If this fellow was involved with the Phantom in some way, he might be able to help locate the crime fighter.

The man was awake, and could stand or sit or walk across the room if he was told to, but he did not communicate verbally, or engage with his surroundings in any meaningful way. He obeyed certain commands as a dog would, without question or understanding. The most complex activity he seemed capable of was feeding himself with a spoon, and this was done in a purely mechanical fashion. If you put food in front of him, he would eat it. If you didn't, he would, presumably, starve to death.

The Embalmer took a blood sample and carefully analyzed it.

It took him two days to find what he was looking for. It was a "zombie drug," of the kind used by certain Voodoo practitioners in Haiti. It was an organic compound, and quite unique, something from the murky territory between virus and living organism. It could stay in the bloodstream for a very long time if someone didn't know it was there, what it was, and how to get rid of it.

"This is exotic stuff," said the Embalmer. "And it has been expertly modified. I'd like to meet whoever did it."

He prepared an injection for his "patient," a compound that would begin to neutralize what was left of the zombie drug in the man's system. It wouldn't work immediately, of course, but if it were administered daily for a period of time, there ought to be results.

Days passed. The old man still wasn't talking, but the look in his eye was getting sharper. The Embalmer slipped out late each night to procure newspapers and other provisions. There was no word on the Bay Phantom.

He was growing bored.

One evening, he shared a can of pork and beans with the old man, pouring his guest's repast into a bowl and eating his own right from the can.

"I know this is awful," he said, "but we have to make do right now. Boy, I miss the food they served us at the clinic! It really wasn't a bad place. A lot less stressful than it is out here, that's for sure. Maybe we can go back there after we find the Phantom and clean up whatever mess has been keeping him busy."

The old man looked down at the beans on his spoon and said, "It... ain't too bad." Then he looked at the Embalmer and said, "You know what? My name is Paul!" He seemed very pleased, and was in the process of smiling, when his face suddenly fell, becoming expressionless and mask-like once again. The lights had flared briefly, then flickered out again. A face had appeared at the window. Somebody was home, after all!

"Well, well," said the Embalmer. "So you're Paul. Well, Paul, finish your beans. 'Myrt and Marge' will be on soon, and we can't miss that."

This was a very good thing, actually. Now that the old man—*Paul, I must start using his name*—was on the mend, the Embalmer could try to find the Phantom and help him deal with whatever it was he was dealing with.

"If I'm going to get out there and start making a difference, I need my fearsome identity back. The Black Embalmer must live again, fully realized. So I need to rebuild my equipment. Yes, it's time to get back into business. Maybe Paul could be my faithful colored majordomo, like that little gal the Phantom has. Well, poor Paul still has a lot of work to do before he's ready to take on any duties. In the meantime, I can start working on my own end."

CHAPTER THIRTY-TWO
EDDIE

Even though they were friends, there was something about Eddie that made Rickey Harvard uncomfortable. But he could ignore it. Eddie was lonely and nobody seemed to like him; he and Rickey had that in common. And powerful bonds have been forged from much less.

Rickey had met Eddie at Mick's Hot Dogs on Royal Street for lunch. Just like every hot dog joint, Mick's claimed they served the "World's Best Hot Dogs." If that was true, Rickey thought, then there must not be any hot dogs worth a damn anywhere on earth. But, since you could get a dog and a bottle of soda for a dime, that made it a good place to eat.

"It's too bad you lost your job," Eddie was saying. "Working in a graveyard! That must have been loads of fun." It sounded like a joke, but Rickey knew Eddie was serious. That was one of the peculiar things about Eddie: when he said things that sounded like jokes, he was being serious, and when he said things that sounded serious, he was joking.

"It wasn't too much fun," Rickey said, "but it was money. Now that it's run out, I don't know what I'm gonna do. I went to one of them day labor places, but a bunch of guys got into a big fight right there on the sidewalk. I didn't want no part of a place like that."

"It's a bad thing to lose a job during this Depression," said Eddie. "That's how come I left home in the first place. There wasn't nothing for me to do except work on the family farm, and I wasn't gonna make no money doing that. I figured it might be a good idea to see a little bit of the country and maybe find some interesting work. I always wanted to be a doctor, but you have to go to school for ten or twenty years to do that."

"Well, I don't reckon I'll ever be a doctor or a lawyer or nothing like that," Rickey said morosely. "I'd like to get on at one of the shipyards, but you gotta have education to get work there too—unless it's sweeping the floors or something."

"Ain't nothing wrong with sweeping floors."

"Yeah, there is," Rickey said with absolute conviction.

"It's honest work," Eddie pointed out.

"That's the problem with it. I'll tell you, I wouldn't mind being a crook, if I knew how to do it. I don't mean some little stick-up man. I couldn't walk into a drugstore with a gun and start demanding money. I need to get in with somebody, one of these big organizations, where they could train me and all that."

"Hey," said Eddie, "maybe I could get you on at the place where I work. I mean, since you got experience with dead people and that."

"What do you mean? Where do you work?"

"Over to the Donner-Purdy Funeral Home. It ain't a bad place at all. It's real interesting, especially to someone like me, who is real interested in medical things and that type of stuff. You can learn all about how the human body works, and what it looks like on the inside, things like that. Scientific."

"Oh, man, Eddie, I don't know. I'm kinda fed up with dead people right now."

Eddie laughed like Rickey had just told him a good joke.

"Well, you could have a look around there anyhow, see what you think. We could go tomorrow afternoon."

CHAPTER THIRTY-THREE
PURSUIT

Donner-Purdy was new, so it stood to reason they'd have the best equipment. The main thing the Embalmer needed was formaldehyde, but he could use some new tubes and trocars and a few other things. One was constantly running out of this or that, or something would break unexpectedly, and he'd rather have a thing and not need it than the other way around.

It was on Joachim Street, one of those nice, tree-lined neighborhoods that made him acutely uncomfortable. He didn't know the area had been zoned for commercial enterprise. Did a funeral home count as a business? Well, of course it did—they didn't give their services away for free, did they?

The Black Embalmer went out there well after midnight, with a bit of burglary in mind. He parked his vehicle three blocks away, and jogged over to do some reconnoitering.

He didn't like the look of the front. There were too many dark spots and windows behind which some watcher might be lurking. He had an odd feeling about this joint. There was something off.

He went around back, keeping to the shadows, and crept up to a large bush at a rear corner of the building. Slowly and quietly, he inched his head forward and peered around the bush.

Well, this was unexpected. There was a *guard* back here! The man was wearing a generic uniform, the shoulder emblazoned with the logo of a security company the Embalmer had never heard of. That was strange. The Embalmer would be willing to bet that this man's services were not provided by any legitimate firm; to his practiced eye, the guy bore the unmistakable stamp of the hired thug. Well, whatever was going on here, this specimen must have been a prize dipshit to pull this kind of duty.

"Hey," the Embalmer said, stepping around the bush to approach the guard. "I want to show you something. A trick. You'll love this."

"Who the hell are you?" the man said, startled. "Go home and sober up. Beat it, before you get hurt."

"No, no, I'm serious. I learned this trick in Tibet. I think it was Tibet. Maybe I read it in a book. Rider Haggard, or—"

"Look, you—"

"Oh, don't get your dander up, I'm just joshing you. I'm with the milk company. Why else would I be up at this hour? I wanted to find out if you guys were interested in starting up a daily delivery."

"Shit. No, we don't need no milk here. What's wrong with you?"

"Well, that's the question. Okay, you don't want milk, that's fine, but I still owe you a trick." He moved closer, and placed a friendly hand on the guard's shoulder. The guard shifted uncomfortably, and tried to pull back, but the brick wall behind him impeded his retreat. He put his hand on the butt of his holstered pistol.

"Would you believe me," the Embalmer said conversationally, "if I told you I knew how to touch a man in a certain spot—just a *light* touch, mind you—and kill him instantly?"

"No, that's crazy."

"You think so? Well, what would you say if I told you I had just done it to *you*?"

The man's eyes suddenly rolled back in his head and he toppled to the ground.

"That's what I figured," said the Embalmer, with a smile and a nod.

As he dug in the dead guard's pocket for the keys, the Embalmer muttered to himself:

"Now, did I bring my list? No, no need for a list, I only need one thing, that's right. Formaldehyde, and plenty of it."

Unlocking the rear door and stepping inside, he found himself in a small, almost-bare anteroom. He knew immediately that something was wrong. He noticed it as soon as he entered the place. It didn't smell like the rear of a funeral home ought to smell. Didn't look like one either. The door he had just used was steel-plated on the inside. And, of course, an armed guard wasn't standard either.

Mounted to the wall at his right was a rack of shotguns.

The only corpse he could think of that rated *this* kind of security was King Tut.

In the wall on the opposite side of the little room was another door. It had a handle rather than a knob, and there was no keyhole to be seen.

"I declare!" he said. "It'll be easy enough to get through—"

Before he did so, he took from his jacket one of his hoods with a plaster death mask affixed to the front. He pulled it on.

In another moment, the Embalmer was through the door, and he jumped lightly down into the chamber he found there...

Twenty-eight minutes later, the Embalmer made a hasty departure from the Donner-Purdy Funeral Home, a pack of armed men hot on his heels. He burst through the rear door, hopping nimbly over the body of the defunct guard, and tore around the building onto Joachim Street. He had a good lead on his pursuers, and was confident that he would get away clean.

They probably wouldn't shoot at him, because that would attract attention. He hadn't killed any more of them, so there might not be much of a rage/revenge factor. The unfortunate guard hadn't seemed like the type anybody would care about avenging.

"And *no* goddamn formaldehyde," he said angrily.

A knot of angry, armed men spilled out through the door and headed around the corner after him, but stopped short when another man yelled at them through an open window:

"It's okay, he won't get far! I made a call to the other house."

The pursuers stood near the corner of the building.

The Embalmer was jogging down the middle of the street, when two dark figures emerged from the gloom and blocked his way.

A pair of tough guys. They obviously didn't intend to let the Embalmer continue on unmolested. They were armed with long knives. Because knives didn't go BANG! and wake the whole neighborhood up and maybe get the police called. That was good. Knife-wielders, he could work with.

The one on his right pounced forward and tried a quick jab to the gut. The Embalmer caught him by the wrist, twisted said wrist until it broke, caught the knife as it slipped from numb fingers, and slashed the man's throat, almost from ear to ear.

This gave the guy on the left pause. He saw his partner topple onto the pavement, and while he was considering whether to advance or retreat, the Embalmer decided the issue himself. He slashed the man's forearm, caught his second falling knife of the evening in his left hand, and slid this one into its owner's heart.

He pulled the blade from his second attacker, and the man sank to the ground like a dynamited building.

And that was two down. *Way* down.

But now a third loomed up out of the darkness.

He was bigger than the first two, and meaner-looking. He was also empty-handed.

"Oh, come on," said the Embalmer. "Really? I've got two knives, and you—" He fell silent as the man came into the glow of the streetlight.

Wait a minute! Isn't that—

Hell, yes, it was! Roy Markham! The guy he'd busted out of jail with last year.

The guy who had turned out to be the Bay Phantom in disguise!

"Hey," the Embalmer said. "I know you. *You* know *me.*"

"I'm gonna break your neck," Markham snarled.

"Dammit, man, I'm THE BLACK EMBALMER!"

"Pal, I don't give a shit who you are."

"Did you just use profanity?"

Something was going on here. The Phantom was working undercover, that much was clear. As Roy Markham, bad language and everything. Maybe the Phantom had actually listened to what the Embalmer had said to him the last time they spoke. So it would be a bad idea to blow said cover. The right thing to do would be to help *enhance* it.

Markham held up a hand and said, "Stay back, fellas, I've got this!" The pursuers from the funeral home, who had started to move cautiously forward once again, halted in their tracks.

"You want we should plug him from here?" one of the men shouted.

"Not necessary," Markham replied.

All right. Now it's showtime.

The Embalmer gave a great performance, lunging toward Markham, yelling threats and dire promises, swinging his knives like a dervish. Markham used caution, but stood his ground, avoiding every thrust and slash of the Embalmer's blades.

Then Markham knocked one of the knives out of his opponent's hand. The second one followed it moments later.

"Oh my God," the Embalmer exclaimed. "How did you do that? You—you're *not human!*"

Now it was hand-to-hand. The Embalmer landed a couple of punches, but took a great many more. The blows that "Markham" dealt out to him were vicious and brutal, and would have maimed or even killed, had they connected the way he intended them to; his methods bore little resemblance to the Bay Phantom's elegant, almost balletic fighting style. What had gotten into him?

Or maybe something had gotten *out*.

After a couple of minutes, the Embalmer threw up his hands, holding them above his head and backpedaling away from his opponent.

"That's it, I've had enough! I give!"

The fingers of his right hand were curled around a small, metallic sphere. His thumb twitched and there was an audible click.

And then there was light.

It was as though the sun had zoomed around from the other side of the earth and touched down on Joachim Street.

Markham and the men from the funeral home were stunned by it. They all staggered about, groping at the air in front of them, for more than a minute.

By the time they could see again, the Black Embalmer was gone.

The Embalmer had used a fantastic little mechanism that had produced a startling, though harmless, burst of light. The heat had burned the glove and scorched the hand that had held the device, but the Embalmer wasn't complaining. An effect like that was worth a little discomfort. And with just a single chemical charge, the thing could be used four or five times. He had, of course, closed his eyes before he set it off.

Unfortunately, he had dropped the light bomb out there on Joachim Street, and he didn't dare go back to retrieve it just now. He hated to lose it. Penny Carter had given it to him the previous year. It was a good piece of equipment, and probably very expensive.

C'est la vie!

Still, he supposed his little jaunt had been a sort of success. At least he had made a clean getaway, and possibly helped the Bay Phantom in the process.

But his triumph was tempered by sadness.

"If I can't get the supplies I need, then I can't be the Black Embalmer. It just wouldn't work. It would be like Buster Keaton without his little hat."

So, if he couldn't get his preferred identity back, he might as well adopt one that was lying fallow at the moment.

"It wouldn't be difficult at all to look like the Phantom, would it? Not, not at all. He is, thank God, unimaginative. The mask is the most difficult part, and it isn't difficult at all. Some heavy cloth, a couple of blue glass lenses... Hell, why not? If he's operating undercover, it could even *help* him."

The following day, Rickey Harvard met Eddie in Bienville Square, and together, they walked to the Donner-Purdy Funeral Home.

They went into a small office just off the foyer. Behind a desk sat a man in a blue suit. Leaning up against one wall was a man who looked familiar to Rickey. He didn't know who the guy was, but he was sure he'd seen him before. He was hard-looking, with a moustache, and had his arms folded across his chest like a tough guy.

The man at the desk was named Feeney. He seemed like he thought an awful lot of himself, and not much of anybody else.

"Are you crazy, bringing a punk like this in here?" he said, after Eddie had explained Rickey's presence. "I swear, Eddie. I know the Bosses have taken a special liking to you, but you can't be doing stuff like this."

If Eddie felt chastened, he didn't show it. The expression on his face very seldom changed at all, and it did not do so now.

"Well, I'm sorry," he said, not sounding sorry or anything else. "If I'd of known it would cause a problem—"

"How the hell would it not?" said the other man. "Today of all days! You dumb little turd."

Eddie did not react on the surface, or even immediately below it—but deep down in him, something twitched.

"Okay, Markham, that'll surmise," Feeney said. "Eddie, you ought to know better, especially after what—Well, you ought to know better." He pointed a finger at Rickey. "You take a hike. Eddie, I want to have a talk with you."

So that was that. The job opportunity had lasted all of five seconds, and Rickey was out on the street. Well, he didn't want to work in a place like this, anyhow. It smelled more like a barbecue joint than a funeral home, and it looked like it was run by roughnecks. He remembered where he'd seen that Markham guy before: he had been at the center of the fight in front of that day labor place a while back. Fine people they hired here! Rickey walked down the steps to the sidewalk, cursing under his breath.

Bad luck, that was all he ever had. He walked along, staring down at the ground. As he crossed the street in the middle of the block, he saw something lying in the gutter.

It was a shiny sphere, perhaps two inches in diameter.

Maybe it was some kind of Mardi Gras trinket. None of the parades came this far north, but someone walking home could have dropped it. Or maybe there had been some kind of revelry up here. It looked like someone had splashed red paint around on the pavement.

He picked the thing up. It looked kind of expensive; it was heavy and made of burnished metal, which Rickey found very impressive. Most cheap trinkets were made out of tin and weighed practically nothing. It had what looked like a little button on one side, and something like a small camera lens on the other. He peered into it, thinking it might be one of those little peep show viewers, with a picture of a naked lady inside. But he saw nothing, apart from the reflection of his own eye.

He tossed it back into the gutter and started walking.

Then he stopped.

The little gadget *was* a pretty thing, in its way. It might be worth money. Or maybe it was a good luck charm.

He went back, picked it up, and slipped it into his pocket.

"Well, Markham," Feeney said, after he had finished chewing out and dismissing poor Eddie, "the bosses were pleased with your performance out there last night. If that guy really was the Black Embalmer—and I believe he was, because some of our guys had some trouble with him at

Magnolia Cemetery the other night—then you proved yourself ineluctable by coming out of it alive. Not only that, but he didn't land a single punch on you!"

"Aw, he's a creampuff," Markham said modestly.

"No, he ain't. He's killed probably two dozen guys. I don't know why he's messing with us. He's as mellifluous as ol' Doctor Piranha was, maybe worse."

"Overrated."

"Be that as it may—You just earned yourself a little promotion. We're gonna have to move most of our operation after this. The bosses have acquired a larger facility north of here. You're gonna start working there soon. This is of tantamount importance. In fact, the bosses want to meet you in person some time during the next couple days. We'll work out the logarithms for that, they like to stay as synonymous as possible. But they think maybe you have the right stuff to move up—*way* up. And you can take your little sidekick with you."

CHAPTER THIRTY-FOUR
MISSIONS

Joe Perrone had told Gladys that he would be going "undercover" for a while, in hopes of infiltrating the gang. That was all he could tell her, he had said, because that was all he had known. He would be in touch. Gladys was to make herself at home at Tull House for the duration.

She had decided to do just that. And, while waiting for word from Perrone, she could take a crack at solving a new, minor mystery that had first manifested itself a couple days after Perrone's departure.

Someone had been getting into the kitchen. After a couple days' investigation, Gladys determined that the intruder was stealing small quantities of oatmeal. She first noticed it because she ate oatmeal every morning.

Did ghosts like oatmeal? She couldn't imagine how any flesh-and-blood marauder was gaining access to the place. All of Perrone and Mirabelle's security systems were in place and working properly, so far as she could determine.

But Gladys still wasn't sure that Penny or someone else wasn't somehow listening to what went on in Tull House. She had learned to recognize the murmuring of the "ghosts," but every now and then she heard a noise that didn't fit. A footfall that sounded like it had some weight behind it, a door somewhere opening and shutting. These things always came in the wee hours between midnight and dawn.

Even if Penny Carter had planted listening devices in the house, she couldn't possibly be physically getting in and out... could she? And, even if she was, why *oatmeal* of all things?

Gladys might have suspected mice, if mice were able to open a container, remove some of its contents, and replace the lid.

While giving the house a long-overdue cleaning, she had searched. And searched. And searched.

It was in Perrone's private library that she made her chilling discovery. Not a microphone or a hidden camera. Nothing to do with any possible surveillance.

It was a book. She was pulling volumes off the shelves to examine the depths of the bookcases when a title caught her eye:

Typee: A Peep at Polynesian Life

There was that strange word that had been written on the paper fragment they had found in Myrtle's room.

Typee.

She took the book down from the shelf, and saw that it was by Herman Melville. She had read *Moby Dick* and *The Confidence Man*, but she couldn't recall ever hearing of this one.

She opened the book and thumbed through it, stopping to read brief passages here and there. After a few minutes of this, her blood started to run cold.

"Oh no," she whispered. "Oh, Jesus. Oh my dear, dear Lord Jesus. Myrtle, honey, what did you get yourself into?"

Over the next few nights, the Bay Phantom reappeared on the streets of Mobile. Whether or not his presence was a comfort and a blessing depended on who you talked to.

"You just earned yourself a promotion."

The Phantom seemed to have adopted a new philosophy toward crime fighting. Those who approved of draconian punishments for relatively minor offenses cheered the masked man's new approach, while more liberal elements looked askance at his methods.

On Monday night, he confronted a flasher in Bienville Square. The deviant ended up with a broken jaw and a knee that would never again operate as it had been designed to.

On Tuesday, a would-be mugger ended up in Providence Hospital with a fractured skull, six broken ribs, and his own inexpensive .38 revolver inserted into a part of his body that was not meant to accommodate even a small firearm.

Wednesday evening, a man named Homer Pentecost, a self-anointed lay preacher and chronic layabout, was doing what he did three or four times a week: drunkenly abusing his wife, Clothilde. On this occasion, the noise he made was sufficient to carry out into the street. At 9:34 p.m., the Bay Phantom entered the Pentecost residence and subdued Homer. The masked man then asked Clothilde if she happened to have a pair of pliers handy. She did, and she cheerfully handed them over. According to a press report the next day, doctors said that the fingers on both of Homer's hands had been so severely damaged that amputation had been considered, but that they had decided to leave them on and see what happened over the next few weeks.

As for the pair of would-be rapists the Phantom caught up with on Thursday, the families announced that both services would be closed-casket affairs. It should be noted that the Phantom did not actually kill them himself; but, given the choice of fighting him hand-to-hand, or attempting to flee across the railroad tracks before the train could hit them, they had chosen the latter.

Gladys Turnbull learned of these incidents shortly after each one occurred.

She was neither pleased nor encouraged by these reports. Something was dreadfully wrong.

She needed to talk with some people she knew...

Feeney called Markham into the office at Donner-Purdy and informed him that the gang would be moving stuff from the funeral home up to a place in Chickasaw they called "the Farm." The property had been acquired some time back, and, since the incident with the Black Embalmer, the mysterious Bosses had decided to shut down Donner-Purdy and move everything up there.

"We'll take you up tomorrow," Feeney informed him. "The Bosses want to meet you for lunch today. In less than half an hour, as a matter of fact. You can't know where they are, so we'll have to blindfold you. Don't take it personal, it's a rule."

Feeney produced a blindfold, and Markham let him tie it over his eyes. Then he was led out to a car.

The car made dozens of turns, right and left, during the short drive. And the turns came in rapid succession; the car could not have traveled more than two or three blocks between each one. So they were surely within two or three miles of their starting point when they finally came to a stop.

Out of the car, across a sidewalk, up a few steps, across a porch, through a door. Across a hardwood floor, through another doorway, down a flight of stairs.

The blindfold was removed.

"Welcome, Mister Markham! Do come and join us."

Markham blinked several times to get his eyes working properly again. As things gradually became clearer, he looked around.

The room was large, dark, and cold. Tapestries covered the walls, and deep, black shadows clustered in every corner. Against the far wall, obscured by the gloom, was what appeared to be a large, old pipe organ. Shapes against one wall, covered with black sheets, might have been furniture or equipment of some sort.

The chamber was dominated by an enormous dining table of some heavy, dark wood. It looked as solid as a slab of marble. Probably an antique. Perrone might recognize what it was and where it was from. That was the kind of crap he knew about—but he wasn't here right now.

The only light came from a large candelabrum in the center of the huge table.

It was eerie, like the set of one of those haunted house movies.

Two men sat at the table, one at each end. Markham recognized them; Perrone had seen them at that silly get-together. The guys from the Transatlantic Whatever-the-hell Guild. The stocky man at the end of the table closest to where Markham stood was that Hans Kebler character. The other one, slim and a bit oily-looking, was Johnny Till.

There was a place setting in the middle, on the right side.

"Welcome, friend. I am Hans Kebler and this is Johnny Till. Do please have a seat and be comfortable."

Markham lowered himself into the chair that was obviously waiting for him.

The dim, flickering light gave an otherworldly quality to his hosts' faces. Their flesh seemed to shift and undulate ever so slightly.

Till's narrow wooden face—the word "saturnine" drifted up from Perrone's vocabulary—was mostly in shadow. The light from the candles seemed to gravitate toward Kebler. Till's eyes were invisible in their pools of darkness, while Kebler's gleamed.

"We have looked into your background, Mister Markham," Kebler informed him. "You have covered your tracks well, but no man may render himself completely invisible. We are impressed by what we have learned. You do not place much value on human life, do you?"

"Not most of 'em, no. I value mine. I want what I want, and if I can take it, I will. Why not? Anybody gets in my way, that's their lookout."

Kebler and Till smiled and exchanged a nod.

"You get better and better, buddy," Till said. "Have you done military service?"

"I fought for the North," Markham said without thinking, then wondered why he had said such a thing.

"You are having a small joke?" Kebler said.

"Ah—Hell, yeah. I gotta be honest, I never saw any percentage in sticking my neck out for a bunch of yahoos in Washington. That stuff hasn't got anything to do with me and mine."

"That is good," said Kebler. "That is excellent, sir." He leaned closer and lowered his voice, as though there were someone lurking nearby who might overhear a secret. "You must not take any talk of patriotism too seriously, Mister Markham. What is a country, after all, but a patch of land? An area on a map defined by arbitrary and ever-shifting lines. The Transatlantic Patriots League is merely, as you Americans say, a 'front.' We have other concerns, deeper ones. Concerns that cut to the bone, as the saying goes.

"Working with us, you will be well-paid, and, as you advance, there will be other benefits as well.

"But now it is time to dine."

He clapped his hands. A door behind Markham opened, and a procession of waiters, four of them, filed in, bearing platters.

The men who served the food looked like walking cadavers. Their skin was sallow and yellowish, and the pupils of their dull eyes were dilated almost to the limits of the irises. Drugs, probably. But they did their jobs efficiently, with no wasted movements, no distractions. They did not require any verbal instructions.

A plate was placed on the table in front of Markham.

"Pork roast, with carrots and boiled potatoes," Till said, as an identical plate was placed before him. "Enjoy."

Kebler and Till tucked into their own plates. There was no dinner conversation.

Markham ate, giving the food as little thought as possible. He didn't chew the meat very thoroughly, swallowing it in chunks just small enough to go down without choking him. He drank only a few sips of water as he ate.

After they had finished and the dishes were cleared away, the interview resumed.

"Have you any religion, Mister Markham?" Kebler wanted to know.

"Not so's you'd notice."

"Do you think women should have been given the right to vote?" Till asked.

"Hell, no."

"What about Negroes?"

"*Double* hell, no."

"But your good friend, Mister Barrow, is colored."

Markham shrugged. "He's useful. He's a damn good fighter. And too dumb to ask questions. You know how those people are."

Kebler nodded. "I am pleased to hear that. One should not reject a useful Negro for reasons of personal distaste. That is their purpose, after all.

"A man with your talents could go far in this organization. We're planning some things, Mister Markham. Our movement is gaining ground in Europe, and we hope to duplicate our success here. We have money, and money equals influence. We are using that, at the level of city government, in order to build our base of power, both here and abroad.

"Perhaps you will be initiated, Mister Markham. This meeting was an important first step. Not many come this far. Digest that which you have taken in, and we will talk again soon."

Feeney returned and the blindfold was once more tied over Markham's eyes. He went through the earlier procedure, this time in reverse.

Feeney let him out of the car downtown.

Markham then did a series of curious things. First, he went into Woolworth's and bought a small tin bucket, a roll of heavy tape, some brown wrapping paper, and a bottle of milk.

Then he found a secluded spot behind the building. After making sure he wasn't being observed by anyone, he forced himself to regurgitate into the bucket.

He emptied the milk bottle onto the ground and rinsed it out at a nearby tap. Without looking too closely, he transferred the contents of the bucket into the milk bottle, which he capped and sealed with tape. Then he dug through a trash can until he found a small cardboard carton, of a particular size and shape. He shredded some of the wrapping paper, wadded it up, and put it into the box, making a snug nest for the milk bottle. He wrote a brief note on a scrap of paper, tucked it in next to the bottle, wrapped the rest of the paper around the box, and secured it with tape.

He took the package to the downtown post office, wrote an address across the front, and mailed it. The thing ought to arrive at its destination very soon, probably the following day, or the one after that.

That night, Markham got up a quietly dressed himself, then left the house where he'd been staying—across and down the street from the funeral home—via a rear window, as he had done several times previously. He had a mission. It was important, he knew. It kept nagging at him, the way Joe Perrone used to do. He knew he'd get no peace unless he went ahead and did it.

They'd have to get up pretty early in the morning to begin the move, so he might as well get it done now.

He walked to the Church Street Graveyard, unaware that he had acquired a shadow.

It wasn't a good shadow; in fact, it was rather clumsy. But Markham was too focused on his mission to notice anything.

This shadow, clad in dungarees, a red plaid shirt, a short jacket, and a red plaid cap, stumbled along after Markham all the way to the old cemetery.

***

While acting as understudy for the Phantom, the Embalmer had tried and failed to come up with some kind of a plan.

He was worried.

Part of him wanted to just storm the funeral home again, while another part thought it was wiser to trust the Phantom, and leave it to him.

But...

Maybe the Phantom had gotten in over his head. Whoever was operating that funeral home was dangerous and depraved on a level seldom encountered in this part of the world. Was the crime fighter aware of the things the Embalmer had seen in there? Surely not, surely not. He probably didn't know what he was dealing with, the poor Pollyanna. And maybe he had carried something too far and gone nuts for real! Maybe the crime fighter no longer knew a hawk from a handsaw. The fact that he was cussing again, and what that might imply, had not been lost on the Embalmer.

The more The Embalmer thought about it, the less he liked it. He was under too much stress. First the situation with Myrt, now this.

Well, there was nothing he could do about the former, but the latter might not be beyond him.

I can't keep dithering around like Hamlet; I need to run a sword through somebody.

And, to do that, he needed to talk with some people...

CHAPTER THIRTY-FIVE
STRANGE ALLIES

Gladys Turnbull glanced around the dimly-lit speakeasy. There were only two or three other patrons, and they were paying no attention to the group at her table.

"I'm worried about the Boss," she said, glancing back and forth between her two companions. "I haven't seen him for days, and I'm afraid he's gone completely nuts."

"Indeed," said Shorty Red. "I haven't heard from him either, and the reports I've had of his recent activities are... alarming. And now, with Louis locked up, I'm at a loss as to how I should proceed."

"I don't buy Rickert as the killer of Charlie Tate," said Tom Dart. "But that idiot Poitier is dead-set on railroading him right into the chair. And nobody has any interest in stopping it."

"The Boss could do it—if we knew where he was," Gladys said morosely. "I'm afraid he's in terrible trouble."

"He isn't the only one in trouble," came a voice from the darkness at the back of the room. "If he's gone off his rocker, you need to be worried over what *he* knows about *you*."

Gladys, Shorty, and Dart all drew their guns at once and stood, aiming at the spot from which the strange, muffled voice had seemed to come.

"Step out where we can see you," Shorty said menacingly. "And no tricks."

"Oh, puh-leez," came the voice again, from the other direction this time. "If I meant you dopes any harm you'd ready for the coroner by now."

The quartet whirled around. Standing in the middle of the room, ten feet from their table, was the Black Embalmer. The masked madman had them covered with a Thompson submachine gun.

"Just put that artillery away," he said in a light, conversational tone. The four lowered their weapons, but did not return them to their respective holsters. "I've got the drop on you, as they say in the movies, but I'm not here for a massacre. Believe it or not, I'm worried about the Bay Phantom too. I know what's going on, more or less, and I want to help him. I think I'm the only one who really can, but I can't do it by myself—and you goofballs couldn't do it in a hundred years without me. So we need to call a truce if we want to save the Bay Phantom."

"How do we know you're on the level?" Tom Dart asked.

The Embalmer snickered. "*On the level!* That's cute, Detective Sergeant. I don't trust you lot either, but I am proposing an alliance based on desperation, not good faith, of which there will never be more than zero. And I'm prepared to make a gesture."

He squatted down and placed the machine gun on the floor, then stood up straight and spread his arms. "Shoot, if you must, this old plaster head, but if you do, the Bay Phantom might be as good as dead."

A very uncomfortable silence followed, during which the other patrons slunk out of the joint through the front door. The bartender looked on impassively. One might get the impression that he had seen much worse than this.

"Oh, hell," Tom Dart finally said. "Sit down and talk."

A few minutes later, the group, now four in number, sat around the table sipping the drinks the bartender had just brought them. The Black Embalmer had removed his bizarre plaster mask. Gladys, for one, was surprised to see that he was rather young and not too bad looking.

"I've been helping the Phantom, or trying to," the Embalmer was saying. "He doesn't seem to be very grateful for my input, but it didn't prevent him from taking up a suggestion of mine that was, in retrospect, perhaps a little unwise."

"What did you do to him?" Gladys asked coldly. Her anger and distaste were palpable. It occurred to the Embalmer that the next pummeling he received might not come from Shorty Red.

"Nothing!" he said indignantly. "Not a damn thing! You are one suspicious broad. Like I said, I've been helping him. Yes, I'm a criminal, a madman, a reprobate, et cetera. But the Phantom and I—Well, there are certain ties that bind. I have more in common with him than any of *you* do."

"Actually," Shorty said, "that may be the truth."

"Of course it is. Anyhow, one of the main rules of war is *know your enemy.* The Bay Phantom, bless his little heart, lacks my depth of experience with the profoundly mad and anti-social. That is to say, on the surface he does. But in here..." He tapped the side of his head. "That's a different story. He has a great dark beast inhabiting the depths. A few months ago, he let it out, a little bit, and he gave it a name: Roy Markham."

He didn't tell them about his own encounter with the Phantom's "alter ego," nor did he mention his own recent activities *as* the Bay Phantom. He gave them no details of the things he had observed in the funeral home.

They probably wouldn't have believed him anyhow. Vague hints were more plausible than the incredible truth.

"Your employer," he said, "has attempted to infiltrate a certain criminal organization, I believe. But I'm afraid he may have bitten off more than he can chew, and it might be too late for him to spit it out. And the center of it is the Donner-Purdy Funeral Home. Of that, I could not be more certain."

He implied that something godawful was going on in the place, while claiming not to be in possession of any details.

"How do you know all this?" Gladys demanded. She had an idea of what might be going on, based on that damn book. But she didn't want to say anything to anybody but the Bay Phantom himself. She was afraid to come right out and state her suspicions; for fear that the Embalmer would confirm them.

"I just do," he said. "The Phantom and me—Well, we're not friends, exactly, but we kind of understand some things that other people don't. We don't agree on things, but once you get past a certain level, that doesn't really matter. So I have insight, and I'm telling you about it because I want to help him, and I know you do too."

"Well, aren't you sweet," Gladys said sourly.

"I sort of am, in a way."

For the Embalmer's benefit, Shorty related the recent encounter with the Mummifier.

"What?" the Embalmer exclaimed, after Shorty had described the strange weapon. "Why, that's just a cheap knockoff of my gimmick! Doing things to living people you're only supposed to do to dead ones! Well, that fancy, newfangled gear can't beat the old-fashioned methods."

"Actually," Shorty said, "mummification predates modern embalming by a considerable—"

"Yeah, but not with wires and electricity! Wait'll I get my hands on that bum!"

"Well, there's no doubt that he's connected with that funeral home in some way. Maybe you'll get a chance."

"*If* we bring this nut in with us," Dart interjected, hooking a thumb at the Embalmer. "And that's a mighty big if."

"You will," said the Embalmer, "if you've got any sense at all. Which is an even bigger if."

They parked a block away from the Donner-Purdy Funeral Home, under the shadow of a big old live oak. The four of them were in Shorty's car—Shorty and Gladys in front, Tom and the Embalmer in back.

"It's guarded," said the Embalmer, "and they'll be extra careful now, after my visit."

"What visit?" Dart asked.

"The visit I paid them. That's how I learned what's going on."

"Which is what?" Shorty wanted to know.

"Diabolical. Absolutely. As something of an arch-fiend myself, I know diabolical, trust me. And they are it."

"They're being protected," said Dart. "The Phantom tried to point me in their direction before he—Well, anyhow, I nosed around and I found a brick wall. Some of the families that have had dealings with them made complaints, but every one of them got slapped down. Somebody has deep pockets."

"It doesn't look like anybody's there," Shorty said. "There aren't any lights. Of course, that doesn't necessarily mean anything, but—"

"Look!" Gladys exclaimed, pointing.

A pair of large panel trucks had rolled to a stop in front of the funeral home. Three men climbed down from each vehicle, and all six went inside the building. The drivers remained behind their respective wheels.

Ten minutes later, two of the men came back out, carrying a large table, which they loaded into the back of one of the trucks. Two more men brought a cart piled with metal cylinders, and these went into the truck too. It went on in this vein for some time, the men coming and going, filling the trucks with furniture and equipment of various kinds.

"What are they doing?" Gladys wanted to know.

"Well, obviously, they're moving," said the Embalmer. "I guess I scared them."

"Moving in the middle of the night?"

"That's what criminals do," the madman said. "The detective and the crook here can verify that."

"*Ex*-crook," Shorty said.

Dart snorted.

"So what do *we* do?" Gladys asked.

"It would be difficult to get in right now," said Shorty. "Impossible to do it unnoticed. I say we follow one of the trucks whenever they leave."

Dart concurred, as did Gladys. The Embalmer went along with it, even though he felt more inclined to pursue an inadvisable and possibly suicidal course. It was important to learn to work with others, after all. The Phantom had told him that.

Finally, after three-quarters of an hour, the men secured the truck doors and climbed back into the roomy cabs.

"Let's go," Dart said.

When the second truck pulled out, they fell in behind it.

"Don't get too close," Dart fussed.

"I know how to trail a vehicle," Shorty said.

Things went well for a few miles. The trucks went north, and appeared to be heading for Chickasaw. Before they reached the city limits, the truck they were following came to an abrupt halt, right in the middle of the road. The taillights winked out.

"Oh, shit," Dart said through gritted teeth.

Something struck the windshield, right in front of Shorty. There was a pinging noise, and a tiny crack appeared in the glass.

"Was that a rock?" Gladys asked.

There were two more pings, and two more small cracks appeared.

"Slugs," Shorty said. "This glass is bullet-proof."

"Ram them!" the Embalmer shouted, raising a fist.

"Oh, for God's sake," Dart said. "Nobody's ramming anybody. Shorty, I think we might need to retreat. Strategically."

The giant nodded. "There's no way now that we're going to learn their destination, no matter what happens. We don't know how many men are in that truck, or what they have."

ping-krak!

ping-krak!

"There go two more," Gladys said, removing a revolver from her purse.

"You might as well put that away," Shorty said, putting the vehicle in reverse. "We're not going to get any good shots."

"They might not even have known for sure that we were following," Dart suggested. "Maybe they're just trigger-happy."

"Could be, I guess," Shorty allowed.

Shorty swiftly backed up, down the street, away from the truck. No more bullets hit the windshield. When he judged the distance to be sufficient, he backed into a side street, then turned and headed the automobile back the way they had come.

"If this had been a movie, we would've rammed them," the Embalmer complained. "It would have worked out all right, and this whole thing would have been over in less than an hour. But you've gotta draw it out, like 'Myrt and Marge.' It's nerve-wracking."

"You listen to that program?" Gladys asked.

"I can't talk about it right now. Not until I know Myrt is safe."

They returned to the funeral home.

The place was dark. Dart tried the front door, while Shorty checked the back. Locked. And the doors and shuttered windows were obviously stout enough to repel an assault.

"Going by what I saw when I was in there," the Embalmer said, "I'll bet this place could withstand a mortar attack."

"Not that I would dare try to break in," Dart said. "Not without a warrant."

"Well, then, *get* one," the Embalmer suggested.

"It's not that easy. I can't just snap my fingers."

"I thought cops just did whatever they felt like. You're ruining it for me."

There wasn't much of anything they could do. Employing all the stealth they could muster, the group entered an abandoned house on the corner of Constitution and Joachim, from the front windows of which the funeral home was just visible. It wasn't the best vantage point, but they dared not try to get closer.

They sat there until a little after sunrise. There was no further activity at the funeral home.

"I'm going to see if I can find me a judge and try to get him to issue a warrant," Tom said. "I don't know what I'll use for probable cause; I may have to lie. But I know that place is crooked, so I'll worry about the consequences later. If anything happens, get to a phone and call headquarters. Leave a message for me with the dispatcher. I don't know where I'll be, but I'll check in every half hour. If any more of them pull out, just do whatever your common sense tells you—that only goes for Shorty and Gladys, by the way. And be careful."

When Tom had gone, Gladys questioned the Embalmer:

"What did you see in there, anyhow? You never did say exactly."

"Bad things. Really bad things. They would turn your stomach. But I didn't learn anything about specific plans. I did see something tacked up to one of the walls in the cellar. A diagram, a plan. Something about a tunnel or tunnels. I only got a glimpse of *that*, right before I was discovered. Anyhow, that's not the big thing. It's what they're *already* doing."

"Why won't you tell us what that is?"

"Nag, nag, nag—that's all you do."

They were silent for a while.

"This whole thing was a mistake," the Embalmer suddenly said, out of the blue. "I need to hook up with someone I can trust. Don't you think so? Yes, you're quite right, I couldn't agree more."

Gladys looked around and saw that the Embalmer seemed to be staring at a blank wall as he spoke.

"Who the hell are you talking to?" she asked irritably.

"I don't know their names. Well, one of them I call Carl, because he looks like a Carl, but the rest are sort of like extras. It doesn't matter. One of them might actually be Jesus, but I wouldn't dare tell anyone that. They'll lock you up for that kind of talk."

"The Lord have mercy," Gladys said, shaking her head. "And you're out running around loose."

"So I am. And I think I'll do some running now. See you yeggs later."

The "Farm" was in Chickasaw, or close to it. It was way off the beaten track, and Markham wasn't sure whether it was inside the city limits or not.

Markham still didn't know the purpose of the Farm, but he had his suspicions. Of course, no crops were grown there, nor was there any livestock in evidence. Still, the meat the gang was selling had to come from *somewhere*.

The property was surrounded by a high fence. At one end was a loading dock attached to a warehouse. Large, unmarked cartons were stored in the warehouse, along with rows of metal cylinders that looked like oxygen tanks. Those were coming in from somewhere, delivered by large trucks, and then being loaded onto smaller trucks that the gang used locally.

For the time being, Markham and Barrow were part of the warehouse crew.

At the rear of the property, an area that was off-limits to him, there were rows of long, narrow buildings that looked a bit like closed-off chicken coops. There were no windows; only a single door at one end of each building. They were surrounded by an interior fence topped with barbed wire. Trucks came and went from there too, but they used a different entrance.

✳✳✳

Markham and Joe Barrow were not permitted to come and go as they pleased, but they were driven into Mobile three evenings a week to amuse themselves however they wished.

On one such excursion, Markham left Joe on Royal Street, to watch a parade go by, and found a payphone. He placed a call to the office of Dr. Ambrose V. Atticus.

Atticus answered after the third ring:

"Hello?"

"Doctor, this is—" Markham cleared his throat. "This is Joe Perrone talking. Speaking. Have you had an opportunity to analyze the, ah, *material* I sent you? Uh-huh. I see. Well, that's what I was afraid of. I think I understand now why they formulated that poison the way they did. No, I'd better not say just yet. I'm sorry to spring it on you like I did, but—No, I haven't heard anything about—Who did *what*? Oh, I see. Well—I'll do something about it. Look, I have to go. I'll be in touch. Yes, Doctor, I will. Thank you. Goodbye."

Markham replaced the receiver and took several deep breaths.

Perrone's suspicions had been correct.

The doctor had confirmed it. Atticus had also told him something about an embalmer and an old man who had escaped from some clinic somewhere. Those things sounded familiar; Perrone knew about them, they meant something to him, but not to Markham.

The important thing was that the material he had sent to Atticus, the regurgitated meal he had eaten with Kebler and Till, at their elegant dining table, had contained human flesh.

And *that* was the secret behind the strange poison that was automatically eradicated after a certain period of time. Not only did the neutralizing agent render the poison untraceable—it prevented it from spoiling the meat.

CHAPTER THIRTY-SIX
BY PENNY SAVED

"They're crazy," said Penny Carter. "I mean, they are very, very sick. Pots and kettles, I know, but I've never *eaten* anybody. Have you?"

"God, no," said the Embalmer, making a face and putting his tongue out. "Not to my knowledge. I'm basically a vegetarian, except I have a fondness for seafood."

Penny hadn't been difficult to find—not for him. There were only four places she could have been, and he had found her at number three. He had just finished giving her an uncensored version of what he had learned the night he got into the Donner-Purdy Funeral Home.

"Uh-huh," she said. "Well, anyway, I thought I knew what I was dealing with. I thought it was the same thing as last year, a power play by a well-financed gang of thugs. But this is different. I simply cannot have widespread cannibalism and wholesale murder going on in my backyard."

"No, that's terrible for business."

"They tried to blackmail me," she said. "Can you believe the nerve?"

"What have they got on *you*?"

"Nothing! Some 'compromising' photos, taken years ago. How they found out about them and located them, I don't know. But I mean, really! Dirty pictures? Who gives a shit? I told them they could plaster them all over downtown, for all I cared."

"That's priceless."

"I had the photos stashed in a safe in one of the family warehouses. The gang probably just broke in there hoping to find valuables or something incriminating, and got lucky. They *did* manage to trace a lot of our blind assets, but I was able to secure most of them. And they've been buying highly-placed cops right out from under me.

"Anyhow, when the blackmail fell flat, they threatened me. You know, dismemberment, death, the usual. I was defiant at first, because I have a reputation, but then I started acting a little scared. Finally, I agreed to stay out of their way. My idea was to let them build whatever they're wanting to build, *then* take it away from them. But that was before I knew what they were really up to."

"So, what now?"

"We better start taking them out," she said resolutely, "before this crap goes much further."

"The place is fortified. I got lucky that first time, and now they're on their guard. Anyhow, they've been moving out of the funeral home."

"Yeah, well, they might not be done yet, and even if they are, they might have left something behind. I think I may know something helpful. And then, on top of that, I have a *very* unique asset. I've been working with him, and I think he'll be able to lend a hand. He's been out of it for a few months. I knew how to wake him up, so we did that. He's a little... difficult to manage, but he has been unusually receptive to me. I think he's ready. I just need to get his equipment. *That* can't be duplicated, and I don't have anybody on the inside who would dare steal it for me, so... I guess it's time for a raid. And we might as well get it over with immediately."

Louis Rickert had been held for almost 24 hours before he was formally charged and arraigned. Then he was held for a while longer before they decided to start interrogating him.

He had been offered his one phone call, but declined it. Who the hell was he supposed to call? He was afraid of what Shorty's reaction would be.

If he didn't want to call an attorney, one would have to be appointed, and that would take time.

He had to squirm out of this thing himself, without any help from the Phantom or his other comrades. It would be too embarrassing, otherwise.

To his dismay, he had been informed that Alice Tague was missing, and foul play was suspected. She had been snatched by a masked man not long after he had left her to take the ring to the pawn shop. Since Louis was a known associate, they had questioned him about that too. They told him they hadn't found a body—yet.

It seemed like they wanted to put him in the electric chair twice.

And poor Alice! He was worried sick. What had happened to her? Had whatever it was happened because of him?

Following his latest interrogation session, which had produced nothing but frayed nerves and strained bladders, a couple of cops named Davis and Carnes were leading him back to his cell on the other side of the building. His mind worked furiously as he plodded along between them, but it was like a man running a drill press with nothing on the work table.

"There's no way you killed Charlie Tate," said Davis. "I dunno what the hell's wrong with Poitier."

"Right," said Carnes. "You'd have a hard time strangling a kitten."

"That's a damn lie!" Louis spat. "I've never strangled a kitten, but if I took it into my head to do it, you can bet it'd get done. I never killed Charlie Tate, though. You got that part right."

"If I was to bring a kitten in here," Davis said, "could I get you to strangle it for me?"

"You could bring your mother in," Louis shot back, "if you knew where to find her."

"You just earned a crack on your head, soon as we get you back to your cell."

"Aw, nuts."

It was time now for another prayer. Silently, inside his head, Louis made this appeal:

Dear Sir, how are you? Doing well, I hope. This is Louis Rickert. You probably remember that time you dropped a big statue of Jesus on top of that guy that was about to kill me. Thanks again, by the way. Well, I got another problem now. You may already know that I got arrested for something I didn't do. Matter of fact, I was trying to do good and help a poor sick fallen woman. You look kindly on that kind of stuff, right? Well, anyhow, it's a long story, but here I am, and I might get railroaded all the way into the chair. So, if you aren't too busy, I was hoping you might get me out of here some kind of way. The sooner the better, if you know what I mean. I'll be waiting, so if you could just maybe put a rush on it, I'd be awfully grateful. And please look after Alice too, she's a sweet kid. I guess that's it. Take care. Yours truly, Louis P. Rickert, friend and associate of the Bay Phantom, a good guy.

They were walking across the main lobby—which was deserted at the moment, the desk sergeant having repaired to a broom closet for a snort of whiskey—headed back to the detention cells, when there was a terrific BOOM! and the front doors were blown off of their hinges. Louis and his two escorts were knocked to the floor.

"Holy shit, what the hell?" Davis exclaimed, getting back to his feet. Carnes helped Louis up.

"Damn," said Carnes, "there's glass and shit all over the place."

Eight men emerged from the cloud of dust and smoke that had

billowed into the lobby. They were nicely-dressed, in sharp suits, and they had bandannas tied over the lower parts of their faces, like Wild West desperadoes. They were armed, not with six-shooters, but Thompson submachine guns.

Two men, a redhead and a blonde, seemed to be in command.

"You!" barked the redhead, jabbing a finger at Davis. "Take us to the property room, now!"

"Yeah, sure," said Davis. "Whatever you want. Watch that Tommy gun, I'm not gonna make trouble. You fellows can have whatever you want out of this damn place."

"You got a key that'll fit?"

"Why don't you just blow the door off?"

"We're not supposed to make too big of a mess."

"The front doors weren't even locked, and you blew *them* off."

"That's called making an entrance. The Boss wanted us to make a *statement*, and that was it. Now you know we mean business. Come on, open that door for us."

"I will," said Davis, "keep your shirt on. It's one of these here keys... Yeah, this one."

He led them down a short hallway off the lobby, to a large room with a door made of chain-link fencing. It had a padlock on it. Davis unlocked the door and threw it open.

"Have at it, boys," he said.

The men went in and rummaged around on the metal shelves.

They found what they wanted—the stuff was packed into three large tin tubs on the floor against one wall.

"This is it," said the blonde. "Come on, let's get these out of here."

Three of the men lifted the tubs and carried them out of the evidence room.

"What you want *that* junk for?" Davis asked.

"I don't," said the blonde. "The Boss does."

One of the gang had been eyeing Louis. He spoke up:

"Say, who is this mug? He looks a little familiar."

"Oh, that's just Louis Rickert," one of the others said dismissively. "He's a two-bit punk."

"Hey!" Louis exclaimed, offended.

"What are you in for?" the redhead asked. "Jaywalking?"

"Actually," Davis said with some amusement, "we got him for murder one."

"No kidding? Did he croak a shoeshine boy?"

"Oh, no," said Carnes with a slight smirk. "He's the one cut off Charlie Tate's head! He's a vicious man!"

"Is that the truth, Rickert?" asked the redheaded hood.

"Well, what if it is?" Louis snarled, defiant.

The two head goons looked at each other.

"I thought that new gang in town done that," said the blonde.

"Yeah," said the redhead. "Hey, maybe he's in with them. If so, the Boss'll want to talk to him."

Then they returned their attention to Louis, seeming to look on him with new eyes.

"Now, wait a minute, fellahs," said Louis, suddenly drained of defiance and indignation. "I'm in custody here, and I couldn't..."

"We can't stop you fellows if you wanna take him," Davis said with a smile. "You got the upper hand!"

"Yeah," said Carnes, struggling not to laugh. "But you better be careful. He's vicious! It took six of us to bring him in!"

"No kidding?" said the redhead. "The Boss has been saying we need some hard guys. This could be like a double bonanza."

So the raiders took Louis Rickert along with them, tossing him into the back of a panel truck, along with the boxes of whatever it was they had stolen from the property room. One of the mob got in there with him, to make sure he didn't mess around with the stuff, but the guy didn't say a word to Louis the whole time.

Which wasn't all that long, as it happened.

Louis didn't know where he was when they let him out of the truck. He didn't recognize the big house they led him into, but he knew it couldn't be very far from downtown. It was secluded, though, back behind a bunch of trees and bushes that would make it invisible from the road.

He accompanied the men into the house—not at gunpoint, but not a free agent, either. He wondered what the hell he had got sucked into this time.

His escorts brought him into a living room full of expensive-looking furniture, with strange old paintings hung on the walls, and a large radio set in one corner.

"Sit down there," one of the men told him, pointing to an overstuffed sofa.

Louis sat. Two of the men remained with him, while the others went on deeper into the house. The men didn't say anything to Louis. They just stared at him. Somewhere, a clock ticked. Louis looked around the room, but didn't see it.

"You fellows been to any parades this year?" he asked at one point.

His only answer was the ticking of the invisible clock.

Presently, a tall, red-haired woman drifted into the room. Louis politely rose from his seat.

The woman looked him up and down and said, "So you're Louis Rickert, the desperado, eh? What did you do, exactly?"

"I didn't do anything," Louis said, studying the woman's face and form. There was something familiar about her. "It's a frame or something. They say I, uh, decastrated Charlie Tate."

The woman laughed. "Now, *that* I would pay to see! But I think you mean *decapitated*, don't you?"

It was then that a light went on in Louis' head. "Holy—" He swallowed hard. "I know you! You're that redhead!"

This, he was certain, was the woman who had posed so provocatively for the postcard he had taken from that punk the other day.

"Well, I'm one of them anyhow," she said. "And, now that I think about it, *you* look kind of familiar. Don't you work for old—" She made circles of her thumbs and forefingers and held them over her eyes, like the lenses of a pair of goggles.

"Naw!" Louis said, too quickly and too loud. "I don't work for the Bay Phan—" He cut it off, but not soon enough.

She clapped her hands. "I knew it!"

Louis cursed.

"Don't worry," she said. "It's okay. I'm on his side too."

"You are?"

"Uh-huh. Sure, I'm a crook, just like you. Penny Carter, the redheaded crook, that's me. But there are crooks and then there are *monsters*, right?"

"Well, yeah, I guess so."

"You *know* so. Like that shit last year, those Klan bastards. And now we've got something that is arguably worse. Do you know what this new gang has been doing?"

"Well, they been forcing restaurants to buy their meat, I know that."

"Yes, but do you know what that meat *is*?"

"Meat is meat."

She shook her head. "It's not as simple as that. Some meat comes from cows, some comes from chickens. Meat is basically muscle tissue. Pigs have it, turkeys have it, dogs and cats have it. And do you know what else has it?"

Louis shook his head dumbly. Something nasty was about to rear its head, he just knew it.

"Human beings, Louis. *People*. People have it."

It took a little while, but once the first domino finally toppled, the others quickly followed.

The new gang was forcing meat on restaurant owners.

The meat was human flesh.

One of the restaurant owners who tried to resist, Charlie Tate, and been murdered, and his body had been taken away.

Charlie Tate's body had been made out of meat.

Charlie Tate had been married recently.

Married people wore gold rings on their fingers.

Louis had eaten a hamburger at Woolworth's, one of the restaurants forced to buy the meat.

The hamburger had contained a gold ring.

The gold ring had been engraved with Charlie Tate's name.

When the final domino fell, the color drained out of Louis' face and he clapped both his hands over his mouth.

"The bathroom's right over there," Penny said with a smile.

CHAPTER THIRTY-SEVEN
ASH MONDAY

Tom Dart had spent much of the previous day trying to obtain a warrant, and his forehead was getting sore from banging it against so many brick walls.

In spite of his earlier reckless declaration, he had not resorted to blatant fabrication when it came to probable cause. And his "suspicious activities observed" and "reports from confidential informants" hadn't been enough to sway any of the judges he had approached at their homes or in various social settings.

It had been strongly suggested that he was beginning to make a nuisance of himself, and that he might want to find other ways to occupy his time.

He had checked in with Gladys and Shorty. They had no idea where the Embalmer had gone or what he was doing. And there had been no activity at all at the funeral home. That was either good luck or a complete catastrophe.

And then there had been that raid on headquarters, the theft of the Werewolf's gear and the liberation of Louis Rickert.

What the hell was *that* all about? He didn't think Rickert could have been in on it, even though those two pinheads, Davis and Carnes, said they believed he was. Had that screwball Black Embalmer been behind it? It would be just like him to pull such a stunt in order to "help out." Well, at least nobody had been killed, which made the incident a change of pace, if nothing else.

He had helped with the cleanup, checked in once more with Gladys and Shorty, then gone home for a few hours' sleep.

Meanwhile, the Donner-Purdy Funeral Home was just sitting there, possibly full of evidence, its operators possibly getting further and further away from the possibility that they would ever face justice for whatever the hell they'd been doing.

Today, he decided he would just have to confide in his superior officer.

It took a while. Branch was out of the office, and no one seemed to know where he had gone. Was he on an assignment? Nobody knew, but since it wasn't his day off, he probably was.

He picked up his phone and rang the front switchboard.

"Is Branch in yet?" he asked for the seventeenth time.

"Yeah, I was just about to ring you. He just walked in, probably headed for his office. You want me to put you through to his phone?"

"No, that's okay. I'll just go down there. Thanks."

Branch's office was on the opposite side of the building from Dart's. Anxiously, he got up and headed that way.

He walked quickly across the lobby to the hallway on the other side. This wing of Headquarters was virtually deserted. The men that weren't out on the streets for Mardi Gras—which was continuing full swing, in spite of everything—were busy with the damage to the front of the building. The contents of several of the offices were being moved to the rear.

He stopped at a door near the end of the hall, and tapped on it, then pushed it open without waiting for an invitation.

"I need to talk to you," Tom said.

"What's the matter, Tom?" Branch, seated behind his desk, looked up at the intruder. There was no warmth in his eyes. "I'm really busy right now, and—"

"It's the Donner-Purdy thing again," Dart interrupted.

"Oh, Tom, for the—"

"No, Alvin, I'm serious. Something big is going on, and we got to do something. I don't know what you know, but you need to hear what I have to say."

Branch sighed sharply. "All right, damn it. Lock the door, Tom. Nobody else needs to hear any of this."

Tom shut the door and turned the bolt.

"You're asking the wrong kind of questions, son," Branch said seriously. "Something's going on with that Donner-Purdy place."

"I *know* that! That's why I—"

"*What* do you know? What kind of information do you have?"

"Well, Alvin, I'd like to kind of keep that to myself, just for the time being."

"So do you or do you not have sufficient probable cause to get a search warrant?"

"I might have." He glanced at Branch's desk, and something caught his eye. It was one of the department's standard warrant application forms. It was partially completed. He could read the name on it...

Irene Maude

"What is this, Alvin?" he said, tapping the sheet with a forefinger.

Branch closed his eyes and took a deep breath. "Tom. I've been working on this thing, and I've made progress. I'm ready to get a warrant. I was just filling out the application to take to Judge Corril."

"Well, that's great! I'm behind you all the way, Alvin."

Branch shook his head.

"Let it go. This is bigger than you, Tom. There are international complications. I've been keeping an eye on that Irene Maude. I'm sorry I had to keep you in the dark. But she's the lynchpin, the big cheese. The funeral home is part of it, but there's a lot more to that iceberg. There have been some suspicious deaths, and everything points to Maude as the culprit."

"That makes sense. So she's tied in with that bunch that was at Donner-Purdy, and—"

"Wait, Tom, What do you mean *was* at Donner-Purdy? What's going on, son?"

"I don't know, Alvin. But *something* is, and I feel like if I don't make a move right now—Let's work together on this. I know a few things you might not, and I'm not afraid of consequences. I can't let it go, Alvin—I *won't!*"

Branch studied him for half a minute. "Damn it, Tom. Very well. Then there's only one thing I can do."

He leaned forward and began to rise from his chair, and then...

BANG!

Branch's eyes went wide, shock and confusion registering in them for half a second, before blood poured down over them, and the light behind them went out. He pitched forward onto the desk.

One look at Branch told Tom that his mentor was in need of last rites, rather than first aid. The shot had struck right behind Branch's left ear and torn away a large chunk of his head. More brain matter had spilled out onto the desk than remained in the cranial cavity.

At the window behind Branch, for just a second, Tom saw a face. It blurred, then vanished.

I'm going nuts, Tom thought, as he dashed for the window. *That looked like Frankenstein.*

Tom shoved the sash all the way up, noting a bullet hole in the glass. There was no screen, and he climbed out into the passage between this building and the next. One end of the passage was a blank wall, so the shooter must have gone the other way, out to the street. And so that was where Tom Dart went.

He dashed out onto Royal Street, looking first right, then left. The ragged edge of the Mardi Gras crowd trailed all the way down to City Hall, and there were too many people on the street for Dart's liking.

Yes, there he was. That tall, Frankenstein sonofabitch was hard to miss —*and* he was wearing a purple turban.

The shooter was just a block away, across Government Street, plunging into a knot of people on the sidewalk.

"Oh, no you don't," Tom vowed. Fortunately, the shooter's head was easily visible above those of most of the revelers. And, even if he found a crowd of people his own size, the turban was an unmistakable marker.

Dart couldn't shoot at him, not in the crowd. But he couldn't let him get away.

Alvin is dead, I couldn't help him, no way he could survive the wound I saw, there goes his killer, my job is to lay my hands on him.

And, for the moment, that was that.

It was a fine day, unseasonably warm, but with a gentle, pleasantly fishy-smelling, breeze coming in off the Bay. Tom Dart didn't notice and wouldn't have cared. Likewise, the throngs of gaily-clad citizens who lined both sides of Royal Street were featureless obstacles to him, blocking the space between him and his quarry.

He dodged around people, shoving some out of the way, practically vaulting over the heads of others, leaving a trail of irate parade goers hurling curses at his back; but they soon forgot and returned to their debauches.

He got closer to the turban, then further away. All these damn people, going every which way—it was like swimming in a blender. But he never lost sight of the head.

At the next block, the man vaulted one of the crowd control barricades that had been set up along the curb, and dropped to the street; the maneuver slowed him down, and he stumbled. Dart put on speed, and used the broad back of a man who had stooped down to tie his shoe to boost himself over the barricade. The tall man had recovered and reached the opposite side of the street.

Dart almost had him, but he slithered over the other barricade, just inches from the detective's outstretched hands. Dart vaulted over, and the chase resumed. The detective was gaining on the fleeing killer, but not fast enough.

As he passed a street vendor, Dart grabbed several strings of cheap purple and green glass beads hanging from a pole on his pushcart. Ignoring the man's indignant shouts, he closed the gap between himself and the tall man. When he was close enough, Dart gave it one extra burst of speed and jumped onto the killer's back.

"You are *not* getting away."

He wrapped the strings of beads around the man's throat and pulled back.

The cheap colored-glass ornaments bit into the flesh of the man's neck as he staggered about, stiff-legged, with Tom Dart on his back. Revelers on the sidewalk backed away, realizing they were witnessing a genuine life-and-death struggle, not a drunken pantomime.

"You dirty sonofabitch!" Dart gritted.

"Hey, there's kids out here!" someone yelled indignantly.

Dart twisted and pulled. The tall man gasped and fell to his knees, almost dislodging his garroter.

Dart wanted to stop, to take the killer into custody, but he just kept pulling the strings of beads tighter and tighter. It was as though he was

"...*everything points to Maude as the culprit.*"

no longer capable of anything else but this. What he wanted didn't matter. This was how it played out.

But another factor entered the equation. Strings of inexpensive Mardi Gras beads are not generally an implement of choice among experienced stranglers. The reason for this soon became apparent.

As Dart pulled tighter, the cords all snapped at once, scattering beads everywhere and freeing the tall man. Tom Dart fell backwards. The man, wheezing, got to his feet and ran, crouching down as he plunged into a knot of people.

Dart gave chase, but the guy had evidently wised up and ducked down as he ran.

Three blocks later, an exhausted and dispirited Tom Dart found an unwound purple turban, discarded in the gutter.

Gladys returned to the house on Constitution, parking one street over and walking the rest of the way. She found Shorty Red there, keeping the vigil.

"Any action?" she inquired.

"Not a bit," Shorty said morosely.

He stood up and stretched, made a circuit of the room, to get the blood flowing in his legs. Then he went back to the window and peered out.

Gladys stood in the middle of the room, rubbing her hands together, fretting. Her little secret had been nagging at her, and she decided to broach the subject with Shorty.

"Shorty, have you ever read a book called *Typee*?"

"By Melville? Sure. The one about Polynesia. With the cannibals."

Gladys shuddered. "Yes. I'm afraid—"

"Wait a minute," he said. "Look."

Gladys stepped up beside him and saw two large vehicles that had just stopped at the curb in front of the funeral home.

"Yep, that's them," Shorty said. "Same trucks."

Several men climbed down from the cabs and headed for the front door.

"What should we do?" Gladys asked.

"I guess we should just watch them."

"Okay, but let's get a little closer, at least."

When they arrived at the funeral home, Markham and Joe were told they wouldn't be allowed down in the lower levels, underneath the building proper. Markham made careful note of the men who *were* allowed down there, and kept a special eye on them.

The Bosses were there too, riding in the other truck. They had come to supervise the removal of certain secret items from certain secret rooms. They kept to themselves, not mixing with the rank and file men who were busy removing less sensitive stuff.

Momia was there too, supervising the dismantling of the unused embalming room. The idiotic Eddie had tagged along as well, and was prowling around somewhere, smiling his creepy smile.

After everyone had scattered to complete their assignments, Markham and Barrow found themselves alone in the Viewing Room. They were to remove the paintings from the walls and tote them out to one of the trucks. But Markham had another idea, one he quickly outlined for Barrow.

Then he moved to the red door at the rear of the room. Nobody had gone down there yet. He slipped a lock pick out of his pocket and applied it to the keyhole.

It was a good lock. He used up half a minute getting it open.

"You keep a lookout, Joe," he said. "I'm going down there."

"Be careful."

In a curtained alcove behind Joe Barrow, there stood a watcher. He had seen what had just happened. Markham had picked the lock on that door and gone downstairs, where he wasn't allowed to go. The watcher smiled. He turned around and crept down a narrow passage that led to the hallway where the secret rooms were.

There wasn't much for Markham to see. The door had opened onto some stairs, which led down to a large chamber. The place had been mostly cleared out, it appeared, but a few odds and ends remained. To his left was a big, old pipe organ, probably the one Perrone had heard playing that sissy music that night he got clocked in Irene Maude's cellar. Too big to move, Markham reckoned. He didn't think it was the same one he had seen in Kebler and Till's dining room, but—Well, it *might* have been. This might have been the room he was brought to that day.

If so, it looked a lot different now.

There were ten or twelve metal cylinders scattered about on the floor, ranging in size from a foot to four feet long and six to ten inches in diameter.

A couple of maps were tacked to the wall.

He pulled one of them down. It looked familiar, in that irritating way that had become familiar to him. He rummaged through Perrone's memories. When he found what he wanted, he felt a chill.

"Oh, holy shit," he whispered. He was looking at a diagram of the network of underground tunnels beneath Mobile that Perrone used as the Bay Phantom! How the hell had they gotten their hands on *this*? The map was far from complete, with many of the tunnels missing from the diagram, but that wasn't much of a relief. Nobody should have even *this* much information.

"Mister Markham, I am truly surprised and disappointed," came a voice from the top of the stairs behind him.

He turned around slowly.

"Yes, surprised and disappointed," Hans Kebler said, shaking his head sadly.

"I echo that sentiment," said Johnny Till. "We had such high hopes for you."

Till held a shotgun, which was pointed at the head of Joe Barrow. Kebler was brandishing a pistol. They descended the steps into the chamber.

"Well, well," Markham said with a sneer. "What a sweet pair of fairies you two make!"

They had him cold. There was no way to squirm out. Markham's only hope was to throw them off somehow, shake them up, force them to make a mistake. They had the upper hand, it appeared, but the fact was that Joe Barrow's life was not that important right now, and neither was Roy Markham's. Oh, he wanted the kid to live, and he wanted to live too, but those things were overshadowed by the fact that Kebler and Till had to be destroyed. And it might as well be right here and right now.

Markham did not share Perrone's notions of bringing them to "justice." That was too uncertain, too many things could go wrong. While the lawyers and the courts dithered, these two would continue eating food and breathing air, and they might eventually end up back out on the streets. Shit like that happened all the time.

They had to die. Horribly if possible, but above all, *quickly*.

Markham's insult seemed to have angered Till just a bit. His gaze became a glare, and his finger tensed on the trigger of the shotgun.

Shoot me, *not him*, Markham silently willed him, *move the barrel of that gun away from the boy's head and try to use it on* me.

"Till," he said, "have I ever told you how much you remind me of a bulldog's asshole?"

Joe Barrow bit his lip to keep from laughing. Till's glare turned white-hot for a second, and the shotgun twitched slightly in Markham's direction. He might just crack.

Kebler, though, was a different story.

His icy calm seemed untouchable. A barb might prick Till's skin, irritate it; but Kebler's was too thick, or too numb.

"You like to make insults," said the German. "You like to sound clever. Well, it is true, sir, that you are *very* clever. You infiltrated us, and we suspected nothing. Interestingly, the only one who *did* suspect anything was the idiot. What that says about us as a species, I cannot be sure. In some ways, our idiot is a prodigy—quite remarkable. But the things at which he excels require no intellect, a commodity he is not overburdened with.

"He has just informed us that he followed you to the Church Street Graveyard, where, according to him, you opened a grave and climbed down into it. At first, I wasn't sure what to make of that, but now I believe I have it. That particular grave doesn't contain a corpse, does it? No, I think it must be an entrance to something. The most obvious thing being the system of subterranean tunnels employed by Doctor Piranha years ago. And rumored lately to be used by the Bay Phantom.

"That, coupled with the information that he had just seen you come down here, told us all we needed to know. You have some connection with the Phantom, I think. Perhaps more than a connection. He was one of the few people ever to best the Black Embalmer—just like you. Yes, and I don't believe an ordinary thug, as you pretend to be, could have hoodwinked us so thoroughly."

Kebler had made a brief circuit of the room as he spoke, leaning in to snatch the map out of Markham's hand, and now he stood behind Markham with a revolver. Till was in front of him, at the foot of the stairs, far enough away that Markham couldn't make a grab for the gun. Till shoved Barrow toward the middle of the room, instructing him to stand against the wall, too far away to reach either of them before they could open fire.

Suddenly, they all became aware of a loud rumbling sound, seemingly coming from the other side of the rear wall.

Kebler and Till looked at one another.

It was a split second, but that was all Joe Barrow needed.

He dashed forward and punched Till in the face. The shotgun clattered to the floor, spinning toward Markham. Till hit the floor too, six feet in the other direction.

Kebler struck Markham over the head, putting him on his knees, and was about to put a bullet into the back of his skull. But Joe was too quick for him. A solid jab put the German on the floor with his compatriot.

"Kid, you just turned the tide," said Markham. He picked up the shotgun and made ready to use it on either of the two masterminds, should they attempt a break. Barrow had snatched Kebler's pistol. He didn't seem comfortable with it.

Markham, on the other hand, seemed quite at ease with his firearm.

"Get on your knees, both of you," he barked at the Guild leaders.

They complied, both wearing annoying smirks.

"The rest of our men are upstairs," Kebler said. "You won't get out of here alive."

"I know," Markham said calmly, thumbing back the hammer. "And I think it's better for everybody that you two don't survive this, either. Goodbye, fellas."

"Roy!" Joe exclaimed, horrified. "You can't just—just *execute* them!"

"And why the hell can't I?" As far as Markham was concerned, he had already pulled the trigger. It would have been done by now if Barrow hadn't piped up.

"'Cause it ain't right! And we gotta get out of here! I don't know what's happening behind that wall, but—"

The noise had continued while they had fought, and now the wall bulged out in the middle, chunks of plaster falling into the room. The rumbling turned into a metallic shrieking. The wall crumbled, then the middle section collapsed completely.

And something stepped into the room, wading through the rubble, crushing small chunks of plaster beneath its enormous hind paws...

Markham recognized the newcomer from Perrone's Bay Phantom memories.

The Werewolf.

✳✳✳

Thirty minutes earlier, one street over—

Two vehicles pulled up and parked at the curb in front of Mauvais Rêve. One was a sleek, two-seat roadster, the other was a large panel truck. The roof of the truck scraped the low-hanging branches of the live oaks

Penny Carter and Louis Rickert stepped out of the car. The Black Embalmer climbed down from the passenger side of the truck.

The trio went up to the porch, and Penny knocked on the door.

Irene Maude opened the door a crack and poked her nose through the gap. "Yes?"

"Are you Irene Maude?" Penny asked, in a clipped, businesslike voice.

"You know I am, Miss Carter. We've met before."

"I know, I just wanted to sound like a cop. It might surprise you to learn that I know everything."

"Everything? In the world? You are to be commended."

"Indeed I am. Knowing everything in the world means I know what *you've* been up to."

"I don't know what you're referring to."

"Yes, you do. I know what you've been doing with regard to Kebler and Till. I know *all* about it, and I know about the houses too."

"The houses?"

"Specifically, the tunnel in between them."

This seemed to rattle Madame Maude. "Oh. I see."

"Yes, I'll just bet you do," Penny said knowingly.

Actually, she didn't know as much as she claimed to, but she knew plenty, and the suppositions she had made had proven sound so far, and were even now leading to fresh ones. So she would continue.

Madame Maude opened the door all the way.

"Anyhow," Penny said, "I have brought along a—"

"Boss," came the voice of one of Penny's bodyguards, out on the sidewalk, "somebody's coming this way. A man and a woman. And it looks like the woman's got a *sword*."

"Ah! Now that's what I call timing. They're on their way here, Gus, let them come. And there should be another man and woman close behind them. Let them all pass."

Milt Cabal and Winona Dirge were puzzled by the welcome they received. They hadn't known what to expect, but it never would have been this.

"Mister Cabal and Miss Dirge," said Penny. "I'm pleased to see you."

"We called your number when we got into town," Cabal said, "and your representative said to meet you here."

"You were followed, of course."

"Right, just like you said. I believe they caught on to what we were doing."

"Well, certainly. They are both of well above average intelligence."

"They should be right behind us," Winona put in. "We left the car a couple of blocks away, so they'd be more likely to trail us on foot."

"They will. Let's give them a few moments."

"Miss Carter," Cabal said, "this whole thing is—"

"Almost done," Penny interrupted. "One more act to go, and you two can earn your fee and be on your way."

"The whole thing?"

"Absolutely. I'll even throw in a bonus."

"But what about Doctor Piranha? He's—"

"He's *here*," said Doctor Piranha.

Everyone on the porch turned to look. Piranha was standing in the middle of the path leading from the sidewalk. Next to him stood Mirabelle Darcy. The men on the street wore expressions that ranged from puzzlement to panic.

"Boss, we never saw him—I mean, we were watching for them, then, all of a sudden…"

"It's okay, boys. He does that. Evidently, she does too."

"Hello, Penny," said the doctor.

"Why, I declare," Penny said comically, pressing the back of a hand to her forehead. "It's that dreadful Doctor Piranha. I might just succumb to the vapors!" She turned to address the assassins. "I thought I hired you two to rub him out, but here he is!"

Winona raised a forefinger. "But you said—"

"Never mind what I said. I've seen the light! It was wrong of me to try to take the law into my own hands, to play *God*! Can you forgive me, Doctor?"

"I suppose I can, Miss Carter, just this once."

Mirabelle rolled her eyes and shook her head.

Piranha turned to her and said, "Come on now, Miss Darcy. You knew it all the time. Did you ever have even a particle of doubt about what was really going on?"

"No, not really. You weren't on the defensive at all when I came into your cell. Just lying idly in your bunk, as I recall, even though you supposedly knew that people were coming to kill you. One doesn't even have to be a super-genius to have noticed that. I went along with it because what the hell good would anything else have done?"

"Before I met you," Piranha said, "I thought I might fool you. I knew within five minutes of your arrival that it had been a pointless charade. But—since you were going along with it, *I* went along with it because—" Out came the fishy smile. "What the hell good would anything else have done?"

Mirabelle shook her head. She had an expression on her face, and she herself wasn't sure whether it was a smile or a grimace.

"And there was more to it than just having Miss Carter hire these two and presumably supply them with equipment," she said. "I don't care how well-equipped they were, they couldn't have caused everything we saw at the prison that night. They had inside help, didn't they?"

Piranha shrugged his shoulders a quarter of an inch.

"Nobody helped us!" Winona protested. "We didn't have an inside man."

"Not that you were aware of," Mirabelle said. "But that whole thing was prepared long before you got there. For one thing, during the brief blackout periods, *someone* had to be working the phones and the shortwave radio, assuring the outside world that nothing was amiss, or else the place would have been swarming with law enforcement within minutes. Not that I care, I just hate loose ends like that. The warden was certainly in on it, and probably a few others as well. No more than twenty men would be required."

"Sixteen," Piranha whispered.

Winona Dirge and Max Cabal exchanged a look of dismay.

"I know who you work for," Penny said to Mirabelle, "and I also know who you *work* for. Don't worry, I'm not going to make an issue out of it."

Mirabelle ignored Penny and said hello to Winona.

"Again," she added, "I'm sorry for what I did to you."

Winona shrugged. "Eh, what the hell? It's just business. I'd have done the same thing."

The Embalmer cocked his head and studied Mirabelle for a few moments.

"Hey," he said. "I recognize you. You're that colored gal that hangs around with the Phantom. When I went through that underground thing and ended up at that house, you were there and so was Sigmund Freud. How's he doing?"

"All right, so far as I know."

"Great! So that whole thing really *did* happen! That's a relief. Listen, I'm on your boss' side right now, and we've got a problem."

"What are you babbling about?" Mirabelle demanded angrily.

"I'm not babbling! Jesus, I'm speaking plain English, and I think I'm remarkably lucid right now. Look, the only other time you saw me, my face was all bunged up from having the shit beaten out of me by Shorty Red. I'm the Black Embalmer! Remember?"

Of course she did. There was no way she'd ever forget this lunatic. She knew that Perrone, or his masked alter-ego, had developed some kind of weird friendship with the madman. And the Embalmer was just crazy enough to be sincere.

"I know what you've been doing, Madame Maude," said Penny. "I figured it out. Put all the little pieces together." She pantomimed assembling a jigsaw puzzle. "You've been patient and worked hard. And now I've come to end it for you."

"How do you plan to proceed?"

"I'll show you."

Penny walked out to the curb and banged on the side of the truck with her fist.

The rear doors opened. The men standing close to the vehicle stood back. *Way* back.

Something emerged, led by other men, very large men, with long metal poles attached to a heavy steel ring around the neck of...

...the Werewolf.

Two members of the group at the front of the house said, "Oh my God," one in French. Two others opted for, "What the hell—?" Piranha said nothing, and Mirabelle said, "Holy shit!" The Embalmer patted his hands together in restrained applause.

Seven feet tall. Covered in gray and black fur. The Werewolf stood on the street behind the truck, shifting its immense weight from foot to foot, making metallic clanking and grinding sounds. Somewhere beneath the fur and steel was the ferocious, nearly-mindless wreck of man who had been responsible for so much carnage during the brutal gang wars of the previous year.

Mirabelle remembered her first encounter with the beast, on the streets of the French Quarter in New Orleans. The monster had come close to killing Mister Perrone, the Bay Phantom.

The armored costume looked the same, except for the hands; the old claws had been replaced with wide, flat, spade-shaped appliances with razor-sharp edges.

"What in the *hell* are you doing with *him*?" Mirabelle demanded.

"Giving him an opportunity to serve the greater good," said Penny. "I'll explain everything to you, Miss Darcy, but not right away. What you need to know now is that there is a particularly vicious new gang operating in Mobile. We are going to dismantle them. The Bay Phantom has gone undercover to infiltrate them, and he may be having some difficulties."

Mirabelle looked at Piranha.

"I don't know anything about *this*," he said. "I just wanted to come back for a short while and do what needs to be done for a certain party."

"Madame Maude," Penny said, as the men with the poles guided the beast up the walk toward the house, "meet *Monsieur Loup Garou*. Or perhaps we should start calling him the Mole. He is going to finish your tunnel for you, and deal with whatever is at the other end of it."

Irene Maude shrugged, and held the door open for her guests.

The Werewolf and his handlers went first. The men guided the monster carefully across the hardwood floor of the front parlor, in between the antique furnishings, through the dining room, and down the hall toward the kitchen.

Penny followed, side-by-side with Madame Maude, then came Louis and the Embalmer and the two assassins, with Mirabelle and Doctor Piranha bringing up the rear.

"I have now seen everything," Winona Dirge declared.

"No, you have not," Milt Cabal averred.

Louis Rickert sniffed the air. "He don't smell like a dog. He smells like axle grease."

"This can't possibly be a good thing," Mirabelle Darcy muttered. "It is mathematically impossible for this not to end in disaster."

"We'll see," said Doctor Piranha.

"Right through that door," Penny said, when they reached the kitchen. "There shouldn't be a cellar, but there is. Somebody put a great deal of work into digging it out and shoring it up, making it waterproof. It was done a long time ago, shortly after the Grandine family bought it."

Madame Maude unlocked the door. Down the stairs they all went, following the restrained Werewolf into the unlikely cellar.

There wasn't much to see down there, and the few interesting items scattered about were eclipsed by what lay in the middle of the floor.

The bodies of two women.

One of them was obviously dead—the knife embedded to the hilt in her chest seemed pretty conclusive—but the other seemed to be breathing.

Penny turned to Madame Maude.

"Is this what it looks like?" she asked.

"I don't know what it looks like to you. And I don't know how these poor girls come to be here, though I have a strong suspicion. Mohammed has gone to deal with it, in fact."

Penny nodded. "It seems we're just in time, then."

Doctor Piranha was not a medical doctor. In fact, he had no doctorates in anything, from anywhere. Neither did Mirabelle, but she had learned a lot about medicine from Doctor Atticus, so she took the lead. She crouched down and made sure that the girl with the knife in her was actually deceased, then turned her attention to the other, gently rolling the woman over onto her back.

"No wounds that I can see," Mirabelle muttered. She patted the girl's cheeks. "Hey. Hey, honey, wake up. Are you okay?"

The girl's eyelids fluttered, then opened wide.

Louis, jolted by sudden recognition, dropped to his knees beside her.

"Alice!" he said. "Oh, jeez, what happened?"

"Louis? I—I don't know. Somebody grabbed me and... I think I got hit on the head and I got taken someplace and... I don't know, Louis. Heck, I don't know where I am *now*. Are you really here?"

"Far as I can tell. What happened to you?"

"I told you I can't remember. I think I saw a woman and a tall man, and they—Oh, God—" Her eyes fluttered some more, this time remaining closed after they were done.

"She's gone back to sleep," Mirabelle said. "She's just exhausted. Probably been drugged."

Off to the side, Madame Maude and Penny conferred in low voices.

"That knife came from my kitchen," said Madame Maude, pointing to the dead woman.

"Of course it did," Penny said. "I'm sure it's got your fingerprints on it. I'll bet these two were brought in through that window. Look at the paint chips on the floor there. They've sure got it in for you."

"Oh, I don't doubt that."

"I think she'll be okay, short-term," Mirabelle said. "She's malnourished, but she hasn't been injured. God knows what kind of drugs she's been fed. But I think there's something else wrong with her, something organic. Maybe tuberculosis."

"She's been sick for a while," said Louis. "I was—I tried to raise some money for her to go home to her folks and get some treatment. It didn't turn out too good. I wish I could figure out something to do for her."

"Really?" she said. "I guess there's more to you than I used to think."

Mirabelle stood up and stretched, remembering how skeptical she had been when the Bay Phantom first decided to hire Louis Rickert as an agent.

"How do you know anything about me?" said Louis, looking her up and down. "I don't—Oh, wait, I recognize you. Yeah, you're Paper Bag Girl! I saw you that day at Cathedral Square. You look a little different without that bag on your head, but I recognize your suit, and your, ah—I recognize your suit."

Mirabelle just nodded, not bothering to deny anything. She crouched down again and felt Alice's forehead.

"Did you retire or something?" Louis went on. "Oh, I'm Louis Rickert, by the way, I work with the Bay Phantom too. I guess you already knew that, though. I'm sort of his right hand man. I help him plan everything out, and I handle most of the legwork."

"Is that a fact?"

"Oh, yeah, it sure is."

"Well, then, where is he now?"

"Ah—Well, we don't exactly know. According to that Embalmer character, he went undercover to, uh, filter into this gang, and—Well, we don't know what's going on with him right now."

"And," said Penny Carter, who had just loomed up over them, like a sudden storm cloud, "we are going to find out. If they have harmed him in any way, I will destroy them even more thoroughly than I was already going to destroy them. If they're holding him prisoner, we'll get him back. And if they've killed him—Just call me King Lear."

Mirabelle studied Penny Carter's face and decided that she was sincere. Penny was a horrible woman, but it seemed that she genuinely cared for Joe Perrone. As much as she was capable of, anyhow, which wasn't enough, so far as Mirabelle was concerned. But it was something, especially under the circumstances.

"Miss Carter," she said, "I promise I will stop fantasizing about murdering you until after all this is over."

Penny smiled. "Okay," she said. "Let's get moving."

She walked across the cellar and along the short tunnel to where the excavation ended.

"A man and a woman might be able to get all the way through in another two or three days," she said, stepping back to the doorway. "Now watch this."

The Werewolf had stood quietly, apparently exhibiting patience. Now

Penny motioned it forward, and it obeyed, joining her at the tunnel entrance.

Penny placed a hand on its shoulder, as calmly as though she were petting a puppy, and said, "Plow into that dirt, and when you get through, keep going. You'll be in another house. I don't know what we'll find there, but I want you to raise pure holy hell."

To the astonishment of everyone else present, the great shaggy head bobbed up and down. The movement produced a muffled clanking noise.

"Well, go to it!" Penny urged. "Unhook that collar, boys!"

The monster moved forward, into the tunnel, and attacked the wall of dirt and debris at the far end; furiously plunging his hands into the clay, tearing out huge chunks and flinging them backwards.

"So *there's* the tunnel," the Embalmer exclaimed. "I knew there would be a tunnel somewhere!"

"He could probably get into the other house through their front door," said Penny, "but I like an element of surprise. There's something kind of Biblical about a savage monster coming up out of the ground to smite your enemies."

While the Werewolf dug, Penny explained as much of the situation to Mirabelle and Piranha as time and the limits of her own knowledge would permit. The Embalmer tossed in a few details here and there.

Presently, the shoveling and thudding in the tunnel gave way to screeching and grinding. The Werewolf had apparently hit some concrete and metal, and was very industriously tearing it apart

"He's just about through," said Penny.

"If you really do know the truth about me," Madame Maude said, "you'll let me come along."

Penny nodded. "Yeah, I guess you've earned it. Maybe there'll be something left for you when I get through."

To the assassins, she said: "Everybody on the other side over there is guilty. Show no mercy, and do not waste time assessing situations. You're still in the running for that four million bucks, but the job has changed."

The Werewolf crashed through the last of the barrier, into a room beyond. The two assassins were right behind him. They spread out, moving toward opposite ends of the large room.

Lots of things happened then, and very quickly.

Joe Barrow pivoted and held the pistol up, trying to decide which of the three menacing figures he ought to threaten with it.

A squad of men pounded down the stairs into the chamber. They were halfway across the room before they could even begin to process what was down there.

The Werewolf tore into them.

Joe Barrow, more or less by reflex, fired a shot at the beast. The bullet ricocheted off with a metallic whang.

Winona Dirge took advantage of Barrow's moment of distraction, and was about to remove his head with her sword. As the lethal arc commenced, Markham let loose with a blast from his shotgun. Winona's blade shattered, the largest piece spinning end over end across the room.

Right into Milt Cabal's throat.

He had no time for even the briefest of final words. His carotid was severed instantly, as was his windpipe. He looked slightly confused and profoundly irritated.

Winona turned to look at him, saw what had happened, and froze. As Cabal dropped to the floor, grief twisted her features, then anger. She paused for a moment to think about what had happened, and who she needed to get revenge against. Before she could decide, the Werewolf, swinging his sharp, spade-like claws around with mindless abandon, opened her up from her collarbone to her pelvis.

Kebler and Till, on the edge of the sanguinary melee, recovered themselves and ran for the stairs.

Markham fired at Till, striking him in the hip, but failing to drop him. The two Guild leaders made it to the stairs and disappeared. Markham and Joe charged after them, slowed up a bit by the necessity of dodging blood, bodies, and slashing claws.

Winona Dirge looked down at what had just befallen her, dropped the stub of sword, and said:

"Ha! And my old man used to say I didn't have any guts. Guess this proves—"

Her proof slithered out of her abdominal cavity through the terrible breach, and made a wet pile on the floor. A second later, Winona Dirge followed.

"That was perfect," said the Embalmer, stepping through the new entrance to the chamber with Penny and Piranha. "I hope my final words are pithy, yet ironic, like that. What a nice twist."

Penny stepped in front of the Werewolf—who had run out of victims, and was now prowling around the perimeter of the room, snout in the air—and held up a hand.

"That's enough, little pal," she said.

The monster became still and quiet. Penny got close and reached up to stroke its head.

"Good boy," Penny purred. "You did good. Yes, you did."

"Jesus, that is disturbing," said the Embalmer. "But in a good way."

"Those two got a terrible deal," Piranha said, shaking his head over the remains of Dirge and Cabal.

"Well, at least we don't owe them four million bucks," Penny pointed out.

"True, but money isn't everything," Piranha pontificated.

"*Jesus holy motherloving God!*"

Mirabelle had stepped into the chamber, with Madame Maude, and the scene she found had provoked her outburst. Bodies and parts of bodies and blood covered most of the floor space. The Werewolf had accomplished all of this in less than a minute. Maude surveyed the gruesome decor and became very pale, but stayed silent.

"It *is* a bit much, isn't it?" said Piranha.

"I don't know how to react to this," Mirabelle said. "I mean, where does one start? I should probably throw up. Oh my God, there's poor Winona!"

She looked at Penny with tears in her eyes and scowled. "How did you manage to gain control of this creature?" she asked, jabbing a forefinger at the untethered but docile Werewolf.

"I don't know," the red-headed crime boss replied. "It was a surprise to me too. I guess he just likes me."

"Some people," Mirabelle said, shaking her head. She gave Winona a last look.

"Sorry, sweetheart," she whispered.

"All the cannon fodder has been slaughtered!" Kebler shouted to nobody in particular. Till had disappeared somewhere, and Kebler was in the foyer, headed for the front door. Barrow and Markham weren't far behind. They had emerged from the stairwell and dashed through the Viewing Room. In the foyer, Barrow snatched an urn from a table and threw it, catching the German in the back of the head before he could reach the door. Kebler pitched forward, bounced off the doorframe, and fell to the floor.

Barrow and Markham started forward to deal with their foe.

"We'll get *one* of the bastards, anyhow," Markham growled.

"They can run," said Barrow, "but they can't hide."

However...

The Mummifier stepped from the Viewing Room behind them, raised his weapon, and pulled the trigger. The twin projectiles shot out, one finding Barrow's back, the other striking Markham's.

Then the weird current passed along the wires.

The effect, divided as it was, was not lethal, but it wasn't negligible, either.

They stopped abruptly and jerked backward, as though the slender wires had arrested their motion and yanked them back.

They were unconscious when they hit the floor.

Kebler, on the other hand, had not been knocked out by the urn. He and the Mummifier dragged Markham and Barrow out to one of the trucks and threw them into the back. The Mummifier climbed in with them, and Kebler got behind the wheel.

Shorty and Gladys, having witnessed the arrival of the vehicles, had left the house on Constitution and crossed the street, where they had hidden behind a bush to watch whatever might unfold. Now they emerged and charged toward the scene of the action.

They each fired a shot at the cab of the truck. Both of them struck the driver's side door. Neither of them disabled the vehicle or its operator. The engine roared to life and the truck peeled away from the curb.

Shorty and Gladys rushed up the steps and into the funeral home, where they encountered the others. Gladys hugged Mirabelle and Shorty shook her hand. Both of them ignored Penny Carter, after a couple of quick, disapproving looks.

"They're gone," Mirabelle said glumly

"Well, we might find something in here that will tell us where they went," Gladys suggested.

Louis Rickert wandered in through the cellar door in the Viewing Room.

"Louis!" Gladys exclaimed. "You're out of jail!"

"Oh, hi, uh, Gilda," he said distractedly. "I kind of got sprung, but not on purpose." He turned to Penny. "Miss Carter, I think Alice needs to get to a doctor."

Penny went back downstairs and had her men attach their poles to the Werewolf's collar. They led him back through the tunnel he had dug, through Madame Maude's house, and on out to the truck, where he was once again locked into the compartment.

They would also transport Alice Tague to the hospital. She had regained consciousness again, and could sit in the roomy cab with the driver—and one other. Louis insisted on accompanying her.

Those who remained searched the rest of the funeral home. The Embalmer had disappeared, muttering something about his "faithful assistant," who needed checking on. But he had told Penny all about what he had seen during his first incursion into the funeral home. She had relayed the information to the others. Gladys, in particular, was affected by it.

They conducted their search with this disturbing revelation in mind.

And they found—

Shortly after Penny's men and their charges left in the truck, there was another arrival at Mauvais Rêve.

Finding the upper floors unoccupied, Mohammed went down to the basement, and was puzzled by the fact that there was only one dead woman down there now. He followed the now-completed tunnel into the Donner-Purdy house.

He was stunned by the carnage in the cellar. It took him a few seconds to compose himself and work up the nerve to cross the floor to the stairs. He held his breath, kept his gaze fixed on the ceiling, and ignored the unpleasant squishing sounds his footsteps made.

He found Madame Maude in the Viewing Room.

"Madame Maude!" he exclaimed, relieved to see her alive and intact. "We were right about Branch. But what has happened *now*?"

"The whole thing has blown open, Mohammed. These people know about the Guild, and I believe this redhead knows all about us."

Just then, the others returned from their search. They all looked grim and shaken. Madame Maude introduced Mohammed to those who didn't know who he was, and Penny gave him a brief rundown of recent events. Most of them.

"Well, thanks to God for one thing," he said. "I am glad that one of the women survived. Had I known, I would have stayed to render aid. But I assumed that both of them were dead, so I rushed to prevent what would surely come next. However, I'm afraid I may have—"

The front door banged open and Tom Dart crossed the foyer and burst into the Viewing Room.

"Hey," he said, "what's going on in—" Then he saw Mohammed. Ignoring the other occupants of the room, he pulled his gun from its holster and drew a bead on the man's head.

"*There* you are, you sonofabitch."

"Now, settle down," Penny said, holding up her hands. "Before you do anything rash, you'll want to hear what Madame Maude has to say."

Dart glared at her. He and Penny Carter had an unpleasant history. It was no longer an active topic, thanks largely to the Bay Phantom, but it had not been forgotten.

"This man killed Alvin Branch!" he snapped. "I was chasing him and I lost him. I looked around for—Well, to hell with that! I came here to check on things, and here the sonofabitch is! And what are all the rest of you doing in here?"

"Alvin Branch was working with the Guild!" Madame Maude said.

"She's telling the truth," said Penny. "She is absolutely on the level."

"And I'm supposed to take *your* word for that?" Dart said, angry and incredulous. "What the hell are *you* doing here, anyhow?" He turned to his Bay Phantom comrades. "Shorty? Gladys? What's this all about?"

"Leave them alone," Penny snapped. "They didn't bring me here. What do you *think* I'm doing? I'm protecting my interests! Doing *your* job!"

"Why you—You're dirty as hell, Penny Carter!"

"Well, no shit, Sherlock! You've never heard of a gang war? And if you think *I'm* dirty, wait'll you hear what the Guild has been up to."

Dart, fed up with Penny for the moment, turned his gaze to Madame Maude.

"Just who the hell are you, really?"

Penny said, "She's a cop, for Christ's sake. Check on her, you'll find out."

"I will."

"Do. First, listen to what she has to say, then check all you want."

"All right. But this sonofabitch is under arrest. And he's damn lucky I don't just put a slug into his head right here and now."

"Oh, settle down, you're not impressing anybody. If you didn't suspect I was telling the truth, you'd have done something already. And there's something else you need to know about."

"What else could there possibly be?" Tom asked.

"We found a kitchen upstairs," she said. "It was almost completely cleared out. But the Embalmer got a good look at what was there a few days ago, and he told me all about it. Knowing what I knew, a couple of things we found up there that we might otherwise have overlooked took on a very distressing significance.

"Kebler and Till were living here, and having their meals prepared in the kitchen. To put it bluntly, they've been eating human beings."

Dart was, for once, speechless. He turned to Gladys Turnbull. She just nodded.

Madame Maude, who was hearing this information for the first time, was obviously hit hard by it, but didn't seem terribly shocked.

"I realize now," she said, shaking her head slowly, "that I have suspected something of the sort, but I never dared articulate it, even in my own mind. I have no problem believing it now."

"So, who the hell are you, really?" Tom Dart asked again. "And what the hell are you up to?"

"I've been after Kebler and Till for years," Madame Maude said. "I work for the International Criminal Police Commission. A few people refer to it as Interpol, but that isn't official. I'm French, and I was part of the conference that founded the organization in 1923.

"And it was in 1923 that Kebler and Till first surfaced in Berlin.

"Keep in mind, that was an eventful time in the Weimar Republic, for both good and ill. The economy had been wrecked by the War and its aftermath, and was only just starting to come out of the hyperinflation that followed the war and the Treaty of Versailles.

"They could be called salad days, I suppose, but they spawned a certain level of decadence and a high degree of hedonism. Berlin in the 1920s! All things to all people. Bauhaus, Fritz Lang, Brecht and Weill, and so forth. Those things were on the bright, shiny side of the 'decadence.' However, there was a very dark underside, typified by the likes of Kebler and Till.

"They had begun their Transatlantic Patriots movement a year or so after the war ended. In the beginning, it was merely an anti-Semitic, nationalist group that paid lip service to strengthening the ties between the 'Aryan' peoples of Germany, England, and the United States. 'Aryan' being a word with no clear meaning, that could be redefined to include or exclude almost anything.

"But Kebler and Till weren't interested in politics, not really. And, while they did accept many notions of racial purity that were current, this did not seem to be their true focus, either. Their Patriots Guild served as their entree into the loftier European social circles. In 1923, they opened their doors in what could arguably be called the cultural capitol of Europe—Berlin. This, I believe, was where they first found customers for their ghastly wares."

"Tell us about those wares," Penny said.

"So-called 'French postcards,' sent from Hell by Jack the Ripper. Horrible pictures, dreadful things. Oh, they had the ordinary kind, the sort that I gather they've been selling here in Mobile. They could make an excellent living on those alone, and nobody would care very much. But it was the *others*, the 'special' pictures, that drew our attention.

"Young girls murdered and butchered before the cameras! Awful, bloody scenes. Of course, the pictures could have been 'staged,' but—" She shook her head emphatically. "They were too authentic for that. When one has seen enough dead bodies at murder scenes, one develops a certain sense for such things. Photographic experts said the same thing.

"As we would eventually learn, Kebler and Till were involved in the white slave trade as well, and that is how they procured their 'models.' As for the 'technicians' who produced the pictures, rumor has it that they employed such demonic degenerates as Peter Kürten and Fritz Haarmann. Both of whom, now that I think of it, were reputed to have eaten the flesh of their victims.

"They were known to frequently entertain Aleister Crowley as well, and that may have been the genesis of their interest in the occult.

"These ghastly pictures of theirs sold for unbelievable sums of money. And the perpetrators enjoyed protection from the highest quarters! I have intelligence suggesting that members of most of the old royal families of Europe were among their most ardent customers! And they were affiliated with Adolf Hitler and his gang as well. I understand that many of their most valued consumers are to be found in the upper echelons of the Nazi party.

"Having established themselves in Berlin, they sought new lands. First, London, where they spent a year. Then they moved again. It was in Paris that I attached myself to them, as it were.

"I had learned that they were interested in the occult. They are a superstitious pair, and rather cowardly at bottom. They were constantly seeking advice from the 'spirit world,' patronizing any number of quack mediums. I introduced myself to them and made myself... *useful*. I told them the things they wished to hear, and there was an added benefit: It seemed that seances and psychic demonstrations and the like attracted the kind of people they were interested in cultivating. Rich, with grandiose ideas about themselves and the world, and very little practical sense. I had to be careful, of course. I couldn't let them know what I suspected."

"So you pretended to be a psychic," Dart said, intrigued in spite of himself. "How did you pull that off?"

"Well, I *am* psychic, a little bit. Not enough to have divined what they were really up to. I knew there was a terrible darkness about them, but— Well, I have a bit of ability, as I say, and what I don't have, I know how to fake.

"I have a reputation for being rather flighty. I worked hard to create the appearance. My head is in the spirit world, you see, and I'm barely aware of what goes on around me. There is value in camouflaging one's true self."

Mirabelle nodded. That much she understood well.

"Still, they never let me get close to anything. When they expressed their intention to move their operation to America, I thought I might turn it into an opportunity. They felt that it would be a safer place for them. Were there to be any further conflicts in Europe, even if the United States once again became involved, it was likely that, as in the Great War, the fighting would remain in Europe and never reach American shores.

"I decided to use my influence to steer them in a direction of my own choosing. I volunteered to research available properties for them, and that is what led me to the story of the Grandines, who had purchased Mauvais Rêve from the estate of the original owner.

"The Grandines were secret abolitionists. I learned all about it in a book I found years ago at a shop in Paris."

"I have the same book," Penny interjected. "Read it when I was a girl."

"Whatever the hell you are now," Dart mumbled.

"They owned both of the houses," Madame Maude went on. "Mauvais Rêve, and the one we are sitting in now, having built this one shortly after they purchased the first. And they made a secret tunnel connecting them.

At the time, there was no Joachim Street; this building was at the edge of a wooded area, and was used as a hiding place. Fugitive slaves could come and go from here at night. Both houses had cellars that were well-concealed.

"In the years since then, after the Civil War and Emancipation, both houses were sold to others. This house was built onto, to the point where it now almost touches the house I've been renting.

"I was delighted to find that both properties could be made available for lease or purchase to anyone willing to pay extortionate sums of cash. Money was not a problem for Kebler and Till."

"That's how I first knew about this thing," Penny said. "In a roundabout way, I actually own these houses, and the realty company you dealt with was one of mine. The whole deal piqued my interest, since I knew the history, though I didn't know how significant it would become—Well, go on, please."

"I used my influence," Maude continued. "Suggested the Joachim Street section of the old Grandine estate to their agent, and Mauvais Rêve for me. I was pleased when they accepted the arrangement. That way, I might finally be able to obtain some evidence. They never knew this property was connected to the house I rented for myself."

"And you brought them right here," Mirabelle said angrily. "To Mobile. Knowing, or believing, that they were killers."

"They were determined to come here! It was their idea, not mine. What else could I do? Shoot them down in the street?"

"Why not?"

"That is not how I have been taught to do things. I work for Interpol, I am not a masked vigilante—or an unmasked one, for that matter. These *criminals* must be dealt with by the law, for all to see, or nothing is accomplished." She sighed and shook her heard. "That said—if I had known what I was actually dealing with—I don't know. Perhaps you're right."

"No, I'm sorry. You're doing it the right way. I'm just upset."

Madame Maude nodded. "I knew they were producing the pornography, and I believed they were killing the girls, but I never dreamed they were doing... all this. I should have asked more questions. Why were they always connected with funeral homes and other places of the dead? I believed it was because of Till, his upbringing. It was the business his family had been in, you see. He had grown up with it. I never really saw anything suggestive in that. He owned an interest in a mortuary in Berlin, and a crematorium in Paris. I suppose a lot of evidence went up *that* chimney...

"At any rate, we all set up here a few months ago. The tunnel had been closed off, but not completely filled in. I suppose this was done at some point after the Grandines sold their properties. Mohammed and I located the entrance, down in the cellar."

"The Embalmer mentioned that he saw some kind of reference to a tunnel when he got in here," Gladys said. "If their plans hadn't been upset by his breaking in, they probably would have either blocked if off completely, or used it against you somehow."

Tom had listened to all of this absolutely stone-faced. Now he turned to Mohammed.

"And what do *you* have to say for yourself?"

"They're crazy," said Mohammed, "but not stupid. I did small jobs for the gang, but never really gained their full trust. I don't know if they had any reason to suspect us of treachery—perhaps they were just making sure. But they had that detective, Branch, shadowing us. He discovered our end of the tunnel, and probably other things as well. He certainly found out what we were really up to. He got into our cellar today and planted evidence against us—those poor women. When you met with him, he had returned to headquarters to draw up an application for a warrant—that was my surmise. He would have had no trouble obtaining it, of course, and we would have been in some very hot water.

"He didn't know I was right behind him. I observed him leaving after he planted that ghastly evidence, and I followed him."

"And then you shot him down," Dart said stonily. "In the back."

"Detective Dart, you didn't see what I saw from my spot at the window. He was reaching for a pistol that was taped to the underside of his desk. That's why I shot him. Obviously, he felt that *you* were coming too close to the operation."

Dart's eyes got wide, but the rest of his face remained immobile. Memories of his recent conversations with Branch returned to him, but they seemed new and sinister. Anomalies he had ignored at the time suddenly started making horrible, depressing sense.

He had to pull himself together. His feelings and uncertainties didn't matter. Penny Carter was nuts, but he believed she was telling the truth. He believed Madame Maude. That was what he had to deal with.

"Okay," he said through gritted teeth. "Okay. I can't report any of this, not just yet. If we're lucky, nobody around here saw anything. Let's just look this place over, then lock it down. Maybe there are some clues left as

"I was pleased when they accepted the arrangement."

to where the rest of them went. I'll figure out what to do about it *officially* later on.

"All those bodies downstairs will just have to stay where they are for the time being," Penny said.

"Bodies?" Dart repeated.

Penny nodded. "About a dozen."

Dart just shook his head.

In fact, eleven members of the gang were dead. They lay strewn across the floor of the cellar, in approximately seventy-four completely detached pieces. The two hapless assassins brought the total to thirteen.

"Oh, and there's another one over in the other house," Penny added. "And there was a live one too."

"Fantastic."

Tom accompanied Mohammed, about whom he still had mixed feelings, back over to the other house to check out the dead girl in the cellar.

While he was there, he used the telephone to place a transatlantic call— to the headquarters of the International Criminal Police Commission in Vienna, Austria. Mohammed offered no information, no phone numbers, no names. He wanted Dart to do it all on his own, so there would be no suspicion of trickery. Dart obtained the phone number from a friend of his who worked for the Department of Justice in Washington, and he worked his way through the bureaucracy in Vienna until he reached the man he needed to speak with: a Doctor Johannes Schober, who confirmed Madame Maude's story, and offered his assistance.

Tom thought that was a good idea—*if* it could be done without involving anyone in the police department or the city government of Mobile. He gave the ICPC head a short briefing on what he had discovered.

"I can't trust anybody in my own department," he concluded. "I have no way of knowing who has been bought off and who hasn't."

If Alvin, of all people, had been corrupt, how could Dart trust *anybody*?

Schober, who had a deep understanding of politics, crime, and money, agreed. He said the ICPC would send an operative to Mobile as soon as possible.

Madame Maude was left alone in the Viewing Room. The others were exploring the house again, looking for anything they might have missed earlier.

She walked around rather aimlessly, examining furniture and fittings as though they were rare and puzzling artifacts from a mysterious, lost civilization. She was feeling a bit stunned. It seemed that her long quest had finally come to an end—almost. The criminals were exposed, but they were still at large, and might escape justice after all.

She was running her fingers back and forth on the lower edge of a gilt picture frame, when a faint noise came to her from the other side of the room. She turned around.

The curtains covering a little alcove rustled, then parted, and Johnny Till hopped out from behind them on one foot. In his right hand, held like a club, was a jointed wooden leg, complete from foot to upper thigh.

"So, you didn't get away after all," Madame Maude said.

"No, one of those bastards shot me. Hit my artificial leg, then the bullet ricocheted up into my *non*-artificial hip. I had to hide and patch it up. Hurts like a sonofabitch."

"Well, that's good, anyhow."

He hopped forward and swung at her with the artificial leg. She ducked out of the way.

"Hold still, you dirty slag," he snarled. "You're responsible for all this!"

"I am not dirty. I do not know what a slag is."

"You know what *dead* is," he said, hopping closer and swinging the leg again.

"Yes, but you don't seem capable of making me that way. I think you'll get there before I do."

She grabbed the leg and yanked on it, pulling Till off-balance. He hopped frantically, struggling to remain upright, and let go of the leg. He managed to avoid a spill, and he now stood, teetering slightly from side to side, glaring at Madame Maude.

"Well, that was ridiculously easy," she said.

"Oh, I never meant to kill you with *that* thing. I just wanted you closer and unsuspecting."

Till suddenly lurched forward and bit Irene Maude on the neck.

She pulled back, and bashed him over the head with his own wooden leg. This knocked him to the floor. She flung the wooden leg across the room, produced a little revolver from inside her jacket, and aimed it at Till.

She touched the spot on her neck. The skin was broken, a little chunk of it was missing, but the wound was not deep. There was only a little dab of blood on her fingers when she looked at them.

Till sat on the floor where he had fallen, smiling up at her, his jaw working slightly.

"Something is amusing?" she said.

He nodded and swallowed.

"You," she said, "are under arrest. Do not attempt to resist further."

"All right," Till said. "Shit, I give up. You may get me to trial, Maude, but a conviction is something else. And I'll tell you one more thing. My teeth are coated with poison. I have been immunized against it. You have not. You'll be dead before this day is over, and there's *nothing* you can do about it. They'll never find the poison. It'll look like a plain old coronary. And I will not reveal any information about my organization. What organization? Prove that one exists, and that I am part of it! I may very well end up walking free, after all is said and done."

"I believe you," said Madame Maude. "And Miss Darcy had the correct idea about you, I think."

She nodded, touching the wound on her neck again with her free hand.

"Therefore," she said, "you are *not* under arrest. Remember what I told you earlier."

She squeezed the trigger. The small-caliber bullet entered Till's head squarely between his eyes. He brushed a hand across his face, as though shooing away a fly.

Then he died. He slumped forward a bit, but remained in his seated position on the floor.

"Too late for self-defense," Madame Maude remarked, "and too soon for revenge. Ah, well."

Drawn by the shot, Mirabelle and the others rushed back to the Viewing Room.

"Who the hell is this?" Mirabelle demanded.

"Johnny Till, of course" said Madame Maude.

"What have you done?" Piranha asked.

"I should think it obvious. I am still holding the smoking gun, you see."

"We could have interrogated him," Mirabelle said.

"Are you not ever satisfied?" Madame Maude said pettishly. "Anyhow, do you think he would have talked?"

"I didn't even know him."

"I did. I finally did. And you were right the first time."

Mirabelle, never one to fret over spilled milk, shrugged and said, "Shit. Okay, then."

Madame Irene Maude was taken to Providence Hospital by Shorty Red. The emergency room physician could find nothing wrong with her—apart from a minor wound on her neck, which he easily treated—though she was obviously weak and in distress. Blood tests were ordered, hurriedly conducted, and showed nothing amiss. She complained of a headache and a dry mouth. Shorty persuaded them to keep her for observation.

She would pass away two hours later. She gave every appearance of having succumbed to a heart attack.

Searching further, the Phantom's friends and Doctor Piranha discovered a large, hidden room at the back of the house. Mirabelle had noticed a slight misalignment of the wood paneling in one of the pantries. This proved to be a concealed door. It had three heavy locks, all of which were open; the head honchos must not have had time to secure it before everything hit the fan. The room had been soundproofed and the door was made of steel-plated oak.

There wasn't much in there, but what they found suggested that the worst might be yet to come.

Mirabelle, Piranha, Gladys and Penny gathered in the Viewing Room to discuss it.

"I found a map of downtown," said Mirabelle. "It looks like tomorrow night's parade route has been marked out on it. And I found some other things too. Some fragments of notes, and a few more gas cylinders. Two of them contained sulfur dichloride. And another one had ethelyne in it."

"They were making $C_4H_8Cl_2S$," said Piranha. "Using the Depretz method to synthesize it."

"Looks that way," Mirabelle agreed.

"Wait, now," said Gladys, "what are we talking about here?"

"Sulfur mustard," Mirabelle said grimly. "In other words, *mustard gas.*

And, judging by all the space in there, and the evidence that there were a great many more canisters at one time, they synthesized a *lot* of it."

Tom Dart stopped back by Donner-Purdy before returning to his office.

"Rickert needs to keep out of sight until I can figure out a way to clear him," he said. "It should be doable once we round up the rest of these bastards, but I can't do anything right now."

"He went to the hospital with that girl, Alice," said Gladys. "She's not well."

"Good, he can be useful for once in his life, then. I've gotta go back to headquarters and deal with this shit—*somehow.* I'll be in touch."

The police department was in total disarray, following the raid on the property room and now the death of Branch. Nobody knew whether or not the two incidents were related.

The front of the building had been boarded up pending permanent repairs.

Tom Dart filed a report on the murder of Alvin Branch and his own subsequent actions. The unidentified shooter had gotten away, and there were no leads as to his identity or current whereabouts.

Dart found the pistol, a .22 with a noise suppressor attached, that had been taped on the underside of Branch's desk, along with other incriminating evidence. For example, a heavily-annotated floor plan of Mauvais Rêve, with various points of ingress marked out in red ink. One of these led into the cellar where the dead girl and the living one had been discovered.

Tom held back most of the information he had, preferring to keep it to himself until this mess was closer to resolution. He knew he didn't dare show his hand until the scales were tipped overwhelmingly in his favor. He knew what the city officials on the gang's payroll would do to him if he did anything rash.

He also knew that, once the whole truth came out, Branch's reputation would be destroyed. He still wasn't sure how he felt about that.

Goddamn it, Alvin, he thought. *Goddamn you. Goddamn this whole goddamn business.*

In the days to come, a search of Branch's automobile would yield ropes and a gag. It would be determined that these had been used to secure the unconscious Alice Tague when she and the deceased girl were transported to Mauvais Rêve by Branch. Hairs found on the rear floorboard and in the trunk would match samples from the heads of the unfortunate women.

It would also become apparent that Alice Tague had been drugged and confronted with actors made up to resemble Madame Maude and Mohammed. Maude and Mohammed would have been looking at a murder one rap, with a living witness to bolster it.

✳✳✳

The Friends of the Phantom, as Gladys had humorously suggested they call themselves, moved their operations, such as they were, into Mauvais Rêve, making use of the tunnel to continue their search of the funeral home.

Late that evening, an ICPC man, who was based in New Orleans, arrived to begin his own discreet investigation in the Donner-Purdy house. Madame Maude had passed away by this time. The agent received the news with a grim nod and a flash of strong emotion deep in his eyes. Then he got to work, helping the other sift through what little was left on the premises.

All they knew about the gang's other base was that it was north of downtown Mobile, and that covered a hell of a lot of ground. Shorty Red had volunteered to work his way through some of the territory, keeping an eye out for anything suggestive. He made periodic reports by telephone.

He obtained no leads on the gang's whereabouts, but he learned interesting things. Things that involved methane and dead people.

Mirabelle took one of the reports over the phone and relayed the disturbing information to the others:

"A cemetery in Saraland was—Well, they're saying 'vandalized,' but it goes way beyond that. Graves were opened and their contents... taken. And there's another report of a similar incident out in Semmes."

"Holy hell," said Penny.

"Also, an unspecified quantity of methane was stolen from an industrial lab where they were doing research into methanogens."

"Into *what*?" Gladys asked.

"Methanogens," Mirabelle repeated. "microorganisms that produce methane as a metabolic byproduct in anoxic conditions."

"Oh, yeah, right. *Those* manothogens."

"Mustard gas and methane," Mirabelle said musingly. "Whatever they're planning, it won't be good."

Penny Carter took an opportunity to have a private word with Doctor Piranha.

"There's something I need from you," she said.

"That seems to be the nature of our relationship. One of us needs something, the other supplies it. Unlike most human interaction, it is beautifully straightforward and uncomplicated. State your case, Penny, and I'll do my best for you."

"Joe Perrone has had a lot of dealings with a fellow named Doctor Ambrose Atticus," Penny explained. "So I had him followed, whenever it was possible. He goes over to a little private clinic in Baldwin County two or three times every week. I had a hunch it might have something to do with the old man Joe rescued at that Klan rally last year. I knew, from interrogating one of Hector Sams' men, that Hector believed this old man had been responsible for what happened to his brother. We know that wasn't so, but it was true that the old guy had been seeing Gerald in the capacity of a faith healer or some such thing around the time *another party* was performing the experiments that would eventually turn him into the Werewolf. Hector blamed this man. I knew he hadn't done it, but I thought he might have some insight. I thought he might know some way to bring Gerald back to normal, after I had used the Werewolf to mop up the new gang."

"Bring him back to *normal*?"

"Yes! Don't act so shocked. I do have redeeming qualities. I just don't allow myself to be ruled by them. Anyhow, I tried to put the snatch on the old man, if he was there, which it turned out he was—but something went wrong. My crew isn't sure what happened. My point being, you're the only one who can do anything for Gerald."

"Yes, and I have a feeling you aren't the only woman who will insist on it. Of course I will. But what about this old man? Who is he?"

"I never learned his name. And I don't know where he is now, though I have developed some suspicions."

Some time later, Mirabelle found Doctor Piranha standing on the second floor veranda. He was leaning on the railing, looking out over what he could see of the city from here. She took a place beside him and looked up at the sky. Gladys had gone to join Shorty on his thus-far fruitless search for the Guild's new headquarters.

Mirabelle had had a long talk with Gladys, who knew about the Markham business from the Embalmer. What Gladys didn't know was that the recent antics attributed to the Bay Phantom had actually been the Embalmer's work.

"He's gone off the deep end," she said to Piranha. "We've got to find him and fix him."

"Yes, we must. You can blame me if you like."

She sighed, reminding herself painfully of Perrone. Of Joe.

"What good would *that* do?" she said. "I could blame myself too, I suppose. I could blame *him.* I could blame your parents, or Penny Carter, or President Hoover, or the Man in the Moon. There's nothing to be gained from that."

"You're right."

They were silent for a while, just looking up at the sky.

"Well, Miss Darcy," Piranha said presently.

"Well, indeed, Doctor Piranha. They have Mister Perrone. Gladys saw a couple members of the gang carry 'Markham' out and put him and another man into a truck. Is he playing them, or has he overplayed his hand? Does he even know what he's doing? Is he even still alive?"

Silence for more than a minute.

"There's an east wind coming, Miss Darcy," Piranha said.

"Tell me something I don't know. Hell is empty and all the devils are here."

"To whom, exactly, are you referring?"

She thought about it for a moment.

"I don't know," she said.

CHAPTER THIRTY-EIGHT
FAT TUESDAY

February 9, 1932

Rickey Harvard was roaming around downtown on Fat Tuesday evening, with no real aim in mind, taking in Mardi Gras without enjoyment. He was just about out of money, and had no job prospects at all. More and more lately, he had been thinking about being a criminal. It would probably be good work, if he could find it. He had no idea how to get started, though.

He wandered along Saint Francis Street, feeling extravagantly sorry for himself. He stuck a hand in his pants pocket and felt the two dimes that represented all his worldly wealth.

Then something caught his eye. A tall redhead was walking up the sidewalk on the other side of the street. She looked awfully familiar to Rickey.

Now, where do I know her from? Wait a minute, she looks just like—oh, gosh, could it be?

By golly, it was! The redhead from the picture cards! He was sure of it.

She was accompanied by an odd group of people: A little colored girl, very dark-skinned, wearing a close-fitting pair of black trousers and a black blouse, with boots and a little backpack; a strange, fishy-looking man; another man Rickey thought he recognized as a police detective; a short, blonde woman; and an oddball decked out in a dress suit and a long cape.

Without knowing what he might accomplish by doing so, Rickey crossed the street, and started following them. It seemed like some kind of a sign. Maybe the good luck charm he had found was starting to work. He trailed the redhead and her friends, staying about a quarter of a block behind them. Maybe they were going someplace to take some more pictures! That stuff was against the law, so it was crime. And it would be an excellent kind of crime for Rickey to get into.

He had never seen what a colored woman looked like without clothes; he wondered if they had all the same parts as white girls.

He trailed them two blocks east on Saint Francis Street, and around the corner onto Royal Street.

"Hey! Rickey! How's the boy?"

Someone was calling to him from the doorway of Mick's Hot Dogs as he passed. Rickey slowed down and looked.

Of all people, it was Eddie. This was a fine time for him to pop up.

"Oh, hey, Eddie," Rickey said, shifting his eyes back to the group he'd been following. "I'm kinda busy right—"

"I been looking for you" Eddie said, stepping forward and putting a hand on Rickey's arm to stop him.

"Well, you found me. What's going on?"

"It's about my bosses from the funeral home."

"What?" Rickey asked, hope rising in his breast. He instantly forgot about his quarry. "They changed their minds? They want to hire me after all?"

"Well—Not *that*, exactly. They had to close down the funeral home. I don't know all the facts about that, but there's a *new* job. I think you could help with it, and I'm sure the Bosses will think so too."

"Really? What is it? How much does it pay?"

"It's easier to show it to you than to say it. You just follow me, Rickey, and we'll fix you right up. Your troubles are over."

He followed Eddie over to Dauphin Street, just west of Bienville Square, where the street was torn up.

"Hey, did you get a job with the city street crew?" Rickey asked, on the verge of being impressed.

"You'll see."

Eddie walked right up to the edge of the street, where all the pavement had been torn up. There was a wooden ladder there, propped against the lip of the excavated area, leading down into the darkness below the level of the street.

"I don't see nobody around here," Rickey said, starting to become a little nervous. "They take Fat Tuesday off or something?"

Eddie started down the ladder, and Rickey followed.

It was like another world down there; a world of dirt and busted-up concrete and huge metal pipes and deep, black shadows.

"The Boss is down here," Eddie said, "he's doing some overtime work."

"Oh, I see," said Rickey, who did not. He was starting to wonder if this was such a good idea. He remembered all the misgivings he had about Eddie, and they began to loom large, down there in the darkness under the streets.

The walked into one big tunnel, and soon they came to three smaller ones that branched off of it. Eddie took the one to the far left, and Rickey followed. It was pretty dark down here, but there was a faint, shimmery light somewhere ahead, probably at the end of this section of tunnel.

Soon, they emerged into a large chamber, lit with a string of small, dim bulbs, hung from the walls and ceiling.

There were rows and rows of metal tanks, grouped together according to size and color, and weird machines attached to the tanks, with rotating gears and gauges with quivering needles. Parts of it looked like the insides of a gigantic clock.

Off to one side were three large barrels, lashed together, with bundles of wires coming out of the tops. All the wires were twisted together into one very thick bundle, which led to a black box on the floor.

It looked like the headquarters of some kind of mad scientist, like in *Frankenstein*.

Oh, God, Rickey thought, *that's what they're doing! Making monsters!* They probably used dead bodies from the funeral home, just like the doctor, whose name Rickey couldn't remember, did in the movie when he made Frankenstein.

A man was standing with his back to Rickey and Eddie, fiddling with one of the Frankenstein machines.

"Look what I found," Eddie announced. "This is that boy you wanted to get back. I caught him for you, all by myself."

The man turned around. He was mean-looking, with a puffy face and a small, unpleasant-looking moustache.

"Well, that's something, I suppose," said Hans Kebler. "Though it no longer matters, since Donner-Purdy is a lost cause. He probably didn't see anything important anyhow, and no doubt lacks the wit to make anything of it if he did. But one must be careful, Eddie. I have tried to impress that upon you. *You're* the one who brought him into the funeral home. Now, bring him over here and let's kill him."

"Are we going to eat him?" Eddie asked.

The man made a face. "You can, if you want. I prefer more refined fare."

The intrepid band that had scoured the downtown streets all day was comprised of Mirabelle, Gladys, Doctor Piranha, the Black Embalmer, and Penny Carter. Shorty Red had elected to continue his search to the area to the north of the city.

The Embalmer had turned up back at Mauvais Rêve and joined the others on their reconnaissance. He was clad in a dark suit and a long, black cape. Today of all days, he probably wouldn't attract much attention.

For most of the day, they had walked the parade route, back and forth, looking for anything suggestive. It proved to be a frustrating, impossible task, since they didn't know what they were looking for, nor did they know what to filter out of their observations. Everything looked suspicious, nothing looked significant.

Two parades had gone off without incident. The third and final parade would soon begin.

Tom Dart, having pursued such inquiries as he'd been able to, and come up with nothing, joined them as the last parade got underway. They could hear all the hubbub coming from blocks away, on Government Street. All of them were weary. They stopped for a while on Royal Street, leaning against a wall as the floats appeared and began their procession.

Mirabelle watched, stone-faced, as the lead float, carrying the Krewe of the Paper Bag Girls passed. A dozen or so idiotic debutantes in black dresses, with brown grocery sacks pulled over their heads, stood and waved to the crowd.

A few more floats followed. They all seemed just alike to the watchers.

Then came the horror.

They smelled it before they saw it.

"Jesus, what is that stench?" Penny said, pinching her nose.

Then they heard the screaming.

Then they saw the float.

Much later, Gladys Turnbull would sit in front of her typewriter in her glassed-in office in the *Mobile Press* building, trying to dredge up some combination of words that would adequately describe the lumbering horror that rounded the corner from Government Street, three blocks away, to crawl up the middle of Royal Street.

Most of what she came up with would be unpublishable, and even then did not convey a tenth part of the dreadful impact the grisly spectacle had on her and the other parade-goers. She realized that most of it would have to be left to the readers' imaginations, with the sincere hope that none could possibly be depraved enough to come close to the reality of it.

It was, like the other floats, a flatbed truck, being pulled by a dark gray cab. The trailer carried a riser that was draped in black cloth. That was the first thing she noticed as the thing rounded the corner. Then she saw the boxes. Large rectangular crates of some kind, mounted upright around the edges of the float.

As the float drew closer, it became apparent that these crates were actually caskets. Warped, dilapidated, streaked with red mud, as though they had only recently been dug up. Some of the lids were hanging open a few inches, and Gladys saw human remains in various stages of decay. Some were virtually mummified with age, while others appeared disturbingly fresh.

All five senses were engaged. The stench was so bad she could taste it, feel it on her hands and face. She closed her mouth tight and breathed shallowly through her nose, to avoid taking too much of it into her.

The float reached the point where Gladys and the others stood.

Above the caskets, on top of the float, were a group of men in long, white coats, wearing grotesque, flabby-featured face masks that appeared to be made of pale, soft leather, stitched together up the sides. They reached into large baskets and tossed objects to the crowds along the sidewalks.

Not moon pies, not colorful beads.

Hands. Human hands, severed at the wrists.

Their authenticity was confirmed by the Black Embalmer, who caught one in midair and examined it.

"Even *I* would not go *that* far," the Black Embalmer said solemnly, tossing the hand to a smiling little girl standing on the sidewalk to his left. "This is nothing but overkill."

By now, a number of parade goers had begun to panic, screaming and trying to flee. All of this was more than bad enough. And so, of course, it got worse.

The krewe members turned from their baskets of hands and picked up submachine guns.

✻✻✻

The float slowed down. Standing toward the front, slightly apart from the ghastly krewe, was a man in a heavy leather apron and a welder's mask.

He held a microphone close to the bottom edge of the mask and spoke: "Here we are!" he said, his voice amplified by two large speakers mounted at the rear of the trailer. "Fat Tuesday, also known as 'Shrove Tuesday.' The day before Ash Wednesday. And, by tomorrow, that is what all of you will be—ashes!"

"Hoo-boy!" Gladys said. She and the others were walking north on the sidewalk now, easily pacing the slow-moving float.

"Today is the day you should be considering your sins," said the man in the welding mask, "and preparing yourself for your penance during Lent. Instead, you are out here celebrating your own foolish excesses.

"Well, you need not worry about Lent; your penance has already been arranged. Your sins cannot be forgiven. You had in your midst something bright and beautiful, and a few among you chose to reject it, destroy it. Christ died one death for the sins of all. Tonight, you will die hundreds of deaths for the sins of a few.

"Your death will come from below, from the very earth itself, and you will not escape. You will burn and you will suffer! There are secret places under your feet, they almost destroyed you once, and they've been waiting. They're coming for you, I'm here to tell you now! You will *all* pay!"

"*From below...*" Mirabelle repeated. "Oh, shit."

"What?" said Piranha.

"Tunnels," said Mirabelle.

"What?"

"*Tunnels.* The Embalmer said something about tunnels. Plural. There is a tunnel running between those two houses, and that kept us from wondering too much about it. But that's just *one* tunnel. The gang was interested in something else, some *other* tunnels. Maybe they've discovered *your* tunnels. The ones you used and the Phantom uses now! And I'll bet they're going to flood them with mustard gas. But where would they be?"

Piranha frowned and rubbed his chin. "Close to here, I would think. So many people, concentrated within a space of a few blocks—And they wouldn't have to occupy the entire network, they'd just need a central point from which to launch the attack."

"Dauphin Street!" Mirabelle said, snapping her fingers. "All that excavation over there! That could be their access point. If they've been buying off City Hall, it would be simple to get control of a project like that."

"I've got to get down there,' said Piranha. "If they're using that spot as a staging area, I can still stop them."

"*We* can. Come on, follow me."

Leaving the others to deal with the nightmarish float, they wormed their way through the crowd almost a block south, stopping at the entrance door of a small restaurant.

"There's an alley behind this place," Mirabelle said. "We can cut through."

The door was closed and locked. Piranha smashed the glass with a forearm, and kicked what remained out of the way. He and Mirabelle ducked inside, ran through the deserted cafe to the back, and exited via the rear door.

"That's the sonofabitch that stole my gimmick!" said the Embalmer. "All right, I've had enough. Time to put these dogs to sleep."

From inside his cloak he produced a mask and hat, which he quickly donned.

The Mummifier ranted on, as the float crawled ever so slowly northward.

"And see this pitiful thing tied to the board beneath my feet! Who do you suppose it is? Why, it is the Bay Phantom! Yes, that's who it is! The Bay Phantom! And a poor, deluded black boy who dared to stand with him! See what they have come to!"

Lashed to the front of the float with rough ropes were two figures. A pair of men, one black, one white. Gladys had glimpsed them before, and assumed that they were just two more corpses. But now she could see that they were moving ever so slightly.

And the white man, now that she really looked, seemed familiar.

The Embalmer glanced at his companions and saw that Gladys, Tom, and Penny wore looks of sheer horror on their faces. The Embalmer wore a mask on his—and behind that, a look of grim determination.

"Some of you will be fortunate, though, and die immediately," the Mummifier declared. "You are the lucky ones!" He waved a hand at the men with the machine guns. "Open fire, boys!"

Triggers were depressed. An awful chattering began, and bullets ripped into fabric and flesh up and down the sidewalks on both sides.

"I'm gonna take care of this!" the Embalmer shouted. "Draw their fire!"

Gladys, Penny, and Tom ducked around behind a pair of mailboxes, drew their weapons, and started shooting at the masked krewe members. The villains ducked and fired back, as the spectators standing nearby cleared out of the way as best they could. Rounds from the machine guns peppered the heavy steel mailboxes, throwing sparks. The Mummifier dashed to the rear of the float, out of the line of fire.

The crowds on both sides of the street surged first one way, then another, but they were too densely packed at this point for anyone to get anywhere. Fresh corpses, chewed up by slugs, stood upright among the living, unable to fall. No one dared run out into the street, so they pressed back against the glass fronts of the stores and offices. Something would have to give pretty soon.

Like glass. And human flesh.

The Embalmer hopped up on the running board of the cab and pulled the door open. The driver looked around, startled. The last thing he ever saw on this earth was the masked and cloaked form of the Bay Phantom, and he passed into the Great Beyond believing that the famous crime fighter had cut his throat with a butcher knife.

The Embalmer dragged the body out of the cab and let it fall to the street, before getting behind the wheel, applying the brakes, shifting into park, and shutting off the engine.

Then he climbed up onto the roof of the cab and found himself face to face with a badly battered Roy Markham. His face was bruised and his cheeks were glazed with dried blood.

"It *is* you! Markham! Hey, wake up!"

He patted Markham's cheeks a few times, then slapped them.

"Come on, man! Open your eyes! This is serious!"

Markham stirred, and his eyes fluttered open.

"I... can't move," he said.

"Bullshit. Of course you can. Reach down inside and find what you need. You've got reserves you haven't even touched yet."

With his bloody butcher knife, the Embalmer cut the ropes binding the Phantom and the young black man. When the cords fell away, both of them slumped down into seated positions.

"Listen to me," said the Embalmer, taking Markham's chin in his hand. "This is your teachable moment, don't waste it. Right here, *right now*, you need to accept the fact that people who dress up in weird costumes or wear disguises to fight crime without being paid for it *are not like everyone else*! Unless you get that through your head, you will go insane. You don't have to be exhausted. That's for everybody else. You are an *aberration*! Get up and *act* like one!"

"All... All right," said Markham.

"Here, this stuff is yours." The Embalmer removed the hat, the mask, and the cape, and thrust them at Markham. "*You're* the Bay Phantom, I'm not. 'Give me my robe, put on my crown; I have immortal longings in me.' Put this stuff on and *do what you have to do!*"

And he did. He stood, unsteady but tall, and accepted the garments offered to him by his friend, the madman. He put the cloak around his shoulders. As he did so, something happened. Something inside him, something essential and fundamental, began to push against the alien interloper that had made itself at home inside him for the past several days.

"No more Markham," he said, as he prepared to don the mask and hat.

The Embalmer plucked the false moustache from the Phantom's lip. "No more Markham," he repeated.

"Never again. And no more of *this!*" Just before he slipped the mask over his head, he looked the Embalmer in the eye and said, "Thank you. Please take him to safety, if you would." He indicated the limp form of Joe Barrow.

"Absolutely. Now, go get 'em!"

As the Embalmer scooped up Joe Barrow and hopped down to the street, the Bay Phantom climbed up to the pinnacle of the float to confront the dealers in horror and death. The machine guns swung around to cover him. Without a word, he moved forward.

Scores of people would see what happened next, and none of them would ever forget. Most of them would feel transformed, as though they had witnessed a phenomenon belonging to another world—a higher, mythical plane that revealed itself on that day, in that place. It was a puzzling revelation, a fulfillment of a cryptic prophesy, the work of a mysterious higher power, something that happened once in a hundred generations. It was the Miracle at Fatima, the stone rolled away from the empty tomb, the Great Chicago Fire, the Battle of Waterloo.

For years, the eyewitnesses would pick through their memories, searching for hidden meanings, sometimes supplying their own when none could be found. In the weeks ahead, some of them would suddenly find religion, while others would abruptly lose theirs. Many would quit their jobs and seek lives of quiet seclusion, while others would migrate to troubled corners of the country and the world, to pursue charitable work. Criminals would repent and go straight; honest citizens would become thieves.

None of them, not a single one, would remain unchanged.

The machine guns erupted again, chattering madly and spraying lead in the Bay Phantom's direction. Somehow, the masked man ducked and dodged his way through the hail without sustaining so much as a scratch. Bullets pelted his cloak, and two small holes appeared in the crown of his hat, but the man was not touched.

Using fists and feet he disarmed all of the krewe members, then he pitched them, one by one, into the street, where they were dealt with by the agitated crowd. A bit barbaric, perhaps, but these men had chosen to sow the wind; that they should now reap the whirlwind was no more than just.

Soon, the only one left was the Mummifier.

He had retreated to the rear edge of the float. There was nowhere for him to go. The parade goers, transformed into a single, vengeful organism, seethed below him, beckoning. He turned to confront the Phantom.

"I'm not done yet!" he shouted. "I still have this!"

He raised his bizarre weapon and took aim.

The Bay Phantom didn't say a word—just held up his bare right hand, like a traffic cop halting oncoming vehicles.

The Mummifier pressed the trigger.

The projectiles struck the palm of the Phantom's hand and ricocheted off, arcing down and to the sides, embedding themselves in the wood and metal of the float.

That was the moment. Though it was night, it felt as though the sun emerged suddenly from behind a black cloud that had hidden it for an age.

The horror was broken; the Bay Phantom had shattered it with his bare, empty hand.

The unwieldy backpack worn by the Mummifier began to sputter and spark. The man tried to remove it, struggling with the straps, but it was in vain. The backpack erupted in flames, and the Mummifier was engulfed. The villain was nothing now but a ball of fire, listing to the left and to the right, wobbling, juddering closer to the edge of the float. The crowd below him parted just before he toppled over into the street.

"And there," the Embalmer said reverently, "but for the grace of God go I." He and the Phantom's other friends had taken charge of Joe Barrow. The young man seemed to have suffered no permanent harm, and had already regained consciousness.

The Bay Phantom walked to the edge of the float and looked down at the burning lump.

He never said a thing, but in the years to come, spectators would credit him with all manner of poignant, cryptic, or inspirational remarks. Many would be moved to tears by the recollection, their spirits buoyed up by the words of empowerment and consolation. It seemed that each of them had heard whatever it was they needed the Phantom to say to them at that moment.

Voices were raised in raucous cheers, all up and down Royal Street. Screams of terror were forgotten, the Mummifier and his henchmen were history. There would be mourning and painful reckonings in the near future, but for now—for *right now*—the Bay Phantom stood tall, and the people stood with him.

The Phantom raised his arms and nodded his head. He backed slowly toward the other edge of the float.

And then, his work accomplished, the Phantom went limp and toppled backward, off of the float, and fell to the sidewalk below...

Eddie was stronger than he looked. He pinned back Rickey's arms, holding him by the wrists, while Kebler approached.

Rickey closed his eyes tight and started praying, or trying to. He couldn't really think of what he ought to say, what would be likely to get the best and quickest results. He was pretty sure he was about to die, and he would probably come back as an ugly, spooky ghost, and he'd never see the redhead again. All he'd ever be able to do from now on was to rise up out of graves all over town and scare poor people that were just trying to live their lives.

Kebler patted him down, to see if he had any weapons on him, or anything else of interest.

He reached into Rickey's pocket and removed the "good luck charm."

"What is this?" Rickey heard him say. "I've never seen anything quite like it. Looks a bit like one of those old Stanhope balls, but there's a—"

Click!

The insides of Rickey's eyelids lit up red, the way they do when you point your face right at the sun with your eyes closed. He felt heat on his face and heard the man squawk:

"Aoow! What the devil?"

Rickey opened his eyes. The weird guy and Eddie were standing there, blinking, tottering around with their arms stuck out, not really looking at anything.

Like they were blind.

The Lord must have done it. The Lord was all the time striking people blind for one reason or another. Rickey thanked Him sincerely and ran like hell back through the tunnel, towards Dauphin Street.

Behind him, Eddie groped his way around the space, narrowly avoiding a collision with Kebler, and bumping into one of the methane tanks, knocking it over. The nozzle opened up, and the thing started to hiss. Whatever was coming out of it smelled worse than his family's hog pen up in Wisconsin.

"Oh, for gosh sakes," he said. "First I go blind, now this."

He groped around for the toppled tank, found it, and managed to close the valve, after quite a bit of fumbling.

"What did that imp do?" Hans Kebler said. "I am dizzy."

Eddie's vision was starting to come back. Whatever that flash of light had been, the effect from it didn't seem to be permanent. He blinked his eyes furiously until he could see well enough to get around.

... where he was caught by his friends: Tom Dart, Gladys Turnbull, Joe Barrow, the Black Embalmer, and Penny Carter.

Just barely conscious, The Bay Phantom looked up at the faces above him, and, behind his mask, he smiled.

As blackness encroached on him once again, he focused on one of the faces.

"Gladys," he said. "Thank goodness. Please—Please go down to my laboratory and leave a bit of oatmeal for the mouse."

Then he lost consciousness.

"That was a good day's work," the Embalmer declared, apparently to a mailbox on Royal Street. "If I needed a sign, this was it. I know what I have to do. First, though, we must get Paul back in shape so he can help out."

"None of the tunnels actually run under Dauphin Street itself," Mirabelle said, as she and Piranha reached the site of the street work, "but there's a main artery not far to the south. If they got into *that*—"

"Yes, I recall that one. Anything released in there would quickly spread through the whole network."

"And then through the sewers, up into the streets. If they just blew holes in two or three of the junction points—Goddamn medieval drainage system."

They picked their way through the equipment, which stood idle today, and found a wooden ladder that would take them below the pavement.

It didn't look as though much actual work had been going on down here. A lot of excavation, but no obvious repairs. They found what looked like a recently-dug tunnel going south under the block.

"Yep," Mirabelle said, "I think this is it."

They followed the tunnel for about thirty yards before they encountered a dilemma.

"It branches off here and goes in three different directions," Mirabelle said.

"There's no way of knowing which way to go," said Piranha. "There are tracks all over the place. I suppose we can—"

They were interrupted by the sound of footfalls, coming toward them from the tunnel to the left.

A young man charged out of the tunnel mouth, frantic, wide-eyed. Piranha caught him by the collar.

"Oh Jesus," the young man wailed, "there's some Frankenstein guys back there and they're crazy as hell and they're gonna blow something up or something and they want to *eat* people and they—Oh, Lord, are you *with them?*"

"Settle down," said Piranha. "We've come to stop them. Where are they?"

"Back there!" He pointed back down the tunnel from which he had just emerged. His voice was brittle with terror. "That way!"

"Show us."

"Oh, no, I ain't going back there—"

"Yes, you are," Doctor Piranha said, in a voice Rickey would never, if he lived to be five hundred years old, have the nerve to disobey. "Go."

Piranha released Rickey's collar. Rickey turned around and he went. Piranha stayed behind him, keeping a light grip on his upper arm.

Well, Rickey thought, *they got struck blind, so maybe it'll be okay.*

"Good Lord, it *stinks* down here," Mirabelle said, pinching her nose.

"Worse than the chicken processing plant."

Sure enough, it smelled like somebody had passed an enormous amount of gas. Rickey hoped it wasn't coming from him.

"I think we may have located the stolen methane," Piranha remarked.

Rickey slowed down as the drew close to the light at the end of this particular tunnel.

"This is it," he whispered, pointing. "There they are."

Piranha released Rickey's arm and said, "Go home."

"Yessir," he whispered, then scurried away.

"You must be Hans Kebler," Piranha said casually, standing in the entrance to the chamber. "Word is that you're planning some kind of mayhem down here."

Kebler turned around, leveling a machine gun at his visitors. He did not seem particularly perturbed. Completely inappropriate affect. Mirabelle looked forward to the time when she would no longer be interacting with psychopaths all day long.

"Well, well," said Kebler. "Step just a bit closer, into the light, please."

Mirabelle and Piranha stepped forward. Kebler squinted at them, studying them for almost a minute. His vision had returned completely, but he still wasn't sure he was seeing what he was seeing.

"Could it be? Oh, it must! I know who you are, sir. Doctor Piranha, the master criminal! I did not know you kept a colored wench, Doctor."

Mirabelle snarled. Piranha held up a hand.

"That remark is so vile," he said, "I'll do you a favor and won't take it into consideration when I decide how I'm going to kill you."

"How magnanimous! Well, Doctor, I don't know why you have taken an interest in me. Were you behind my recent misfortunes? Have you come now to deliver the traditional gloating monologue? Doesn't the villain usually do that when he believes he has the hero in his power?"

"That's how you've cast this? You're the hero?"

"Of course! You are the criminal here, sir. I have never so much as received a traffic ticket! Yes, I am the hero—the hero of a great and senseless tragedy. I made an attempt to improve this world, and my efforts have been spurned. I do not know what has become of Johnny Till, but—"

"Your partner was captured by the police," Mirabelle said. "He's been spilling his guts ever since."

"I don't believe that's true. I think it more likely that he is dead. But it doesn't matter. All I have left is my compound to the north, and that will soon be gone. It is bound to be discovered now, so it is best to sacrifice it. The orders have been given."

"I think you probably have other resources," Piranha said, "for all the good they'll do you. When did you start eating human flesh, Herr Kebler?"

Kebler smiled then, like a dedicated philatelist who has just been asked a casual question about postage stamps.

"Why, during the Great War, of course. When I was so famously stranded in No Man's Land with the American, Johnny Till. We had both 'become lost' from our units. If anybody ever suspected us of deliberate desertion, they never said it out loud. It was sheer coincidence that we both chose to abscond at the same time—or so we used to believe. We have since learned to recognize the hand of destiny."

"One moment, Herr Kebler," Piranha interrupted. "No Man's Land was never more than a few hundred yards wide, and sometimes as narrow as ten. You couldn't have been far from your respective trenches. How could you have been lost there for an extended period?"

"Do you know, Doctor, that you are the first person ever to raise that objection? Even the journalists back in 1918 let it pass unremarked. Probably because 'No Man's Land' has such a dramatic ring to it. Perhaps my whole story is a lie, or perhaps we were someplace else—or perhaps our experience was a metaphysical one. Be that as it may, you asked me and I am telling you. Wherever we might have been, we had no idea what we were doing. And that was our great good fortune. Had we not been so woefully inept, we might never have made our great discovery."

"Oh, very well. Are we approaching the point, Herr Kebler? I have places to be."

"Oh, yes, yes, you do, Doctor," Kebler said, rubbing his free hand over his stomach. "I'll be as brief as I can without doing an injustice to the material.

"We had a series of misadventures, and poor Johnny ended up with a shattered ankle. It was painful and prevented him from moving freely. An untenable situation.

"And, on top of that, we were out of provisions, and could not locate fresh ones. We had water, but that was all. And we had to be very careful about even that, boiling it and letting it cool before drinking. No food to be had where we were. A few grubs, something that looked like a cockroach with fur, a bit of dry grass.

"How could you have been lost there?"

"Two potentially lethal difficulties. At first, we did not appreciate the fact that each provided an ideal solution for the other. Pain and starvation give birth to desperate innovation. It was as startling a revelation as only the most obvious things can be. We had our food supply with us, of course—on the hoof, as it were.

"We were starving. Johnny's leg would soon become infected if it weren't removed. Two plus two, Doctor. There could be only one answer."

"Yes," Piranha said dryly, "I believe I see where this is heading. But do go on. Perhaps you have one or two surprises."

"I had some medical supplies with me. Some opiates I had earmarked for recreational use were shanghaied back to their original purpose. In a little over an hour, Johnny was rid of his troublesome leg, and we had the makings of a fine repast!

"We ate. It was quite good, as a matter of fact, though anything would have been ambrosia to starving men. But that wasn't where it ended. No, no.

"We discovered something wonderful. We saw other worlds. There in that moribund land between battle lines, we communed with the spirits of the dead! Would that I could describe it for you, but it's one of those things you just have to experience for yourself.

"But, alas, a leg does not last forever, not even one as substantial as Johnny's was...

"And so, tit for tat, as they say. I had two perfectly good legs, and Johnny was a quick learner. I have always believed in pulling my own weight. So..."

"Another foregone conclusion, Herr Kebler," Piranha said. "Feel free to get to whatever point you're trying to make, without further, ah, culinary diversions."

"Yes, yes. I apologize if I'm boring you. I'm disappointed that you're not getting the point, Doctor. The *essence*—something quite different from the spirit—permeates the body, even after death and dismemberment. It is all quite scientific, if somewhat arcane. Animal magnetism, Doctor— *lebensmagnetismus*. Have you read Mesmer? He was on the right track, but did not go far enough. The magnetic fluid of one organism may be absorbed by another organism, and along with it, the best of the first organism's traits! Eugenics without breeding, survival of the fittest without evolution!

"Well—all good things do come to an end, and so it was with our wondrous odyssey in No Man's Land. When we did finally make it to what passes for civilization, the war had ended. We had been gone for forty days; the significance of which I trust will not escape you.

"Now that everyone was friends again, Johnny and I became heroes. A bit of a nine day wonder we were, but we parleyed it into something much bigger. Our Transatlantic Patriots Guild was genuine enough in its way, but it also provided 'cover' for much higher purposes."

"Right. You were a pair of high-rolling grifters, yes? Selling your gruesome pornography while fleecing well-to-do idiots."

"Money is not unimportant, Doctor. It is not an end in itself, but it can make life much smoother. We chose the wealthiest citizens we could entice to our table. Some we ate; others we used in different ways. Those with the largest bank accounts made up the largest share of our larder. If we could induce them to part with some of their money beforehand, we did. If not, *ce'st la vie!*"

"People with lots of money aren't necessarily the best physical or mental specimens," Piranha pointed out.

"That isn't the point, Doctor," Kebler said. "You are too materialistic, I think. The ability to inherit money, or to make it in other ways, is an expression of what people refer to as 'good luck.' It is just as valuable a commodity as strong bones and good teeth. We were not looking to improve our physical conditions, but rather our spiritual ones."

Mirabelle laughed. Kebler ignored her and continued his lunatic monologue:

"And then we came here. America was to be our Promised Land. Europe had grown moribund and dangerous. America is brash and reckless. Dangerous in its way, yes, but filled with vitality and charming naïveté. We found converts of all kinds. Some shared our beliefs, some shared their money. While still others—"

"As the Bard put it, 'A man may fish with the worm that hath eat of a king, and eat of the fish that hath fed of that worm.' "

"And which are you?" Piranha asked. "The worm or the king?"

"Why can't I be both, Doctor? And the fisherman too?"

"At any rate, here in this city, we saved the best victuals for ourselves, the flesh of the elite, and we allowed the dregs to feast on the dregs. The meat we supplied to the restaurants around Mobile came from the lowest of the low—whores, derelicts, and so forth.

"Thus, the working classes, the ones who eat in those establishments, will be degraded, brought down, made less able to resist us. They were to be our cattle, our servants. You see now? Our way of life can be a double-edged sword. But we knew how to control it. This place was to be our petri dish, where we would perfect a model we could take worldwide."

Then he fell silent. It seemed that Kebler had said all that he had to say.

"So, what now?" Mirabelle asked. "You gonna eat *us*?"

Kebler wrinkled his nose. "Not *you*! Why, the very idea! I would no more eat a Negro than I would a Jew. Absolutely revolting."

"If you're saying you'd find me hard to stomach, the feeling is mutual."

"That is good. I have no desire to be found appealing by members of the, ah, *darker* races. I do not know who *you* are, or under what authority you presume to intrude on my operations." He looked at his watch. "You will be disposed of. Doctor Piranha will, of course, grace my table later this evening. His intellect will raise me higher; I have no intention of risking my mind by ingesting an inferior specimen such as yourself."

Piranha laughed out loud at this. It was the first time Mirabelle had ever heard the man express merriment. She was just a little bit surprised that it sounded like pure and innocent joy, not the diabolical cackle of a sinister mastermind.

"Oh," Piranha gasped, "if you only knew what you were saying, Herr Kebler! If there were any substance to your insane theories, you'd be passing up a chance to rule the world!"

If Kebler was puzzled by this attitude, he didn't show it. His self-absorption was impressive.

"Fortunately," he said, "all of my clockwork here is in motion, so you cannot prevent anything." He held up his machine gun, just in case the intruders had failed to notice it, or had forgotten.

"My organization has been damaged, perhaps mortally. Everything I strove to do is in ruins. I know when to call it quits. I may get away, return to Europe, or I may not. I have associates there, but my reputation will surely suffer from this humiliation, and the people to whom I refer will not stand by me in times of trouble. I may or may not recover from this— but I promise you that this accursed city won't.

"First, the mustard gas will be released, under pressure, from these canisters. Thirty minutes later, the methane will follow it. Ten minutes after that, the explosives will detonate. I will not be here, and neither will you. I have killed this city, and I shall go out into the world and see if I can rebuild what I have lost. With your intellect added to my own, Doctor, I might just have a fighting chance."

"That was the *old* plan," said Piranha. "It didn't take me and my comrade into account."

"Oh, that doesn't matter. I am going to kill you both now."

"With what? You don't dare fire that gun down here, with the methane fumes in the air."

"Oh, *methane*," Mirabelle said. "I thought that was *him*."

Kebler nodded. "Very good. I have been outsmarted by circumstance, yes? But—I do not know if the two of you are carrying firearms, but if so, you are under the same prohibition as I."

"Herr Kebler," said Piranha, "the holes in your reasoning are large enough to accommodate vast herds of cattle. I can only conclude that you are mentally ill."

"Be quiet, and let me tell you how I'm going to kill you!"

"Oh, very well."

"Thank you. I am going to kill you with gas. I am something of a prodigy when it comes to airborne toxins. Members of Herr Hitler's government have consulted with me on the subject. What I have here in *this* tank is a non-flammable poisonous compound." He indicated a squat metal canister painted bright blue. "I can release a lethal stream of it well before you could hope to reach me."

Piranha and Mirabelle exchanged a glance. Both of them wore slight smiles.

"Miss Darcy, how good are you at holding your breath?" Piranha whispered.

"I could do two minutes if I had to."

"Splendid. And you still have your rebreather in your backpack?"

"Of course."

"All right then. Let's get ironic on this bastard."

Mirabelle had to admit that she liked certain elements of the Doctor's style.

Mirabelle took a deep breath and held it as Piranha started moving. He walked calmly toward Kebler, seemingly in no hurry at all. Kebler pulled a gas mask over his head and twisted the valve at the top of the canister. A jet of gas hissed out, just barely visible as a yellowish mist. The stream turned into a faint cloud that billowed around Piranha and Mirabelle.

She got her rebreather out of her backpack and slapped it into her mouth. Piranha just kept walking. He would cover the thirty or so feet between him and Kebler in a few seconds.

It occurred to Hans Kebler that something was wrong. He examined the nozzle of his precious tank, hit it three times with his fist. He slapped it one final time, then looked up into the eyes of Doctor Piranha. Those eyes seemed to burn right through the lenses of Kebler's gas mask, through his brain, and down his spine.

Piranha caught Kebler by the shirtfront and ripped off his gas mask.

"Breathe, Herr Kebler," he said. "Neither I nor my 'colored wench' are affected by your gas."

"You—You said—you wouldn't—hold that remark—against me."

"When you insult a lady, there are always consequences."

Kebler smiled. "It—It is unpleasant, but—I partially immunized myself against—the gas. It—won't—kill me."

"Ah. Well, then, it seems you have bested me after all. My congratulations."

Piranha placed his hands firmly on either side of Kebler's head and twisted until the man's neck snapped.

"And what do you see *now*, Herr Kebler?" Piranha whispered, so softly that he himself wasn't certain he had actually said it. "I would so love to know." He let Kebler's body slump to the floor.

Then, out loud, over his shoulder, he said:

"Should I have resisted that impulse, Miss Darcy?"

"Probably, but who really gives a shit? Let's dismantle this bomb and get the hell out of here."

Eddie, who had been hiding in a recessed spot next to the chamber entrance, well away from the cloud of yellow gas, quietly slipped down the tunnel, following the path Rickey had taken, as Mirabelle and Doctor Piranha dismantled Hans Kebler's sickening legacy.

CHAPTER THIRTY-NINE
QUADRAGESIMA

Then came the cleanup.

The two Joes, Perrone and Barrow, were taken to Tull House by Gladys Turnbull. Shortly after arriving and putting the unconscious master of the house to bed, she was joined by Mirabelle Darcy and Doctor Piranha. The latter was introduced as a "family friend."

Piranha and Mirabelle examined Perrone and determined that his physical condition was good. He had taken a beating recently, and was exhausted, but he would recover. The examination revealed the secret behind the defeat of the Mummifier:

Perrone had used Mirabelle's flesh-like gloves as Markham, to perform the function for which they had originally been created. It would not have done for the criminal to have left Perrone's fingerprints all over everywhere. And the one on his right hand had still contained the pad he had used to secure a sample of the Guild's poison—the pad with the metal backing. They had not been discovered when "Markham" and Barrow were beaten and bound to the float. He had received a terrible pummeling to his head and his body, but his hands had been left alone.

The history of Empires often depends on such trifles.

Joe Barrow divulged the existence and location of the Guild's "farm" in Chickasaw, though he had no knowledge of its actual function. "Markham" had never shared his ghastly suspicions.

Tom Dart immediately relayed the information to the Alabama State Police and the Department of Justice in Washington. He also notified the International Criminal Police Commission, who had an operative on the scene in Mobile, ready to move at a moment's notice: the ICPC man who had taken unofficial charge of the unofficial investigation at Mauvais Rêve and Donner-Purdy. The Mobile P.D., as an entity, was unaware of these crime scenes. The whole thing was irregular enough to provoke an international incident if it became common knowledge. But Madame Maude had been well-liked, and the ICPC knew what to expect from corrupt local governments the world over. As for Tom Dart, he didn't give a damn about any possible consequences, not this time.

Nobody at City Hall was going to interfere.

The facility was raided, and fourteen members of the gang were taken into custody. Acting under Hans Kebler's final orders, these "elite troops" had killed a score of their fellows and set some of the buildings on fire. They were about to make their escape when the authorities descended on them. The fires were extinguished before the structures could be badly damaged.

Before the day was done, more than one of the men on the scene would wish that the whole thing had been allowed to burn.

The chicken coop-like buildings at the rear of the property can only be described as a combination barracks and abattoir.

The source of the black market meat had been found.

This information would never be made public by the government or any law enforcement agency. The men who penetrated that part of the compound were sworn to secrecy, a vow none of them would ever break. Within five years, more than a dozen of them would be dead. Most would die in one of two ways: suicide or complications from alcohol and/or drug abuse.

Nothing resembling the Guild's compound would be seen again until 1945, when the Allies would liberate the German death camps at the end of World War Two.

All of the unused meat stocked at the restaurants on the Guild's list was confiscated by federal authorities. Some discussion was had on the prospect of trying to identify it in hopes of arranging some kind of decent burials. But no workable plan could be devised, so, in the end, it was destroyed in large industrial incinerators.

The police gathered up as many of the gruesome "throws" as they could find. Some had probably disappeared down storm drains, while others had undoubtedly been taken home as morbid souvenirs by the sort of people who ought to be supervised at all times, but weren't.

Fingerprinting would be undertaken in an effort to fix the number of victims, and identify at least some of them.

Twenty-four innocent parade goers had been killed by machine gun fire. Memorials were held for days, all over the city.

Joe Barrow, conscious and active, though a little the worse for wear, expressed concern for his friend, the man he knew as Roy Markham. He related the story of his and Markham's infiltration of the gang. Mirabelle felt that Joe Barrow deserved to know the truth about his friend, so she told it to him. He took it well. He seemed delighted to learn that there was so much more to "Roy Markham."

"I *knew* he wasn't a bad guy," Joe Barrow said. "I *knew* it!"

Eddie had hitched a ride almost all the way to Montgomery. The truck driver had let him out in Wetumpka, about 200 miles northeast of Mobile. He stood by the side of the road for thirty minutes or so, his grip and his rucksack at his feet, his thumb stuck out, before a car finally stopped for him.

It was boxy, dark green 1930 Plymouth. The driver was an older woman, maybe around forty. She reminded Eddie a little bit of his mother. Just a little bit.

"Hop in," she said.

He did, heaving his gear over into the back seat..

"Where you headed, big boy?" she asked, kind of flirty.

"I'm on my way back home," he told her. "Plainfield, Wisconsin."

"Well, well. How'd you get all the way to Alabama?"

"Oh, the wind just blew me down here I guess. I was looking for something to do."

"Did you find it?"

"Yes, ma'am, I'd have to say I did."

"Well, that's fine, then. You got a name?"

"Yes, ma'am. Name's Eddie."

They rode in silence for a little while. When they got past Montgomery, back out in the country, Eddie spoke up:

"I'm kinda hungry. You think you could pull off the road right up ahead there?"

He reached back and got his grip from where he had tossed it.

"There's nothing there," the lady said. "No restaurant, no store, no nothing."

"That's right. Perfect spot. I got my lunch with me."

"Where? In that grip?"

"No, my tools are in there. I'm gonna fix lunch myself. Just pull over, you'll see."

"Huh. Well, whatever you say, I guess. You're a strange one, Eddie."

"I used to think so. But I found out I ain't as uncommon as I figured.

That's what getting out in the world and seeing things can do for a person. Yeah, that's good, just pull off the road a little bit, under them trees over there..."

It was a long way back to Plainfield, Wisconsin, and the Gein family farm, and a man could not travel on an empty stomach...

Perrone was kept sedated while Piranha and Mirabelle ran a series of exhaustive tests. He was semi-conscious at times, and Mirabelle told him he had been badly injured during the Guild investigation, and needed time to recover.

He believed her.

He always believed her.

During her off hours, she drank wine and cursed herself for a treacherous little shit.

"Somehow, this Markham personality took over," Piranha said to her one evening, as they planned their strategy for the next few days.

"Seems that way," she agreed, "according to what Gladys and Joe Barrow have told me. He was doing some pretty atrocious things as the Bay Phantom too, during the same period."

"I think perhaps an electrolyte imbalance, or some other chemical mischief, may have started a chain reaction that affected his brain. The two hemispheres began working more in tandem, but also kept certain things back from one another. The id and the super-ego meshed, but tried also to pull away from each other. This left the ego as a very confused moderator between the two. But I think it's organic, not psychological."

"He's had a few traumas in his life," Mirabelle pointed out.

"Yes. But he should be more stable."

"He wears a mask and fights crime."

"You pretend to be a housekeeper, when you could do literally almost anything in the world. And you spend your vacations breaking into prisons."

"Touché."

Piranha was silent for a while, seemingly deep in thought, then:

"You love my brother."

"I never said I didn't."

"And I presume he loves you."

"He'd damn well better!"

"Yes. Well—I'm not *entirely* sure what went wrong with Joe—"

"Maybe the original work was shoddy," Mirabelle said without any inflection.

"Perhaps," he allowed. He was, it seemed, comfortable enough with Mirabelle's intellect not to let his own ego get in the way when she pointed out something like that. "I was young. I may have been too self-confident. The procedures must have caused some kind of glandular destabilization over a period of years, bringing on the imbalance I spoke of. That's the only thing I can figure, and it admittedly doesn't entirely account for this Markham business."

"Can you fix it?"

"Yes. I'm *sure* I can. *If* I can get the materials I need."

"Tell me what they are. If I don't have them, I'll get them."

He told her, in great detail. She had most of it on hand. The rest, she obtained within a few hours.

The intervention was mostly chemical, with a minor surgical component. Mirabelle assisted Piranha every step of the way. Piranha was working in territory that had never been anything more than theoretical in her experience. She was able to make a few connections that had previously eluded her.

Doctor Piranha—Anthony Perrone—had learned how to make superhumans. That was the only way to put it. Subjects of his treatments would develop greatly increased strength and stamina, and would heal at an incredibly rapid rate.

The side-effects of his experiments on Gerald Sams had been disastrous. The poor boy's mind had been hopelessly scrambled.

Of course, Piranha had done the same things to himself, once he was convinced that he had perfected the procedure. He had to have had help with that, but he volunteered no information. He and Mirabelle agreed that there was no way to determine whether or not his own mind had been affected, all things considered.

And then he had done it to his little brother. Why? Had he had some inkling of the tragedy that would one day overtake the Perrones?

Again, he offered no enlightenment.

"His mind will be clearer," Piranha said, after he and Mirabelle had finished and carried Perrone to his bedroom. "The deterioration has been checked, and will reverse itself over a period of time. A few weeks or months, no more than half a year. He may experience further disorientation while this is going on, but it's nothing serious. And he will still heal rapidly and enjoy almost superhuman stamina. In fact, these things may increase. And he may start wondering about them. You might wish to concoct an explanation that doesn't include me."

"I'll come up with something. I can't be honest, goddammit, not about this. Well, it's on me, I guess. But we're not done yet. Next, we're going to fix Gerald Sams, and undo whatever you did to him."

In a facility owned by Penny Carter, Mirabelle and Doctor Piranha repeated their "repair work" on Gerald Sams. It was more involved, and more dangerous, than it had been with Joe Perrone, since the damage had gone so much deeper.

The treatment seemed to be successful. Time would tell.

When it was done, only a few small matters remained. Piranha seemed eager to return to Leavenworth now that things had been settled, and Mirabelle couldn't say she'd be sad to see him go.

"You get bored in there," Mirabelle said to him. "I understand that, even though you say that's where you want to be. But when the opportunity arises to play an intricate game, you take it."

"You may be right, Miss Darcy. I have never articulated it to myself in that way, but you may be right."

"There's just one thing I don't get," she said. "How did you know I was leaving, and when, and what I was going to do? You had to have known, in order to arrange for those assassins to be at Leavenworth at the same time I was. How do you know what goes on in Tull House? How do you get your information?"

"I could be coy about it, but I won't bother. Tull House is haunted, right?"

"It does seem to be. I don't claim to know very much about psychic phenomena, but I know better than to look for plausible explanations where they just don't fit, but... Wait a minute. Are you saying what I think you're saying?"

"Of course I am. You know that."

"I know you're *saying* it, but—How does it work?"

"I'm not going into that. I have to temporarily turn my back on every scientific principle I have always lived by when I... make use of that resource. And it isn't as reliable as an electronic device would be, but one must work with what one has."

"So, you're suggesting that there really is something in the house, then. A ghost."

"Oh, yes. More than one, in fact. There are... *presences*. I suppose they are what people refer to as ghosts. And it is possible to communicate with them, even from afar, by employing certain rituals.

"Here's what I know about them: They are not malicious, nor are they particularly benevolent. They are confused about their own identities. They believe themselves to be the spirits of deceased human beings. This conviction on their part is unshakable. I myself do not know. They may be, or they may not. Perhaps they are just echoes, or some strange species of creature self-deluded into mimicking our dead. Of all the questions that remain unanswered to me, that one nags at me the most. I have been aware of them for a long time—since *before* Piranha—and I covet their secrets."

Mirabelle was silent for what seemed like a very long time. Finally she shook her head sadly and said:

"I have to say I'm a little disappointed you'd resort to a tale like that. I can't guess at your motives, so I suppose you've put one over on me. Talking to ghosts! The very idea!"

He looked at her. His mouth wasn't quite closed, and there was something in his eyes that didn't seem to belong there. He actually seemed a bit... hurt.

"I'm sorry you feel that way, Miss Darcy," he said. "You're like me: You know enough not to believe in anything, and not to rule anything out. The ideal thinker would never stray from that territory."

"Yes. And the ideal thinker also does not stray through the looking glass when a more conventional portal is handy. A friend of mine suspected that Penny Carter planted listening devices in Tull House. Nothing has been found, but it's a large house, and Penny is both smart and wealthy. And, of course, you and Penny are—whatever you are. I'll figure it out one of these days, unless I don't. It's not a big deal either way."

He wasn't angry. He seemed sad, deflated. Mirabelle felt as though she were being cruel, and she almost faltered. She had actually drawn breath to speak what was on her mind, but stopped herself.

You could trust him today, maybe, she said to herself. *But what about tomorrow, or the day after that? You know what he's already done, what he's capable of. And, really, what good could you hope to do?*

She dismissed her conscience, to be dealt with later or never, and brought up the subject of Piranha's return to Leavenworth.

"We must decide how best to accomplish it," she said. "I've done some asking around. Your warden at Leavenworth wasn't able to keep your absence secret for very long. The state police got involved, then the Department of Justice.

"A reward will be offered; the money is already earmarked, but the offer has not yet been made public. They're still looking, they don't want a panic. I mean, Doctor Piranha! It would be like if Jack the Ripper had been caught, then escaped. But they're getting very nervous. The bulletins will be going out any time now."

"I shouldn't wonder."

"If someone were to somehow hand you over to the authorities in the very near future, I have no doubt that the reward would be paid, if only to keep the whole thing quiet."

"Yes. Are you in need of some extra cash, Miss Darcy?"

"No, Doctor Piranha, I am not. But I know somebody who is."

✳✳✳

"Holy hell, Alice," Louis Rickert said, "look at that guy over there! No, don't *look* at him. Oh, jeez, do you know who that is?"

They were at a table in one of Louis' favorite speakeasies, ostensibly celebrating the dropping of all the bogus charges that had been lodged against him by the police.

"Since I can't look at him," said Alice Tague, "no, I don't."

"Why, that's—" Louis decided he'd better not say the name. "That's a *wanted man*, right there. He's got a reward out for him! Oh boy, this is our lucky night."

"How so?"

"I'll tell you what: You go over there and talk to him, keep him right where he is, in case he's thinking about leaving. I'll go call the cops."

"I don't know, Louis. Is he dangerous?"

"Aw, no. He don't hurt women. He, uh, took a pledge against it or something. You'll be safe."

"I still don't know. It seems kind of—"

"The reward is ten grand."

Her eyes got wide, and she risked a look at the fugitive. "That guy right over there?"

Louis nodded. "Yeah. Pretend you're like a b-girl or something. Just keep him there for a few minutes. I'll go out and use a pay phone."

"You're sure about this?"

"This time I damn sure am. You go on, and I'll head out to a phone."

John Doe, aka "Doctor Piranha" was quietly taken into custody by the Mobile Police Department. Four hours later, he was handed over to federal marshals, who, without any fanfare, escorted him back to Leavenworth, Kansas.

Two weeks later, a reward of ten thousand dollars was presented to Alice Tague. She offered to split it equally with her friend, Louis Rickert, who refused to accept any of the money, with only slight reluctance and regret. Alice returned to Huntsville and her family, and received the medical treatment she needed.

Alice would die in 1991, at the age of 86, leaving four children and nine grandchildren.

Alvin Branch's treachery was a bitter pill for Tom Dart to swallow. It was still hung up halfway down his throat when he was promoted to Branch's chair as Senior Detective Lieutenant in charge of the Homicide Squad. He had wanted to refuse the appointment, but some dark sense of duty forced him to accept. He didn't know why. Was it now his job to atone for another man's sins?

And then there were a few more ominous implications, which he began to consider.

He had never learned who in the department, other than Branch, had been working for the Guild. But he knew a lot of people had been bothered by his inquisitiveness. Of course, the Guild was no more, but those who had been on their payroll would not forget. And how long would it be before someone else took the Guild's place? Penny Carter was once more firmly in control, so he believed, but how could he know anything for sure?

Why had he been promoted so quickly?
Was someone setting him up to knock him down?
He would have to be careful in the future.

Joe Barrow stayed at Tull House for a few weeks, helping Mirabelle around the house while Mister Perrone recuperated. Mirabelle, had, of course, informed him that Joe Perrone was Roy Markham was the Bay Phantom. Perrone trusted Barrow with the information, and so did Mirabelle.

When Perrone was up and around, which didn't take him long, he taught Barrow a few interesting things about fighting, and Barrow did the same for him. In that respect, their accidental friendship was very beneficial to both of them. And it was beneficial in other ways too. They went fishing a few times, and even worked together on an old car Perrone had acquired somewhere. And they talked, sometimes long into the night, about everything and nothing. Observing them together, Mirabelle saw a boy in need of a father figure who understood him, and a man in need of a surrogate son, to whom he could pass on some of his wisdom, both mundane and arcane. She was happy that both of them had found what they needed, if only for a short while.

"I'll miss you when you go," she told him one day. "Even though it'll be less confusing with only one Joe on the premises again."

"Yes, ma'am. I'm mighty grateful to you."

"What will you do now?"

"Oh, I guess I'll head back North, figure out what I want to do with myself."

"You're very good with your fists. The sweet science, I think they call it."

"Yes, ma'am. Maybe I'll become that kind of scientist. I've done a lot of sparring at the Brewster Street recreation center, back in Detroit. Mama thought I was there learning to play the fiddle. But these hands weren't made for that.

"I'll be seventeen in just a few weeks. About time I got serious about something."

"Yeah, an old man like you better hurry if he wants to make his mark. What do you think you'll do?"

Barrow shrugged. "I dunno. I worked at the Ford plant for a while, but

I didn't much care for that. I like boxing, and these fists—these fists right here—saved my own life, and Mister Perrone's too. I figure that's a sign. Anything *that* important is something I oughtta be doing. Don't you think so, Miss Mirabelle?"

"If that's what your heart tells you, then yes."

"Seems like a person's color don't matter quite so much if they have something they can do really well. I mean, look at you, everything you've done. You didn't let being black stand in your way."

"Hm. For a long time, Joe, I did. But I'm starting to come out of my shell, I think. Being black's not an affliction, though some people see it that way."

"Well, that's good. I'm gonna do the same thing."

"If you set your mind to it, I don't doubt you'll make good. I'll bet that, in the future, lots of people will know the name Joe Louis Barrow."

In that, Mirabelle would prove to be two-thirds correct. Later that year, young Joe would drop the "Barrow," and go on to achieve lasting fame as a boxer, under the name Joe Louis.

He would commence his career as an amateur later in 1932, at the ripe old age of 17, not long after his return to Detroit. His professional career would begin in 1934, and he would go on to become the World Heavyweight Champion in 1937, with his celebrated defeat of James J. Braddock.

The "Brown Bomber" would be one of the most famous and feted boxers of all time, retaining the Heavyweight title for almost 12 years.

For all his fame, the course of his life would be neither smooth nor easy. But whenever the chips were down, and they often were, he would draw comfort and inspiration from his memories of the time he had spent with Joe Perrone and Mirabelle Darcy.

CHAPTER FORTY
THEM

There were a lot of things Mirabelle didn't like about recent events. And there was virtually nothing she could do about any of them.

She still didn't know how the Guild had obtained details of the Phantom's network of tunnels. Had they discovered them by accident, and then mapped them out? The existence of the tunnels was not common knowledge any more, but references to them could be found in the public domain.

Or, had Piranha been behind it? Had he hoped they would finish what he had started years ago? Had something happened that made him change his mind? She might never know the truth about that, and it irked her. And if he *did* have a change of heart—why?

Because of me?

She shuddered at the thought. Best to just leave that one alone.

There was one thing, however, over which she could exercise a bit of control...

She knew that Piranha hadn't got his information from hidden microphones, because she had never spoken her own plans out loud to anyone else. But that didn't mean they were safe from observers of a different kind. Observers who could see that which was invisible and hear that which was unspoken. It would have taken Piranha a lot of time to get enough data to act on, but time was one thing he had plenty of.

Piranha had been truthful.

Mirabelle had not.

One evening shortly after Piranha had been taken back "home," Mirabelle climbed a wooden ladder in the hall outside her bedroom, up into the attic. Compared to the rest of the house, it was uncluttered, containing only one item of interest: Mirabelle's electronic radio jammer. It prevented any listening devices from functioning anywhere in the house. It was always on, blocking the frequencies that such devices typically used—and had been, continuously, for the last eight months.

But that wasn't why she had come up here.

Months earlier, after a hypnosis session with Sigmund Freud, she had remembered some things her father had taught her when she was a little girl.

If you listen in a certain way, Paul Darcy had said, *you can understand them. If you speak from that understanding, they can hear and understand you. Conversation is not easy, but it is possible, if you are gentle, sincere, and patient.*

Her father, Paul Darcy, had been a sort of houngan, a Wise Man, one who trafficked with invisible powers. He was lost to her when she was just a little girl, and most of her memories of him had been buried until the hypnosis called them out of their tomb. Little lessons, bits of folklore, how to talk to the spirits. That had been one of Paul Darcy's great passions: communication with those discarnate, disjointed minds that seemed to have little or no insight themselves into their own nature and condition.

Reaching into a pocket of her skirt, she took out four votive candles. Then she sat down on the floor, arranged the candles in front of her, and lit them. When all four were going, she said a brief prayer in Latin.

The temperature in the room dropped. Though she had been prepared for it, Mirabelle found it disconcerting. *What could possibly cause that? Some kind of energy transfer?*

She shoved the thoughts back down into the depths of her mind. It didn't matter. She took several deep breaths.

"You've all done some good," she said. "You were extremely helpful."

Something answered her.

It was a voice, but not just one. Many voices, maybe five, maybe twenty, maybe a hundred, whispering to her in strange, sibilant harmony, all of them saying the same words:

Yes yes Miss Mirabelle so glad you're here I we are glad had fish for dinner and lit all the lamps but one don't need no more help today the one who went away is back and won't be blamed for nothing hello hello Miss Mirabelle your presence is very warm there is light

They didn't always make sense, and they had a tendency to stray into other subjects—or complete nonsense—during a conversation.

How Piranha had managed to do it from such a distance was not at all clear to her. Nor did it really need to be. She had learned of his ethereal surveillance months ago, when she first began her experiments with her father's techniques. The entities had liked her better than they did Piranha, and Mirabelle was able to enlist them as ectoplasmic "double agents."

She had known everything Piranha had learned about her activities and plans. Her "friends" had given her the secret details of the prison layout. She had not known about the assassins specifically, but she had been cautioned to expect something. She had known that Piranha intended all along to accompany her to Mobile. And she had decided, for Joe's sake, that it would be best if he did.

"This is the last time I'll call on you this way," Mirabelle said. "I'm not at all comfortable with it, but I do appreciate the help. You'll remember everything I asked of you?"

Yes yes Miss Mirabelle no more telling things to the man in the prison he doesn't need to know what goes on in here you say we believe you thank you thank you light mass prayers and the water comes in when we

"You're drifting," Mirabelle said gently. "Please focus just a while longer."

Yes yes Miss Mirabelle I we will thank you no more talking to Piranha and I and we did as you asked before and only told him what you wanted us to tell him and we found out things and told you and didn't tell him we told you

"You did, yes, and I thank you for that. Things worked out very well, as it happened."

Glad we are glad glad Miss Mirabelle you have been polite and listened and said the prayers and lighted a candle in the hallway and we won't talk to anybody outside here any more one of us does not talk to nobody but he gets inside and he ran away for a while but now he has come back not you the other one he is here but he won't talk we made him come back when the man returned here see what a jolly bonnet I've got be sure and leave something for the mouse

"I can see you're having trouble staying tethered, so I'll leave you now. Thank you again, and you can be sure that I'll continue with the prayers and the candles, if they make you feel better."

Communicating with these entities made her a bit giddy. It gave her a strange and uncomfortable feeling of freedom, liberation—it was so much different from the orderly way in which she had always trained herself to think and react.

And, in that moment, she suddenly realized why her scoffing had affected Piranha the way it had. The insight was startling.

This, she now understood, was his only possible escape, this contact with these simple, mysterious voices, who obeyed no scientific laws and were unbound by logic—the only hope he had of leaving the cold prison of his own mind. He had respected her, and she had ridiculed it. Had she caused him to doubt his own experiences? Or had he himself failed to believe in them, and so sought a confirmation from her? Was he a madman who would never be free, no matter where he went?

Yes yes Miss Mirabelle they do thank you yes plant nice things in the garden thank you goodbye goodbye Miss Mirabelle your daddy will be happy and proud he is near goodbye goodbye

"Yes, I—Wait, what? What do you mean? You said my daddy *will be* happy and proud? Not *is*? Not *would be*?"

She sat quietly for almost ten minutes, but there was nothing more. The voices were silent.

Mirabelle extinguished the candles and went down to the kitchen, where she selected a bottle of wine to take with her to her bedroom.

EPILOGUE

Charles Hoy Fort passed away on May 3, 1932, at Royal Hospital in The Bronx, New York. The cause of death was listed as "unspecified weakness." It was likely that he had succumbed to leukemia, but this was impossible to determine, given the poor state of his health overall.

He was interred in the Fort family plot at the Albany Rural Cemetery.

His final book, *Wild Talents*, would be published later in the year.

And Fort would in fact "come back as an adjective." Decades after his death, the word "Fortean" would appear in the Oxford English Dictionary, defined as, "Relating to or denoting paranormal phenomena."

Joe Perrone and Mirabelle Darcy traveled to Albany to attend his funeral. They were gone for a week.

They had barely discussed the events surrounding the downfall of the Transatlantic Patriots Guild—or the "Cannibal Guild," as Mirabelle was calling it. Perrone was recovering nicely from the beating he had taken while he was a captive of the Guild, and the coma it had brought on. That was the truth as he knew it; he had no idea what had happened afterward, and the involvement of Doctor Piranha would never be part of the "official" record, so long as Mirabelle could keep it concealed.

But there were other mysteries, other things that could be approached gingerly.

On the train trip home from Albany, Mirabelle, in a reflective mood brought on by Fort's passing, started a conversation:

"Do you remember the time you spent as Roy Markham?" she asked.

He thought for a while, then said, "Yes, but—I remember it in the same way I remember, let's say, *The Phantom of the Opera*. It is as though I watched Markham's 'performance' on a movie screen, while sitting by myself in a darkened theater. Some things stand out, others do not. And there are jump cuts between important scenes, spans of time for which

I cannot account at all. Kebler and Till and the rest of the gang are just characters I saw playing their parts. A strange psychological phenomenon. I don't plan to let myself go that way again."

"That's good."

"Yes. The only person who seems real to me today is Joe Barrow."

"Yeah, he's a good kid. I think he kept you from crossing some lines you might not have been able to uncross."

"I know he did."

They were silent for a while after that.

"What do you remember about your brother?" Mirabelle asked presently.

"Anthony? Well... not a great deal, I'm afraid. He was always a bit aloof. I do recall that he taught me to play chess."

"You're very good at it. You beat me three times out of five, on average."

"You mean you don't allow me to win?"

She scowled at him. "Don't you dare insult me like that. I've never done that—with *anybody*—and I never will."

"Yes, I apologize for that. You're right. But why are you curious about Anthony all of a sudden? I can't recall you ever interacting with him at all when we were young."

"I was just wondering," she said. "I guess he was a real character, huh?"

"I suppose he might have been. He had virtually no influence on me."

"Mmm."

They were silent again for a minute or two. Then:

"What about your father?" Perrone asked. "Do you remember much about him?"

Perrone had learned that both Paul Darcy and the Black Embalmer had gone missing from the clinic. Strangely, he wasn't worried about them. Whatever had happened, and would happen, would be all right. He knew that the Embalmer had helped him during that horrible parade, and that was significant. He knew his strange friend wouldn't harm Darcy, and might even help him. How he knew this, he couldn't say, but nothing could induce him not to believe it.

Mirabelle frowned. "Oh, I recall a few things. What made you think of him?"

"Just thinking about lost family."

"Lost," she said. "Is that what they are? Lost and found. I honestly don't know which is worse."

"What?"

"Nothing, Joe. Nothing."

She was happy to drop that particular subject. She had something else she wanted to bring up, while she was in this mood:

"You know," she said, "a lot of people in Mobile were eating human flesh for a while. Should we... you know, *tell* them? Should we make some kind of announcement?"

"I don't know that I would advocate that," Perrone said.

"They have a right to know," Mirabelle replied, knowing full well what she was doing.

"Granted. However, think of the harm that knowledge could do. The *trauma* it would engender. On top of all the disappearances, and the deaths at the parade—No, I feel inclined to ignore their right to know in favor of their right not to be plagued by nightmares for the remainder of their lives."

"Well, yeah, but—"

"Consumption of human flesh is not inherently harmful, so long as the, ah, *meat* is free of disease. It seems that the Guild was quite scrupulous in the preparation of their wares. There will be no ill effect from it. This is truly a case where what people don't know will not hurt them. If they did know, it would change nothing—except for their *minds*, how they *see* themselves. Some would never recover, Mirabelle. You know that."

"Okay—So, you're saying, basically, that potentially harmful information can justifiably be kept from people, if the revelation would do more harm than good."

"I suppose I am."

Mirabelle smiled wanly. Here was what she had been fishing for, and it did her almost no good at all. Joe Perrone had stated a doctrine that ought to absolve her guilt.

It wasn't working.

Maybe tomorrow...

They returned home to a stack of mail, most of it for Mirabelle. But there was one thick envelope addressed to Joseph Perrone.

"I suppose it's a love letter from Penny Carter," Mirabelle said sourly.

"Now, Mirabelle—"

"Wait a minute—it's from Charles Fort. He—He must have mailed it just before he died."

Mirabelle, who had remained dry-eyed for the past couple of days, felt herself tearing up once again.

"Go ahead and open it Mirabelle," Perrone said. "He was your friend too."

She got herself under control and slit the envelope open, extracting several sheets of paper. A hand-written letter from Fort.

"He found out some information about Tull House," she said, deciphering Fort's eccentric handwriting. It occurred to her with a pang that his script had been further distorted by his terminal condition. "Something happened here in the closing days of the Civil War, he says. A week before Lincoln was assassinated, actually.

"The man who owned the house then was shot by Confederate troops, right here in this room—Through that window." She pointed to the front of the living room.

"No details on how or why. The man's name was Carl Rudy. He was a Southerner who fought for the North in the Civil War."

"Well, that must have endeared him to his fellows."

"Well, it says here that he was an Abolitionist, couldn't stand the slave trade. There was a rumor that his mother or grandmother had been a slave—that was never confirmed. But that was about his only redeeming quality. He was a mean, ruthless sonofabitch."

"I'm sure poor Charles didn't write *that*."

"I'm paraphrasing. Rudy was a murderer, probably several times over. After they shot him, he lived long enough to curse God and everybody in the world and swear he'd come back."

"Scoundrels tend to do that. They seldom make good on it."

"What authority are you citing for that? Hang on, there's a little more here. Hmmm, 'Carl Rudy' wasn't his real name. This wasn't discovered until later. He had changed it ten years earlier to duck a murder rap in Georgia. It seems his real name was—"

She turned the page over and continued reading. She had drawn a breath to speak when her eyes got wide, and she found herself momentarily unable to say anything at all.

"Mirabelle, what's the matter?"

"Oh, my God."

"What is it?"

"I—I need to sit down."

And she did just that, still staring at the letter, looking as close to dumbfounded as Perrone had ever seen her.

"Mirabelle, what *is* it?"

"His real name was Roy Markham."

THE END

ABOUT OUR CREATORS

AUTHOR –

CHUCK MILLER - was born in Ohio, lived in Alabama for many years, and now resides in Norman, Oklahoma. He is a Libra whose interests include monster movies, comic books, music and writing. He holds a BA in creative writing from the University of South Alabama.

He is the creator/writer of TALES OF THE BLACK CENTIPEDE, THE INCREDIBLE ADVENTURES OF VIONNA VALIS AND MARY JANE KELLY, THE BAY PHANTOM CHRONICLES, and THE MYSTIC FILES OF DOCTOR UNKNOWN JUNIOR. He has also written stories featuring such classic characters as Jill Trent: Science Sleuth, Armless O'Neil, The Griffon, and others.

Miller received the BEST NEW WRITER OF 2011 Award from Pulp Ark. His first novel, the critically acclaimed "Creeping Dawn: The Rise of the Black Centipede" was published in 2011 by Pro Se Press. The second installment in the Black Centipede series, "Blood of the Centipede" was published in 2012. "Black Centipede Confidential" is slated for release in 2013. Also due in 2013 is "Vionna and the Vampires," the first installment of "The Incredible Adventures of Vionna Valis and Mary Jane Kelly."

http://theblackcentipede.blogspot.com/

INTERIOR ILLUSTRATOR –

KEVIN PAUL SHAW BRODEN, - initially seeking a career in comic books, took art courses throughout his education - only to eventually discover that no matter what the media, he was a storyteller at heart. Kevin received a BA in Art (emphasizing Narrative Illustration) from California State University, Fullerton (Fullerton, CA); before that, he worked on the HORNET newspaper as a reporter/illustrator while earning his AA at Fullerton College.

One of Kevin's early jobs teamed him with some of the talent that launched Supreme for Image Comics. You can even find a special "thank you" to Kevin in SUPREME #1. He storyboarded the music video for

BiGod20's "One," as well as videos for John Wesley Harding and Kristin Hersch as part of Summer Arts in Humboldt, CA. Also, he's been contracted to do illustrations for commercials and television series pitches. The textbooks GARDNER'S GUIDE TO WRITING AND PRODUCING ANIMATION and GARDNER'S GUIDE TO PITCHING AND SELLING ANIMATION feature all interior art done by Kevin. With his wife and creative partner, Shannon Muir, Kevin created the online comic FLYING GLORY AND THE HOUNDS OF GLORY, which has been in existence over 15 years. His artwork has also been seen as the interior illustration for Ralph L. Angelo, Jr's "Against Fire and Stone" tale in LEGENDS OF NEW PULP FICTION by Airship 27 Productions, the cover art for the anthology NEWSHOUNDS from Pro Se Press (which also features his story "Stop the Presses!"), and as cover art for self-published e-books he's authored and released which include the REVENGE OF THE MASKED GHOST series and the CLOCKWORK GENIE MYSTERIES.

Oh, and yes, he does have FOUR NAMES. It's a family thing, but it comes in quite handy... FOUR NAMES OF PROFESSIONAL CREATIVITY.

COVER ARTIST -

ADAM BENET SHAW –Accomplished painter, illustrator, and comics creator, Adam has garnered acclaim across a number of artistic media. After completing studies at the Cleveland Institute of Art in Ohio, the Edinburgh College of Art in Scotland and Watts Atelier in California, Shaw was selected as an emerging American artist to watch by European gallery owners and exhibited in London, England. He has been featured in "New American Painting", selected multiple times for the Arkansas Art Center's Delta Exhibit, and shown at the prestigious "Red Clay Survey" at the Huntsville Museum of Art. His work has also been shown in over 50 group and solo shows in the US and internationally.   His figurative paintings are a prominent part of a 140-foot mural entitled "The History of Cotton" at the National Cotton Exchange Museum, St. Jude's Children's Research Hospital, the National Contact Bridge Museum, and a treasured part of private and corporate collections. He has created storyboards for several motion pictures, including Paramount Pictures' film "Black Snake Moan" directed by Craig Brewer, stage design for operas and corporate events, and character illustrations for the gaming industry. His published graphic novel work includes the series "Dead In Memphis", "Bloodstream" for Image Comics, "David: The Illustrated Novel" from Shepherd King Publishing and "Harpe: America's First Serial Killers" from Cave-in-Rock Publishing. He shares his love of art through teaching and workshops at his studio in the Broad Avenue Arts District in Memphis. Recently he has been painting book covers for pulp publishers Pro Se Productions and Airship 27 Productions.

For your consideration...

In the middle 1930s, Chicago was one of the fastest growing metropolises in the country. Situated on mighty Lake Michigan, it was the home to millions of hard working Americans looking to better themselves. The Windy City was also shackled by its bootleg history, a time of violent gang wars that had permanently established a brutal underworld empire second to none. Corruption was the order of the day and both the police and government were in the pay of the mob bosses.

Frank "Mac" McCullough was a foot-soldier in one of the city's toughest families until he was ordered to rough up his uncle; a decent man with a gambling problem. The innate decency in Mac rebelled and suddenly he found himself up against the very men he had once admired and followed. Determined to put an end to their lawlessness, he put a bag over his head as a crude disguise only to become labeled the Bagman by the press.

Now writer BC Bell tells the amazing stories of old Chicago's most unique hero. Aided solely by a tough, black WW I veteran named Crankshaft, Mac wages war against the mobs in fast-paced, non-stop action tales pulp fans will cheer. Airship 27 Productions is thrilled to present pulpdom's newest avenger, THE BAGMAN.

www.ingramcontent.com/pod-product-compliance
Lightning Source LLC
Chambersburg PA
CBHW051632260626
47170CB00004B/1148